BLOOD HUNT

BLOOD HUNT

A Novel

IAN RANKIN

LITTLE, BROWN AND COMPANY
New York   Boston

Little, Brown and Company
Time Warner Book Group
1271 Avenue of the Americas, New York, NY 10020
Visit our Web site at www.twbookmark.com

First Little, Brown edition: March 2006
Originally published in the United Kingdom in 1995 under the author name
Jack Harvey

Library of Congress Cataloging-in-Publication Data

Rankin, Ian.
    Blood hunt : a novel / Ian Rankin — 1st American ed.
    p. cm.
    ISBN 0-316-00911-3
        1. Journalists — Crimes against — Fiction. 2. Murder victims'
families — Fiction. 3. Brothers — Death — Fiction. I. Title.
PR6068.A57B58 2006
823'.914 — dc22   2005050419

10 9 8 7 6 5 4 3 2 1

Q-FF

Printed in the United States of America

To Kit

Then you carried your ashes to the mountains:
will you today carry your fire into the valleys?
Do you not fear an incendiary's punishment?
— *Nietzsche,* THUS SPAKE ZARATHUSTRA

PART ONE
THE BLOODING

ONE

HE STOOD ON THE EDGE of the abyss, staring down.

Not afraid, not feeling anything very much except the burn-ing in his lungs, the damp ache behind his legs. He knew staring was never a one-way thing. It was reciprocal. Okay, he thought, get your staring finished, get it over and done with now. The fall, he thought — it isn't the fall that kills you, it's the ground at the end of it. It's gravity, the fatal pull of the planet. There was water at the bottom of the chasm, the tide rising, foam churning against the sheer sides. He could hear the water, but in what was left of the daylight he could barely see it.

He took a deep breath at last and drew back, stretching his spine. There was an hour left till dusk: not much time. They wouldn't find him now. He'd had one piece of luck about seventy-five minutes ago, but reckoned he was allowed one lucky break per mission.

At least they were quiet now, his pursuers. They weren't yelling ill-considered commands back and forth, their words car-rying on the sweet, still air all the way to where he lay listening. And they'd split into two-man patrols: also well-learned. He wondered whose idea that had been. They would know by now that time was against them, know too that they were tired, cold, and hungry. They'd give up before he did.

3

That was the edge he had on them. Not a physical edge — some of them were younger, fitter, stronger than him — but a psychological one. The sharpest edge there was.

He looked up and listened, breathed in the wet bracken, the small dull buds, the charged air. There were thunderclouds in the distance, moving farther away. A torrent of rain had swept the land yet again. There was nothing worse for the spirits than a periodical drenching. Their spirits, not his. They weren't within a mile of him. They weren't anywhere close. None of them would be blooded today.

He checked himself. Overconfidence. It had to be avoided. The most dangerous part of a mission, *any* mission, was the last part — those final few hours, or minutes, or even seconds. Your brain starts winding down, your tired body doing the same. And you start to make mistakes. He shook his head roughly, feeling the pain across his shoulders. He was carrying seventy-five pounds, which would have been nothing five or ten years before — he'd carried double that in the Falklands; some Special Air Service missions in the Gulf War had carried even more — but now he'd been carrying the rucksack for thirty-six hours, and the pack was wet and heavy.

He set off again after checking his map, walking backwards through the mud, sometimes circling so he crossed over his own tracks. He took a pride in all this confusion — a confusion his pursuers probably wouldn't even notice. They had, perhaps, turned back already. But this wasn't about *them* at all. It was about him. He'd never doubted it for a moment.

He started to climb again, with his back to the ground, heels pushing into the soil, his rucksack transferred to his chest. Near the top of the ridge he paused, listened, and heard a sound he could identify all too easily: paper tearing, being crushed. The ball of silver foil bounced close to him and stopped. He could hear no footsteps, no advance, no retreat — and no conversation. A sentry, then; a lone lookout. Maybe part of an observation post, which would mean two men. They had, after all, split into two-man patrols. He heard a bar of chocolate being snapped in two. He became certain he was dealing with a stand-alone; the other man must be out on recce.

The close of daylight being so near, it was tempting to take a prisoner, a hostage. But he knew it was only tempting because he was tired. Overconfidence again. He was trying to evade the enemy, not engage it. But if feet shuffled towards the overhang, if toecaps sent crumpled earth showering down, if a pair of eyes wondered what was below . . . The gun was ready.

He hugged the soil and grass, feeling the damp soaking into his back. To take his mind off it, he did a little mental check, ensuring he was ready for anything.

He was.

A sigh from above, barely ten feet away. Then: "Sod this for a lark," and the sound of feet shuffling away, a throat being cleared, phlegm hawked onto the ground. Minus points, he thought — traces left for any pursuer: a gob of spit, some silver foil. Plus speaking out loud. Very minus points.

One day, he thought, one day not so very long ago, I'd have crept up behind you and dug my knife into your throat. Not a slit — a throat was tougher than you thought; a slit often wouldn't be enough — you went for maximum damage in minimum time, and above all you wanted to get the voice box. So you stuffed the point of the dagger into the throat and poked around with it.

Jesus.

He had that nightmare sometimes. Not so often these days. It worried him that he didn't dream about Joan and Allan. He never dreamed about them at all, yet they were his whole life — they were his saving.

He was wondering where the other man was, the one the chocolate-eater had gone to find. Last thing he wanted was for the bastard to stumble on him lying here, exposed, with the rucksack on his chest getting in the way of his gun.

Go back down the slope, or head up over the rise? He gave it another minute, then wormed his way upwards, peering over the lip. Open countryside, a rounded dip to the land like a giant saucer; and a hundred yards away, stumbling along, the chocolate-eater. He recognized the young man, even from behind, even in this light and from this distance. He recognized his useful bulk, not too much of which was flab. A quick check of the map confirmed he was headed back to the enemy base. He wasn't looking for anyone. He just wanted to be indoors with a mug of something hot and wet. He'd had enough.

A final look at the map, committing it to memory. Soon it would be too dark to read, and the use of a torch, even the thinnest pencil-lead beam, was dangerous. So dangerous it was verboten during most active missions except in the direst emergency. There'd be no dire emergency this time.

He tracked the chocolate-eater, keeping a steady distance. After a while a tall, thin man joined up with the chocolate-eater and they had a muted discussion, pointing their arms in various directions like windblown weather vanes. Together they set off for camp, unaware that they were being watched by the very man they were supposed to capture at any cost.

Eventually, the "camp" itself came into view: two olive-green Land Rovers with roofs that had once been white. There were three men already there, hovering around a steaming kettle on a Campingaz stove. They were shuffling their feet and checking their watches.

He knew this land fairly well by now, and decided to get closer. It would mean a hike of a couple of miles, around to the other side of the encampment where the ground cover was thicker. He set off, crouching low, crawling on his belly when necessary. Another two-man patrol was coming home, and passed within a hundred yards of him. He made himself part of the scenery. They weren't really concentrating anymore — they were too close to home, not expecting anything. The most dangerous time.

At one point he heard a cry of "Come out, come out!" followed by laughter. The laughter had an embarrassed edge to it. They'd be even more embarrassed if he walked into their camp, his gun trained on them.

He was where he wanted to be now, separated by the vehicles from the campfire and the men. They hadn't set guards; they hadn't done anything. Overconfidence. He lay his rucksack on the ground and started to crawl in towards their position. He knew his target. He was going to crawl right under one of the

Land Rovers and point his gun up at them as they drank their tea. Then he was going to say hello.

"Hello."

The voice behind him, over him. A woman's voice, sounding amused, as well she might. He rolled over onto his back and looked up at her, at the gun she was carrying. In her free hand, she held his rucksack. She was tutting now, shaking her head.

"Traces," she said. She meant the rucksack. He'd made no attempt to hide it. She glanced at her wristwatch. It was a man's chronometer with a time-lapse function.

"Thirty-six hours and three minutes," she said. "You almost didn't make it."

They were close enough to the Land Rovers for her voice to carry. The men in their camouflage uniforms came around to the back of the vehicles to see what was happening. He stood up and looked towards them, finding the chocolate-eater.

"Traces," he said, tossing the ball of silver paper. It landed in the young man's tin mug and floated in his tea.

They couldn't head back until everyone had returned to camp. Eventually, the last few stragglers came limping home. One of them, the car dealer, had twisted his ankle and was being supported by his two friends, one of whom — a school PE instructor — had badly blistered feet, the result of wearing the wrong kind of socks with nearly new boots.

"I think I've caught pneumonia," the man with the blisters said. He looked at the man they'd all been trying to catch for the past day and a half. Ten of them against one of him, within an area of six square miles outside which he was not allowed to operate. He was removing his belt-kit, always the last thing he shed. It comprised his survival kit, knife, compass, first-aid kit, water bottle, and chocolate bars. The PE instructor hobbled over and touched his arm, then his chest.

"How come you're not soaked like the rest of us?" He sounded aggrieved. "There's not a bit of shelter out there, hardly a bloody tree. You been cheating, Reeve?"

Gordon Reeve stared at the man. "I never need to cheat, Mr. Matthews." He looked at the other men. "Anyone know how I kept my clothes dry?" Nobody spoke up. "Try some lateral thinking. How can you keep your clothes dry if you've nothing to cover them with?" They still didn't answer. Reeve looked towards his wife. "Tell them, Joan."

She had placed his rucksack against a Land Rover and was using it as a seat. She smiled towards Reeve. "You take them off," she said.

Reeve nodded at the men. "You take them off and you stash them in your pack. You let the rain do its stuff, and when it stops you get dry again and you put your nice dry clothes back on. You've been cold and wet and miserable for a while, but you're dry afterwards. One final lesson learned, gentlemen." He took a mug from the ground and poured a brew into it. "And by the way, you were crap out there. You were absolute crap."

They drove back to the house for debriefing. The Reeves had turned the stables into an annex that included a shower room with a dozen spray nozzles; a changing room with metal lockers, so each man could store his civvy clothes and all the other paraphernalia of the life they were leaving behind for seventy-two hours; a well-equipped gym; and a small conference room.

The conference room was where Reeve did most of the initial teaching. Not the physical stuff — that was done in the gym, or outside in the courtyard and surrounding countryside — but the other lessons, the show-and-tell. There was a monitor and a video machine; a slide projector; various blackboards, wall maps, and diagrammatic charts; a big oval table and a dozen or so functional chairs. There were no ashtrays; no smoking was allowed indoors. Smoking, as Reeve reminded each new intake, is bad for your health. He wasn't talking about lung cancer; he was talking about traces.

After showering, the men dressed in their civvies and headed for the conference room. There was a bottle of whiskey on the table, but none of them would sniff a drop until the debriefing —

and then there'd be just the single glass apiece, as most of them were driving home after dinner. Joan Reeve was in the kitchen, making sure the oven had done its work. Allan would have laid the table, then made a tactical retreat to his room to play another computer game.

When they were all seated, Gordon Reeve stood up and went to the blackboard. He wrote the letter *P* seven times with lime-green chalk. "The seven *P*'s, gentlemen. Not the seven dwarves, not the Magnificent Seven, and not the seven moons of Jupiter. I couldn't name the seven dwarves, I couldn't name the Magnificent Seven, and sure as shit sticks to your arse I couldn't name the seven moons of Jupiter. But I can tell you the seven *P*'s. Can you tell *me?*"

They shifted in their seats and offered up a few words. When they got a word right, Reeve chalked it on the board.

"Piss," he said, writing it down. "Planning . . . Poor . . . Proper . . ." He saw they were struggling, so he turned away from the board. "Proper Planning and Preparation Prevent Piss-Poor Performance. I could add an eighth *P* today: Procedure. You were a shambles out there. A barefoot Cub Scout blind from birth could have avoided you these past thirty-six hours. An elephant looking for the graveyard could have avoided you. The British Ladies' fucking Equestrian Team and their horses could have given you a run for your money. So now it's time to evaluate exactly what went so bloody disastrously wrong."

They exchanged sad glances; his captives. It was going to be a long time till dinner.

After dinner and good-byes, after seeing them all off in their cars, waving them back to their real lives, Reeve went upstairs to try to convince Allan that it was bedtime.

Allan was eleven and "bookish" — except that in his case the adjective referred to computers, computer games, and videos. Reeve didn't mind in the least that his son wasn't the outdoor type. Friends thought maybe Reeve would have preferred a musclebound son who was good at football or rugby. Friends were wrong. Allan was a lovely-looking kid, too, with a strawberry-cream complexion and peach fuzz on his cheeks. He had short fair hair which curled at the nape of his neck, and deep blue eyes. He looked like his mother; everybody said so.

He was in bed, apparently asleep, when Reeve opened the door. The room was still warm from computer-use. Reeve went over and touched the top of the monitor — it was hot. He lifted the plastic cover off the hard drive and found it was still switched on. Smiling, Reeve nudged the mouse and the screen came to life. A game screen was held on pause.

He walked over to the bed, crunching magazines and comics underfoot. The boy didn't move when Reeve sat down on the bed. His breathing sounded deep and regular; too deep, too regular.

Reeve stood up again. "Okay, partner, but no more games, right?"

He'd opened the door before Allan sat bolt upright, grinning. Reeve smiled back at him from the doorway. "Get some sleep . . . or else."

"Yes, Dad."

"How are you getting on with that game?"

"I'll beat it, just you wait. Uncle James always sends me games that're too hard."

Uncle James was Reeve's brother, a journalist. He was working out in the States, and had sent Allan a couple of computer games as a very belated birthday-and-Christmas-combined present. That was typical of James; kids always forgave him his forgetfulness because he made it up to them once a year or so.

"Well, maybe I can help you with it."

"I'll do it myself," Allan said determinedly. "There's one screen I can't get past, but after that it'll be okay."

Reeve nodded. "What about homework, is it done?"

"Done. Mum checked it this afternoon."

"And do you still hate Billy?"

Allan wrinkled his face. "I *loathe* Billy."

Reeve nodded again. "So who's your best friend now?"

Allan shrugged.

"Go to sleep now," his father said, closing the door. He waited in the hall, listening for the crackle of footsteps on paper as Allan left the bed and headed for the computer. But he didn't hear anything. He stayed a little longer, staring along the passageway. He could hear Joan downstairs, watching television. The dishwasher was busy in the kitchen. This is home, he thought. This is my place. This is where I'm happy. But part of him was still crouching in the rain while a patrol passed nearby . . .

Downstairs, he made a couple of mugs of instant coffee and headed for the living room. This had been a farmhouse once, just a couple of rooms and an attic reached by a ladder. Reeve imagined that in the winters the farmer brought his animals into the house, keeping them warm and using them as central heating. The place had been uninhabited for eight years when they bought it. Joan had seen potential in the house — and Reeve had seen potential in the seclusion. They were close enough to civilization, but they were on their own.

It had taken time to settle on this location. The Scottish Borders would have provided better communications; clients driving up from London could have done the trip in half a day. But Reeve had finally opted for South Uist. He'd been here on holiday once as a child and had never really forgotten it. When he persuaded Joan to come with him to see it again he pretended it was just a holiday, but really he'd been sizing up the place. There were a few villages nearby; but for the most part there was nothing at all. Reeve liked that. He liked the wilderness and the hills. He liked the isolation.

Most of his clients came from England, and didn't mind the travel. For them, it was part of the overall experience. They were a mixed lot: hikers looking for something more; gung-ho apocalyptic types, shaping up for the final showdown; trainee bodyguards; all-purpose masochists. Reeve provided intensive training that was partly field craft, partly survivalist. His aim, he told them at the outset, was to get them to use their *instincts* as well as any skills they might learn along the way. He was teaching them to survive, whether it be in the office or on a wind-chilled mountaintop. He was teaching them to survive.

The final test was the pursuit. It was never a no-win situation for the weekend soldiers. If they planned, prepared, and worked together, they could find him easily within the time allotted. If they read their maps, found themselves a leader, split into pairs, and covered the ground systematically, there was no way he could elude them. The area wasn't that big, and boasted few enough hiding places. It didn't matter if they couldn't find him, just so long as they learned their lesson, learned that they might have found him if only they'd gone about it the right way.

The chocolate-eater was going to be somebody's bodyguard someday. He probably thought being a bodyguard was all about being big and holding a clean driving license; a sort of chauffeur with clout. He had a lot to learn. Reeve had met a few heavyweight bodyguards, international types, political types. Some of them had been in Special Forces at the same time as him. Chocolate-chops had a long way to go.

He never told clients he'd been in the SAS. He told them he was ex-infantry, and mentioned a few of his campaigns: Northern Ireland, the Falklands . . . He never went into detail, though he was often pressed. As he said, none of that was important; it was the past. It was just stories — stories he never told.

The living room was warm. Joan was curled up on the sofa, tending to the immediate needs of Bakunin the cat while they both watched TV. She smiled as she took the mug from him. Bakunin gave him a dirty look for daring to interrupt the stroking session. Reeve made a tactical withdrawal and sank into his favorite chair. He looked around the room. Joan had decorated it, doing her usual thorough job. This is what home is all about, he thought. This is fine.

"You slipped up today," she said, her eyes still on the TV.

"Thanks for making me look good."

"Sorry. I didn't know that was my job."

Did she want an argument? He didn't need one. He concentrated on the coffee.

"Did you get all their checks?" she asked, still not looking at him.

"They're in the drawer."

"In the cashbox?"

"In the drawer," he repeated. He couldn't taste the coffee.

"You gave them their receipts?"

"Yes."

She didn't say anything after that, and neither did he, but she'd managed to get beneath his skin again. She could do it so easily. He'd been trained for most things, but not for this. Joan would have made a great interrogator.

This is home, he thought.

Then the phone rang.

TWO

THE CO-WORLD CHEMICALS BUILDING was situated on the corner of B Street and Fifth Avenue in downtown San Diego. That put it about sixteen miles north of the Mexican border, which was a lot closer than Alfred Dulwater liked. The place was practically a foreign country as far as he was concerned. He knew, too, that the city's Gaslamp Quarter started only a couple of blocks south of the CWC building, and though the city had cleaned the place up and now advertised it to tourists as "historic," it was still as full of panhandlers and bums as it was overpriced restaurants and knickknack shops.

Dulwater came from Denver. As a kid, he'd taken a map of the USA and drawn two diagonals through it, one from Seattle to Miami, the other from Boston to San Diego. In so doing, he'd managed to prove to himself that Denver, Colorado, was just about at the heart of the blessed United States. Okay, Topeka had actually been nearest the cross-sights, but Denver was close, too.

He didn't live in Denver these days, though. The private investigation company he worked for — indeed, was the newest junior partner in — operated out of Washington, DC. The image a lot of people had of PIs was the usual fictional one: grubby men chain-smoking on motel stakeouts. But Alfred Dulwater's firm, Alliance Investigative, wasn't like that. Even its name made it sound more like an insurance company than some two-bit outfit. Alliance was big and prosperous and worked for only select clients, most of them big corporations like Co-World Chemicals. Dulwater didn't mind at all working for CWC, even on something which seemed so trivial, but he did mind that Kosigin kept bringing him to San Diego. Usually, a report would be delivered by trusted messenger service. It was very unusual for a client to demand that a junior partner deliver the report personally; in the present case it was not just one report, but several, requiring several trips to Southern California — crazy economics, since the subject was living and working locally. It meant Dulwater had to fly out here, rendezvous with his team of investigators, read through their report, and then carry the same to San Diego, like he was a damned postman.

Still, Kosigin was paying. As old man Allerdyce at Alliance said, "He who pays is king." At least for a day.

Mr. Allerdyce was taking a close interest in this investigation. It seemed Kosigin had approached him personally and asked him to take on the case. This was a simple surveillance, with background biography and clippings. They were to look for the usual — dirt buried beneath the fingernails of the subject's past — but were also to report on his workday activities.

Which, really, as Dulwater had suggested to Mr. Allerdyce, was a bit beneath them; they were *corporate* investigators. But Allerdyce had sat behind his huge oak desk and pouted thoughtfully, then waved his fingers in the air, dismissing the complaint. And now *he* wanted regular reports from Dulwater, too. Dulwater wasn't stupid; he knew that if he kept in with the old man, did a good job, and kept quiet, then there might be advancement. And he lived for advancement.

No Mexicans seemed to work in the CWC building. Even the doorman, the security guard who checked Dulwater's identity, and the cleaner polishing the brass rails on the wall between the four elevators were all male, all white. Dulwater liked that. That had class. And the air-conditioning pleased him, too. San Diego was warm-to-hot; it was like that all year, except when it got *real* hot. But there were sea breezes, you had to admit that. It wasn't a baking or steamy heat. It would've been quite pleasant if

Dulwater hadn't been trussed into a blue woollen three-piece with a tie constricting his neck. Damned suit and shirt used to fit — but then he'd added some weight recently, since the injury to his knee stopped his weekly squash torture.

There was a gym in the CWC building. It was one floor below the lobby, and one floor up from parking. Dulwater had never been that far down, but he'd been right to the top, and he was going there again. The security guard came with him to the elevator and turned his key in the lock, pressing the button for the fourteenth floor. You couldn't simply press the button, you needed the key as well, like in some of the hotels Dulwater had stayed in, the ones with penthouse and executive levels. The doors closed, and he tried to stop seeming nervous. Kosigin wasn't the biggest fish within the multinational; he was maybe number five or six in the States, which made him seven or eight in the world. But he was young and arrogant with it, and Dulwater didn't like his attitude. In another life, he'd have punched him out and then given him a sharp-toed kick in the lumbar region for good measure.

But this was business, and Kosigin was king for the duration of the meeting. The doors opened, bringing Dulwater out onto the thick, silent carpeting of the fourteenth floor. There was a reception area, with only three doors leading off. Each door led to an office, and each office covered several hundred square feet, so that they didn't feel like offices at all; they felt more like temples. The secretary, who was actually known as a "personal assistant," smiled at him.

"Good morning, Mr. Dulwater." She still pronounced it *dull-water*, even though on his first visit he'd corrected it to *doo-latter*. In truth, the family back in Denver said *dull-water*, too, but Alfred didn't like the sound of that, just as he'd hated all the jibes and nicknames at school and college. When he left for Washington, he'd decided to reject *dull-water* and become *doo-latter*. He liked *doo-latter*. It sounded like it had class.

"Mr. Kosigin will be about five minutes. If you'd like to wait inside . . ."

Dulwater nodded and approached the door to Kosigin's office, which the secretary unlocked with a button beneath the lip of her desk. Then he walked in.

That was another thing. He'd looked at Kosigin's name and thought *koss-eegin*, like the Soviet guy in the fifties — or was it sixties? But the name was pronounced *kossigin*, rattled off in a single breath, all the letters short and hard. There was a hardness to Kosigin's office which matched both his name and personality. Even the works of art looked harsh and brutal: the paintings were full of squared-off objects, geometric shapes in dull colors; the sculptures looked like either disfigured people or things that had gotten too close to a heat source. And even the view, which should have been fantastic, was somehow harder, crueler than it merited. You couldn't quite see the waterfront — there were other, taller buildings in the way. He thought he could see the shiny Marriott through a gap in the downtown buildings, but the way it reflected light it could have been anything.

True to his investigator's skills, Dulwater didn't spend much time on the view but walked over to Kosigin's desk, just to see what was there. The answer as usual was disappointingly little. It was an ornate antique desk, maybe French, with bowed legs that looked like they'd snap if you put any weight on them. It was quite long but narrow, and didn't seem to square with Kosigin's chosen chair, a workaday swivel model with red covers and black plastic armrests. Dulwater got the feeling Kosigin did his real work elsewhere. On the desk's surface were a blotter pad, a tray of pens and stuff, and a small Anglepoise. It could've been a student's desk; it could have been *any*body's desk.

He took stock of the rest of the room. There was a lot of bare parquet floor between himself and the living area. This comprised a sofa and two chairs, all done in black crushed leather; a large and well-stocked liquor cabinet, with empty decanter and crystal glasses on top; and a couple of TV sets, one of which seemed to be switched on permanently. It was showing C-Span with the sound on mute.

Some of the wall space was taken up with tall freestanding wooden cabinets, locked, and never opened in Dulwater's presence. He didn't know if they were empty or full, if they contained files or Kosigin's shoe collection. Hell, maybe they were secret doors to other offices. It didn't much matter. What mattered was that Kosigin was keeping him waiting. He put his briefcase — rigid, mat-black, almost impossible to open without both keys, official Alliance issue — on the low table next to the working TV and sat himself down on the sofa. There was no remote for the TV that he could see, but he found the control panel on the front of the set, eased its cover aside, and changed channels. There was a Rolling Stones tribute on MTV, so he left it at that and sat back to watch, not bothering with the sound.

He wondered again about the surveillance. Surely a corporation like CWC, one of the globe's chemical giants, could and would afford its own security operatives. Why hadn't Kosigin handed the pissant job to them? And why was old man Allerdyce taking such a close interest? It wasn't as though he was afraid Dulwater would screw up; he'd assured him of that. Why then? What was it about this guy James Reeve, this asshole Anglo with the boring personal habits and the peripatetic job? That wasn't Dulwater's concern, just like Mr. Allerdyce had said. What was his phrase? "We are the means, not the end." It sounded great when he said it, but what the fuck did it mean?

He walked over to one of the windows and looked directly down onto the street below. One block south was an orange-and-green trolley-bus on its tourist route, one of the old city trolleys almost colliding with it. He hoped the tourists would have more sense than to get off in Gaslamp.

"Mr. Dulwater."

He hadn't even heard the door opening, but when he turned, Kosigin was already halfway to his desk. He wasn't looking at Dulwater, though; he was looking over towards the TV and the briefcase. The briefcase wasn't supposed to leave Dulwater's hands. It made going to the john an interesting outing, but those were the explicit instructions. Dulwater went over to retrieve the case. By the time he got back to the desk, Kosigin had unlocked a drawer and brought out a remote. He pointed it towards the distant TV and flipped back to its original channel. Dulwater almost apologized, but didn't. Apologies made you weak. Besides, what had he done wrong?

He sat down opposite Kosigin and watched the man put the remote back in the drawer and relock it with a key he tucked into his vest pocket. For a few seconds, all he had was a view of the top of Kosigin's head, with its thick salt-and-pepper hair, curling and luxuriant. Maybe he had it dyed like that to look older. When he looked up, Kosigin almost seemed like a teenager, with bright healthy cheeks and sparkling eyes with no wrinkles or creases. His burgundy silk tie shimmered with life. Then he slipped on his metal-rimmed glasses and changed again. He didn't need to harden his face; the glasses did that for him. And the voice — the voice was pure authority.

"Now then, Mr. Dulwater."

Which was Dulwater's cue to unlock the briefcase. He took one key from his jacket pocket and slipped off his left shoe to retrieve the second key from where he had taped it to the heel of his sock. The case was fireproof, bombproof, and tamperproof; if anyone attempted to open it without both keys, a small incendiary wiped out the contents. Dulwater opened the case with ease, Kosigin avoiding eye contact as he waited for the investigator to place the file on his desk. The first time they'd met, Dulwater had held out the file and Kosigin had sat like a dummy until Dulwater realized what was wanted of him: Kosigin didn't want any contact with the investigator, not so much as linkage by a document folder. So now Dulwater placed the file on the desk, and when he'd taken his hand away, Kosigin slid the file a bit closer and opened it, leafing through the sheets of paper.

It was a thick report this time: further background, biographies of friends, colleagues, family. It had taken hundreds of man-hours to compile, including use of investigators overseas. It was utterly thorough.

"Thank you, Mr. Dulwater."

And that was it — no small talk, no drink, no eye contact, even. Alfred Dulwater was dismissed.

After the investigator had gone, Kosigin took the file over to one of the leather chairs and made himself comfortable. He glanced up at the TV whenever he turned to a new sheet, but otherwise had eyes only for the report. He didn't like Dulwater — the man was oversized and slow-witted — but he had to concede that Allerdyce ran an impressive operation.

He reread the report, taking his time. He didn't want to make the wrong decision, after all, not when it might be such a *serious* decision. James Reeve the journalist was no longer just a thorn in CWC's side, and the man would not take a warning. Money had been attempted; threats had been attempted; physical threats, too. But the journalist was either very stupid or simply overconfident.

Kosigin read for a third time the updated biography. Several things caught his eye: a failed marriage which ended in acrimony and legal debts; a drinking problem; flirtation with narcotics — some speed and coke, plus grass, but then nearly everyone in California did grass — several unsuccessful relationships since the marital breakup. No children. And now a story that was going nowhere — a state of affairs which might just break Reeve. There was one brother, but no one of importance. And no powerful friends, no real allies.

He buzzed Alexis and asked her to bring him coffee, decaffeinated with one percent milk. Then he took out his leather-bound address book and made a telephone call to Los Angeles.

"It's me," he said into the receiver. "How soon can you get down here?"

THREE

Jᴀᴍᴇs Rᴇᴇᴠᴇ ᴡᴏᴋᴇ ᴜᴘ ᴛʜᴀᴛ ᴍᴏʀɴɪɴɢ feeling the usual apprehension.

He'd really tied one on the previous night, but there was nothing so unusual in that. In the course of his life he'd been kicked out of more bars than he cared to remember. His motel room looked unfamiliar to him, until he caught sight of the large suitcase — his suitcase — its contents spewing out onto the olive-green carpet. Yes, that looked familiar all right. He'd seen that suitcase look the same way all over the USA, Europe, and the Far East. The case had probably done more traveling than most of the world's population.

It took him a couple of minutes to reach the bathroom, what with getting dizzy and having to sit on the end of the bed for a moment, screwing shut his eyes against the headache and the white flashes. It was the kind of thing Vietnam vets should get: huge phosphor explosions across the glaze of his eyeballs.

"I'm not cut out for drinking," he told himself, reaching for the first cigarette, knowing it was a mistake even as he did so, even as he placed it between his lips, even as he lit it and inhaled.

He almost had to pick himself up off the floor after that. God, it hurt, and it tasted foul. But it was necessity. Sheer addiction, like with the drink. Some men were built for alcohol; they had large frames which soaked up the juice, and brains which rejected all thought of a hangover. On the other hand, he was lean and lanky — and by Christ he got hangovers. He guessed by now his liver must be about the size of a sheep's head. It was a wonder it hadn't pushed all his other organs aside, knocked them out of the game. He loved drinking but hated getting drunk. But of course by the time he was getting drunk, the defenses were all down, so he kept on drinking. It was a problem. It surely was a problem.

So why did he drink?

"I drink therefore I am," he reasoned, rising once more from the bed. He smiled through the pain. Maybe his brother would have appreciated the philosophy. Or maybe it was the wrong kind of philosophy. He'd never been able to figure Gordon out, not for a minute. He suspected — no, hell, he *knew* — Gordon had been in the SAS or one of those other quasisecret branches of armed service. He knew it just as surely as he knew the bathroom was only another three hundred yards away. Maybe if I crawl, he thought, maybe everything would be easier if I resorted to all fours, returning to nature, communing with my fellow beasts. Hell, this is California, the idea might catch on. Every other idea in the world had. You could get Tai Chi with your chili or send your kids to Satanist preschool. Every loony in the world seemed to have landed here with their One Idea, some life-changing thing that might take off. You'd always find at least *one* sucker, one easy-to-dupe disciple.

I'm a journalist, he thought. I'm a persuader. I could have half of Beverly Hills crawling on all fours and talking to the dogs and cats in no time. What I can't do, right now, is find my way to the bathroom.

He was sweating when he finally crawled up to the toilet, the sweat cooling his back and brow as he threw up in the bowl. He hauled himself up and sat, resting his head against the cold porcelain sink. He was beginning to feel better, his heart rate slowing, even starting to consider the day ahead, his agenda, things that must be done. Like phone Eddie. Then he'd try to talk to that pharmacist again. But first he had to phone Eddie.

He pulled himself up to standing and stared into the mirror. Most of the glass was covered with dried toothpaste. A woman he'd had back here a few nights before had left a message for him. She'd been gone by the time he got up. He'd stumbled through to the bathroom and leaned against the sink, rubbing his head against the cool mirror. When he'd finally looked up, he saw he'd smeared away whatever the message had been and had red and white stripes of toothpaste clogged in his hair.

When he went back into the bedroom, he saw he'd plugged the laptop in some time the previous night, which showed fore-thought; the batteries would be charged up by now. He couldn't live without his laptop. Just as some people had cats, and held them in their laps and stroked them, he had his computer. It was like therapy; when he picked it up and started to work the keys, he felt his worries evaporate. It felt stupid when he said it to people, but it made him feel immortal; he was writing, and that writing would one day be published, and once something was published it became immortal. People would store it, hoard it, keep it for reference, read it, devour it, cross-reference it, trans-fer it to other media like microfiche or CD-ROM. His laptop was a hangover cure, a panacea. Maybe that was the reason he wasn't afraid of Co-World Chemicals. Maybe.

He sat on the bedroom floor and went through his recent notes. The thing was shaping up — at least, he hoped it was. There was a lot of speculation in there, stuff that needed, as any editor would tell him, meat on its bones. And by meat they'd mean validation. He needed to get people to talk on the record. Hell, even *off* the record would do for the moment. He could still let an editor have a listen to off-the-record remarks. Then maybe that editor would have a check made out to him so he could bol-ster his flagging finances.

The catch was, he was in hock to Giles Gulliver in London, and the bugger was refusing to front him any more cash until he'd seen a story he could run with. Catch-22. He needed more money if he was going to be able to give Giles that story. So now he was looking for a spin-off, something he could sell elsewhere. Jesus, he'd already pitched at a couple of travel editors, pieces about San Diego, the border, Tijuana, La Jolla. He'd do the zoo or Sea World if they wanted it! But they didn't want anything from him. They knew his reputation. Knew several of his reputations. They knew he was bad with deadlines, and didn't write nice little travel articles to be read over the Sunday cornflakes and coffee. That wasn't journalism anyway — it was filler, an excuse for a cramming of ads, and he'd told three travel editors exactly that. Also that they could go bugger themselves.

Which left him running out of money fast, and reduced to cheap motels where they cleaned the rooms once a week and skimped on the towels. He had to work faster. Either that or take CWC's money, use it to placate Giles, and buy a holiday with whatever was left. Everyone would be happier that way. Maybe even *he'd* be happier. But it didn't work like that. There was a story out there, and if he didn't get it, it would nag him for months, years even. Like the time he had to give up on the Faslane story. He'd been working for a London paper then, and the proprietor had told the editor to rein him in. He'd fumed, then resigned, then decided he didn't want to resign — so they fired him. He'd gone back to the story, working freelance, but couldn't get any further with it, and no one wanted to publish what he had except *Private Eye*, who'd given it half a page at the back of the mag.

God bless the Fourth Estate!

He had another cigarette, then pulled the phone off the bedside cabinet.

Once, he would have been living in a Hyatt or Holiday Inn, maybe even a Marriott. But times had changed, and James Reeve with them. He was meaner now; meaner in both senses. He left smaller tips (when he tipped at all: that guy in *Reservoir Dogs* had a point), and he was less pleasant. Poor people can't afford to be pleasant; they're too busy barely getting by.

Eddie's phone kept ringing and ringing, and Reeve let it ring until it was answered.

"What? What?"

"Good morning, sir," Reeve said sweetly, smoke pouring down his nose, "this is your requested alarm call."

There were groans and hacking coughs at the other end of the line. It was good to feel you weren't alone in your afflictions.

"You scumbag, you loathsome string of shit, you complete and utter douchehead."

"What is this?" said Reeve. "Dial-a-Foulmouth?"

Eddie Cantona wheezed, trying to speak and laugh and light a cigarette all at the same time. "So what's our schedule?" he finally said.

"Just get over here and pick me up. I'll think of something."

"Thirty minutes, okay?"

"Make it half an hour." James Reeve hung up the phone. He liked Eddie, liked him a lot. They'd met in a bar in the Gaslamp Quarter. The bar had a western theme and sold ribs and steaks. You ate at a long, hewn wooden bench, or at hewn wooden tables, and at the bar they served the tap beer in Mason jars. It was an affectation, yes, and it meant you didn't get a lot of beer for your money — but it was good beer, almost good enough and dark enough to be English.

Reeve had come into the dark, cool bar after a hot, unprofitable walk in the sunshine; and he'd drunk too many beers too quickly. And he'd got talking to the man on the stool beside him, who introduced himself as Eddie Cantona. Reeve started off by saying there was a football player called Cantona, then had to explain that he meant soccer, and that the player himself was French.

"It's a Spanish name," Eddie persisted. And it was, too, the way he said it, turning the middle syllable into *toe* and dragging the whole name out — whereas in England the commentators would try to abbreviate it to two syllables at most.

The conversation could only improve from there, and it did, especially when Eddie announced that he was "between appointments" and owned a car. Reeve had been spending a fortune on cabs and other modes of transport. Here was a driver looking for short-term employment. And a big man at that — someone who just might double as bodyguard should the need arise. By that point, Reeve had figured on the need arising.

Since then he'd been offered money to quit the story. And when he'd turned the offer down, there had been a silent beating in a back alley. They'd caught him while Eddie was off somewhere. They hadn't said a word, which was the clearest message they could have given.

And still James Reeve wanted the story. He wanted it more than ever.

*   *   *

They drove out to La Jolla first to visit the retired pharmacist unannounced.

It was a white-painted clapboard house (Eddie pronounced the word "clabbard"), a bungalow with not much land around it. It had a green picket fence, which was being freshly redecorated by a whistling workman in overalls. His van was parked with two wheels on the curb, its back doors open to show a range of paint cans, ladders, and brushes. He smiled and said, "Good morning to you" as James Reeve pushed open the stubborn gate. There were bells hanging from the latch, and they chimed as he closed it behind him.

He'd been here before, and the old man hadn't answered any of his questions. But persistence was a journalist's main line of attack. He rang the doorbell and took one pace back onto the path. The street wasn't close to La Jolla's seafront, but he guessed the houses would still be worth at least a hundred and fifty thou apiece. It was that kind of town. Eddie'd told him that Raymond Chandler used to live in La Jolla. To James's eye, there didn't seem much worth writing about in La Jolla.

He stepped up to the door again, tried the bell, then squatted to peer through the mail slot. But there was no mail slot. Instead, Dr. Killin had one of those mailboxes on a post near the gate, with a red flag beside it for when there was mail. The flag was down. James went to the only window fronting the bungalow and looked in at a comfortable living room, lots of old photographs on the walls, a three-seat sofa with floral covers taking up way too much room. He remembered Dr. Killin from their first, only, and very brief meeting. Killin had reminded him physically of Giles Gulliver, a knotted strength beneath an apparently frail exterior. He had a shiny domed bald head, the skull out of proportion to the frame supporting it, and thick-lensed glasses behind which the eyes were magnified, the eyelashes thick and curling.

The old fart wasn't home.

He walked back down the path and wrestled with the gate again. The painter stopped whistling and smiled up at him from his half-kneeling position.

"Ain't in," he informed James Reeve, like this was news.

"You might have said before I went three rounds with that damned gate."

The painter chuckled, wiping his green fingers on a rag. "Might've," he agreed.

"Do you know where he is?"

The man shook his head, then scratched his ear. "I was told something about a vacation. But how do you take a vacation when you live in paradise?" And he laughed, turning back to his task.

James Reeve took a step towards him. "When did he leave?"

"That I don't know, sir."

"Any idea when he'll be back?"

The painter shrugged.

The journalist cursed under his breath and leaned over the fence to open the mailbox, looking for something, anything.

"Shouldn't do that," the painter said.

"I know," said Reeve, "tampering with the U.S. Mail."

"Oh, I wouldn't know about that. But see, you got green paint on your shirt."

And so he had.

Dismissing the offer of mineral spirits, in need of another kind of spirit altogether, he stomped back to the car where Eddie was waiting for him. He got into the passenger seat.

"I heard," said Eddie.

"He's been scared off," Reeve declared. "I know he has."

"You could leave a business card or something, ask him to get back to you." Eddie started the engine.

"I did that last time. He didn't get back to me. He never let me past the front door."

"Well — old folks, they do get suspicious. Lot of muggings around."

James Reeve turned as best he could in the seat, so he was facing Eddie Cantona. "Eddie, do I look like a mugger?"

Eddie smiled and shook his head, pressing the accelerator. "But then you don't look like the Good Humor man either."

The painter watched them go, waved even, though they'd already forgotten about him. Then, still grinning, he wiped his hands as he walked to his van. He reached into the passenger side and took out a cell phone, holding it to his face. He stopped smiling only when the connection was made.

"They were just here," he said.

That afternoon, Eddie dropped his employer off downtown, on the corner of Eighth and E. James Reeve had some work to do at the public library. He sometimes typed his notes into the laptop there, too — it was better than his motel room, a hundred times better. Surrounded by busy people, people with projects and ideas, people with *goals*, he found his own work, his own goal, became more focused.

Plus, the library was only four blocks from Gaslamp, which meant he could get a beer afterwards. Eddie had a couple of things to do, but said he might be in their regular haunt by six. If he still hadn't arrived by the time James felt like going home, the bar would call him a cab. It was an eight-dollar ride, including tip.

The story was slowing down, he decided. Here he was in San Diego, which should have been the heart of it, and he wasn't getting anywhere. He had Preece and the pesticide research, but that was years back. He had a rape, also ancient history. He had stories from two retired investigators. He had Korngold . . . but Korngold was dead.

He had Agrippa and the bank accounts. Maybe if he went back to England, concentrated on that particular corner of the puzzle, talked to Josh Vincent again; the union man's story was almost enough in itself. But he'd already pitched that at Giles Gulliver, who'd pooh-poohed it, saying the *Guardian* had run a similar story the year before. He'd checked, and the *Guardian* hadn't been following the same tack at all — but there'd been no persuading Giles, the stubborn old bastard.

So there was little enough for him to add to his files. He had other names, and had tried telephone calls, but no one wanted to meet him, or even talk on the phone. This was a shame, as he'd had his little recorder beside him, the microphone attached to the telephone earpiece. All his recordings showed so far was evasiveness on a grand scale, which didn't mean anything. Americans were wary of callers at the best of times. Blame all the cold-callers out there, interrupting lunch or dinner or a postprandial snooze to drum up money for everything from the Republican Party to Tupperware parties. He'd even had someone call him in his motel room, trying to sell him language courses. *Language courses!* Maybe they tried every room in every motel. Barrel-scraping was what it was.

Barrel-scraping.

He sighed, turned off the laptop, folded it away, and decided he could use a beer, Mason jar or no Mason jar. As he pushed through the library's main door the heat hit him again. It was very pleasant; almost too pleasant. You could go crazy in a place like this, with only slight fluctuations in temperature all year. Almost no rain, and the streets clean, and everyone so polite to you; it could get to you.

He found himself in the dimly lit air-conditioned bar, sliding onto what had become his favorite stool. The barmaid was new and wore cutoff denims and a tight white T-shirt. Her hair was tied back with a red bandanna, another one loose around her throat. Her legs, arms, and face were tanned and smooth. You just didn't get girls like that in England — not with that all-over even tan and that unsullied complexion — yet here they were thick on the ground. Then he looked in the long mirror behind the bar, seeing not only his own reflection, but those of his fellow drinkers. Who was he kidding? Imperfections were staring him in the face. Men — men in love with beer — pasty-faced and thick-paunched, with greasy thinning hair and little stamina. Here's to the lot of us, he thought, draining his first jar.

The drinker on the stool next to him didn't look in the mood for conversation, and the barmaid needed everything repeated twice, unable to comprehend his accent. "I haven't got an accent," he told her, then had to repeat that, too. So when Eddie hadn't turned up by 6:30, he thought about calling him. After all, he was Eddie's employer, and Eddie's job was to ferry him around. But that wasn't exactly fair, he decided, after a moment's thought. He was paying Eddie peanuts, and the guy was with him most of the day as it was — though he got the feeling Eddie hung around so he could pick up some free drinks and maybe even a free dinner.

He decided he wasn't hungry. He'd had enough. He just wanted to go back to his lousy motel and sleep for twelve or so hours. He asked if the barmaid could call him a cab, remembering to shorten the *a* in *cab* so she'd understand the word.

"Sure," she said.

Then the silent drinker next to him decided it was time to bow out, too. He walked out of the bar without saying a word, though he did nod in James's general direction, and he left a couple of dollars on the bar for the server, which was pretty generous. While she had her back to him, making the call, James slipped one of the dollars along to his own section of bar and left it there. Times were hard.

A minute later, the driver stuck his head into the bar.

"Mr. Reeve!" he called, then went back outside again. James Reeve slid off his stool and said so long to the assembly. He'd only had the four beers, and felt fine — maybe a little depressed as he picked up his laptop, but he'd been worse. He *would* do something with the story, something lasting, something immortal. He just needed a little more money and a lot more time. He couldn't just let it go, not when it affected the whole damned planet.

There were a couple of panhandlers directly outside, but he brushed past them. They never really bothered him. They took one look at him — his height, his pallor — and decided there were better options. The driver was holding the rear door open for him. The cab was unmarked, that struck him as he got in. And something else struck him, just a little too late.

He hadn't given the barmaid his name.

So how did the driver know it?

PART TWO
GHOSTS

FOUR

As HE DROVE SOUTH, Gordon Reeve tried to remember his brother, but the phone call kept getting in the way.

He could hear the operator telling him he had a call from the San Diego Police Department, then the detective's voice telling him it was about his brother.

"Very unfortunate circumstances, sir." The voice had betrayed no emotion. "It appears he took his own life."

There was a little more, but not much. The detective had wanted to know if he would be collecting the body and the effects. Gordon Reeve said yes, he would. Then he'd put the phone down and it rang again. He was slow to pick it up. Joan had been standing beside him. He remembered the look on her face, sudden shock and incomprehension mixed. Not that she'd known Jim well; they hadn't seen much of him these past few years.

The second phone call was from the British Consulate repeating the news. When Reeve told them he already knew, the caller sounded aggrieved.

Gordon Reeve had hung up the phone and gone to pack. Joan had followed him around the house, trying to look into his eyes. Was she looking for shock? Tears? She asked him a few questions, but he barely took them in.

Then he'd got the key to the killing room and gone outside.

The killing room was a single locked room attached to the outbuildings. It was fitted out as a cramped living room. There were three dummies dressed in castoff clothes — they represented hostages. Reeve's weekend soldiers, operating in teams of two, would have to storm the room and rescue the hostages by overpowering their captors — played by two more weekend soldiers. The hostages were to come to no harm.

Reeve had unlocked the killing room and switched on the light, then sat down on the sofa. He looked around him at the dummies, two seated, one propped upright. He remembered the living room of his parents' home, the night he'd left — all too willingly! — to join the army. He'd known he would miss Jim, his older brother by a year and a half. He would not miss his parents.

From early on, Mother and Father had led their own lives and had expected Jim and Gordon to do the same. The brothers had been close in those days. As they grew, it became clear that Gordon was the "physical" one, while Jim lived in a world of his own — writing poetry, scribbling stories. Gordon went to judo classes; Jim was headed to university. Neither brother had ever really understood the other.

Reeve had stood up and faced the standing dummy. Then he punched it across the room and walked outside.

His bag packed, he'd got into the Land Rover. Joan had already called Grigor Mackenzie who, hearing the circumstances, had agreed to put his ferry to the mainland at Gordon's disposal, though it was hours past the last sailing.

Reeve drove through the night, remembering the telephone call and trying to push past it to the brother he had once known. Jim had left university after a year to join an evening paper in Glasgow. Gordon had never known him as a serious drinker until he became a journalist. By that time, Gordon was busy himself: two tours of duty in Ulster, training in Germany and Scandinavia . . . and then the SAS.

When he saw Jim again, one Christmas when their father had just died and their mother was failing, they got into a fight about war and the role of the armed forces. It wasn't a physical fight, just words. Jim had been good with words.

The following year, he'd moved to a London paper, bought a flat in Crouch End. Gordon had visited it only once, two years ago. By then Jim's wife had walked out, and the flat was a shambles. Nobody had been invited to the wedding. It had been a ten-minute ceremony and a three-month marriage.

After which, in his career as in his life, Jim had gone freelance.

All the way to the final act of putting a gun in his mouth and pulling the trigger.

Reeve had pressed the San Diego detective for that detail. He didn't know why it was important to him. Almost more than the news of Jim's death, or the fact that he had killed himself, he had been affected by the *means*. Anti-conflict, anti-army, Jim had used a gun.

Other than stopping for diesel, Gordon Reeve drove straight to Heathrow. He found a long-term parking lot and took the courtesy bus from there to the terminal building. He'd called Joan from a service station, and she'd told him he was booked on a flight to Los Angeles, where he could catch a connecting flight to San Diego.

Sitting in Departures, Gordon Reeve tried to feel something other than numb. He'd sometimes found an article written by Jim in one of the newspapers — but not often. They'd never kept in touch, except for a New Year's phone call. Jim had been good with Allan, though, sending him the occasional surprise.

He bought a newspaper and a magazine and walked through duty-free without buying anything. It was Monday morning, which meant he'd no business to take care of at home, nothing pressing until Friday and the new intake. He knew he should be thinking of other things, but it was so hard. He was first in line when boarding time came. His seat on the plane was narrow. He discarded the pillow but draped the thin blanket over him, hoping he would sleep. Breakfast was served soon after takeoff; he was still awake. Above the clouds, the sun was a blazing orange. Then people started to pull down the shutters, and the cabin lights were dimmed. Headsets clamped on, the passengers started to watch the movie. Gordon Reeve closed his eyes again, and found that another kind of film was playing behind his eyelids: two young boys playing soldiers in the long grass . . . smoking cigarettes in the bathroom, blowing the smoke out of the window . . . passing comments on the girls at the school dance . . . patting arms as they went their separate ways.

Be the Superman, Gordon Reeve told himself. But then Nietzsche was never very convincing about personal loss and grief. Live dangerously, he said. Hate your friends. There is no God, no ordering principle. You must assume godhead yourself. Be the Superman.

Gordon Reeve, crying at thirty thousand feet over the sea. Then the wait in Los Angeles, and the connecting flight, forty-five minutes by Alaska Airlines. Reeve hadn't been to the USA before, and didn't particularly want to be here now. The man from the consulate had said they could ship the body home if he liked. As long as he paid, he wouldn't have to come to the States. But he had to come, for all sorts of jumbled reasons that probably wouldn't make sense to anyone else. They weren't really making sense to him. It was just a pull, strong as gravity. He had to see where it happened, had to know why. The consulate man had said it might be better not to know, just remember him the way he was. But that was just so much crap, and Reeve had told the man so. "I didn't know him at all," he'd said.

The car-rental people tried to give him a vehicle called a GMC Jimmy, but he refused it point-blank, and eventually settled for a Chevy Blazer — a three-door rear-drive gloss-black wagon that looked built for off-roading. "A compact sport utility," the clone at the desk called it; whatever it was, it had four wheels and a full tank of gas.

He'd booked into the Radisson in Mission Valley. Mr. Car Rental gave him a complimentary map of San Diego and circled the hotel district of Mission Valley.

"It's about a ten-minute drive if you know where you're going, twenty if you don't. You can't miss the hotel."

Reeve put his one large holdall into the capacious trunk, then decided it looked stupid there and transferred it to the passenger seat. He spotted a minibus parked in front of the terminal with the hotel's name on its side, so he locked the car and walked over to it. The driver had just seen a couple of tourists into the terminal and, when Reeve explained, said "sir" could follow him, no problem.

So Reeve tucked the Blazer in behind the courtesy bus and followed it to the hotel. He unloaded his bag and told the valet he didn't need any help with it, so the valet went to park his car instead. And then, standing at the reception desk, Reeve nearly fell apart. Nerves, shock, lack of sleep. Standing there, on the hotel's plush carpet, waiting for the receptionist to finish a telephone call, was harder than any thirty-six-hour pursuit. It felt like one of the hardest things he'd ever done. There seemed to be fog at the edges of his vision. He knew it must be exhaustion, that was all. If only the phone call hadn't come at the end of a weekend, when his defenses were down and he was already suffering from lack of sleep.

He reminded himself why he was here. Maybe it was pride that kept him upright until he'd filled in the registration form and accepted his key. He waited a minute for the elevator, took it to the tenth floor, finding his room, unlocking it, walking in, dumping the bag on the floor. He pulled open the curtains. His view was of a nearby hillside, and below him the hotel's parking lot. He'd decided on this hotel because it was the right side of San Diego for La Jolla. Jim had been found in La Jolla.

He lay down on the bed, which seemed solid and floating at the same time. He closed his eyes, just for a minute.

And woke up to late-afternoon sun and a headache.

He showered quickly, changed his clothes, and made a telephone call.

The police detective was very obliging. "I can come to the hotel if you like, or you can come down here."

"I'd appreciate it if you could come here."

"Sure, no problem."

He took the elevator back down to the ground floor and had some coffee in the restaurant, then felt hungry and had a sandwich. It was supposed to be too early for food, but the waitress took pity on him.

"You on vacation?"

"No," he told her, taking a second cup of coffee.

"Business?"

"Sort of."

"Where you from?"

"Scotland."

"Really?" She sounded thrilled. He examined her; a pretty, tanned face, round and full of life. She wasn't very tall, but carried herself well, like she didn't plan to make waitressing a career.

"Ever been there?" His mouth felt rusty. It had been a long time since he'd had to form conversations with strangers, social chitchat. He talked at the weekenders, and he had his family — and that was it. He had no friends to speak of; maybe a few old soldiers like him, but he saw them infrequently and didn't keep in touch between times.

"No," she said, like he'd said something humorous. "Never been outside South Cal, 'cept for a few trips across the border and a couple of times to the East Coast."

"Which border?"

She laughed outright. "Which border? Mexican, of course."

It struck him how ill-prepared he was for this trip. He hadn't done any background. He thought of the seven *P*'s, how he drilled them into his weekenders. Planning and preparation. How much *P&P* did you need to pick up the body of your brother?

"What's wrong?" she said.

He shook his head, not feeling like talking anymore. He got out the map the car-rental man had given him, plus another he'd picked up from a pile at reception, and spread them on the table. He studied a street plan of San Diego, then a map of the surrounding area. His eye moved up the coast: Ocean Beach, Mission Beach, Pacific Beach, and La Jolla.

"What were you doing here, Jim?"

He didn't realize he'd spoken out loud until he saw the waitress looking at him. She smiled, but a little uncertainly this time. Then she pointed to the coffeepot, and he saw that he'd finished the second cup. He nodded. Caffeine could only help.

*   *   *

"Mr. Reeve?" The man put out his hand. "They told me at reception I'd find you here. I'm Detective Mike McCluskey."

They shook hands, and McCluskey squeezed into the booth. He was a big fresh-faced man with a missing tooth which he seemed to be trying to conceal by speaking out of the other side of his mouth. There were shoots of stubble on his square chin where the razor hadn't done its job, and a small rash-line where his shirt collar rubbed his throat. He touched his collar now, as though trying to stretch it.

"I'm hellish sorry, sir," he said, eyes on the tablecloth. "Wish I could say welcome to San Diego, but I guess you aren't going to be taking too many happy memories away with you."

Reeve didn't know what to say, so he said thanks. He knew McCluskey hadn't been expecting someone like him. He'd probably been expecting someone like Jim — taller, skinnier, in less good all-around shape. And Reeve knew that if the eyes were the window on a man's soul, then his eyes were blackly dangerous. Even Joan told him he had a killer's stare sometimes.

But then McCluskey wasn't what Reeve had been expecting either. From the deep growl on the telephone, he'd visualized an older, beefier man, someone a bit more rumpled.

"Hell of a thing," McCluskey said, after turning down the waitress's offer of coffee.

"Yes," Reeve said. Then, to the waitress. "Can I have the bill?"

"We call it a check," McCluskey told Reeve when they were in the detective's car, heading out to La Jolla.

"What?"

"We don't call it a bill, we call it a check."

"Thanks for the advice. Can I see the police report on my brother's suicide?"

McCluskey turned his gaze from the windshield. "I guess," he said. "It's on the backseat."

Reeve reached around and picked up the brown cardboard file. While he was reading, a message came over McCluskey's radio.

"No can do," McCluskey said into the radio at the end of a short conversation.

"Sorry if I'm taking you away from anything," Reeve said, not meaning it. "I could probably have done this on my own."

"No problem," McCluskey told him.

The report was blunt, cold, factual. Male Caucasian, discovered Sunday morning by two joggers heading for the oceanfront. Body found in a locked rental car, keys in the ignition, Browning pistol still gripped in the decedent's right hand . . .

"Where did he get the gun?"

"It's not hard to get a gun around here. We haven't found a receipt, so I guess he didn't buy it at a store. Still leaves plenty of sellers."

Decedent's wallet, passport, driver's license, and so forth were still in his jacket pocket, along with the car rental agreement. Rental company confirmed that male answering the description of James Mark Reeve hired the car on a weekend rate at 7:30 P.M. Saturday night, paying cash up front.

"Jim always used plastic if he could," Reeve said.

"Well, you know, suicides . . . they often like to tie up the loose ends before they . . . uh, you know, they like to make a clean break . . ." His voice trailed off. Suicides; the next of kin. McCluskey was used to dealing with howling uncontrollable grief, or a preternatural icy calm. But Gordon Reeve was being . . . the word that sprang to mind was *methodical*. Or businesslike.

"Maybe," Reeve said.

Decedent's motel room was located and searched. No note was found. Nothing out of the ordinary was found, save small amounts of substances which tested positive as amphetamine and cocaine.

"We've had the autopsy done since that report was typed," McCluskey said. "Your brother had some booze in his system, but no drugs. I don't know if that makes you feel any better."

"You didn't find a note," Reeve stated.

"No, sir, but fewer suicides than you might think actually bother to leave a note. It looked like there'd been a message of some kind left on the mirror of the motel bathroom. He, uh . . . looks like it was written with toothpaste, but then wiped off. Might indicate the state of mind he was in."

"Any obvious reason why he would commit suicide?"

"No, sir, I have to admit I can't see one. Maybe his career?"

"I wouldn't know about that, I was only his brother."

"You weren't close?"

Reeve shook his head, saying nothing. Soon enough they arrived in La Jolla, passing pleasant bungalow-type houses and then larger, richer residences as they neared the oceanfront. La Jolla's main shopping street had parking on both sides of the road, trees sprouting from the sidewalk, and benches for people to sit on. The shops looked exclusive; the pedestrians wore tans, sunglasses, and smiles. McCluskey pulled the car into a parking bay.

"Where?" Reeve asked quietly.

"Two bays along." McCluskey nodded with his head.

Reeve undid his seat belt and opened the car door. "I'll be fine on my own," he told the detective.

There was a car in the second space along. It was a family model, with two kids playing in the back. They were boys, brothers. Each held a plastic spaceman; the spacemen were supposed to be battling each other, the boys providing sound effects. They looked at him suspiciously as he stared in at them, so he went and stood on the sidewalk and looked up and down the street. Jim's body had been found at six o'clock Sunday morning, which meant two o'clock Sunday afternoon in the UK. He'd been on the moor, chased by a group of weekend soldiers. Playing soldiers: that's how Jim had summed up his brother's life. At 2:00 P.M. it had been raining, and Gordon Reeve had been naked again, clothes bundled into his rucksack — naked except for boots and socks, crossing the wetland. And he hadn't felt a thing; no twinge of forewarning, no sympathetic gut-stab at his brother's agony, no fire in the brain.

McCluskey was standing beside him. Reeve turned his back and rubbed at dry, stinging eyes. The boys in the car had stopped play-

IAN RANKIN

ing and were looking at him, too. And now their mother was coming back with a young sibling, and she wanted to know what was
happening. Reeve walked quietly back to McCluskey's unmarked
car.

"Let's go," he said.

"Deal," said McCluskey.

They drank one drink apiece in an overpriced hotel bar. Reeve
insisted on paying. The detective wanted a beer, and though
Reeve knew he wasn't supposed to touch alcohol, he ordered
a whiskey. He knew he must be careful; his medication was back
in Scotland. But it was only one whiskey, and he deserved it.

"Why La Jolla?" he asked.

McCluskey shrugged. "I don't have an answer to that, except
maybe why not. Guy rents a car, suicide on his mind. He drives
around, and the world looks beautiful to him — so beautiful it
makes him sad, which he hadn't been expecting. And he decides,
fuck it, why not now?" He shrugged again.

Reeve was staring at him. "You almost sound like you've been
there yourself."

"Maybe I have. Maybe that's why I take the suicides. Maybe
that's why I like to spend some time with the still-living." Then
he shut up and sipped the beer.

"No note," Reeve said. "I can't believe it. The one thing in
his life Jim ever loved was words, especially printed ones. I'm
sure he'd've left a note; and a long one at that. A manuscript." He
was smiling. "He wouldn't have wanted to go quietly."

"Well, he created a news story in La Jolla. Maybe that was his
way of saying good-bye, a final front page."

"Maybe," Reeve said, half-believing, wanting to believe. He
finished the whiskey. It was a large shot, easily a double. He
wanted another, so it was definitely time to leave.

"Back to the hotel?" McCluskey suggested.

"The motel," Reeve corrected. "Jim's motel."

*   *   *

42

The room was as it had been.

They hadn't bothered to clean it up and relet it, McCluskey said, because James Reeve had paid until the middle of the week, and they knew his brother was coming and would take all the stuff away.

"I don't want it," Reeve said, looking at the clothes spilling from the suitcase. "I mean, there may be a couple of things . . ."

"Well, there are charities who'll take the rest of it; leave that side of things to me." McCluskey toured the room with hands in pockets, familiar with the place. Then he sat down on the room's only chair.

"Jim usually stayed in better than this," Reeve said. "Money must have been tight."

"You'd make a fine detective, Mr. Reeve. What line of work are you in?"

"Personnel management."

But McCluskey wasn't fooled by that. He smiled. "You've been in armed forces though, right?"

"How could you tell?" Reeve checked the bedside table, finding nothing but a copy of Gideon's Bible.

"You're not the only detective around here, Mr. Reeve. I know Vietnam vets, guys who were in Panama. I don't know what it is . . . maybe you all have the same careful way of moving, like you're always expecting a trip wire. And yet you're not afraid. I don't know."

Reeve held something up. It had been lying beneath the bed. "AC adapter," he said.

"Looks like."

Reeve looked around. "So where's whatever goes with it?"

McCluskey nodded towards the suitcase. "See that carrier bag there? Half hidden under those trousers."

Reeve went over and opened the bag. Inside were a small cassette recorder, microphone, and some tapes.

"I listened to the tapes," McCluskey said. "Blank, mostly. There are a couple of phone calls, sounded like your brother wanted to talk to some people."

"He was a journalist."

"So it says on his passport. Was he here covering a story?"

"I don't know. Haven't you found any notes? There must be a notebook or something."

"Not a damned thing. I wondered if maybe that was another reason for the trip to La Jolla."

"What?"

"To ditch all those kinds of things in the ocean. Clean break, see."

Reeve nodded. Then he held up the cable and the recorder. "It doesn't fit," he said. And he showed the detective that the adapter wouldn't connect with the small machine. "It just doesn't fit."

After the detective had dropped him back at his hotel, Reeve went upstairs to wash. He thought of telephoning Joan, but checked himself. In Scotland, it was the wee small hours of the following morning. He could phone her at 11:00 P.M. his time, but not before. He wasn't sure he'd still be awake at 11:00 P.M. He turned on the TV, looking for news, and found everything but. Then he made his way back downstairs. He used the stairs rather than the elevator, feeling the need for some exercise. At the bottom, he felt so good he climbed back up to the tenth floor and then descended again.

In the restaurant, he had soup, a steak, and a salad. He looked in at the bar, but decided against a drink. The hotel's gift shop was still open, though, and he was able to buy a detailed street map of San Diego, better than the tourist offerings he'd so far been given. Back in his room, he found a couple of bulky phone books in one of the dresser drawers, took them to the table, and started working.

FIVE

THE NEXT MORNING, REEVE WOKE UP early but groggy, and went to the window to check. The strange car wasn't there.

He'd seen it yesterday evening, outside Jim's motel, and had the feeling it followed McCluskey's car back here to the hotel. He thought he'd spotted it in the parking lot; a big old American model, something from the sixties or early seventies with spongy suspension and faded metallic-green paint that looked like a respray.

It wasn't there now, but that didn't mean it hadn't been there before.

He showered and telephoned Joan, having fallen asleep last night without fulfilling his own promise to himself. They spoke for only a couple of minutes, mostly about Allan. She asked a few questions about the trip, about Jim. Reeve's replies were terse; Joan would call it denial — she'd read some psychology books in her time. Maybe it was denial, or at least avoidance.

But there wouldn't be much more avoiding. Today he had to look at the body.

He ate breakfast in a quiet corner of the restaurant. It was buffet-style, with the usual endless coffee. There didn't seem to be many overnight guests, but a bulletin board in the reception area warned that the hotel would be playing host to a convention and a couple of large-scale civic meetings during the day. After three glasses of fresh orange juice and some cereal and French toast, he felt just about ready. Indeed, he felt so good he thought he might get through the day without throwing up.

He went out to the parking lot, not bothering to have the car brought out front for him. He wanted a good look around. Satisfied, he got into the Blazer and put his map on the passenger seat. He'd marked several locations — today's destinations. The biggest circle was around his own hotel.

The green car was sitting at the exit ramp of a lot next to the hotel's. It slid out behind him, keeping too close. Reeve tried to see the driver in his rearview, but the other car's windshield was murky. He could make out broad shoulders, a bull's neck, and that was about it.

He kept driving.

The funeral parlor was first. It was out in La Jolla, not too far from where the body had been found. The vestibule was cream satin and fresh flowers and piped music. There were a couple of chairs, one of which he sat on while he waited to be shown through to the viewing room. That was what the quiet-spoken mortician had called it: the viewing room. He didn't know why he had to wait. Maybe they kept the bodies somewhere else and only hauled them up and dusted them off when somebody wanted to see them.

Finally, the mortician came back and flashed him that closed-lipped professional smile, no hint of teeth. Pleasure was not a factor here. He asked Reeve to follow him through a set of double doors, which had glass panes covered with more cream satin material. All the colors were muted. In fact, the most colorful thing in the place was James Reeve's face.

There was a single open coffin in the room, lined, naturally, with cream satin. It stood on trestles at the end of the red-carpeted walkway. The corpse was dressed only in a shroud, which made it look bizarrely feminine. The shroud came up over the corpse's scalp. Reeve knew his brother had swallowed the Browning, angling it up towards the brain, so probably there wouldn't be much scalp there.

They'd given James's face the only tan, fake or otherwise, of its life, and there looked like rouge on the cheeks, maybe a little coloring on the thick, pale lips. He looked absurd, like a waxwork dummy. But it was him all right. Reeve had been hoping for a fake, a monstrous practical joke. Maybe Jim was in trouble, he'd thought, had run off, and had somehow duped everybody into thinking he'd killed himself. But now there could be no doubt. Reeve nodded his head and turned away from the coffin. He'd seen enough.

"We have some effects," the mortician whispered.

"Effects?" Reeve kept walking. He didn't want to be in the viewing room a second longer. He was angry. He didn't know why, perhaps because it was more natural to him than grief. He screwed his eyes shut, wishing the mortician would stop whispering at him.

"Effects of your brother's. Just clothes, really, the ones he was wearing . . ."

"Burn them."

"Of course. There are also some papers to sign."

"I just need a minute."

"Of course. It's only natural."

Reeve turned on the man. "No," he snarled, "it's highly *un*natural, but I need that minute anyway. Okay?"

The man went paler than his surroundings. "Why . . . uh, of course." Then he walked back into the viewing room, and seemed to count to sixty before coming out again, by which time Reeve had recovered some of his composure. The pink mist was shifting from in front of his eyes. Jesus, and his pills were back in Scotland.

"I'm sorry," he said.

"Quite . . ." The man swallowed back the word *natural*, and coughed instead. "Quite understandable. When will you want the body released?"

That had been taken care of. The coffin would travel to Heathrow on the same flight Reeve himself was taking, then be transported to the family plot in Scotland. It all seemed so ludicrous — burying a brother, traveling thousands of miles with the physical remains. How would Jim have felt? Suddenly Reeve knew exactly what his brother would have wanted.

"Look," he said in the vestibule, "is there any way he can be buried here?"

The mortician blinked. "In La Jolla?"

"Or San Diego."

"You don't want to take the remains back?"

"Back where? He left Scotland a long time ago. Wherever he was at any given point, that was his home. He'd be as well off here as anywhere."

"Well, I'm sure we could . . . burial or cremation?"

Cremation: the purifying fire. "Cremation would be fine."

So they went through to the office to fix everything, including the expenses to date. Reeve used his credit card. There were forms to sign, a lot of forms. A bell sounded, signaling that someone else had come in. The mortician went to his office door and looked out.

"I'll be just one moment," he called, "if you'd take a seat . . ."

Then he came back to his desk and was briskly businesslike. First, he got the details from Reeve and canceled the cargo reservation from LAX to LHR. He called the transport company in England, and caught someone just as they were about to leave for the night, so was able to cancel that, too. Reeve said he could take care of the rest when he got back to Scotland. The mortician was obviously used to having to do these things, or things like them. He smiled again and nodded.

Setting up the cremation was like setting up a dental appointment. Would he want the ashes in an urn, or scattered? Reeve said he'd want them scattered to the four winds, and let them blow where they may. The mortician checked the paperwork, and that was that.

Plastic made these financial transactions so much easier.

The mortician handed over a clear cellophane bag — Jim's effects.

They shook hands in the vestibule. Reeve noticed that the new client wasn't anywhere to be seen, then just as he was leaving, the double doors to the viewing room opened and the man came out.

He was broad across the chest and neck, with legs that tapered to pencil-thin ankles. Reeve ignored him and stepped outside, then hugged the wall beside the door. He looked along the street, and there was the green car, not twenty feet from him. It was an old Buick. He was still standing to one side of the door sixty seconds later when the man came out. Reeve grabbed for a hand, wrenched it up the man's back, and marched him across the pavement to the car, where he slammed him onto the hood.

The man made complaining noises throughout, even as Reeve started searching his jacket pockets. Then he made out a few words, punctuated by gasps of pain.

"Friend . . . his friend . . . Jim's . . . your brother's."

Reeve eased the pressure on the arm. "What?"

"I was a friend of your brother's," the man said. "Name's Eddie Cantona. Maybe he mentioned me."

Reeve let the man's hand go. Eddie Cantona lifted himself slowly from the hood, as though checking the damage — to both himself and the car.

"How do you know who I am?"

Cantona turned towards him and started rubbing his elbow and wrist. "You look like him," he said simply.

"What were you doing out at La Jolla?"

"You saw me, huh?" Cantona kept manipulating his arm. "Some gumshoe I'd make. What was I doing?" He rested his bulk against the wheel well. "Same as you, I guess. Trying to make sense out of it."

"And did you?"

Cantona shook his head. "No, sir, I didn't. There's only one thing I know for damned sure: Jim didn't commit suicide. He was murdered."

Reeve stared at the stranger, and Cantona returned the look without blinking.

"I liked your brother a hell of a lot," he said. "Soon as I saw you, I knew who you were. He mentioned you to me, said he wished you could've been closer. He was mostly drunk when he talked, but they say drunk men speak the truth."

The words rolled out like they'd been rehearsed. This was what Reeve wanted, someone who had known Jim towards the end, someone who might help him make sense of it all. But what had Cantona said . . . ?

"What makes you think," Reeve said slowly, "my brother was murdered?"

"Because he'd no need to rent a car," Eddie Cantona said. "I was his driver."

They sat in a bar two blocks from the funeral parlor, and Reeve told Cantona what McCluskey had told him — how suicides like to make a break.

"If he was going to commit suicide, he wouldn't've wanted to do it in your car," Reeve said.

"Well, all I know is, he didn't kill himself." Cantona shot back his second Jose Cuervo Gold and sipped from his iced glass of beer.

Reeve nursed his orange juice. "Have you talked to the police?"

"Sure, soon as I heard about it on the news. That fellow you were with, McCluskey, he took a sort of statement from me. Leastways, he listened to what I had to say. Then he said I could go, and that was the end of it, haven't heard from the police since. Tried phoning a couple of times, but I never catch him."

"Did my brother ever tell you what he was working on?"

Cantona shrugged his huge rounded shoulders. "Talked about a lot of things, but not much about that. Usually when he was talking he was drunk, which meant I was drunk, too, so maybe he did talk about his work and I just didn't take it in. I know it was to do with chemicals."

"Chemicals?"

"There's a company out here called CWC, stands for Co-World Chemicals. It was to do with them. I drove Jim out to talk to someone who used to work there, a scientist sort of guy. But he wouldn't say anything, wouldn't let Jim over the door. Second time we tried, the guy wasn't at home. On vacation or something."

"Where else did you take him?"

"Well, there was another scientist, only this one wasn't retired. But he wasn't talking either. Then I used to take him to the library downtown, that's where he'd do his research. You know, take notes, all that."

"He took notes?"

"Yes, sir."

"You saw his notebooks?"

Cantona shook his head. "Didn't have anything like that. Had a little computer, used to fold open, with a little bitty screen and all. He'd put these disks in there, and he was all set."

Reeve nodded. Now the cable made sense: it was to recharge the battery on the computer. But there was no computer, and no disks. He ordered another round and went to use the telephone next to the toilets.

"Detective McCluskey please." His call was put through.

"McCluskey here." The voice sounded like it was stifling a yawn.

"It's Gordon Reeve. I've been talking with Eddie Cantona."

"Oh, yeah, him." There was a pause while the detective slurped coffee. "I meant to tell you about him."

"Why didn't you?"

"You want the truth? I didn't know how you'd feel finding out your brother had spent his last few days on earth rattling around every seedy joint in San Diego with a bum at the steering wheel."

"I appreciate your candor." A rustling noise now; a paper bag being opened. "And I apologize for disturbing your breakfast."

"I had a late night; it's no problem."

"Mr. Cantona says my brother had a laptop computer and some disks."

"Oh, yeah?"

"The cable in his room was an adapter so he could charge the battery."

"Uh-huh?"

"Am I boring you?"

McCluskey swallowed. "Sorry, no. It's just, like, what do you want me to say? I know what that old bum thinks; he says your brother was killed. And now he's got you listening to his story . . . and would I be right in thinking you're calling from the pay phone in a bar?"

Reeve smiled. "Good detective work."

"*Easy* detective work. And would I further be right in thinking you've already laid a few drinks on Mr. Cantona? See, Gordon, he'll tell you any damned story he can come up with if it keeps a glass of hooch in front of him. He'll tell you your brother met Elvis and they rode off together in a pink Cadillac."

"You sound like you know something about that state of mind."

"Maybe I do. I don't mean any disrespect, but that's how I see it. There's no secret here; there's no cover-up or conspiracy or whatever you want to call it. There's just a guy who gets tired of it all one day, so he tidies up his life and gets himself a gun. And he does it in private, away from family and friends, and doesn't leave a note. It's a tidy way to go."

"Unless you're the hire company with a car that needs cleaning."

"Yeah, agreed, but those fuckers can afford it."

"All right, McCluskey. Thanks for listening."

"Name's Mike. Let's talk again before you leave, okay?"

"Okay."

"And don't go buying Mr. Cantona too many more drinks, not if he's driving."

Detective Mike McCluskey put down the receiver and finished his pastry, washing it down as best he could with the scalding liquid that passed for coffee from the vending machine down the hall. While he chewed, he stared at the telephone, and after he'd swallowed the last mouthful, he tossed the paper bag into the trash (making eight first attempts out of ten for the week, which was not bad), then reached again for his phone, checking first that there was no one in earshot.

"Fucking Cantona," he snarled, trying to recall the number.

Back in the bar, Reeve sat on his stool and took a mouthful of orange juice. He studied Eddie Cantona, who was studying the cocktail menu and looking like he was settling in for the day. Yes, Eddie looked like a boozer, but not a liar. But then a lot of people were real pros when it came to lying. Reeve knew; he was one of them. He'd had to lie to a lot of people about his real position in the army; he never said SAS or Special Forces, not even to other army careerists. He kept his mouth shut when he could, and lied when he couldn't. Lying was easy, you just said you were in the regiment you'd been in before you joined Special Forces. Some people took pride in their lies. But nothing Cantona had said so far struck Reeve as anything other than accurate. It made sense that Jim would own a portable computer. But then it also made sense that he might ditch it . . .

No, it didn't. He'd been writing a story. He'd have wanted that story published in some form, even after death. He'd have wanted his monument.

"Eddie," Reeve said, waiting till the man had turned away from the menu, "tell me about my brother. Tell me everything you can."

Cantona drove them to the car rental firm. Reeve had memorized the salient details of McCluskey's report, and knew which firm to go to. He'd found the address in the telephone book. He was thinking about his own expensive rental car, the Blazer, and how it was spending more time at rest than in motion.

"You got a wife, Gordon?"

"Yes."

"Kids?"

"A son. He's eleven."

"Jim used to talk about a nephew, would that be him?"

Reeve nodded. "Allan was Jim's only nephew." He had the side window open, his head resting into the airflow.

"You got any photos?"

"What?"

"Your wife and kid."

"I don't know." Reeve got out his wallet and opened it. There was an old photo of Joan, not much bigger than a passport shot.

"Can I see?" Cantona took the photograph from him and studied it, holding it between thumb and forefinger as he rested both meaty hands on the top of the steering wheel. He turned the photo over, revealing a line of Scotch tape. "It's been torn in two," he said, handing the photo back.

"I get a temper sometimes."

"Tell my arm about it." Cantona rolled his shoulder a couple of times.

"They tried treating me," Reeve said all of a sudden, not knowing why he was telling a stranger.

"Treating you?"

"For the violence. I used to get angry a lot. I spent some time in a psychiatric ward."

"Oh, yeah?"

"Now I have pills I'm supposed to take, only I don't take them."

"Mood-controllers, man. Never take a pill that screws with your mind."

"Is that right?"

"Take it from one who knows. I was in Monterey in the sixties, then Oakland. I was twenty, twenty-one. I saw some action. Chemical action, if you know what I mean. Came out of it with a massive depression which lasted most of the seventies, started drinking around nineteen eighty. It doesn't cure anything, but other drunks are better company than doctors and goddamned psychiatrists."

"How come you still have a driving license?"

Cantona laughed. "Because they've never caught me, pure and simple."

Reeve looked out through his open window. "Drinking's one of the things that seems to start me off with the violence."

Cantona said nothing for a minute. Then: "Jim told me you were ex-military."

"That's right."

"Seems to me that might explain things. You see any action?"

"Some." More than most, he might have added. *Row, row, row your boat, Gently down the stream* . . . He cut that memory off at the pass.

"I was in Vietnam for a tour," Cantona continued. "Took some shrapnel in my foot. By that time, I was just about ready to do *myself* an injury to get me out of there. So you still get these spells?"

"What spells?"

"The violence."

"I've tried self-help. I've read a lot of books."

"What, medical stuff?"

"Philosophy."

"Yeah, Jim said you got to like that stuff. Castaneda's about my limit. What stuff do you read?"

"Anarchism."

"Anarchism?" Cantona looked disbelievingly at him. "Anarchism?" he repeated, as though trying the word out for size. Then he nodded, but with a quizzical look on his face. "Does it help?"

"I don't know. Maybe."

"What do the doctors say?"

"They say I'm on my last warning. One more outburst, they'll section me. I think they mean it." He stared at Cantona. "Why am I telling you this?"

Cantona grinned. "Because I'm listening. Because I'm harmless. Besides, it's a damned sight cheaper than therapy." Then he laughed. "I can't believe I'm sharing my car with a goddamned anarchist."

The rental place looked like a used-car lot, dusty cars ranked behind a high fence. There was a metal gate, a chain and padlock hanging off it, and behind it a single-story prefabricated office. Reeve could tell it was the office because there was a big painted sign above it stating just that. Garishly colored notices in the window offered "the best deals in town," "extra-special weekend rates," and "nice clean cars, low mileage, good runners."

"Looks like Rent-A-Wreck before they went upscale," Cantona commented.

They knocked and opened the office door. There was a single room inside with a couple of doors leading off, both open. One showed a storeroom, the other a toilet. A man in shirtsleeves was seated behind the desk. He looked Mexican, in his fifties, and he was showing teeth around a long thin cigar.

"My friends," he said, half rising. "What can I do for you?"

He gestured for them to sit, but Reeve stayed standing by the window, occasionally looking out, and Cantona stayed there with him.

"My name's Gordon Reeve."

"Good morning to you, Gordon." The Mexican wagged a finger. "I seem to know you."

"I think you rented a car to my brother on Saturday night."

The smile melted. The man slipped the cigar out of his mouth and placed it in the overspilling ashtray. "I'm sorry. Yes, you resemble your brother."

"Was it you who dealt with my brother?"

"Yes, it was."

"Do you mind if I ask a few questions?"

The Mexican smiled. "You sound like a policeman."

"This is just for my peace of mind." Then Reeve spoke to the man in Spanish, and the man nodded. Family, he was saying, I have to take these memories back for the family. The Spanish understood these things.

"See," he said in English, "I'm trying to understand my brother's state of mind on that night."

The Mexican was nodding. "I understand. Ask your questions."

"Well, one thing I don't quite yet understand. My brother was last seen drinking in a downtown bar, then it seems he came here. A cab picked him up from the bar. But to get here, he had to pass three or four other car hire firms." In his hotel room, with map and telephone book, Reeve had done his work.

The Mexican opened his arms. "This is perhaps easily explained. For one thing, we have the lowest rates in town, you can ask anyone. Being blunt, if you only need a car so you can drive somewhere quiet and put an end to your life, you do not need a Lincoln Continental. For a second thing, I open later than the other places. You can check this. So maybe they were closed already."

Why would I want to "check this"? Reeve thought, but he nodded his head. "My brother had been drinking," he said. "Did he seem affected by drink to you?"

But the Mexican's attention was on Cantona, who was leaning against the noisy air conditioner. "Please," he said. "It breaks easily."

Cantona got up from the unit. Reeve noticed that the machine was dripping water into a bowl on the floor. He repeated his question.

The Mexican shook his head. "I would not have done business with him if I thought he'd been drinking. I have nothing to gain by seeing my cars wrecked or messed up."

"Speaking of which, where is the car?"

"It is not in the lot."

"That's not what I asked."

"It has gone for repair and . . . detailing. The police smashed the driver's side window to effect entry. Remember, the car was locked from within."

I know that, thought Reeve, but why are *you* telling me? "Before renting the car to my brother," he asked, "did you take a look at his driving license?"

"Of course."

Reeve stared at the man.

"What is it?" the Mexican asked, his grin looking queasy.

"He held a UK driving license, not valid over here."

"Then I should not have rented him one of my automobiles." The man shrugged. "A mistake on my part."

Reeve nodded slowly. "A mistake," he repeated. He asked a few more questions, trivial ones, just to put the Mexican more at ease, then thanked him for his help.

"I am truly sorry about your brother, Gordon," the Mexican said, holding out his hand.

Reeve shook it. "And I'm sorry about your car." He followed Cantona to the door. "Oh, you forgot to say which garage is fixing the car."

The Mexican hesitated. "Trasker's Auto," he said at last.

Cantona started chuckling the moment they were outside. "I thought he was going to swallow that cigar," he said. "You really had him going."

"He wasn't a very good liar."

"No, he surely wasn't. Hey, where did you learn to speak Spanish?"

Reeve opened the car door. "There was a time I needed to know it," he said, sliding into the passenger seat.

Daniel Trasker ran what looked like four parts wrecking operation to one part repair. When Reeve explained who he was, Trasker went wide-eyed with shock.

"Hell, son, you don't want to see that car! There's stains on the —"

"It's okay, Mr. Trasker, I don't want to see the car."

Trasker calmed a little at that. They'd been standing outside the wood-and-tin shack that served as Trasker's premises. Most of the work was done in the yard outside. Trasker himself was in his well-preserved early sixties, clumps of curling silver hair showing from beneath an oily baseball cap. His walnut face showed deep laugh lines around the eyes, with oil and dirt ingrained. He wiped his hands on a large blue rag throughout their conversation.

"You better come in."

In the midst of the shack's extraordinary clutter, it took Reeve a while to work out that there was a desk and chair, and even a PC. Paperwork covered the desk like so much camouflage, and there were bits of engines everywhere.

"I'd ask you to sit," said Trasker, "but there's nowhere *to* sit. If someone's writing me a check, I sometimes clear some space for them, but otherwise you stand."

"Standing's fine."

"So what is it you want, Mr. Reeve?"

"You know my brother was found in a locked car, Mr. Trasker?"

Trasker nodded. "We got the car right here."

"Police smashed the window to get in."

"That they did. We got the replacement part on order."

Reeve stood close beside the older man. "Is there any way someone could have locked the car afterwards? I mean, after my brother died?"

Trasker stared at him. "What's your point, son?"

"I'm just wondering if that's possible."

Trasker thought about it. "Hell, of course it's possible. All you'd need's a spare set of keys. Come to think of it . . ." Trasker's voice trailed off.

"What?"

"Let me go check something." He turned and left the shack. Reeve and Cantona followed him outside, but he turned back to them, holding up his hands. "Now, let me do this by myself. That car's not something you should be seeing."

Reeve nodded, and watched Trasker go. Then he told Cantona to stay where he was, and began to follow the old man.

Around the back of the shack, and past heaps of wrecked cars, Reeve saw that there was another low-slung building, double-garage size. Half a dozen tall gas cylinders stood like metal sentries outside a wide door, which stood open. There was a car jacked up inside, but Trasker squeezed past it. Reeve looked around him. He was five or six miles outside San Diego, inland towards the hills. The air was stiller here, not quite so fresh. He had to decide now, right now. He took a deep breath and made for the garage.

"What is it?" he asked Trasker.

The old man shot up from his crouching position and swiveled on his heels. "Nearly gave me a damned heart attack," he complained.

"Sorry." Reeve came forward. Trasker had opened the door of the car and was studying it. The car James Reeve had died in. It was smarter than Reeve had expected, a good deal newer, as good certainly as anything in the Mexican's lot. He approached it slowly. The seats were leather or Leatherette, and had been wiped clean. But as he bent down to peer inside, he could see stains against the roof. A rust-colored trajectory, fanning out towards the back of the car. He thought of touching the blood, maybe it was still damp. But he tore his gaze away from it. Trasker was looking at him.

"I told you to stay put," the old man said quietly.

"I had to see."

Trasker nodded, understanding. "You want a moment to yourself?"

Reeve shook his head. "I want to know what you were looking at."

Trasker pointed to the interior door-lock on the driver's side. "See there?" he said, touching it. "Can you see a little notch, low down on the lock?"

Reeve looked more closely. "Yes," he said.

"There's one on the passenger door-lock too."

"Yes?"

"They're sensors, son. They sense a beam from a remote-control key ring."

"You mean you can lock and unlock the doors from a distance?"

"That's right."

"So what?"

"So," said Trasker, digging into his overall pockets and pulling out a key on a chain, "here's what came with the car. This is the key that was in the ignition when the police found the car. Now, this is obviously the spare key."

Reeve looked at it. "Because there's no button to activate the locks?"

"Exactly." Trasker took the key back. "You only usually get the one remote-control key ring with a car like this. The spare key they give you is plain, like the one I'm holding."

Reeve thought about it. Then, without saying anything, he walked back to Cantona's car. Cantona was standing in the shade provided by the shack.

"Eddie," Reeve said, "I want you to do something for me."

By the time Daniel Trasker caught up with Reeve, Cantona's car was already reversing out of the yard.

"I want to wait here a few minutes," Reeve said.

Trasker shrugged. "Then what?"

"Then, if I may, I'd like to use your phone."

Carlos Perez was sucking on a fresh cigar when his telephone rang. It was the brother Gordon Reeve again.

"Yes, Gordon, my friend," Perez said pleasantly. "Did you forget something?"

"I just wondered about the car key," Reeve said.

"The car key?" This Reeve was incredible, the way his mind worked. "What about the key?"

"Do you give your customers a spare set, or just the one?"

"That depends on the model of vehicle, Gordon, and other considerations, too." Perez put his cigar down. It tipped from the edge of the ashtray and rolled off the desk to the floor. He walked around the side of his desk and crouched down, the telephone gripped to his ear.

"Did my brother's car have remote locking?"

Perez made a noise like he was thinking. The cigar was beneath his desk. He felt for it, and received a burn on the side of his hand. Swearing silently, he finally drew the cigar out and returned to his chair, examining the damage to his left hand.

"Ah," he said into the telephone, a man who has just remembered. "Yes, that vehicle did have remote locking."

"And it had the key ring, the push-button?"

"Yes, yes." Perez couldn't see where this was leading. He felt sweat glisten on his forehead, tingling his scalp.

"Then where is it now?" Reeve said coldly.

"What?"

"I'm at the garage. There's no such key here."

Key, key, key. "I see what you mean," Perez improvised. "But that key was lost by a previous client. I did not understand you at first. No, there was no remote by the time your brother . . ." But Perez was speaking into a dead telephone. Reeve had cut the connection. Perez put the receiver back in its cradle and chewed on his cigar so hard he snapped the end off.

He got his jacket from the back of his chair, locked the office and set the alarm, and got into his car. Out on the road, he stopped long enough to chain the gates shut, double-checking the padlock.

If he'd checked everything with the same care, he'd have seen the large green car that followed him as he left.

SIX

Kosigin walked down to North Harbor Drive. A huge cruise ship had just docked at the terminal. He stood leaning against the rail, looking down at the water. Sailboats scudded along in the distance, angled so that they appeared to have no mass at all. When they turned they became invisible for a moment; it was not an optical illusion, it was a shortcoming of the eye itself. You just had to stare at nothing, trusting that the boat would reappear. Trust standing in for vision. Kosigin would have preferred better eyesight. He didn't know why it had been deemed preferable that some birds should be able to pick out the movements of a mouse while hovering high over a field, and mankind should not. The consolation, of course, was that man was an inventor, a maker of tools. Man could examine atoms and electrons. He might not be able to *see* them, but he could examine them.

Kosigin liked to leave as little as possible to chance. Even if he couldn't see something with his naked eye, he had ways of finding out about it. He had his own set of tools. He was due to meet the most ruthless and complex of them here.

Kosigin did not regard himself as a particularly complex individual. If you'd asked him what made him tick, and he'd been willing to answer, then he could have given a very full answer indeed. He did not often think of himself as an individual at all.

He was part of something larger, a compound of intelligences and tools. He was part of Co-World Chemicals, a corporation man down to the hand-stitched soles of his Savile Row shoes. It wasn't just that what was good for the company was good for him — he'd heard that pitch before and didn't wholly believe it — Kosigin's thinking went further: what is good for CWC is good for the whole of the Western world. Chemicals are an absolute necessity. If you grow food, you need chemicals; if you process food, you need chemicals; if you work at saving lives in a hospital or out in the African bush, you need chemicals. Our bodies are full of them, and keep on producing them. Chemicals and water, that's what a body is. He reckoned the problems of famine in Africa and Asia could be ended if you tore down the barriers and let agrichemical businesses loose. Locusts? Gas them. Crop yields? Spray them. There was little you couldn't cure with chemicals.

Of course, he knew of side effects. He kept up with the latest scientific papers and media scare stories. He knew there were kids out there who weren't being vaccinated against measles because the original vaccine was produced after research on tissue from unborn fetuses. Stories like that made him sad. Not angry, just sad. Humanity had a lot still to learn.

Some tourists wandered past, a young couple with two children. They looked like they'd been out for a boat ride; rosy-cheeked, windblown, grinning. They ate fresh food and breathed clean air. The kids would grow up straight and strong, which might not have been the case a hundred and fifty years before.

Good chemicals, that was the secret.

"Mr. Kosigin?"

Kosigin turned, almost smiling. He didn't know how the Englishman could sneak up like that every time. No matter how open the terrain, he was always nearly on Kosigin before Kosigin saw him. He wasn't built to hide or be furtive: he stood six feet four inches, with a broad chest and thick upper arms, so that his lower arms didn't quite touch his sides when he let them hang. His legs looked powerful, too, wrapped in tight faded denim, with Nike running shoes on the feet. His stomach was flat, rip-

ples of muscle showing through the stretched black cotton
T-shirt. He wore foldaway sunglasses, with a little pouch for
them hooked on to his brown leather belt, the buckle of which
was the ubiquitous Harley-Davidson badge. The man had wavy
blond hair, cropped high on the forehead but falling at the back
past the neck of the T-shirt. The tan on his face was pink rather
than brown, and his eyebrows and eyelashes were as blond as the
hair on his head. He seemed proud of the large indented scar
which ran down his right cheek, as though a single blemish were
needed to prove how perfect the rest of the package was.

To Kosigin, admittedly no authority, he looked like one of
those TV wrestlers.

"Hello, Jay, let's walk."

That's all the man had ever been to Kosigin: Jay. He didn't
even know if it was a first or second name, or maybe even an initial letter. They walked south towards the piers, past the wares of
the T-shirt and souvenir sellers. Jay didn't so much walk as
bound, hands bunched in his denim pockets. He looked like he
needed to be on a leash.

"Anything to report?"

Jay shrugged. "Things are taken care of, Mr. Kosigin."

"Really?"

"Nothing for you to worry about."

"McCluskey doesn't share your confidence. Neither does
Perez."

"Well, they don't know *me*. I'm never confident without good
reason."

"So Cantona isn't a problem anymore?"

Jay shook his head. "And the brother's flight is out of here
tomorrow."

"There's been an alteration," Kosigin said. "He's not taking
the body back with him. There's to be a cremation tomorrow
morning."

"I didn't know that."

"I'm sorry, I should have told you."

"You should always tell me everything, Mr. Kosigin. How
can I work best if I'm not told everything? Still, the flight out is
tomorrow afternoon. He hasn't changed that, has he?"

"No, but all the same . . . he's been asking awkward questions. I'm sure he doesn't believe the story Perez threw him."

"It wasn't my idea to involve Perez."

"I know," Kosigin said quietly. Jay always seemed able to make him feel bad; and at the same time he always wanted to impress the bigger man. He didn't know why. It was crazy: he was richer than Jay would ever be, more successful in just about every department, and yet there was some kind of inferiority thing at play and he couldn't shake it.

"This brother, he doesn't exactly sound your typical grieving relative."

"I don't know too much about him, just the initial search Alliance did. Ex-army, now runs an adventure-vacation thing in Scotland."

Jay stopped and took off his sunglasses. He looked like he was staring at the million-dollar view, only his eyes were unfocused and he had the hint of a smile on his lips. "Couldn't be," he said.

"Couldn't be what?"

But Jay stayed silent a few moments longer, and Kosigin wasn't about to interrupt again.

"The deceased's name was Reeve," Jay said at last. "I should have thought of it sooner." He threw his head back and burst out laughing. His hands, however, were gripping the guardrail like they could twist the metal back and forth on itself. Finally, he stared at Kosigin with wide greeny-blue eyes, the pupils large and black. "I think I know the brother," he said. "I think I knew him years ago." He laughed again, and bent low over the rail, looking for an instant as though he might throw himself into the bay. His feet actually left the ground, but then came down again. Passersby were staring.

I'm in the presence of a madman, Kosigin thought. What's more, for the moment, having summoned him from L.A., I'm his employer. "You know him?" he asked. But Jay was scanning the sky now, stretching his neck to and fro. Kosigin repeated the question.

Jay laughed again. "I think I know him." And then he pursed his lips and began to whistle, or tried to, though he was still chuckling. It was a tune Kosigin thought he half-recognized — a children's melody.

And then, on the seafront in San Diego, with tourists giving him a wide berth, Jay began to sing:

> Row, row, row your boat,
> Gently down the stream.
> Merrily, merrily, merrily, merrily,
> Life is but a dream.

He repeated the tune twice more, and then suddenly stopped. There was no life, no amusement in his face. It was like he'd donned a mask, as some wrestlers did. Kosigin swallowed and waited for more antics, waited for the giant to say something.

Jay swallowed and licked his lips, then uttered a single word. The word was *good*.

Reeve had got a cab to pick him up from the junkyard. It had taken him to the funeral parlor, where he picked up his rental car. He resisted the temptation of a final look at Jim. Jim wasn't there anymore. There was just some skin that he used to live inside.

Back in his hotel bedroom, he sat at the window thinking. He was thinking about the missing laptop, the laptop's disks. He was thinking that *anyone* could have locked Jim's body in the car. It added up to something — or nothing. The Mexican had been lying, but maybe he was covering up something else, something trivial like the rental car's roadworthiness or his own business credentials. Well, Eddie Cantona was tailing the Mexican. All he could do now was wait for a phone call.

He took the cellophane bag out of his jacket pocket and scattered the contents on the round table by the window. Jim's effects, the contents of his pockets. The police had established his identity, then handed everything over to the funeral parlor.

Reeve flicked through Jim's passport, studying everything but his brother's photograph. Then he turned to the wallet, a square brown leather affair with edges curling from age. Twenty dollars in fives, driver's license, some small change. A handkerchief. A pair of nail clippers. A packet of chewing gum. Reeve peered into the packet. There were two sticks left. A piece of paper had been crumpled into the remaining space. He tore the packet to get it out. It was just the paper wrapper from a used stick of gum. But when he unfolded it, there was a word written in pen on the plain side.

The word was *Agrippa*.

The call came a couple of hours later.

"It's me," Cantona said, "and I hope you feel honored. I'm only allowed one phone call, pal, and you're it."

They were holding Eddie in the same police station Mike McCluskey worked out of, so instead of trying to see the felon, Reeve asked at the desk for the detective.

McCluskey arrived smiling like they were old friends.

Reeve didn't return the smile. "Can you do me a favor?" he asked.

"Just ask."

So Reeve asked.

A little while later they sat at McCluskey's desk in the sprawling office he shared with a dozen other detectives. Things looked quiet; maybe there wasn't much crime worth the name in San Diego. Three of the detectives were throwing crunched-up paper balls through a miniature basketball hoop into the wastebasket below. Bets were being taken on the winner. They glanced over at Reeve from time to time, and decided he was victim or witness rather than perpetrator or suspect.

McCluskey had been making an internal call. He put the receiver down. "Well," he said, "looks straightforward enough. Driving under the influence, DUI we call it."

"He told me he was stone-cold sober."

McCluskey offered a wry smile rather than a remark, and inclined his head a little. Reeve knew what he meant: drunks will say anything. During the phone call, Reeve had been studying McCluskey's desk. It was neater than he'd expected; all the desks were. There were scraps of paper with telephone numbers on them. He'd looked at those numbers.

One of them was for the funeral parlor. Another was the Mexican at the rental company. Both could be easily explained, Reeve thought.

"You phoned the funeral parlor," he said, watching the detective very closely.

"What?"

Reeve nodded towards the telephone number. "The funeral parlor."

McCluskey nodded. "Sure, wanted to double-check when the funeral was. Thought I'd try to come along. Look, getting back to this Cantona fellow, seems to me he palled around with your brother for a few drinks and maybe a meal or two. Seems to me, Gordon, that he's trying to shake you down the same way."

Reeve pretended to be following the basketball game. "Maybe you're right," he said, while McCluskey slipped another sheet of paper over the telephone numbers, covering the ones at the bottom of the original sheet. That didn't matter — Reeve had almost memorized them — but the action itself bothered him. He looked back at McCluskey, and the detective smiled at him again. Some would have said it was a sympathetic smile. Others might have called it mocking.

One of the basketball players made a wild throw. The rebound landed in Reeve's lap. He stared at the paper ball.

"Does the word *Agrippa* mean anything to you?" he asked.

McCluskey shook his head. "Should it?"

"It was written on a scrap of paper in my brother's pocket."

"I missed that," McCluskey said, shifting more papers. "You really would make a good detective, Gordon." He was trying to smile.

Reeve just nodded.

"What was he doing anyway?" McCluskey asked.

"Who?"

"Cantona, Mr. DUI. He telephoned you after his arrest; I thought maybe he had something to tell you."

"Maybe he just wanted me to put up the bail."

McCluskey stared at him. Reeve had become Cantona's accuser, leaving him the defender.

"You think that was all?"

"What else?"

"Well, Gordon, I thought maybe *he* thought he was working for you."

"Have you spoken with him?"

"No, but I was just on the telephone doing you a favor by talking to cops who *have*." McCluskey cocked his head again. "You sound a little strange."

"Do I?" Reeve made no attempt to soften his voice. It was more suspicious if you suddenly changed the way you were speaking to comply with the way you thought the listener wanted you to sound. "Maybe that's because I'm cremating my brother tomorrow morning. Can I see Mr. Cantona?"

McCluskey rounded his lips into a thoughtful O.

"A final favor," Reeve added. "I'm off tomorrow straight after the cremation."

McCluskey took a little more time, apparently considering it. "Sure," he said at last. "I'll see if I can fix it."

They brought Eddie Cantona out of the cells and up to one of the interview rooms. Reeve was already waiting. He'd paced the room, seeming anxious but really checking for possible bugs, spy holes, two-way mirrors. But there were just plain walls and a door. A table and two chairs in the middle of the floor. He sat on one chair, took a pen out of his pocket, and dropped it. Retrieving it from the floor, he checked beneath both chairs and the table. Maybe McCluskey hadn't had enough time to organize a surveillance. Maybe he didn't care. Maybe Reeve was reading too much into everything.

Maybe Eddie Cantona was just a drunk.

They brought him into the room and left him there. He walked straight over and sat down opposite Reeve.

"We'll be right out here, sir," one of the policemen said.

Reeve watched the uniformed officers leave the room and close the door behind them.

"Got a cigarette?" Cantona said. "No, you don't smoke, do

you?" He patted his pockets with trembling hands. "Haven't got one on me." He held his hands out in front of him. They jittered like they had electricity going through them. "Look at that," he said. "Think that's the D.T.'s? No, I'll tell you what that is, that is what's called being afraid."

"Tell me what happened."

Cantona stared wild-eyed, then tried to calm himself. He got up and walked around the room, flailing his arms as he talked. "They must've started following me at some point. They weren't at the rental place — I'd swear to that on a Padres season ticket. But I was too busy watching Mr. Mex. First I knew, there was the blue light behind me and they pulled me over. I've *never* been pulled over; I told you that. I've been too careful and maybe too lucky." He came back to the table and exhaled into Reeve's face. It wasn't very pleasant, but proved Cantona's point.

"Not a drop I'd had," he said. "Not a damned drop. They did the usual drunk tests, then said they were arresting me. Up till that point, I thought it was just bad luck. But when they put me in the back of the car, I knew it was serious. They were stopping me tailing the Mexican." He stared deep into Reeve's unblinking eyes. "They want me out of the way, Gordon, and cops have a way of getting what they want."

"Has McCluskey talked to you?"

"That asshole I talked to about Jim's murder?" Cantona shook his head. "Why?"

"I think he's got something to do with it, whatever *it* is. Where was the Mexican headed?"

"What am I, clairvoyant?"

"I mean, which direction was he headed?"

"Straight downtown, it looked like."

"Did he seem like the downtown–San Diego type to you?"

Cantona managed a grin. "Not exactly. I don't know, maybe he was on business. Maybe . . ." He paused. "Maybe we're over-reacting."

"Eddie, did Jim ever mention someone or something called Agrippa?"

"Agrippa?" Cantona screwed his eyes shut, trying his hardest. Then he sighed and shook his head. "Does it mean something?"

"I don't know."

Reeve stood up and gripped Cantona's hands. "Eddie, I know you're scared, and you've got cause to be, and it won't bother me in the least if you lie through your teeth to get yourself out of here. Tell them anything you think they want to hear. Tell them the moon's made of cheese and there are pink elephants under your bed. Tell them you just want a fresh start and to forget about the past few weeks. You've helped me a lot, and I thank you, but now you've got to think of number one. Jim's dead; you're still here. He'd want you to avoid joining him."

Cantona was grinning again. "Are we engaged, Gordon?"

Reeve saw that he was still holding Cantona's hands. He let them go, smiling. "I'm serious, Eddie. I think the best thing I can do for you right now is walk away and *keep* away."

"You still flying home tomorrow?"

Reeve nodded. "I think so."

"What're you going to do?"

"Best you don't know, Eddie."

Cantona grudgingly agreed.

"There's one last thing I'd like from you."

"What's that?"

"An address . . ." Reeve brought the map out of his pocket and spread it on the table. "And some directions."

He didn't see McCluskey again as he left the police station; didn't particularly want to see him. He drove around for a while, taking any road he felt like, no pattern at all to his route. He stopped frequently, getting out his map and acting the lost tourist. He was sure he hadn't been followed from the actual police station, but he wondered if that might change.

He'd had to learn car pursuit and evasion so he could teach it to trainee bodyguards who'd be expected to chauffeur their employers. He was no expert, but he knew the ground rules. He'd taken a weekend course at a track near Silverstone, an abandoned airfield used for controlled skids and high-speed chase scenarios.

The last thing he'd expected to need this trip were his professional skills.

He looked in the rearview and saw the patrol car draw up behind him. The uniform in the driver's seat spoke into his radio before getting out, checking his holster, adjusting his sunglasses.

Reeve let his window slide down.

"Got a problem?" the policeman said.

"Not really." Reeve was smiling, showing teeth. He tapped the map. "Just checking where I am."

"You on vacation?"

"How could you tell?"

"You mean apart from the map and you being stopped where you're not supposed to make a stop and your license plate being a rental?"

Now Reeve laughed. "You know, maybe I *am* a bit lost." He looked at the map and pointed to a road. "Is this where we are?"

"You're a few blocks off." The officer showed him where he really was, then asked where he was headed.

"Nowhere really, just driving."

"Well, driving's fine — it's the stopping that can be a problem. Make sure parking is authorized next time before you settle down." The cop straightened up.

"Thank you, officer," said Reeve, putting the car into gear.

And after that, they were tailing him. It looked to Reeve like a two-car unmarked tail with a few patrol cars as backup and lookouts. He drove around by the airport and then took North Harbor Drive back into town, cruising the waterfront and crossing the Coronado Bay Bridge before doubling back downtown and up First Avenue. The downtown traffic wasn't too sluggish, and he sped up as he left the high towers behind, eventually following signs to Old Town State Park. He parked in a lot adjacent to some weird old houses which seemed to be a center of attraction, and crossed the street into the park itself. He reckoned one car was still with him, which meant two men: one of them would probably keep watch on the Blazer, the other following on foot.

He stopped to take a drink from a water fountain. Old Town comprised a series of buildings — stables, blacksmith's, tannery, and so on — that might be original and might be reconstructions. The buildings were swamped, however, by souvenir and gift shops, Mexican cafés and restaurants. Reeve couldn't see anyone following him, and went into the courtyard of one of the restaurants. He was asked if he wanted a table, but he said he was looking for a friend. He crossed the courtyard, squeezing past tables and chairs, and exited the restaurant at the other side.

He was right on the edge of the park and skirted it, finding himself on a street outside the perimeter, a couple of hundred yards from where his car was parked. This street had normal shops on either side, and at the corner stood two taxicabs, their drivers leaning against a lamppost while they chatted.

Reeve nodded to them and slipped into the backseat of the front cab. The man took his time winding up the conversation, while Reeve kept low in the seat, watching from the back window. Then the driver got in.

"La Jolla," Reeve said, reaching into his pocket for the map.

"No problem," the driver said, trying to start the engine.

From the rear window, Reeve saw a man jog to the edge of the sidewalk across the street, looking all around. He was slack-jawed from running, and carried a holster under the armpit of his flapping jacket. He might have been one of the other detectives in McCluskey's office; Reeve wasn't sure.

The driver turned the ignition again, stamping his foot on the accelerator. The engine turned but didn't catch.

"Sorry 'bout this," the driver said. "Fuckin' garage told me they fixed it." He got on his radio to tell base that he was "fucked again," and whoever he was speaking to started raving at him for cursing on the air.

The cop was still there, talking into a two-way now, probably liaising with his partner back at the Blazer. Reeve hoped the partner was saying that the suspect was bound to return to his car, so they might as well sit tight . . .

"Hey, man," the driver said, turning in his seat. "There's another cab right behind. You understand English? We ain't going nowhere."

Reeve handed the man five dollars without turning from the window.

"This is for your time," he said. "Now shut up."

The driver shut up.

The cop seemed to be waiting for a message on his radio. Meantime, he lit a cigarette, coughing hard after the first puff.

Reeve was hardly breathing.

The cop flicked the cigarette onto the road as the message came for him. Then he stuffed the radio back into his jacket, turned, and walked away. Reeve opened the cab door slowly, got out, and shut it again.

"Anytime, man!" the driver called to him.

He got into the second cab. The driver was prompt to arrive.

"His engine fuckin' up again?" he asked.

"Yeah," said Reeve.

"Where to?"

"La Jolla," said Reeve. The map was still in his hand. He'd folded it so that his destination wasn't showing. It was something he'd learned during Special Forces training: if you were caught, the enemy couldn't determine from the way your map was folded your landing point or your final destination. Reeve was glad he still knew the trick and had used it without thinking about it, like it was natural, a reaction.

Like it was instinct.

They stopped a few streets away from the one where Dr. Killin lived. It was only a matter of days since James Reeve had been driven there by Eddie Cantona. Reeve didn't think the ex-CWC scientist would have returned; though with Jim out of the picture permanently it was just possible.

Cantona had told him about the man who'd been painting the fence. Why get your fence painted when you were going to be away? More likely that you'd stay put to see the job was done properly. It wasn't like an interior job, where the smell of paint or the mess might persuade you to leave the house while the work was being done. Okay, maybe the painter had just been booked for that time, and wasn't going to rearrange other jobs just so Killin could be there to oversee the minor work. But as Cantona himself had noted, the fence hadn't really *needed* repainting.

The Mexican at the rental company had convinced Gordon Reeve that there was something very wrong about Jim's death, something very wrong indeed. It wasn't just murder; there was more to it than that. Reeve was catching glimpses of a conspiracy, a wider plot. Only he didn't know what the plot was . . . not yet.

Reeve wanted to know if Killin was back. More, he wanted to know if the house was under surveillance. If it was, then either Jim posed a threat to someone from beyond the grave, or there were others who still posed that threat.

Others like Gordon Reeve himself.

So he had a route he wanted the driver to take, and he went over it with him. They would cross Killin's street at two interchanges, without driving up the street itself. Only then, if still necessary, would they drive past Killin's house. Not too slowly, not like they might stop. But slowly enough, like they were looking for a number on the street, but it wasn't anywhere near the number of Killin's house.

The driver seemed bemused by his request, so Reeve repeated what he could in Spanish. Languages: another thing he'd learned in Special Forces. He had a propensity for language-learning, and had specialized in linguistics during his Phase Six training, along with climbing. He learned some Spanish, French, a little Arabic. The Spanish was one reason they'd chosen him for Operation Stalwart.

"Okay?" he asked the driver.

"Is your money, friend," the driver said.

"Is my money," Reeve agreed.

So they took the route Reeve had planned for them. The driver went too slowly at first — suspiciously slow — so Reeve had him speed up just a little. As they crossed the intersection he took a good look at Killin's street. There were a couple of cars parked on the street itself, even though most of the bungalows had garages or parking spaces attached. He saw one freshly painted fence, the color Cantona had said it would be. There was a car half a block down and on the opposite side of the road. Reeve thought he saw someone in it, and that there was a sign on the door of the car.

They drove around the block and came back through another intersection, behind the parked car this time. He still couldn't make out what the sign said. But there was definitely someone in the driver's seat.

"So what now?" the driver said. "You want we should go down the street or not?"

"Pull over," Reeve ordered. The driver pulled the car over to the curb. Reeve got out and adjusted the mirror on the passenger side. He got back into the backseat and looked at the mirror, then got out and adjusted it again.

"What's going on?" the driver asked.

"Don't worry," said Reeve. He made another very slight adjustment, then got back in. "Now," he said, "we drive down the street, just the way we talked about. Okay?"

"Is your money."

As they neared the parked car with the man in it, approaching it from the front, Reeve kept his eyes on the wing mirror. He was just a passenger, a bored passenger staring at nothing while his driver figured out an address.

But he had a perfect view of the car as they passed it. He saw the driver study them, and seem to dismiss them. Nobody was expecting anyone to turn up in a cab. But the man was watchful. And he didn't look to Reeve like a policeman.

"Where now?" the driver asked.

"That car we passed, did you see what was written on the side?"

"Yeah, man, it was some cable company. You know, cable TV. They're always trying to get you to sign up, sign all your money away in exchange for fifty channels showing nothing but reruns of *Lucy* and shitty soaps. They been to my house three, four times already; my woman's keen. They can smell when someone's keen. Not me. So, where now?"

"Turn right, go a block or two, and stop again." The driver did so. "You better fix your wing mirror," Reeve said, so the driver got out to change it back. Reeve had a couple of options. One was to confront the man in the car, give him a hard time. Ask him a few questions while he pressed the life out of him. He knew interrogation techniques; he hadn't used them in a long time, but he reckoned they'd come back to him like riding a bicycle. Just like the map-folding had come back. Instinct.

But if the man was a pro, and the man had looked like a pro — not like a cop, but like a pro — then he wouldn't talk; and Reeve would have blown whatever cover he still possessed. Besides, he knew what he had come to find out. There was still a watch on Dr. Killin's house. Someone still wanted to know whenever anyone went there. And it looked like there was nobody home.

His driver was waiting for instructions.

"Back to where you picked me up," Reeve told him.

He paid the driver, tipped him a ten, and walked back the way he'd come. Back into Old Town State Park. He was in a gift shop, buying a postcard and a stamp and a kite that Allan would probably never use — too low-tech — when he saw the cop from the street corner watching him. The guy looked relieved; he'd probably gone back to his partner and then gotten jumpy, decided to look around. The park was full of tourists who had decamped from some trolley tour; it must've been a hard time for him. But now he had his reward.

Reeve left the shop and sauntered back to his car. He drove sedately back to his hotel, and only got lost once. He was assuming now that he was compromised; they'd be following him wherever he went. And if he lost them too often, they'd know *they'd* been compromised. And they'd either get sneakier — homing devices on his car, for example — or they'd have to gamble on direct assault. Maybe even an accident.

He didn't think it would be a simple DUI.

In his room he wrote the postcard home and stuck the stamp on, then went down to the front desk to mail it. One man was seated in the reception area. He hadn't brought any reading material with him, and had been reduced to picking out some of the brochures advertising Sea World, the San Diego Zoo, and the Old Town Trolley Tours. It was a chore to look interested in them. So Reeve did the man a favor: he went into the bar and ordered himself a beer. He was thirsty, and his thirst had won out over thoughts of a cool shower. He savored the chill as he swallowed. The man had followed him in and ordered a beer of his own, looking delighted at the prospect. The man was around the other side of the bar from Reeve. The other drinkers had the laughing ease of conventioneers. Reeve just drank his drink, signed for it, and then went upstairs to his room.

Except it didn't feel like a room now; it felt like a cell.

SEVEN

NEXT DAY, GORDON REEVE saw the ghost.

Maybe it wasn't so surprising under the circumstances. It was a strange day in a lot of ways. He packed his things away when he woke up, then went downstairs for breakfast. He was the only guest in the restaurant. The breakfast was buffet-style again. He could smell bacon and sausage. He sat in his booth and drank orange juice and a single cup of coffee. He was wearing his dark suit, black shoes and socks, white shirt, black tie. None of the hotel staff seemed to realize he was on his way to a funeral — they smiled at him the same as ever. Then he realized that they weren't smiling *at* him, they were smiling *through* him.

After breakfast, he brought his bag downstairs and checked out, using his credit card.

"Hope you enjoyed your stay with us, Mr. Reeve," the smiling robot said. Reeve took his bag outside. There was no one watching him in the hotel lobby, so there'd be someone out here, maybe in the parking lot. Sure enough, as he approached his car, the door opened on a car three bays away.

"Hey, Gordon."

It was McCluskey. He was wearing a dark suit, too.

"What's up?" Reeve asked.

"Nothing. Just thought you might have trouble finding the . . . thought you could follow me there. What do you say?"

79

What could he say — I think you're a liar? I think you're up to something? And I think you *know* I think that?

"Okay, thanks," Reeve said, unlocking the Blazer.

He smiled as he drove. They were tailing him from in front, tailing him with his own permission. He didn't mind, why should he mind? His business here was almost done, for the moment. He needed some distance. A good soldier might have called it *safe* distance. It was a perfect maneuver: look like you're retreating when really you're on the attack. He knew he wasn't going to learn much more in San Diego without wholly compromising himself. It was time to move camp. He'd been taught well in Special Forces, taught lessons for a lifetime; and as old Nietzsche said, if you remained a pupil, you served your teacher badly.

Someone somewhere had once termed the SAS "Nietzsche's gentlemen." That wasn't accurate: in Special Forces you depended on others as thoroughly as you depended on yourself. You worked as a small team, and you had to have trust in the abilities of others. You shared the workload. Which actually made you more of an anarchist. In Special Forces there was less bull about rank than in other regiments — you called officers by their first names. There was a spirit of *community*, as well as a sense of individual worth. Reeve was still weighing up his options. He could work alone, or there were people he could call. People he'd only ever call in an emergency, just as they knew they could call him.

He knew he should be thinking of Jim at this moment, but he'd thought about Jim a lot the past few days, and he didn't see how another hour or two would help. It wasn't that he'd managed to detach himself from the reality of the situation — his brother was dead, maybe murdered, certainly at the center of a cover-up — but that he'd accepted it so completely he now felt free to think about other things. Mr. Cold Rationalist himself. He hoped he'd stay cool at the cremation. He hoped he wouldn't reach over and thumb McCluskey's eyeballs out of their sockets.

The ceremony itself was short. The man at the front — Reeve never did learn if he was a priest, some church functionary, or just a crematorium lackey — didn't know the first thing about

James Reeve, and didn't try to disguise the fact. As he told Gordon, if he'd had more time to prepare he might've said something more. As it was, he kept things nice and simple. He could have been talking about anyone.

There was a coffin — not the one Reeve had been shown at the funeral parlor, some cheaper model with not so much brass and polish. The chapel had some fresh cut flowers which Reeve couldn't name. Joan would have known them — English *and* Latin tags. He was glad she'd stayed behind with Allan. If she'd come, he wouldn't have taken such an interest, would never have met Eddie Cantona. He'd have signed for the body, shipped it home, and gone back to life as before, trying now and again to remember two brothers playing together.

There were just McCluskey and him in the chapel, and some woman at the back who looked like a regular. Then there was the man at the front, saying his words, and someone behind the scenes working the piped music and finally, the little electric curtain that closed over the coffin. The hum of the conveyor belt was just barely audible.

McCluskey held Reeve's arm lightly as they walked back up the aisle; an intimate gesture, like they'd just been married. The woman smiled at them from her pew. She looked to be sticking around for the next service. Guests were already arriving outside.

"You all right?" McCluskey asked.

"Never better," Reeve said, swallowing back the sudden ache in his Adam's apple. He almost gagged, but cleared his throat instead and blew his nose. "Shame Cantona couldn't have been here."

"He should be out later today. We like to dry the drunks out before we release them back to their bars."

"Did you see him?"

"No."

"He wasn't drunk. He hadn't touched a drop."

"Blood test shows different."

Reeve blew his nose again. He'd been about to say, Why doesn't that surprise me? Instead he said, "Let's get out of here."

"Got time or inclination for a drink?"

"I'm afraid you'd pull me in for DUI."

"Hell, I wouldn't do that," McCluskey said, smiling, "not to a tourist. So where to now? The airport?"

Reeve checked his watch. "I suppose so."

"I'll come with you. Maybe we can have that drink there."

"Why not?" Reeve said, though it was the last thing he wanted. They went to their cars. Other vehicles were arriving, including two large black limos bearing the family of the crematorium's next client. Other cars had arrived early, and the drivers and passengers were waiting to emerge. It looked like a point of etiquette: the chief mourners should be the first to arrive. Reeve's eyes almost met those of one mourner, sitting in his car with his hands on the steering wheel. But the man had turned away a second before.

He was back out on the highway, following McCluskey, when he realized who the man had reminded him of. He nearly lost control of the Blazer, and braked hard. A pickup behind him sounded its horn, and he accelerated again.

A ghost. He told himself he'd seen a ghost. It was that sort of day.

At check-in, Reeve got rid of his bag. He had a few small items of Jim's, but otherwise was taking back practically nothing he hadn't brought with him. Allan's kite was safely layered between shirts. Maybe he could get some perfume for Joan on the plane. Not that she ever wore perfume.

McCluskey was suggesting that drink when his pager beeped. He went to a pay phone and called the station. He looked annoyed when he returned.

"I've got to go, Gordon. Sorry."

"Not your fault."

McCluskey put out his hand, which Reeve felt duty-bound to shake. McCluskey could feel it was of a different quality from their first handshake. Reeve wasn't putting anything into it.

"Well," the detective said, "have a nice flight back. Come see us again sometime."

"Right," Reeve said, turning away. He saw the board pointing him towards his gate, and headed for it. McCluskey waited till he was out of sight, then watched for another minute or so. Then he went out to his car. He was worried about Reeve. He didn't think Reeve knew much, but he did know something was wrong. And now he had Agrippa. McCluskey had considered telling Kosigin that Reeve now held that one word, but that would mean admitting that he'd missed the scrap of paper in the dead man's pocket. Kosigin didn't like mistakes. McCluskey intended to keep quiet about the whole thing.

Jay was leaning against McCluskey's car like he owned not only the car but the whole parking lot, and maybe everything else in the city, too.

"Scratch the paint, I'll kill your whole family."

"My family are all dead," Jay said, lifting his weight from the wheel well.

McCluskey unlocked his door but didn't open it. He squinted into the glare as an airplane lifted into the blue, hanging sky. "Think we've seen the last of him?" McCluskey asked. "I certainly fucking hope so. I didn't like him. I don't think he liked me. I wasted a lot of effort on that fuck."

"I'm sure Mr. Kosigin is grateful. Maybe you'll have a bonus this month."

McCluskey didn't like Jay's insolent smile. But then he didn't like his reputation either. He pulled open the driver's door. "You didn't answer my question."

"I wasn't listening."

"I asked if you thought we've seen the last of him."

Jay grinned. "I think *you've* seen the last of him." He was waving something. It looked to McCluskey like an air ticket. "Mr. Kosigin thinks I should take a vacation . . . back to the old homeland." He paused. "I think he saw me."

"What?"

"Back at the crematorium, I think he got a sideways glance. It would make things more interesting if the Philosopher knew I was around."

McCluskey frowned. "What the fuck are you talking about?"

But Jay just shook his head, still grinning, and walked away. He was whistling something, a tune the detective half-recognized.

It bugged him for days, but he never did place it.

Jeffrey Allerdyce was entertaining a corporate client in the penthouse dining room of Alliance Investigative in Washington, DC.

This meant, in effect, that Alliance's senior partners were entertaining, while Allerdyce looked on from his well-upholstered office chair, which had been brought up one flight to the penthouse by a pair of junior partners (who naturally played no other part in the affair).

Allerdyce did not enjoy entertaining, and didn't see why it was expected of a company. To his mind, if you worked well for a client, that should always be enough. But as one senior partner and a host of accountants had told him, there needed to be more these days. Clients needed to feel wanted, cherished, cosseted. They needed, the senior partner had had the temerity to declare, to feel loved.

As if Allerdyce were entertaining them because he actually *liked* them. The only human being Jeffrey Allerdyce had ever loved was his father. The list of people he had *liked* in his long life wouldn't have filled an address label. He liked dogs — he owned two — and he liked an occasional gamble. He liked pasta with fresh pesto sauce. He liked the *Economist* and the *Wall Street Journal*, though neither as much as he once did. He liked *Inspector Morse* on TV, and the music of Richard Wagner. He would travel far for a live concert, if he could be assured of the quality of the artists involved.

He held the belief that his very distrust and dislike of people had made his agency the success it was. But success had bred the need for further success — bringing with it the necessity for corporate entertainment. He watched with a beady eye from his chair as the hired staff made sure plates were full. They were under instructions not to approach him. He would make his needs, if any, known to a senior partner, and food would be brought to him accordingly.

The affair had been arranged meticulously. A senior partner was allocated someone from the client company. They had to entertain that person, make any necessary introductions, check that glasses were replenished. Allerdyce almost sneered his contempt. One balding man in an expensive suit which hung from him like a dishrag from its peg was gulping at the champagne. Gulping it, swallowing it down, getting it while he could. Allerdyce wondered if anyone knew, or even cared, that it was Louis Roederer Cristal, 1985. The champagne of czars, an almost unbelievably beguiling wine. He had allowed himself one glass, just to check the temperature was correct.

A senior partner, nominally in charge of "the floor," came over and whispered into Allerdyce's ear. It gratified Allerdyce to see that members of the client company, even the CEO, glanced over at the conversation with something like fear — as well they might. The CEO called him J. Edgar behind his back. It was almost a compliment, but was probably said with a certain amount of nervous, defensive laughter. The nickname was apposite because, like Hoover, Allerdyce craved information. He hoarded the stuff, from tidbits to full-scale secret reports. Being at the hub of Washington, and especially at the hub of Washington's *secrets*, Allerdyce had collected a lot of information in his time. He used very little of it in any physical way. It was enough that he knew. It was enough that he could shake the CEO's hand, stare into his eyes, and let the man know with that stare that he knew about the male prostitute the CEO kept in a suite only four blocks from the White House.

That was why they glanced over nervily at the whispered exchange — all of them, all the ones with secrets to hide. When in fact the partner's message had been "Dulwater's outside," and Allerdyce's reply had been "I'll be a few minutes."

As Allerdyce got up slowly from his chair, feet shuffled forward, showing their owners were only too willing to help him to his feet should their help be needed. And when he walked across the floor, the various conversations lost their thread, or trailed off, or became more hushed. And when the door had closed behind him, they all felt the need for another drink.

Dulwater was sitting in a chair near the single elevator. Only one of the building's several elevators had access to the penthouse. The chair he sat in was reproduction Louis Quatorze, and looked like it might break at any moment. Dulwater was quick to rise when his employer appeared. Allerdyce pressed the button for the elevator, and Dulwater knew enough to be silent till it had arrived, they'd entered it, and the doors had closed again. Allerdyce turned his access key, quickly pressed some digits on the small keypad with dexterity, so Dulwater couldn't recognize the code, and stood back. They began the descent to the basement.

"Well?" Allerdyce asked.

"I'm not sure what it adds up to," Dulwater began.

"That's not your concern," Allerdyce snapped. "I merely ask for your report."

"Of course." Dulwater swallowed. There was nothing on paper — his employer's instructions — but he knew it by heart anyway, or hoped he did. There was perspiration on his upper lip, and he licked it away. "Kosigin had brought in some muscle from Los Angeles, an Englishman. They twice had meetings outside the CWC building: once in a downtown café, once on the waterfront. Even with the long-range mike I had trouble picking up the conversation."

From the way Dulwater was speaking, Allerdyce knew he was curious to know why Alliance was now spying on its employers. He admired the younger man's curiosity. He knew, too, that no answer he could give would be satisfactory.

"Both were good choices," Allerdyce mused. "Café . . . waterfront . . . A babble of background noise, other voices . . ."

"And on the waterfront they kept moving. Plus there was tourist traffic."

"So, you've told me what you did *not* learn . . ."

Dulwater nodded. "There was a death, an apparent suicide of the reporter who'd been looking into CWC and whom we had been asked to investigate. The man's brother came to town. That seemed to bother Kosigin. You know Kosigin has a detective in his pocket?"

"Of course."

"The detective tailed the brother. Looked like he was calling favors from half the department."

"And the muscle from L.A., as you so described him?"

Dulwater shrugged. "I don't have a name, not yet. I'll get one."

"Yes, you will." The elevator reached the basement, which housed an underground parking garage. The limos the guests had arrived in were parked in neat rows, their liveried drivers enjoying a smoke and a joke.

"No smoking in the building!" Allerdyce barked before letting the elevator doors close again. He keyed in the penthouse. "Interesting," he said to Dulwater, his voice a dull ripple once more.

"Should I continue?"

Allerdyce considered this. "Where is the brother?"

"Our agents report he's heading out today."

"Do you think we'd learn anything more in San Diego now that he's gone?"

Dulwater gave the answer he thought was expected. "Probably not, sir."

"Probably not," Allerdyce echoed, tapping a finger to his thin, dry lips. "They were watching the brother because they perceived in him some threat. The threat of discovery. Now that he's flown home, does he still pose a threat?"

Dulwater was stuck for an answer. "I don't know."

Allerdyce seemed pleased. "Exactly. And *neither do they.* Under the circumstances, Kosigin might just want to know more about the brother, more than we've already been able to tell him."

"We weren't able to find out much about him," Dulwater confessed.

"Kosigin is a careful man," Allerdyce said. It was part of the man's attraction. Allerdyce had not managed to build up much of a dossier on Kosigin, though he knew just by looking at the man, just from a casual conversation with him, that there were secrets there to be discovered. He was a challenge.

And, of course, one day Kosigin might rise to the very pinnacle of CWC. He was already close, and still so young. "I'm not a chemist," he'd told Allerdyce, as though imparting some confidence, and so perhaps hoping to satisfy Allerdyce's celebrated curiosity. "I don't have to be to know how to run a company. To run a company, I need to know two things: how to sell, and how to stop my competitors selling more than me."

Yes, he was a challenge. That was why Allerdyce wanted him, wanted a nice fat dossier of secrets with Kosigin's name on it. Kosigin had made a mistake coming to Alliance again. Allerdyce had known that CWC employed its own security department. Why hadn't Kosigin used them? Why the need for an outside agency to follow the English journalist? Allerdyce was beginning to form an answer: Kosigin had something to hide from his superiors. And Alliance had worked for Kosigin once before. Allerdyce knew now that the two cases were connected, even if he didn't know why.

The elevator arrived at the penthouse. While Dulwater held the doors, Allerdyce keyed for the elevator to return to the lobby. Then he stepped out, leaving the young man inside, still holding the doors, awaiting instructions.

"This intrigues me," Allerdyce said. "Is your passport up to date?"

"Yes, sir," Dulwater said.

"Then come to my office tomorrow morning at seven. We'll have a further discussion."

"Yes, sir," said Dulwater, releasing the doors.

Allerdyce walked back to the dining-room door but did not open it, not immediately. Instead he pressed his ear to the wood, the way he used to when he was a young boy, tiptoeing downstairs from bed to listen at the living-room door or at his father's study. Listening for secrets, for things that could not be said in front of him. Happiest then — when nobody knew he was there.

PART THREE
MAIN LINES

EIGHT

LONDON SEEMED EVERY BIT as alien to him as San Diego.

He actually found himself carrying out evasion procedures at Heathrow. After depositing his single bag in Left Luggage, he went down to the Underground terminal and moved along the platform, watching, waiting. There were good reasons for not taking his car into London of course, reasons anyone would understand: he was only going into town for a short while; his destination was close to a Tube stop; he'd have to be crazy to drive through London, especially jet-lagged. But also he wanted to know if he was being followed, and this was more easily accomplished on foot.

When a train pulled in, he walked onto it, then came off again, looking to left and right along the platform. Then he stepped in again as the doors were closing. The other passengers looked at him like he was mad. Maybe he was. He looked out of the window. There was no one on the platform. No one was tailing him.

He'd been the same on the airplane. His fellow fliers must have thought there was something wrong with him, the number of times he got up to walk the aisles, visiting the bathroom, or going back to ask the stewardesses for drinks he didn't really want. Just so that he could study the passengers.

Now he was on his way into London, with keys in his pocket he had taken from his brother's motel room. The train ran on the Piccadilly Line and would take him all the way to Finsbury Park. But he came off two stops short on the Holloway Road and took his time finding a taxi, then watched from the back window as the driver talked football at him. He got the driver to take him past Jim's flat and drop him off at the end of the road.

The street looked quiet. It was nine-thirty in the morning. People had gone to work for the day. There was a line of cars on one side of the street, and he looked into each one as he passed. Farther along, workmen were digging a hole in the pavement. They were laughing and trading Irish-accented obscenities.

He dismissed them, then checked himself. Nobody could ever be dismissed entirely. The one-armed beggar could be hiding an Uzi up his sleeve. The innocent baby carriage could be booby-trapped. Dismiss nothing and no one. He would stay aware of them, though they were a low priority.

He'd been to the flat before. It was carved from a four-story house which sat just off the top of Ferme Park Road and almost had a view of Alexandra Palace. Jim had laughed about that when he bought the flat. "The estate agent told me as part of his pitch — *nearly* has a view of Ally Pally! Like that was somehow better than being five miles away! Those bastards'll turn anything into a selling point. If the roof was leaking, they'd say it was a safety feature in the event of a fire."

Reeve tried the mortise key in its lock, but it was already unlocked. So he tried the Yale, and that opened the door. The garden flat had its own front door at the bottom of half a dozen steps, but the ground floor and first and second floors were reached via the main door. In the vestibule, there were two more solid doors. Jim's was the ground-floor flat.

"This was probably a nice family house at one time," he'd told Gordon when showing him around. "Before the cowboys moved in and carved the place up." He'd shown him how a large drawing room to the rear had been subdivided with plasterboard walls to make the kitchen and bedroom. The bathroom would once have been part of the main hallway, and the flat's designer had taken an awkward chunk out of what was left of the living room, too.

"It's ugly now, see?" Jim had said. "The proportions are all wrong. The ceilings are too high. It's like standing shoe boxes on their ends."

"So why did you buy it?"

Jim had blinked at him. "It's an investment, Gordie." Then they'd opened the back door so that Jim could show him that the so-called garden flat had no garden, just a concrete patio. "Besides," said Jim, "this area is *in*. Pop stars and DJs live here. You see them down on the Broadway, eating in the Greek restaurant, waiting for someone to recognize them."

"So what do you do?" Reeve had asked.

"Me?" his brother had replied with a smirk which took years off him. "I walk right up to them and ask if I can reserve a table for dinner."

"Jesus, Jim," Reeve said now, unlocking the flat door.

There were sounds inside. Instinctively, he dropped to a crouch. He couldn't identify the sounds — voices maybe. Could they be coming from the flat below or above? He didn't think so. And then he remembered the hall. There'd been no mail sitting there awaiting Jim's return. Jim had been gone awhile; there should have been mail.

He examined the short hall in which he stood: no places of concealment; no weapons to hand. The floor looked solid enough, but might be noisy underfoot. He kept to one side, hugging the wall. Floors were usually strongest there; they didn't make so much noise. He clenched his hands into fists. Running water, a clatter of dishes — the sounds were coming from the kitchen — and a radio, voices on a radio. These were domestic sounds, but he wasn't going to be complacent. It was an easy trick, lulling someone with sound. He recalled a line from Nietzsche: shatter their ears, and teach them to hear with their eyes. It was good advice.

The kitchen door was open a fraction, as were the other doors. The living room looked empty, tidier than he remembered it. The bathroom was in darkness. He couldn't see into the bedroom. He approached the kitchen door and peered through the gap. A woman was at the sink. She had her back to him. She was thin and tall with short fair hair, curling at the nape of her neck. She was alone, washing her breakfast dishes. He decided to check the other rooms, but as he stepped back into the hall he hit a floorboard which sank and creaked beneath him. She looked around, and their eyes met.

Then she started screaming.

He pushed open the kitchen door, his hands held in front of him in a show of surrender.

"It's all right," he said. "I'm sorry I gave you a fright . . ."

She wasn't listening. She had raised her hands out of the water and was advancing on him. Soap suds fell from her right hand as she lifted it, and he saw she was holding a bread knife. Her face was red with anger, not pale with fear, and her screams would bring people running if they could be heard above the workmen outside.

He waited for her to lunge at him. When she attacked, he would defend. But she seemed to know better. She stopped short, bringing the knife down and turning it from a hacking weapon into something she could stab with.

When she stopped screaming for a second to catch her breath, he spoke as quickly as he could: "I'm Jim's brother. Gordon Reeve. We look alike. Maybe he's mentioned me. Gordon Reeve. I live in Scotland. I'm Jim's brother." He shook the keys at her. "His keys. I'm his brother." And all the time his eyes were half on her, half on the knife, and he was walking backwards into the hall as she kept coming forwards. He hoped he was getting through.

"His brother?" she said at last.

Reeve nodded, but said nothing. He wanted it to sink in first. One concept at a time. She was pumped with adrenaline, and her survival instincts had taken hold. There was fear there, too, prob-ably — only she didn't want him to sense it. And at the back of it all, there would be shock, just waiting for its chance to join the party.

"His brother?" she repeated, like it was a phrase in some new language she'd only just started learning.

He nodded again.

"Why didn't you ring the bell?"

"I didn't think anyone would be here."

"Why didn't you shout? You sneaked up, you were spying on me." She was working herself up again.

"I thought the flat would be empty. I thought you were an intruder."

"Me?" She thought this was funny, but she wasn't lowering the knife. "Didn't Jim tell you?"

"No," he said.

"But you're telling me he gave you the keys? He gave you the keys and he didn't say I was living here?"

Reeve shook his head. "The reason I'm here," he said quietly, weighing up the effect this would have on her, "is that Jim's dead. He died in San Diego. I'm on my way home from the funeral."

San Diego seemed to click with her. "What?" she said, appalled.

He didn't repeat any of it. He was dealing with porcelain now — knife-wielding porcelain, but fragile all the same.

"I'm leaving," he told her. "I'll sit outside. You can call the police or you can call my wife, verify who I am. You can do whatever you want. I'll be waiting outside, okay?"

He was at the door now. A dangerous moment: he'd have to half-turn from her to work the lock, providing her with a moment for attack. But she just stood there. She was like some awful statue as he pulled the door closed.

He sat in the vestibule for ten minutes. Then the door opened and she looked out. She wasn't carrying the knife.

"I've made some tea," she said. "You better come in."

Her name was Fliss Hornby, and she was an ex-colleague of Jim's — which was to say, she still worked for the paper from which he had resigned.

"He didn't really resign," she told Reeve. "I mean, he *did* resign, but then he reconsidered — only Giles Gulliver wouldn't unaccept his resignation."

"I had a policeman friend that happened to," Reeve said.

"Jim was furious, but Giles said it was for his own good. I really think he meant it. He knew Jim would be better off going freelance. Not financially better off, but his stuff wouldn't get spiked so often. He'd have more freedom to write what he liked. And to prove it, he commissioned a couple of pieces by Jim, and took a couple of stories from him which ended up on the inside news page."

They were eating an early lunch in an Indian restaurant on Tottenham Lane. There was a special lunchtime businessmen's buffet: large silver salvers with domed covers, blue flames licking beneath each. But they were just watching their food, rearranging it with their forks; they weren't really eating. They simply needed to be out of the flat.

Reeve had told Fliss Hornby about Jim's death. He'd meant to keep it simple, lying where necessary, but he found the whole story gushing out of him, a taste of bile at the back of his throat, like he'd been puking.

She was a good listener. She had listened through her tears and got up only once — to fetch a box of tissues from the bedroom. Then it had been her turn to talk, and she told Reeve how she'd met up with Jim and a load of other journalists one night in Whitehall. She'd told him that things weren't going well with her, that her boyfriend had become her ex-boyfriend and had threatened her with violence.

"I mean," she told Gordon, "I can look after myself —"

"I've noticed."

"But it was more the atmosphere. It was disrupting my work. Jim said he was going to the States for a month, and suggested I look after his flat. Lance might get bored knocking on the door of an empty flat in Camden. And in the meantime, I could get my head together."

"Lance, that's the boyfriend?"

"Ex-boyfriend. Christ, *boyfriend* — he's in his forties."

Fliss Hornby on the other hand was in her late twenties. She'd been married some time in her past, but didn't talk about it. Everyone was allowed one mistake. It was just that she kept making the one mistake time after time.

They'd demolished a bottle of white wine in the restaurant. Or Fliss had; Reeve had had just the one glass, plus lots of iced water.

She took a deep breath, stretching her neck to one side and then the other, her eyes closed. Then she settled back in her chair and opened her eyes again.

"So what are you going to do?" she asked.

"I'm not sure. I was planning to search the flat."

"Good idea. Jim filled the hall cupboard with all his stuff, plus there are a couple of suitcases under the bed." She saw the look on his face. "Would you like me to do it?"

Reeve shook his head. "He didn't tell you why he was going to the States?"

"He was always a bit hush-hush about his stories, especially in their early stages. Didn't want anyone nicking his ideas. He had a point. Journalists don't have friends — you're either a source or a competitor."

"I'm a source?"

She shrugged. "If there's a story . . ."

Reeve nodded. "Jim would like that. He'd want the story finished."

"Always supposing we can start it. No files, no notes . . ."

"Maybe in the flat."

She poured the last of the wine down her throat. "Then what are we waiting for?"

Reeve tried to imagine anyone threatening Fliss Hornby. He imagined himself hurting the threatener. It wasn't difficult. He knew pressure points, angles of twist, agonies waiting to be explored. He could fillet a man like a chef with a Dover sole. He could have them repeat the Lord's Prayer backwards while eating sand and gravel. He could break a man.

These were thoughts the psychiatrist had warned him about. Mostly, they came after he'd been drinking. But he hadn't been drinking, and yet he was still thinking them.

More than that, he was enjoying them, relishing the possibility of pain — someone else's; maybe even his own. Sensations made you feel alive. He was probably never more alive than when consumed by fear and flight at the end of Operation Stalwart. Never more alive than when so nearly dead.

He telephoned Joan from the flat to let her know what was happening. Fliss Hornby was pulling stuff out of the hall cupboard, laying it along the floorboards so it could be gone through methodically. Reeve watched her through the open door of the living room. Joan said that Allan was missing his dad. She told him there had been potential clients, two of them on two separate occasions. He'd already had her cancel this weekend's course.

"Phone calls?" he asked.

"No, these were personal callers."

"I mean have there been any phone calls?"

"None I couldn't deal with."

"Okay."

"You sound tense."

He had yet to tell Joan what he'd just sat and told a complete stranger. "Well, you know, I've got all his things to sort through . . ."

"I can come down there, you know."

"No, you stay there with Allan. I'll be home soon."

"Promise?"

"I promise. Bye, Joan."

By the time he got through to the hall, the cupboard was half empty.

"You start looking through that lot," Fliss said, "while I haul the rest out."

"Sure," Reeve agreed. Then: "Shouldn't you be at work or something?"

She smiled. "Maybe I *am* at work."

An hour later, they'd been through the contents of the cupboard and had found nothing relevant. Fliss Hornby had burst into tears just the once. Reeve had thought it best to ignore her. Besides, his mind was on his work. They drank herbal tea and then went into the bedroom. At some point, Reeve couldn't work out when, Fliss had tidied the room. When he'd first glanced into it, the bed had been strewn with clothes, the floor with books and magazines. Now everything had been hidden.

She pulled two suitcases out from beneath the bed and lifted the first one onto the bed. It wasn't locked. There were clothes inside. Reeve recognized some of them: a gaudy striped shirt, a couple of ties, a Scotland rugby shirt, saggy, the way all rugby shirts seem to go after the very first wash. The second case contained paperwork.

They spent a lot of time flicking through files, bundles of paper-clipped news cuttings, an old-fashioned card index. Then Fliss found half a dozen computer disks, and waved them at Reeve.

"I may be able to read these here."

Her PC was set up on the desk in the living room. Reeve studied the bookshelves while she booted up.

"These all yours?" he asked.

"No, most of them are Jim's. I didn't bring much from my flat, just stuff I didn't want burgled."

There were a couple of philosophy books. Reeve smiled, picking one out. David Hume's *An Enquiry Concerning the Principles of Morals*. He flicked through, and found a couple of lines had been underlined on one page. He knew which lines they'd be, but read them anyway.

A man, brought to the brink of a precipice, cannot look down without trembling.

He'd spouted philosophy at Jim during a couple of their meetings. He'd quoted Hume at him, this very passage, comparing it with Nietzsche: "If you gaze into the abyss, the abyss gazes also into you." More melodramatic than Hume, probably less factual — but much more powerful. Jim had been listening. He'd appeared bored, but all the time he'd been listening, and he'd even bought a couple of the books. More than that, he'd read them.

Fliss Hornby was sliding the first disk home. It contained correspondence. They read through some of the letters.

"This feels weird," she said at one point. "I mean, I'm not sure we should be doing this. It's almost like desecration."

The other disks dealt with stories Jim Reeve had been working on at one time or another. Reeve was glad Fliss was there; she saved him time.

"Giles used that one," she said of one story. "This one I think turned up unattributed in *Private Eye* or *Time Out*. This one I haven't come across before, but it looks like he hit a dead end with it."

"We're looking for a chemical company, Co-World Chemicals, headquarters in San Diego."

"I know, you told me." She sounded impatient. She tried another disk. It was labeled 1993 and proved to be all old stuff. The other disks were no more helpful.

"Nothing current," she said. "He probably took the current disks with him along with his laptop."

Reeve remembered something she'd said, about journalists only having sources and competitors. "He wouldn't have left any of his notes here anyway," he stated. "Not with another reporter on the premises."

"Where else would he have left them?"

"Could be anywhere. A girlfriend's, a drinking mate's . . ."

"With his ex-wife?"

Reeve shook his head. "She disappeared a while back, probably left the country. Jim had that effect on women." He'd tried contacting her, to tell her the news. Not that she'd have been interested; not that he'd tried very hard.

Reeve remembered something. "We're also looking for the name Agrippa."

"Agrippa? That's classical, isn't it?" Fliss slid a CD into the computer's CD-ROM slot. "Encyclopedia," she explained. She went to Word Search and entered "Agrippa." The computer came up with ten articles, the word appearing a total of twenty times. They scanned all ten articles, but remained none the wiser about what Agrippa had meant to Jim. Fliss tried a few reference books, but the only additional Agrippa she found was in the *Oxford Companion to English Literature*.

"Dead end," she said, slamming shut the last book.

"What about mail?" Reeve asked. "Has he had any letters while he's been away?"

"Plenty. He told me he'd phone and give me an address I could redirect them to, but he never did. Last I spoke to him was when he handed me the front-door keys."

"So where's the mail?"

It was in the cupboard above the sink in the kitchen. There was a teetering tower of it. Fliss carried it to the kitchen table while Reeve cleared a space, moving cups, sugar bowl, and milk bottle. He couldn't hear the pneumatic drill anymore. He looked at his watch, surprised to find it was nearly five o'clock — the best part of the day had gone, used up on a hunt which had so far failed to turn up anything the least bit useful.

The mail looked similarly uninspired. Much of it was junk. "I could have just binned it," Fliss said. "But when *I* come home after a trip, I like there to be a big pile of letters waiting for me. Makes me feel wanted."

"Jim was wanted all right," Reeve said. "Wanted by double-glazing firms, clothes catalogs, the football pools, and just about every fund management scheme going."

There was a postcard from Wales. Reeve deciphered the spidery handwriting, then handed it to Fliss. "Who's Charlotte?"

"I think he brought her to the pub once."

"What about his girlfriends? Anyone come to the flat looking for him? Anyone phone?"

She shook her head. "Just Charlotte. She called one night. Seems he hadn't said he was going to the States. I think they were supposed to be going to Wales together."

Reeve considered this. "So either he was an unfeeling bastard who was giving her the big hint she was being ditched . . ."

"Or?"

"Or something suddenly came up in the States. When did he tell you you could move in?"

"The night before he flew out."

"So he crammed all his stuff into the cupboard in the hall and the suitcases under the bed and off he went." Reeve gnawed his bottom lip. "Maybe he knew they were going to move the scientist."

"Scientist?"

"Dr. Killin — he worked at CWC. Jim went to see him once. Next time he tried, Killin had gone on vacation and the house was under surveillance."

"I got the feeling he'd only had a few days' notice that he was making the trip. He complained at the price of the airfare. It wasn't APEX. What's the matter?"

Reeve was studying an envelope. He turned it over in his hands. "This is Jim's handwriting."

"What?" She gazed at the envelope.

"It's his handwriting. Postmarked London, the day before he flew to the States." He held the envelope up to the light, shook it, pressed its contents between thumb and forefinger. "Not just paper," he said. He peeled apart the two glued flaps. He would never use ready-seal envelopes himself; they were too easy to tamper with. He pulled out a sheet of A4 paper, double-folded. A small key fell out of the paper onto the table. While Fliss picked up the key, Reeve unfolded the paper. The writing was a drunken scrawl.

"Pete's new address — 5 Harrington Lane."

He showed it to Fliss. "What do you reckon?"

She fetched her street guide. There was only one Harrington Lane in London — just off the upper Holloway Road, near Archway.

"It's not that far," said Fliss. Her car was being fixed at a garage in Crouch End, so they called for a cab.

"Yeah," said Pete Cavendish, "like Jim said, you can't be too careful. And I had the garage gutted out, sold my car and my motorbike. I've gone ecology, see. I use a bicycle now. I reckon everybody should." He was in his late twenties, a photographer. Jim Reeve had put work his way in the past, so Pete had been happy to oblige when Jim asked a favor.

Reeve hadn't considered his brother's car. He'd imagined it would be sitting in some long-term car lot out near Heathrow — and as far as he was concerned they could keep it.

Cavendish put him right. "Those places cost a fortune. No, he reckoned this was a better bet."

They were walking from 5 Harrington Lane, a terraced house, to the garage Pete Cavendish owned. They'd come out through his back door, crossed what might have been the garden, been shown through a gate at the back which Cavendish then repadlocked shut, and were in an alley backing onto two rows of houses whose backyards faced each other. The lane had become a dumping ground for everything from potato chip bags to mattresses and sofas. One sofa had been set alight and was charred to a crisp, showing springs and clumps of wadding. It was nearly dark, but the alley was blessed with a single working streetlight. Cavendish had brought a flashlight with him.

"I think the reason he did that," Cavendish said, meaning Jim's letter to himself, "was he was drunk, and he hadn't been to my new place before. He probably reckoned he'd forget the bloody address and never find me again, or his old car. See, Jim had a kind of dinosaur brain — there was a little bit of it working even when he'd had a drink. It was his ancient consciousness."

Pete Cavendish spoke with a hand-rolled cigarette in his mouth. He had a ponytail and gray wizened cheeks. The holes in his jeans weren't there by design, and the heel was loose on one of his sneakers. Reeve had noticed some cans of Super Lager on the kitchen counter. He'd seen Cavendish swig from one before they set off. Ecology and dinosaurs. If Cavendish kept drinking, he'd be seeing green dinosaurs in his dreams.

They passed seven garages before coming to a stop. Cavendish kicked away some empty cans and a bag of bottles from the front of his own private garage, then took the key from Reeve that Jim had mailed to his own home. He turned it in the lock, pulled the handle, and the garage door groaned open. It stuck halfway up, but halfway was enough. The streetlight barely penetrated the interior gloom.

Cavendish switched on the flashlight. "Doesn't look as though any of the kids have been in here," he said, checking the floor and walls. Reeve didn't ask what he'd thought he might find — glue, spray paint, used vials of crack?

There was only the car.

It was a battered Saab 900 of indeterminate color — charcoal came closest — with a chip out of the windshield, the fixings for side mirrors but no actual mirrors, and one door (replaced after a collision) a different color from the rest of the body. Reeve had never let his brother drive him anywhere in the Saab, and had never seen Jim drive it. It used to sit outside the flat with a tarpaulin over it.

"He spent a grand getting it done up," Cavendish said.

"Money well spent," Reeve muttered.

"Not on the outside, on the inside: new engine, transmission, clutch. He could've bought another car cheaper, but he loved this old tank." Cavendish patted it fondly.

"Keys?" Reeve asked. Cavendish handed them over. Reeve unlocked the car and looked inside, checking under the seats and in the glove compartment. He came up with chewing gum, parking tickets, and a book of matches from the same Indian restaurant where he'd eaten lunch.

"The boot?" Fliss suggested. Reeve was unwilling; this would be it, the very last option, their last chance to move any further forward. He turned the key and felt the trunk spring open. Cavendish shone the flashlight in. There was something nestling there, covered with a tartan traveling rug. Reeve pulled off the rug, revealing a large cardboard box advertising its contents to be twelve one-liter bottles of dishwashing liquid. It was the kind of box you picked up from supermarkets and corner shops. He opened its flaps. There were papers inside, maybe half a boxful. He pulled out the top sheet and angled it into the failing flashlight.

"Bingo," he said.

He lifted the box out, and Fliss locked the trunk. The box was awkward rather than heavy.

"Can we call for a cab from your phone?" Reeve asked Cavendish.

"Yeah, sure." They left the garage, and Cavendish locked it tight. "Just one thing," he said.

"What's that?"

"What's going to happen to the car?"

Reeve thought about it for all of two seconds. "It's yours," he told Cavendish. "Jim would have wanted it that way."

NINE

January 13

I suppose if this turns into a story, I'll have to credit Marco with the genesis — though he'd probably stress he's more of a Pink Floyd fan. He wears a T-shirt which must date back to Dark Side of the Moon. *It's black with the prism logo on it — only he says it's a pyramid. Sure, but light doesn't enter a pyramid white and come out the seven colors of the rainbow. It only does that with prisms, so it must be a prism. He says I'm missing the point, maaann. The point is, the album's a concept album and the concept is everyday madness. Pure white light into a myriad of colors. The everyday gone mad.*

But then why is it a damned pyramid? Why not a teacup or a toaster or even a typewriter? Marco laughs, remembering that party of his and how I looked at a poster on his wall and thought it was sailing boats on a rippling blue sea, pictured near sunset with some heavy filtering.

And it wasn't. It was pyramids. It was the poster that came with Dark Side of the Moon *and I was sober when I mistook it. Sober as a judge. Later, I was drunk as a lord and trying to get my hand up Marco's girlfriend's kilt until she reminded me, her mouth shiveringly close to my ear, that Marco had done a bit of judo in his time and part of his left ear was missing. So, fair enough, I retracted my hand. You do, don't you?*

Where the fuck was I? The story. The story.

It's about madness, too: that's why I used the Pink Floyd reference. I could use it as a lead into the story proper. "Tales of Everyday Madness." Was that a book or a film? Did someone give me that at charades one time? Absolutely impossible. Yes, charades, at Marco's party. And Marco's team was making half its titles up. The bastard even dumped in some that were in Italian.

Marco is Italian, and that is also relevant to the story. This is a story he told me last night in the Stoat and Whistle. I said to him, why haven't you told me this before? Know what he said? He said, this is the first serious (not to mention intelligible) conversation we've ever had. And when I thought about it, he was probably right. What's more, he only got round to telling his story because we'd run out of Tottenham jokes. Here's the last one we told. What's the difference between a man with no knob and a Spurs player? A man with no knob's got more chance of scoring.

See, we were desperate.

"Anything?" Fliss asked. She had her own sheaf of paper in front of her, as well as a second mug of coffee.

"I think he was drunk when he typed this."

"Full of spelling mistakes?"

"No, just full of shit."

They were back in the Crouch End flat. They'd brought a carry-out back with them — Chinese this time, with some lagers and Cokes bought from the corner shop. The tin trays of food sat half-uneaten on the living room's coffee table.

"What about you?" Reeve asked.

"Photocopies mostly. Articles from medical and scientific journals. Looks like he was calling up anything he could find on mad cow disease. Plus on genetic patents. There's an interesting article about the company that owns the patent on all genetically engineered cotton. Might not be relevant." She gnawed on a plastic chopstick. The chopsticks had been fifty pence a pair extra. Reeve rubbed his jaw, feeling the need for a shave. And a bath. And some sleep. He tried not to think about what time his body made it; tried to dismiss the eight hours he'd wound his watch forward, and the sleep he hadn't taken on the plane.

He started reading again.

Marco is a journalist. He's over here for a year, more if they like his reports, as London correspondent for some glossy Milan rag. They keep faxing him to say they want more royal family, more champagne balls, more Wimbledon and Ascot. He's tried telling them Wimbledon and Ascot come once a year, but they just keep sending the faxes to their London office. Marco's thinking of chucking it. He used to be a "serious" journalist, real hard copy, until he sniffed more money in the air. Moved from daily to weekly, newspaper to magazine. He said at the time he was just sick of journalism; he wanted easy money and a break from Italy. Italian politics depressed him. The corruption depressed him. He'd had a colleague, a good friend, blown up by a parcel bomb when he tried to zero in on some minister with Mafia connections. Ba-boom, and up and away to the great leader column in the sky. Or maybe the elevator down to the basement, glowing fires and typing up the classifieds.

Marco told me about some of the scandals, and I was matching him conspiracy for conspiracy, chicanery for chicanery, payoff for payoff. Then he told me he covered the Spanish cooking oil tragedy. I recalled it only vaguely. 1981, hundreds died. Contaminated oil — yes?

And Marco said, "Maybe."

So then he told his side of it, which didn't quite tally with the official line at the time or since. Because according to Marco, some of the people who died hadn't touched the oil (rapeseed oil it was — memo to self, get clippings out of library). They hadn't bought it, hadn't used it — simple as that. So what caused the deaths? Marco's idea — and it wasn't original, he got it from other researchers into the area — was that these things called — hold on, I wrote it down — Jesus, it's taken me ten minutes to track it down. Should've known to look first on my fag packet. OPs, that what it says. OPs were to blame. He did tell me what they are, but I've forgotten. Better look into it tomorrow.

"OPs," Reeve said.

"What?"

"Any mention of them in the stuff you're reading?"

She smiled. "Sorry, I stopped reading a while back. I'm not taking it in anymore." She yawned, stretching her arms up, hands clenched. The fabric of her sweater tightened, raising the profile of her breasts.

"Shit," said Reeve, suddenly realizing. "I've got to get a room."

"What?"

"A hotel room. I wasn't planning on being here this late."

She paused before answering. "You can sleep where you are. That sofa's plenty comfy enough; I've fallen asleep on it a few times myself. I'll just check out *Newsnight* if that's all right, see what I've missed today and what I can expect to read tomorrow, and then I'll leave you to it."

He stared at her.

"It's all right, really it is," she said. "You're perfectly safe with me."

She had blue eyes. He'd noticed them before, but they seemed bluer now. And she didn't smell of perfume, just soap.

"We can read the rest over breakfast," she said, switching on the TV. "I need a clear head to take in half of what I'm reading. Bovine spongiform encephalopathy: it doesn't exactly trip off the tongue, does it? And nor does it trip off the eyeballs. Bloody boffins just refuse to call it mad cow disease. I hope to God that's not what this is all about, the beefburgers of the damned — and bloody John Selwyn Gummer stuffing one down his poor sodding daughter's throat. Do you remember that photo?"

"Why do you say that?"

She was engrossed in the TV. "Say what?"

"That you hope it's not about bovine spongy whatsit."

She glanced at him. "Because it's been covered, Gordon. It's old news. Besides, the public are physically repelled by scare stories. They'd rather not know about them. That's why they end up in the *Grauniad* or *Private Eye*. You've heard of the right to know? Well, the good old British public has another inalienable right: the right *not* to know, not to worry. They want a cheap paper with some cartoons and funny headlines and a good telly section. They do not want to know about diseases that eat their flesh, meat that makes them mad, or eggs that can put them in casualty. You tell them about the bow doors on ferries, they still troop on and off them every weekend, heading for Calais and cheap beer." She turned to him again. "Know why?"

"Why?"

"Because they don't think lightning strikes twice. If some other bugger has died that makes it so much less likely that *they* will." She turned back to the TV, then smiled. "Sorry, I'm ranting."

"You have a low regard for your readers?"

"On the contrary, I have a very high regard for *my* readers. They are discriminating and knowledgeable." She turned the sound up a little, losing herself in the news. Reeve put down the sheets of paper he was still holding. Sticking out from below the sofa was a newspaper. He pulled it out. It was the paper Fliss worked for.

"Isn't he a dish?" she muttered, a rhetorical question apparently. She was talking to herself about the news presenter.

Reeve went through to the kitchen to boil some more water. He knew he should call Joan again, let her know the score, but the telephone was in the living room. He sat down at the kitchen table and spread out the paper which he'd brought through with him. He started examining each page, looking for the byline Fliss Hornby. He didn't find it. He went through the paper again. This time he found it.

He made two mugs of instant decaf and took them back through to the living room. Fliss had tucked her legs beneath her and was hugging them. She sat forward ever so slightly in her chair, a fan seeking a better view, though there was nothing between her and her idol. Then Reeve was in the way, handing her the mug.

"You work on the fashion page," he said.

"It's still journalism, isn't it?" Obviously she'd had this conversation before.

"I thought you were —"

"What?" She glared at him. "A *proper* journalist? An *investigative* journalist?"

"No, I just thought . . . Never mind."

He sat down, aware she was angry with him. Tactful, Gordon, he thought. Nil out of ten for leadership. Had he told her he appreciated all she'd done today? She'd halved his workload, been able to explain things to him — bits of journalist's shorthand on the disks, for example. He might have been there all day, and spent a wasted day, instead of which he had something. He had the genesis; that's what Jim had called it. The genesis of whatever had led him to San Diego and his death. It was a start. Tomorrow things might get more serious.

He kept looking at Fliss. If she'd turned in his direction, he'd have smiled an apology. But she was staring unblinking at the screen, her neck taut. Reeve seemed to have the ability to piss women off. Look at Joan. Most days now there was an argument between them; not when Allan was around — they were determined to put up a "front" — but whenever he wasn't there. There was enough electricity in the air to light the whole building.

After *Newsnight* was watched in silence, Fliss said a curt good night, but then came back into the room with a spare duvet and a pillow.

"I'm sorry," Reeve told her. "I didn't mean to imply anything. It's just that you never said anything, and you've been acting all day like you were Scoop Newshound, the paper's only investigative reporter."

She smiled. "Scoop Newshound?"

He shrugged, smiling also.

"I forgive you," she said. "First one up tomorrow goes for milk and bread, right?"

"Right, Fliss."

"Good night, then." She showed no sign of moving from the doorway. Reeve had pulled off his blue cotton sweater and was wearing a long-sleeved white T-shirt. She appraised his body for a moment, and gave a smile and a noise that was halfway between a sigh and humming, then turned and walked away.

He found it hard to sleep. He was too tired; or rather, he was exhausted but not tired. His brain wouldn't work — as he discovered when he tried carrying on with Jim's notes — but it wouldn't be still either. Images flitted through his mind, bouncing along like a ball through a series of puddles. Snatches of conversations, songs, echoes of the two films he'd watched on the flight, his trip on the Underground, the taxicabs, the Indian restaurant, surprising Fliss in the kitchen. Songs . . . tunes . . .

Row, row, row your boat.

He jerked from the sofa, standing in the middle of the floor in his T-shirt and underpants, trembling. He switched on the TV, turning the sound all the way down. Nighttime television: mindless and bright. He looked out of the window. A halo of orange sodium, a dog barking in the near distance, a car cruising past. He watched it, studied it. The driver was staring straight ahead. There were cars parked outside, solid lines of them on both sides of the street, ready for tomorrow's race.

He padded through to the kitchen on bare feet and switched on the kettle again. Rooting in the box of assorted herbal tea bags, he found spearmint and decided to give it a try. Back in the hallway, he noticed that Fliss's bedroom door was ajar. More than ajar in fact: it was halfway open. Was it an invitation? He'd be bound to see it if he used the kitchen or the bathroom. Her light was off. He listened for her breathing, but the fridge in the kitchen was making too much noise.

He waited in the hall, holding the steaming mug, until the fridge switched off. Her breathing was more than regular — she was snoring.

"Morning." She came into the kitchen sleepy-faced and tousling her hair. She wore a thick tartan dressing gown and fluffy pink slippers.

Reeve had been out and purchased breakfast and newspapers. She slumped into a chair at the table and grabbed a paper.

"Coffee?" he asked. He'd bought a packet of coffee and some paper filters.

"How did you sleep?" she asked without looking up.

"Fine," he lied. "You?"

As she was folding a page, she glanced up at him. "Soundly, thanks."

He poured them both coffee. "I've found out what OPs are."

"Oh?"

"I've been doing some more reading."

"You *were* up early. So, what are they?"

"Organophosphorus treatments."

"And what are those when they're at home?"

"Pesticides, I think. Marco and others think the Spanish cooking oil thing was all to do with pesticides."

She drank greedily from her mug and exhaled. "So what now?"

He shrugged.

"Are you going to talk to Marco?"

Reeve shook his head. "He's got nothing to do with it. He's just a catalyst. Jim wasn't researching the Spanish incident, he was looking at BSE."

"Bovine spongiform thingy."

"Encephalopathy."

"How did he make the leap from cooking oil to BSE?"

"He remembered something he'd heard."

So I phoned Joshua Vincent, and told him he probably wouldn't know me. He said I was correct in that assumption. I explained that some time ago the paper had received a press release from his organization, the National Farmers' Union, concerning BSE. He told me he wasn't working for the NFU anymore. He sounded bitter when he said it. I asked him what had happened.

"They sacked me," he said.

"Why?"

"Because of what I said about BSE."

And I began to sniff my story. Now if only I can persuade Giles to fund me . . .

"So what are you doing today?" Fliss asked. She'd had a shower, dried her hair, and was dressed.

"Trying to find Joshua Vincent."

"And if you can't?"

Reeve shrugged again; he didn't want to consider failure, though really it should be considered. With any plan, there should be a fallback position.

"You could talk to Giles Gulliver," she suggested, dabbing crumbs of toast from her plate.

"That's an idea."

"And then?"

"Depends what I learn."

She sucked at the crumbs. "Don't expect too much from Giles, or anyone like him."

"What do you mean?"

She grabbed the newspaper and opened it to a full-page advertisement, placed by Co-World Chemicals. "Don't bother reading it," she said. "It'll put you back to sleep. It's just one of those feel-good ads big corporations make up when they want to spend some money."

Reeve glanced at the ad. "Or when their consciences are bothering them?"

Fliss wrinkled her nose. "Grow up. Those people don't have consciences. They've had them surgically removed to make room for the cash-flow implants." She tapped the paper. "But as long as Co-World and companies like them are throwing money at advertising departments, publishers will love them, and the publishers will see to it that their editors never print anything that might upset Sugar Daddy. That's all I'm saying."

"Thanks for the warning."

She shrugged. "Will you be here this evening?"

"I don't know. Maybe. I'll have to see how it goes."

"Well, I'll probably be late. There's a second Giannini's opening in Covent Garden and I'm invited."

"Giannini's?"

"The designer."

"Hold the front page," he said. She scowled and he held up his hands. "Just a joke."

"I want to know what you find, no matter what. Even if it's only a phone call from Scotland, let me know."

"Sure, it's the least I can do."

She left the kitchen and returned again wearing a coat and carrying a briefcase. She made show of adjusting the belt on the coat. "Just one thing, Gordon."

"What's that?"

"What are you going to do about the flat?"

He smiled at her. "It's yours for as long as you want it."

Finally she looked at him. "Really?" He nodded. "Thanks."

Maybe he'd found his fallback position. If he didn't get any further with Jim's story, he could always track down her ex-boyfriend and make a mess of the rest of his life. She came over and pecked him on the cheek.

Which was payment enough in itself.

He found a telephone number for the NFU, but nobody could give him a forwarding address for Joshua Vincent. A woman who had tried to be helpful eventually passed him on to someone who had more questions than answers, wanting to know who he was and what his connection was with Mr. Vincent.

Reeve put down the telephone.

Maybe Vincent lived in London, but there were several Vincent J's listed in the phone book. It would take a while to talk to them all. He went to Jim's notes again. They were a hodgepodge of the detailed and the rambling, of journalistic instinct and alcoholic excess. There were jottings on the backs of some sheets. He hadn't paid them much attention, but laid them out now on the living-room floor. Doodles, circles, and cubes mostly, and a cow's warped face with a pair of horns. But there were names and what looked like times, too, and some telephone numbers. There were no names beside the numbers. He tried the first one and got a woman's answering machine. The second just rang and rang. The third turned out to be a bookmaker's in Finsbury Park. The fourth was a central London pub, the one Fliss and her journalist colleagues used.

The fifth was another answering machine: "Josh here. Leave your message and I'll get back."

An evasive message. Reeve severed the connection and wondered what to say. Eventually he dialed again.

"Josh here. Leave your message and I'll get back."

He waited for the tone.

"My name's Gordon Reeve, and I'm trying to locate Joshua Vincent. I got this number from my brother's notes. My brother's name was James Reeve; I think Mr. Vincent knew him. I use the past tense because my brother is dead. I think he was working on a story at the time. I'm hoping you can help me. I'd like to find out why he died."

He gave the flat's telephone number and put down the receiver. Then he sat down and stared at the telephone for fifteen minutes. He made more coffee and watched it for another fifteen minutes. If Vincent was home and had listened to the message straightaway, even if he wanted to check James Reeve *had* a brother, he would have been back by now.

So Reeve telephoned Fliss's paper, spoke to Giles Gulliver's assistant, and was put through to the editor at last.

"Good God," Gulliver said. "I can't believe it. Is this some sort of joke?"

"No joke, Mr. Gulliver. Jim's dead."

"But how? When?"

Reeve started to tell him, but Gulliver interrupted. "No, wait — let's meet. Is that possible, Mr. Reeve?"

"It's possible."

"Just let me check my diary." Reeve was put on hold for the time it took him to count to sixty. "Sorry about that. We could have a drink at midday. I've a lunch appointment at one, so it would make sense to meet at the hotel. Would that suit you? I want to hear everything. It's quite ghastly. I can hardly take it in. Jim was one of —"

"Where's the hotel, Mr. Gulliver?"

"Sorry. The Ritz. See you there at midday."

"Good-bye, Mr. Gulliver."

And still Joshua Vincent didn't call.

In Jim's notes, Giles Gulliver had always been "the old boy" or "the old duffer." Reeve was expecting a man in his sixties or even seventies, a newspaperman of the old school. But when he was shown to Gulliver's table in the Ritz bar, he saw that the man half-rising to greet him from behind a fat Cuban cigar could only be in his early forties — not much older than Reeve himself. But Gulliver's actions were studied, like those of a much older man, a man who has seen everything life has to throw at him. Yet he had gleaming eyes, the eyes of a child when shown something wondrous. And Reeve saw at once that the phrase "old boy" was perfect for Giles Gulliver. He was Peter Pan in a pinstripe.

"Good man," Gulliver said, shaking Reeve's hand. He ran his fingers through his slicked hair as he sat back down again. They had a corner table, away from the general babble of the bar. There were four things on the table: an ashtray, a portable telephone, a portable fax machine, and a glass of iced whiskey.

Gulliver rolled the cigar around his mouth. "Something to drink?" Their waiter was standing ready.

"Mineral water," said Reeve.

"Ice and lime, sir?"

"Lemon," said Reeve. The waiter retreated, and Reeve waited for Gulliver to say something.

Gulliver was shaking his head. "Hellish business. Surprised no one told me sooner. I've got a sub working on the obit." He paused, catching himself. "My dear chap, I'm so sorry. You don't want to hear about that."

"It's okay."

"Now tell me, how did Jim die?"

"He was murdered."

Gulliver's eyes were hidden by the smoke he'd just exhaled. "What?"

"That's my theory."

Gulliver relaxed; he was dealing with a theory, not a story.

Reeve told him some of the rest, but by no means all of it. He wasn't sure of his ground. On the one hand, he wanted the public to know what had happened in San Diego. On the other, he wasn't sure whose life he might be endangering if he *did* go public — especially if he went public without proof. Proof would be his insurance. He needed proof.

"Did you know Jim was going to San Diego?" Reeve asked.

Gulliver nodded. "He wanted three thousand dollars from me. Said the trip would be worth it."

"Did he tell you why he was going?"

Gulliver's phone rang. He smiled an apology and picked it

up. The conversation — the side of it Reeve could hear — was technical, something to do with the next day's edition.

Gulliver pressed the Off button. "Apologies." He glanced at his watch. "Did Jim tell me why he was going? No, that was one of the irritating things about him." He caught himself again. "I don't wish to speak ill of the dead . . ."

"Speak away."

"Well, Jim liked his little conspiracy; and he liked to keep it his own secret. I think he thought it gave him more power: if an editor didn't know what the story might be, he couldn't come straight out and say no. That's how Jim liked to play us. The less he told, the more we were supposed to think he had to tell. Eventually, he'd give you the story, the story you'd shelled out for, and it was seldom as meaty as you'd been led to believe."

Listening to Gulliver, especially as the whiskey did its loosening, Reeve could hear hard edges and jagged corners that were a long way away from the public school image Gulliver presented to the world. There was street market in those edges and corners. There was street smart. There was city boy.

The fax bleeped and then started to roll out a page. Gulliver examined the sheet and got on the telephone again. There was another technical discussion, another glance at the Piaget watch, a tug at the crocodile wristband.

"He didn't tell you anything?" Reeve persisted, sounding like he didn't believe it.

"Oh, he told me snatches. Cooking oil, British beef, some veterinarian who'd died."

"Did he mention Co-World Chemicals?"

"I think so."

"In what connection?"

"My dear boy, there *was* no connection, that's what I've been saying. He'd just say a couple of words, like he was feeding an infant egg from a silver spoon. Thinking he was stringing one along . . ."

"Someone killed him to stop the story."

"Then prove it. I don't mean prove it in a court of law, but prove it to *me*. That's what you want, isn't it?" Gulliver's eyes seemed clearer than ever. He leaned across the table. "You want to finish what Jim started. You want an epitaph which would also be a revenge. Isn't that right?"

"Maybe."

"No maybe about it. That is what you want, and I applaud you. I'll run with it. But I need more than you've given me, more than Jim gave me."

"You're saying I should finish the story?"

"I'm saying I'm interested. I'm saying keep in touch." Gulliver sat back and picked up his glass, washing the ice with the amber liquid.

"Can I ask a question?" Reeve said.

"We only have a minute or so."

"How much does CWC spend a year on advertising in your paper?"

"How much? That's a question for my advertising manager."

"You don't know?"

Gulliver shrugged. "CWC's a big company, a multinational. They own several subsidiaries in the UK and many more in Europe. There's UK production and some importation."

"A multimillion-pound industry, with a proportionate advertising budget."

"I don't see —"

"And when they advertise, they do it big. Full-page ads in the broadsheets and — what? — maybe double-color spreads in the financial glossies. TV as well?"

Gulliver stared at him. "Are you in advertising, Mr. Reeve?"

"No." But, he might have added, I was well briefed this morning by someone on your fashion page. The fashion page, apparently, was a sop to certain advertisers.

Another glance at the watch, a rehearsed sigh. "I have to go, unfortunately."

"Yes, that is unfortunate."

As Gulliver rose, a hotel minion appeared and unplugged his fax. Fax machine and telephone went into a briefcase. The cigar was stubbed into the ashtray. Meeting most definitely over.

"Will you keep in touch?" Gulliver implored, touching Reeve's arm, letting his hand rest there.

"Maybe."

"And is there any good cause?" Reeve didn't understand. "A charity, something like that. You know, for mourners to make donations to, as a mark of respect and in memory."

Reeve thought about it, then wrote a phone number for Gulliver on the back of a paper napkin. "Here," he said. Gulliver waited for elucidation. "It's the number of a bookie's in Finsbury Park. They tell me Jim owed them a ton and a half. All contributions gratefully received."

Reeve walked out of the hotel thinking he'd probably never in his life met someone so powerful, someone with so much influence, a shaper and changer. He'd shaken hands with royalty at medal ceremonies, but that wasn't the same.

For one thing, some royalty were nice; for another, some of them were known to tell the truth.

Giles Gulliver on the other hand was a born-and-bred liar; that was how you worked your way up from market stall to pin-stripe suit. You had to be cunning, too — and Gulliver was so slippery you could stage ice dancing on him and still have room for the curling rink.

The phone was ringing as he barged into the flat. He willed it to keep ringing and it obliged. His momentum took him onto the sofa as he snatched the receiver. He lay there, winded, trying to say hello.

"Is that Gordon Reeve?"

"Speaking."

"My name's Joshua Vincent. I think we'd better meet."

"Can you tell me what my brother was working on?"

"Better yet, I think I can show you. Three stipulations."

"I'm listening."

"One, you come alone. Two, you tell nobody where you're going or who you're going to meet."

"I can accept those. And number three?"

"Number three, bring a pair of Wellies."

Reeve wasn't about to ask questions. "So where are you?"

"Not so fast. I want you to leave Jim's flat and go to a pay phone. Not the nearest one. Try to make it a pub or somewhere."

Tottenham Lane, thought Reeve. There are pubs along that stretch. "Yes?"

"Have you got a pen? Take down this number. It's a call box. I'll wait here no longer than fifteen minutes. Is that enough time?"

Reeve thought so. "Unless the telephones aren't working. You're taking a lot of precautions, Mr. Vincent."

"So should you. I'll explain when we meet."

The line went dead, and Gordon Reeve headed for the door.

Outside in the street, just before the corner where the quiet side road connected with Ferme Park Road, there was a dull-green British Telecom box, a metal structure three feet high which connected the various landlines into the system. A special key was used by technicians to open the box's double doors. The key was specialized, but not difficult to obtain. A lot of engineers kept their tools when they left the job; an ex-BT engineer could open a box for you. And if he'd moved to a certain line of work, he could fit a call-activated recorder to any of the lines in the box, tucking the recording device down in the base of the structure, so that even a normal BT engineer might miss it.

The tape kept spooling for a few seconds after the call had ended. Then it stopped, awaiting retrieval. Today was a retrieval day.

TEN

It was a two-hour trip from London. Reeve didn't bother going out to Heathrow to retrieve his car. For one thing, it would have taken time; for another, Vincent wanted him to travel by public transport. Reeve had never heard of Tisbury. As his train pulled in, he saw beyond the station buildings a country town, a narrow main road snaking uphill, a soccer field turning to mud under the feet of the children playing there.

It had been raining stair rods the whole journey, but now the clouds were breaking up, showing chinks of early-evening light. Reeve wasn't the only one getting off the train, and he studied his fellow travelers. They looked tired — Tisbury to London was a hell of a distance to commute — and had eyes only for the walk ahead, whether to parking lot or town house.

Joshua Vincent stood outside the station with his hands in his Barbour pockets. He was quick to spot Reeve; no one else looked like they didn't know quite where to go.

Reeve had been expecting a farming type, tall and heavy-bodied with ruddy cheeks or maybe a sprouting beard to match the wild hair. But Vincent, though tall, was rake-thin, clean-shaven, and wore round, shining glasses. His fair hair was thinning badly; more scalp showing than follicles. He was pale and reticent and could have passed for a high-school science nerd. He was watching the commuters.

"Mr. Reeve?"

They shook hands. Vincent wanted them to wait there until all the commuters had left.

"Checking I wasn't followed?" Reeve asked.

Vincent gave a thin smile. "Easy to spot a stranger at this railway station. They can't help looking out of place. I'm so sorry to hear about Jim." The tone of voice was genuine, not overwrought the way Giles Gulliver had been, and the more affecting for that. "How did it happen?"

They walked to the car while Reeve started his story. Through several tellings, he had learned to summarize, sticking to facts and not drawing conclusions. The car was a Subaru 4x4. Reeve had seen them around the farming towns in the West Highlands. He kept on talking as they drove, leaving Tisbury behind them. The countryside was a series of rises and dips with irregular wooded sections. They chased crows and magpies off the rough-finished road, then rolled over the flattened vermin which had attracted the birds in the first place.

Vincent didn't interrupt the narrative once. And when Reeve had finished, they drove in silence until Reeve thought of a couple of things to add to his story.

As he was finishing, they turned off the road and started bumping along a mud track, churned up by farm machinery. Reeve could see the farm in front of them, a simple three-sided layout around a courtyard, with other buildings dotted about. It was very much like his own home.

Vincent stopped in the yard. A snapped command at a barking untethered sheepdog sent it padding back to its lair. A lone lamb bounded up to Reeve, bleating for food. He had the door open but hadn't stepped out yet.

"I'd put your boots on before you do that," Vincent warned him. So Reeve opened the bag he'd brought with him. Inside were all Jim's notes plus a new pair of black Wellingtons, bought in the army surplus store near Finsbury Park Station. He kicked off his shoes and left them in the car, then pulled on the boots. He swiveled out of his seat and landed in a couple of inches of mud.

"Thanks for the tip," he said, closing the door. "Is this your place?"

"No, I just stay here sometimes." A young woman was peering at them through the kitchen window. Vincent waved at her, and she waved back. "Come on," he said, "let's catch a breath of air."

In the long barn farthest from the house, two men were preparing to milk a couple of dozen cows, attaching clear plastic pumps to the teats. The cows' udders were swollen and veinous, and complaints filled the shed. Vincent said hello to the men but did not introduce them. The milking machine shuddered as Reeve passed it. The two men paid him no attention at all.

On the other side of the milking shed, they came to a wall beyond which were darkening fields, trees silhouetted in the far distance.

"So?" Reeve asked. He was growing impatient.

Vincent turned to him. "I think people are trying to kill me, too."

Then he told his story. "What do you know about BSE, Mr. Reeve?"

"Only what I've read in Jim's notes."

Vincent nodded. "Jim contacted me because he knew I'd expressed concern about OPs."

"Organophosphorous materials?"

"That's right. Have you heard of ME?"

"It's a medical complaint."

"There's been a lot of controversy over it. Basically, some doctors have been skeptical that it exists, yet people keep coming down with the symptoms." He shrugged. "The letters stand for myalgic encephalomyelitis."

"I can see why it's called ME. The *E* in BSE stands for something similar."

"Encephalopathy. Encephalon just means the brain, from the Greek *enkephalos*, meaning 'within the head.' I learned that a few years ago." He stared out over the fields. "I've learned a lot these past few years." He looked back at the farm. "This place is organic. Do you know how BSE is supposed to have started?"

"I read something in Jim's notes about animal feed."

Vincent nodded. "MAFF — that's the Ministry of Agriculture — relaxed their rules in the 1980s, allowing the rendering industry to take a few shortcuts. Don't ask me why it happened or who was responsible, but it happened. They removed two processes, saving time and money. One was a solvent extraction, the other a steam-heat treatment. You see, the rendering industry was rendering down sheep and cows to feed to other cows. Bits of meat and bone were going into the feed cake."

"Right." Reeve buttoned up his jacket, still damp from a dash through the rain to catch the train. The evening was growing chilly.

"Because those two processes had been removed, prions got into the feed cake. Prion protein is sometimes called PrP."

"I saw it in the notes, I think."

"It causes scrapie in sheep." Vincent raised a finger. "Remember, this is the accepted story I'm giving you. So the feed cake was infected, and the cows were being given the bovine form of sheep scrapie, which is BSE." He paused, then smiled. "You're wondering what all this has to do with Spanish cooking oil."

Reeve nodded.

Vincent started to walk, following the wall along the back of the milking shed. "Well, the Spanish blamed contaminated cooking oil and left it at that. Only, some of the victims had never touched the oil."

"And some of the cows who hadn't eaten the infected feed still caught BSE?"

Vincent shook his head. "Oh, no, the point is this: some farms — organic farms — who *had* used the so-called infected feed didn't catch the disease at all."

"Hang on a second . . ."

"I know what you're thinking. But organic farms are allowed to buy in twenty percent conventional feed."

"So you're saying BSE had nothing to do with feed cake, infected or otherwise?"

Vincent smiled without humor. "Why use the past tense?

BSE is still with us. The 'infected' feed cake was banned on the eighteenth of July 1988." He pointed into the distance. "I can show you calves less than six months old who have BSE. Vets from MAFF call them BABs: Born After the Ban. There've been more than ten thousand of them. To date, nearly a hundred and fifty thousand cows have died in the UK from BSE."

They had come back to the farmyard. Vincent opened the Subaru. "Get in," he said. Reeve got in. Vincent kept telling his story as he drove.

"I mentioned ME a little while back. When it first came to be noticed, it was supposed to have its roots in everyday stress. They called it Yuppie Flu. It isn't called that nowadays. Now we call it Farmers' Flu. That's because so many farmers show symptoms. There's a man — used to be a farmer, now he's more of a campaigner, though he still tries to farm when they let him — who's trying to discover why there's an increase in the occurrence of neurological diseases like ME, Alzheimer's, and Parkinson's."

"What do you mean, 'when they let him'?"

"He's been threatened," Vincent said simply. "People helping him have died. Car crashes, unexplained deaths, accidents . . ." He turned to Reeve. "Only four or five, you understand. Not yet an epidemic."

They were winding down country lanes barely the width of two cars. The sun had gone down.

Vincent put the heater on. "It may just be coincidence," he said, "that BSE started to appear around the same time that MAFF was telling farmers to protect against warble fly in their cattle by rubbing on an organophosphorus treatment. What some of us would like to know is whether OPs can cause prions to mutate."

"So these OP chemicals are to blame?"

"Nobody knows. It sometimes seems to me hardly anybody *wants* to know. I mean, imagine the embarrassment if it turned out a government directive had started the whole thing off. Imagine the claims for compensation that would be put in by the farmers suffering from OP poisoning. Imagine the cost to the agrichemical industry if they had to withdraw products, carry out expensive tests . . . maybe even pay compensation. We're talking about a worldwide industry. The whole farming world is hooked on pesticides of one kind or another. And on the other side of the coin, if pesticides had to be withdrawn, and new ones created and tested, there'd be a gap of years — and in those years yields would decrease, pests would multiply, farms would go out of business, the cost of every foodstuff in the supermarket would rocket. You can see where that would lead: economic disaster." He looked at Reeve again. "Maybe they're right to try and stop us. What are a few lives when measured against an economic disaster of those proportions?"

Reeve shivered, digging deeper into his coat. He felt exhausted, lack of sleep and jet lag hitting him hard. "Who's trying to stop you?"

"Could be any or all of them."

"CWC?"

"Co-World Chemicals has a lot to lose. Its worldwide market share is worth billions of dollars annually. They've also got a very persuasive lobby which keeps the majority of farmers and governments on their side. Sweetened, as you might say."

Reeve nodded, getting his meaning. "So there's a cover-up going on."

"To my mind undoubtedly, but then I would say that. I was suddenly fired from my job, a job I thought I was good at. When I began to be persuaded that the feed-cake explanation just wasn't on, I spoke twice about it in public, sent out a single press release — and next thing I knew my job was being 'phased out.'"

"I thought the National Farmers' Union was supposed to be on the side of farmers."

"It *is* on the side of farmers — or at least, it's on the side of the majority of them, the ones with their heads in the sand."

"Where are we going?"

"We're nearly there."

Reeve had half-thought he was going to be returned to the railroad station, meeting over. But, if anything, the landscape had grown less populous. They turned up a track and arrived at a high mesh gate topped with razor wire. A fence of similar height, similarly protected, stretched off either side. There were warning notices on the gate, picked out by the 4x4's headlights, but nothing to say what the fence and razor wire were protecting.

When Reeve followed Vincent out of the Subaru, a smell hit the back of his throat and he nearly gagged. It lay heavy in the air; the smell of dead flesh.

"We have to walk around the perimeter to get a good look," Vincent said. He turned on his flashlight. "It's a good job of invisible landscaping. You'd really have to be keen before you got to see what's inside."

"There's something I might as well ask you," Reeve said. "God knows I've asked everyone else. Does the word *Agrippa* mean anything?"

"Of course," Vincent said casually. "It's a small R and D company, American-based."

"My brother had the word written on a scrap of paper."

"Maybe he was looking into Agrippa. The company is at the forefront of genetic mutation."

"Meaning what exactly?" Reeve recalled something Fliss Hornby had said: Jim had been reading up on genetic patents.

"Meaning they take something and alter its genetic code, to try to make a better product. 'Better' being their description, not mine."

"You mean like cotton?"

"Yes, Agrippa doesn't have the patent on genetically engineered cotton. But the company *is* working on crops — trying for better yields and resistance to pests, trying to create strains that can be grown in hostile environments." Vincent paused. "Imagine if you could plant wheat in the Sahara."

"But if you produced resistant strains, that would do away with the need for pesticides, wouldn't it?"

Vincent smiled. "Nature has a way of finding its way around these defenses. Still, there are some out there who would agree with you. That's why CWC is spending millions on research."

"CWC?"

"Didn't I say? Agrippa is a subsidiary of Co-World Chemicals. Come on, this way."

They followed the fence up a steep rise and down into a valley, then climbed again.

"We can see from here," Vincent said. He switched off his flashlight.

It was a single large building, with trucks parked outside, illuminated by floodlights. Men in protective clothing, some wearing masks, wheeled trolleys between the trucks and the building. A tall thin chimney belched out acrid smoke.

"An incinerator?" Reeve guessed.

"Industrial-strength. It could melt a ship's hull."

"And they're burning infected cattle?"

Vincent nodded.

"Did you bring Jim here?"

"Yes."

"To make a point?"

"Sometimes a picture is worth a thousand words."

"You should never tell a journalist that."

Vincent smiled. "Burning the cattle isn't going to make it go away, Mr. Reeve. That's what your brother understood. There are other journalists like him in other countries. I'd guess each one is a marked man or woman. If BSE gets to humans, it's called Creutzfeldt-Jakob disease. Believe me, you wouldn't wish it on your worst enemy."

But Reeve could picture himself syringing a strain of it into the arm of whoever had killed his brother.

There were other neurodegenerative diseases, too — motoneuron disease, multiple sclerosis — and they were all on the increase. Their conversation on the way back to the farm was all one-way, and all bad news. The more Josh Vincent talked, the more zealous he became and the angrier and more frustrated he sounded.

"But what can you do?" Reeve asked at one point.

"Reexamine all pesticides, carry out tests on them. Use less of them. Turn farms into organic cooperatives. There *are* answers, but they're not simple overnight panaceas."

They parked in the farmyard again. The dog came out barking. The lamb trotted over towards them. Reeve followed Vincent into the kitchen. Once inside the door, they took off their boots. The young woman was still at the sink beneath the window. She smiled and wiped her hands, coming forward to be introduced.

"Jilly Palmer," said Vincent, "this is Gordon Reeve."

They shook hands. "Pleased to meet you," she said. She had a flushed complexion and a long braid of chestnut-colored hair. Her face was sharp, with angular cheekbones and a wry twist to her lips. Her clothes were loose, practical.

"Supper's ready when you are," she said.

"I'll just show Gordon his room first," Vincent said. He saw the surprise in Reeve's face. "You can't get back to London tonight. No trains."

Reeve looked at Jilly Palmer. "I'm sorry if I —"

"No trouble," she said. "We've a bedroom going spare, and Josh here made the supper. All I had to do was warm it through."

"Where's Bill?" Vincent asked.

"Young Farmers'. He'll be back around ten."

"Don't be daft," said Vincent, "pubs don't shut till eleven."

He sounded very different in this company: more relaxed, enjoying the warmth of the kitchen and normal conversation. But all that did, in Reeve's eyes, was show how much strain the man was under the rest of the time, and how much this whole conspiracy had affected him.

He thought he could see why Jim had taken on the story, why he would have run with it where others might have given up: because of people like Josh Vincent, scared and running and innocent.

His room was small and cold, but the blankets were plentiful. He took off his coat and hung it on a hook on the back of the door, hoping it would dry. His dark pullover was damp, too, so he peeled it off. The rest of him could dry in the kitchen. He found the bathroom and washed his hands and face in scalding water, then looked at himself in the mirror. The image of him injecting BSE into a tapped human vein was still there in the back of his mind. It had given him an idea — not something he could put into use just yet, but something he might need all the same . . .

In the kitchen the table had been laid for two. Jilly said she'd already eaten. She left them to it and closed the door after her.

"She never misses *Coronation Street*," Vincent explained. "Lives out here, but has to get her fix of Lancashire grime." He used oven mitts to lift the casserole from the oven. It was half full, but a substantial half. There was a lemonade bottle on the table and two glasses. Vincent unscrewed the cap and poured carefully. "Bill's home brew," he explained. "I think he only drinks down the pub to remind himself how good his own stuff tastes."

The beer was light brown, with a head that disappeared quickly. "Cheers," said Josh Vincent.

"Cheers," said Reeve.

They ate in silence, hungrily, and chewed on home-baked bread. Towards the end of the meal, Vincent asked a few questions about Reeve — what he did, where he lived. He said he loved the Highlands and Islands, and wanted to hear all about Reeve's survival courses. Reeve kept the description simple, leaving out more than he put in. He could see Vincent wasn't really listening; his mind was elsewhere.

"Can I ask you something?" Vincent said finally.

"Sure."

"How far did Jim get? I mean, did he find out anything we could use?"

"I told you, his disks disappeared. All I have are his written notes from London."

"Can I see them?"

Reeve nodded and fetched them. Vincent read in silence for a while, except to point out where he himself had contributed a detail or a quote. Then he sat up.

"He's been in touch with Marie Villambard." He showed Reeve the sheet of paper. The letters MV were capitalized and underlined at the top. They hadn't meant anything to Reeve or to Fliss Hornby.

"Who's she?"

"A French journalist; she works for an ecology magazine —
Le Monde Vert, I think it's called. 'Green World.' Sounds like they
were working together."

"She hasn't tried contacting him in London." There'd been
no letters from France, and Fliss hadn't intercepted any calls.

"Maybe he told her he'd be in touch when he got back from
San Diego."

"Josh, why did my brother go to San Diego?"

"To talk to Co-World Chemicals." Vincent blinked. "I thought
you knew that."

"You're the first person to say it outright."

"He was going to try and speak to some of their research
scientists."

"Why?"

"Why? Because of the experiment they had carried out."
Vincent put down the notes. "They tried to reproduce BSE the
way it had flared up in the UK, using identical procedures after
consultations with MAFF. They brought in sheep infected with
scrapie and rendered them down, taking the exact same shortcuts
as were used in the mideighties. Then they mixed the feed together and fed it to calves and mature cattle."

"And?"

"And nothing. They didn't exactly trumpet the results. Four
years on, the cattle were one hundred percent fit." He shrugged
his shoulders. "They've got other experiments ongoing. They've
got consultant neurologists and world-class psychiatrists working
on American farmers who show signs of neurodegenerative disease. Bringing in the psychiatrists is a nice touch: it makes everyone think maybe we're dealing with psychosomatic hysteria, that
the so-called disease is actually a product of the human mind and
nothing at all to do with what we spray on our crops and stuff into
and onto our animals." He paused. "You want any more casserole?"

Reeve shook his head.

"The beef's fine, honestly," Vincent said, smiling encourage-
ment. "Reared organically."

"I'm sure," said Reeve. "But I'm full up, thanks."

Well, it was 85 percent truth.

*   *   *

After breakfast, Josh Vincent drove Reeve to the station.

"Can I contact you on the farm?" Reeve asked.

Vincent shook his head. "I'll only be there another day or so. Is there somewhere I can contact you?"

Reeve wrote down his home phone number. "If I'm not there, my wife can take a message. Josh, you haven't said why you're hiding."

"What?"

"All these precautions. You haven't said why."

Vincent looked up and down the empty platform. "They tampered with my car, too. Remember I told you about the farmer?"

"The one who's been campaigning against OPs?"

"Yes. A vet was helping him, but then the vet died in a car crash. His vehicle went out of control and hit a wall; no explanation, nothing wrong with the car. I had a similar crash. My car stopped responding. I hit a tree rather than a wall, and crawled out alive. No garage could find any fault in the car." Vincent was staring into the distance. "Then they bugged the telephone in my office, and later I found they'd bugged my home telephone, too. I think they opened my mail and resealed the envelopes. I *know* they were watching me. Don't ask me who they were, that I don't know. I could speculate though. MI5 maybe, Special Branch, or the chemical companies. Could have been any of those, could have been someone else entirely. So" — he sighed and dug his hands into his Barbour pockets — "I keep moving."

"A running target's the hardest kind to hit," Reeve agreed.

"Do you speak from experience?"

"Literally," said Reeve as the train pulled in.

Back in London, Reeve returned to the apartment. Fliss had left a note wondering if he'd gone for good. He scribbled on the bottom of it "Maybe this time" and put the note back on the table. He had to retrieve his bag and his car and then head home. But first he wanted to check something. He found the page of Jim's notes, the one headed MV. On the back were four two-digit numbers. He'd suspected they were the combination of some kind of safe, but now he knew differently. He found a screwdriver in the kitchen drawer and opened up the telephone: apparatus and handset both. He couldn't find any bugs, so he replaced the screws and returned the screwdriver to its drawer. He got the code for France from the telephone book and made the call. A long single tone told him he'd reached a French telephone.

An answering machine, a rapid message in a woman's voice. Reeve left a short message in his rusty French, giving his telephone number in Scotland. He didn't mention Jim's fate. He just said he was his brother. This was called "preparing someone for bad news." He sat and thought about what Josh Vincent had told him. Something had been telling Reeve it couldn't just be about cows. It was laughable, unbelievable. But Josh Vincent had made it both believable *and* scary, because it affected everyone on the planet — everyone who had to eat. But Reeve still didn't think it was *just* about cows, or pesticides, or coverups. There was more to it than that. He felt it in his bones.

He made another call, to Joan, preparing her for his return. Then he gave the rest of the flat a once-over and locked the door behind him.

An engineer was checking the telephone junction box outside. The man watched Reeve go, then lifted the tape out from the recorder and replaced it with a fresh one. Returning to his van, he wound back the tape and replayed it. A thirteen-digit number, followed by a woman's voice in French. He plugged a digital decoder into the tape machine, then wound back the tape and played it again. This time, each beep of the dialed number came up as a digit on the decoder's readout. The engineer wrote down the number and picked up his cell phone.

PART FOUR
LIVING
DANGEROUSLY

ELEVEN

GORDON REEVE HAD BECOME INTERESTED in anarchism because he needed to understand the minds of terrorists. He had worked in the Counter-Revolutionary Warfare Unit of the SAS. They were happy to have him — he wasn't the only one among them who'd specialized in languages during his early training, but he was the only one with so many.

"Including Scots," one wag said. "Could come in handy if the Tartan Army flares up again."

"I've got Gaelic, too," Reeve had countered with a smile.

After he left the SAS, he retained his interest in anarchism because of its truths and its paradoxes. The word *anarchy* had Greek roots and meant "without a ruler." The Paris students in '68 had sprayed "It is forbidden to forbid" on the street walls. Anarchists, *true* anarchists, wanted society without government and promoted voluntary organization over rule by an elected body. The real anarchist joke was: "It doesn't matter who you vote for, the government always gets in."

Reeve liked to play the anarchist thinkers off against Nietzsche. Kropotkin, for example, with his theory of "mutual aid," was advocating the opposite of Nietzsche's "will to power." Evolution, in Kropotkin's view, was not about competitiveness, about survival of the strongest *individual*, but about cooperation. A species which cooperated would thrive, and grow stronger collectively. Nietzsche on the other hand saw competitiveness everywhere, and advocated self-reliance and self-absorption. Reeve saw merit to both assertions. In fact, they were not separate, distinct arguments but parts of the same equation. Reeve had little time for government, for bureaucracy, but he knew the individual could go only so far, could endure only so much. Isolation was fine sometimes, but if you had a problem it was wise to form bonds. War created bizarre allies, while peace itself could be divisive.

Nietzsche, of course, could convince almost no one of his philosophy — give or take a tyrant or two who chose to misunderstand the whole. And the anarchists . . . well, one of the things Reeve found so interesting about the anarchists was that their cause was doomed from its philosophical outset. To grow, to influence opinion, the anarchist movement had to organize, had to take on a strong political structure — which meant taking on a hierarchy, making decisions. Everyone, from players of children's games to the company boardroom, knew that if you took decisions by committee you came up with compromise. Anarchism was not about compromising. The anarchists' mistrust of rigid organizations caused their groupings to splinter and splinter again, until only the individual was left, and some of those individuals felt that the only possible road to power left to them was the bullet and the bomb. Joseph Conrad's image of the anarchist with the bomb in his pocket was not so wide of the mark.

And what of Nietzsche? Reeve had been one of "Nietzsche's gentlemen." Nietzsche had carried on the work of Descartes and others — men who needed to dominate, to control, to eliminate chance. But while Nietzsche wanted supermen, controllers, he also wanted people to live dangerously. Reeve felt he was fulfilling this criterion if no other. He *was* living dangerously. He just wondered if he needed some mutual aid along the way . . .

He was on a hillside, no noise except the wind, the distant bleating of sheep, and his own breathing. He was sitting, resting, after the long walk from his home. He'd told Joan he needed to clear his head. Allan was at a friend's house, but would be back in time for supper. Reeve would be back by then, too. All he needed was a walk. Joan had offered to keep him company, an offer he'd refused with a shake of his head. He'd touched her cheek, but she'd slapped his hand away.

"I'll only be a couple of hours."

"You're never here," she complained. "And even when you're here, you're not *really* here."

It was a valid complaint, and he hadn't argued. He'd just tied his boots and set out for the hills.

It was Sunday, a full week since he'd had the telephone call telling him Jim had killed himself. Joan knew there was something he wasn't telling her, something he was bottling up. She knew it wasn't just grief.

Reeve got to his feet. Looking down the steep hillside, he was momentarily afraid. Nothing to do with the "abyss" this time; it was just that he had no real plan, and without a plan there would be a temptation to rashness, there would be miscalculation. He needed proper planning and preparation. He'd been in the dark for a while, feeling his way. Now he thought he knew most of what Jim had known, but he was still stuck. He felt like a spider who has crawled its way along the pipes and into the bath, only to find it can't scale the smooth, sheer sides. There was a bird of prey overhead, a kestrel probably. It glided on the air currents, its line straight, dipping its wings to maintain stability. From that height, it could probably still pick out the movements of a mouse in the tangle of grass and gorse. Reeve thought of the wings on the SAS cap badge. Wings and a dagger. The wings told you that Special Forces would travel anywhere at any notice. And the dagger . . . the dagger told an essential truth about the regiment: they were trained in close-combat situations. They favored stealth and the knife over distance and a sniper's accuracy. Hand-to-hand fighting, that was their strength. Get close to your prey, close enough to slide a hand over its mouth and stab the dagger into its throat, and twist and twist, ripping the voice box. Maximum damage, minimum dying time.

Reeve felt the blood rush to his head and closed his eyes for a moment, clearing them of the fog. He checked his watch and found he'd been resting longer than he'd meant to. His legs had stiffened. It was time to start back down the hill and across the wide gully. It was time to go home.

*   *   *

"Jackie's got this really good new game," Allan said.

Reeve looked to Joan. "Jackie?"

"A girl in his class."

He turned to his son. "Playing with the girls, eh? Not in her bedroom, I hope."

Allan screwed up his face. "She's not like a girl, Dad. She has all these games . . ."

"On her computer."

"Yes."

"And her computer is where in the house?"

"In her room."

"Her bedroom?"

Allan's ears had reddened. Reeve tried winking at Joan, but she wasn't watching.

"It's like *Doom*," Allan said, ignoring his father, "but with more secret passages, and you don't just pick up ammo and stuff, you can warp yourself into these amazing creatures with loads of new weapons and stuff. You can fry the bad guys' eyeballs so they're blind and then you —"

"Allan, enough," his mother said.

"But I'm just telling Dad —"

"Enough."

"But, Dad —"

"Enough!"

Allan looked down at his plate. He'd eaten all the fries and only had the cold ham and baked beans left. "But Dad wanted to know," he said under his breath. Joan looked at her husband.

"Tell me later, pal, okay? Some things aren't for the dinner table." He watched Joan lift a sliver of ham to her mouth. "Especially fried alien eyeballs."

Joan glared at him, but Allan and Gordon were laughing. The rest of the meal was carried off in peace.

Afterwards, Allan made instant coffee for his parents — one of his latest jobs around the house. Reeve wasn't so sure of letting an eleven-year-old near a boiling kettle.

"But you don't mind fried aliens, right?" Joan said.

"Aliens never hurt anyone," Reeve said. "I've seen what scalding can do."

"He's got to learn."

"Okay, okay." They were in the living room. Reeve kept an ear attuned to sounds from the kitchen. The first clatter or shriek and he'd be in there. But Allan appeared with the two mugs. The coffee was strong.

"Is milk back on the ration books?" Reeve queried.

"What's ration books?" Allan asked.

"Pray you never have to know."

Allan wanted to watch TV, so the three of them sat on the long sofa, Reeve with his arm along the back, behind his wife's neck but not touching her. She'd taken off her slippers and had tucked her feet up. Allan sat on the floor in front of her. Bakunin the cat was on Joan's lap, glaring at Reeve like he was a complete stranger, which, considering he hadn't fed her this past week, he was. Reeve thought of the real Bakunin, fighting on the Dresden barricades shoulder to shoulder with Nietzsche's friend Wagner . . .

"A penny for them," Joan asked.

"I was just thinking how nice it was to be back."

Joan smiled thinly at the lie. She hadn't asked much about the cremation, but she'd been interested to hear about the flat in London and the woman living there. Allan turned from the sitcom.

"So what's it like in the USA, Dad?"

"I thought you'd never ask." Reeve had spent some time deciding on the story he'd tell Allan. He painted a picture of San Diego as a frontier town, exciting enough and strange enough to keep Allan listening.

"Did you see any shootings?" Allan asked.

"No, but I heard some police sirens."

"Did you see a policeman?"

Reeve nodded.

"With a gun?"

Reeve nodded again.

Joan rubbed at her son's hair, though she knew he hated it when she did that. "He's growing up gun-crazy."

"No, I'm not," Allan stated.

"It's all those computer games."

"No, it isn't."

"What are you playing just now?"

"That game I told you about. Jackie copied it for me."

"I hope it hasn't got a virus."

"I've got a new virus checker."

"Good." At that time, Allan knew only a little more about computing than Reeve and Joan put together, but he was steadily pulling away from them.

"The game's called *Militia*, and what you do is —"

"No fried eyeballs," Joan demanded.

"What happened to the game Uncle Jim sent you?" Reeve asked.

Allan looked embarrassed. "I was stuck on screen five . . ."

"You've given it away?"

Allan shook his head vigorously. "No, it's upstairs."

"But you don't play it anymore?"

"No," he said quietly. Then: "Mum said Uncle Jim died."

Reeve nodded. Joan said she'd had a couple of talks with Allan already. "People grow old and tired, Allan, and then they die. They make room for other younger people to come along . . ." Reeve felt awkward as he spoke.

"But Uncle Jim wasn't old."

"No, well some people just —"

"He wasn't much older than *you*."

"I'm not going to die," Reeve told his son.

"How do you know?"

"Sometimes people get feelings. I've got the feeling I'm going to live to be a hundred."

"And Mum?" Allan asked.

Reeve looked at her. She was staring at him, interested in the answer. "Same feeling," he said.

Allan went back to watching television. A little later, Joan murmured, "Thanks," put her slippers back on, and went through to the kitchen, followed closely by Bakunin, scouting for provisions. Reeve wasn't sure what to read into her final utterance.

The telephone rang while he was watching the news. Allan

had retreated to his room, having given his parents over an hour and a half of his precious time. Reeve let Joan get the phone. She was still in the kitchen, making a batch of bread. Later, when he went through to make the last cup of coffee of the night, he asked who had called.

"They didn't say," she offered, too nonchalantly.

Reeve looked at her. "You've had more than one?"

She shrugged. "A couple."

"How many?"

"I think this was the third."

"In how long?"

She shrugged again. There was a smudge of flour on her nose, and some wisps in her hair, making her look older. "Five or six days. There's no one on the other end, no noise at all. Maybe it's British Telecom testing the line or something. That happens sometimes."

"Yes, it does."

But not more than once in a very blue moon, he thought.

They'd been in bed for a silent hour and were lying side by side staring at the ceiling when he asked, "What about those callers?"

"The phone calls?" She turned her head towards him.

"No, you said some customers had turned up."

"Oh, yes, just asking about courses."

"Two of them?"

"Yes, one one day, one the next. What's the matter?"

"Nothing. It's just we don't often get people turning up like that."

"Well, I gave them the brochure and they went away quite happy."

"Did they come in the house?"

She sat up. "Only as far as the hall. It's all right, Gordon, I can look after myself."

"What were they like? Describe them."

"I'm not sure I can. I hardly paid them any attention." She leaned over him, her hand on his chest. She was feeling his heart rate. "What's wrong?"

"Nothing's wrong," he said. But he swung his legs out of bed and started to get dressed. "I don't feel tired; I'll go down to the kitchen." He stopped at the door. "Anybody else come while I was away?"

"No."

"Think about it."

She thought about it. "A man came to read the meter. And the freezer lorry turned up."

"What freezer lorry?"

"Frozen foods." She sounded irritated. If he kept pushing, the end result would be an argument. "I usually buy chips and ice cream from him."

"Was it the regular driver?"

She slumped back on the bed. "No, he was new. Gordon, what the hell is this about?"

"Maybe I'm just being paranoid."

"What happened in the States?"

He came back and sat on the edge of the bed. "I think Jim was murdered."

She sat up again. "What?"

"I think he was getting too deep into something, some story he was working on. Maybe they'd tried scaring him off and it hadn't worked. I know Jim, he's like me — try that tactic and he'd just be more curious than ever, and more stubborn. So then they had to kill him."

"Who?"

"That's what I've been trying to find out."

"And?"

"And, because I've been doing just what Jim was doing, maybe they're targeting me. The thing is, I didn't think they'd come here. Not so soon."

"Two potential clients, a meter-reader, and a man with a van full of spuds and sprouts."

"That's four callers more than we usually get. Four callers while I was out of the country." He got to his feet again.

"Is that it?" Joan asked. "Aren't you going to tell me the rest?"

He started towards her, just able to make out her shape in the shadows of the curtained room — curtained despite the blackness outside and the isolation of the house. "I don't want to make you a target."

Then he padded downstairs as quietly as he could. He looked around, turning on lights, not touching anything, then stood in the living room thinking things over. He walked over to the TV and switched it on, using the remote to flick channels.

"Usual rubbish," he said, yawning noisily for the benefit of anyone listening. He knew how sophisticated surveillance equipment had become. He'd heard of devices that could read computer screens from a distance of yards, without there being any physical connector linking them to the computer. He probably hadn't heard half of it. The technology changed so quickly it was damn near impossible to keep up. He did his best, so he could pass what he knew on to his weekend soldiers. The trainee bodyguards in particular liked to know about that stuff.

He first checked that there were no watcher devices in the house. These were not so easy to hide: after all, if they were going to view a subject, they couldn't be tucked away under a chair or a sofa. They also took a lot longer to fit. Someone would have had to access the house while Joan was out or asleep. He didn't find anything. Next he put his jacket on and went outside, circling the house at a good radius. He spotted no one, certainly no vehicles. In the garage, he slid beneath both Land Rovers and found them clean — well, not *clean*, but lacking bugs. Before going back indoors he unscrewed the front panel from the burglar alarm. The screws were hard to shift, and showed no signs of recent tampering — no missing paint or fresh-looking scratches. The alarm itself was functioning.

Joan had said she'd let the new clients in as far as the hall. And he would guess she'd probably let the van driver in as far as the kitchen. He took a lot of time over both areas, feeling beneath carpets and behind curtains, taking the cookbooks off the bookshelf in the kitchen.

He found the first bug in the hall.

It was attached to the inside of the telephone.

He went into the kitchen and switched on the radio, placing it close to the phone extension. Then he unscrewed the apparatus and found another bug identical to the first one. Both had the letters *USA* stamped into their thin metal casing. He wiped sweat from his face, and went through to the living room. Despite an hour-long search, he found nothing, which didn't mean the room was clean. He knew he could save a lot of effort by getting hold of a locating device, but he didn't have the time. And at least now he knew — knew his family wasn't safe, knew his home wasn't secure.

Knew they had to get out.

He sat on the chair beside the dressing table in their bedroom. A morning ray of sun had found a chink in the curtains and was hitting Joan's face, moving from her eyes to her forehead as she twisted in her sleep. Like a laser sight, Reeve thought, like an assassin taking aim. He felt tired but electric; he'd spent half the night writing. He had the sheets of printer paper with him on the chair. Joan rolled over, her arm flopping down on the space where he should have been. She used the arm to push herself up, blinking a few times. Then she rolled onto her back and craned her neck.

"Morning," she said.

"Morning," he answered, coming towards her.

"How long have you been up?" She was blinking her eyes again in an attempt to read the sheet of paper Reeve was holding in front of her.

"Hours," he said with a lightness he did not feel.

DON'T SAY A WORD. JUST READ. NOD WHEN YOU'RE READY. REMEMBER: SAY NOTHING.

His look told her he was serious. She nodded, sitting up farther in bed, pushing the hair out of her eyes. He turned to the next sheet.

THE HOUSE IS BUGGED: WE CAN'T SAY ANYTHING IN SAFETY. WE'VE GOT TO PRETEND THIS IS JUST ANOTHER DAY. NOD WHEN YOU'RE READY.

She took a moment to nod. When she did so, she was staring into his eyes.

"So are you going to lie there all day?" he chided, turning the page.

"Why not?" she said. She looked frightened.

YOU'VE GOT TO GO STAY WITH YOUR SISTER. TAKE ALLAN. BUT DON'T TELL HIM. JUST PACK SOME THINGS INTO THE CAR AND GO. PRETEND YOU'RE TAKING HIM TO SCHOOL AS USUAL.

"Come on, get up and I'll make the breakfast."

"I'll take a shower."

"Okay."

WE CAN'T SAY WHERE YOU'RE GOING. WE CAN'T LET ANYONE KNOW. THIS IS JUST AN ORDINARY MORNING.

Joan nodded her head.

"Will toast do you?" he asked.

I DON'T THINK WE'RE BEING WATCHED, JUST LISTENED TO.

He smiled to reassure her.

"Toast's fine," she said, only the slightest tremble evident in her voice. She cleared her throat and pointed at him. He had foreseen this, and found the sheet.

I'LL BE FINE. I JUST NEED TO TALK TO A FEW PEOPLE.

She looked doubtful, so he smiled again and bent forward to kiss her.

"That better?" he asked.

"Better," she said.

I'LL PHONE YOU AT YOUR SISTER'S. YOU CAN CALL HER ON YOUR WAY THERE, LET HER KNOW YOU'RE COMING. DON'T COME BACK HERE UNTIL I TELL YOU IT'S ALL RIGHT. I LOVE YOU.

She jumped to her feet and hugged him. They stayed that way for a full minute. Her eyes were wet when he broke away.

"Toast and tea it is," Reeve said.

He was in the kitchen, trying to hum a tune while he made breakfast, when she walked in. She was carrying a notepad and pen. She looked more together now that she was dressed, now that she'd had time to think. She thrust the notepad into his face.

WHAT THE FUCK'S THIS ALL ABOUT?

He took the pad from her and rested it on the counter.

IT'D TAKE TOO LONG. I'LL EXPLAIN WHEN I PHONE.

He looked up at her, then added a last word.

PLEASE.

THIS IS UNFAIR, she wrote, anger reddening her face.

He mouthed the words *I know* and followed them with *sorry*.

"Had your shower already?" he asked.

"Water wasn't hot enough." She looked for a second like she might laugh at the absurdity of it all. But she was too angry to laugh.

"Want me to cut some bread?" she asked.

"Sure, thanks. How's Allan?"

"Not keen on getting up."

"He doesn't know how lucky he is," Reeve said. He watched Joan attack the loaf with the bread knife like it was the enemy.

Things were easier when Allan came down. Both parents talked to him more than usual, asking questions, eliciting responses. This was safe ground; they could be less guarded. When Joan said maybe she'd have that shower after all, Reeve knew she was going to pack. He told Allan he was going to get the car out, and walked into the courtyard, breathing deeply and exhaling noisily.

"Jesus," he said. He circled the property again. He could hear a tractor somewhere over near Buchanan's croft, and the drone of a light airplane overhead, though the morning was too overcast to see it. He didn't think anyone was watching the house. He wondered how far the transmitters carried. Not very far by the look of them. There'd be a recorder somewhere, buried in the earth or hidden under rocks. He wondered how often they changed tapes, how often they listened. The recorder was probably voice-activated, and whoever was listening was only interested in telephone calls.

Or maybe they just hadn't had time to bug the house properly.

"Bastards," he said out loud. Then he went back into the house. Joan was coming downstairs with a couple of traveling bags. She took them straight out to her car and put them in the trunk. She motioned for him to join her. When he did, she just stared at him like she wanted to say something.

"I think it's okay outside," he said.

"Good. What are you going to do, Gordon?"

"Talk to a few people."

"What people? What are you going to talk to them about?"

He looked around the courtyard, his eyes alighting on the door to the killing room. "I'm not sure. I just want to know why someone has bugged our telephones. I need to get hold of some equipment, sweep the place to make sure it's clean apart from the two I found."

"How long will we have to stay away?"

"Maybe just a couple of days. I don't know yet. I'll phone as soon as I can."

"Don't do anything . . ." She didn't complete the sentence.

"I won't," he said, stroking her hair.

She brought something out of her pocket. "Here, take these." She handed him a vial of small blue pills — the pills he was supposed to take when the pink mist descended.

The psychiatrist had wondered at pink. "Not red?" he'd asked.

"No, pink."

"Mmm. What do you associate with the color pink, Mr. Reeve?"

"Pink?"

"Yes."

"Gays, cocks, tongues, vaginal lips, little girls' lipstick . . . Will those do for a start, Doctor?"

"I get the feeling you're playing with me, Mr. Reeve."

"If I were playing with you, I'd've said red mist and you'd've been happy. But I said pink because it's pink. My vision goes pink, not red."

"And then you react?"

Oh, yes, then he reacted . . .

He looked at his wife now. "I won't need these."

"Want to make a bet?"

Reeve took the pills instead.

*   *   *

Joan had told Allan they were taking Bakunin to the vet. The cat had resisted being put in its carrier, and Allan had asked what was wrong with it.

"Nothing to worry about." She'd been looking at her husband as she'd said it.

Reeve stood at the door and waved them off, then ran to the roadside to watch them leave. He didn't think they'd be followed. Joan drove Allan to school every morning, and this was just another morning. He went back inside and stood in the hallway.

"All alone," he said loudly.

He was wondering if they would come, now that he was alone. He was hoping they would. He had plans for them if they did. He spent the day waiting them out, and talking to them.

"She's not coming back," he said into the telephone receiver at one point. "Neither of them is. I'm on my own." Still they didn't come. He went through the house, organizing an overnight bag, making sure he had the list of emergency telephone numbers. He ate a slice of bread and butter for lunch, and dozed at the kitchen table for an hour (having made sure all the doors and windows were locked first). He felt better afterwards. He needed a shower or bath, but didn't like the idea of them coming in on him when he was in the middle of lathering his back. So he just had a quick wash instead, a lick and a spit.

By late afternoon, he was going stir crazy. He checked the windows again, set the alarm, and locked the house. He had his overnight bag with him. He went to the killing room and unpadlocked and unbolted both sets of doors. Those doors looked ordinary enough from the outside, but were paneled inside with beaten metal, an extra deterrent to intruders. In the small hallway outside the room proper, he knelt down and pulled at a long section of baseboard. It came away cleanly. Inside, set into the wall, was a long narrow metal box. Reeve unlocked it and pulled the flap down. Inside was an assortment of small arms. He had large-bore weapons, too, but kept those in a locked cabinet in what had been the farmhouse's original pantry. He picked up one of the guns. It was wrapped in oiled cloth. What use was a killing room without weapons? In his Special Forces days, they'd almost always trained with live ammo. It was the only way you came to respect the stuff.

Reeve had live ammo for the handguns. He was holding a 9mm Beretta. Guns were always heavier than people expected. He didn't know whether that was because most people equated guns with childhood, and childhood meant plastic replicas, or because TV and cinema were to blame, with their blithe gun-toting goodies and baddies, guys who could fire a bazooka and still go ten rounds with the world-champion warlord — whereas in real life they'd be checking into the emergency room with a dislocated shoulder.

The Beretta was just heavy enough to warn you it was lethal. In the killing room they used blank ammunition. Even blanks could give you powder burns. He'd seen weekend soldiers scared shitless, frozen with the gun in their hand like someone else's turd, the explosion echoing in the chambers of their heart.

Maybe he needed a gun. Just to scare these people. But you could only scare someone if you were serious and if they could see exactly how serious you were by the look in your eyes. And he wouldn't be serious if the gun wasn't loaded . . .

And what use was a loaded gun if you didn't intend to use it?

"Fuck it," he said, putting the Beretta back in its cloth. He rummaged around behind the other packages — he had explosives in there, too; almost every other soldier brought *something* with them back into civvy life — until he found another length of oiled rag. Inside was a black gleaming dagger, his Lucky 13: five inches of rubberized handgrip and eight inches of polished steel, a blade so sharp you could perform surgery with it. He'd bought it in Germany one time when they'd been training there. Its weight and balance were perfect for him. It had felt almost supernatural, the way the thing molded to his hand. He'd been persuaded to buy it by the two men on weekend leave with him. The knife cost just under a week's wages.

"For old times' sake," he said, slipping it into his overnight bag.

*　　*　　*

He crossed by ferry to Oban, which was where the tail started.

Just the one car, he reckoned. To be sure, he led it a merry dance all the way to Inveraray. Just north of the town he pulled the Land Rover over suddenly, got out, and went to the back, looking in as though to check he hadn't forgotten something. The car behind was too close to stop; it had to keep going right past him. He looked up as it drew level, and watched the impassive faces of the two men in front.

"Bye-bye," he said, closing the back, watching the car go. Hard to tell from their faces who the men were or who they might work for, but he was damned sure they'd been following him since he'd hit the mainland: most cars would have stuck to the main road through Dalmally and south towards Glasgow, but when Reeve had headed on the much less popular route to Inveraray, this one had followed.

He started driving again. He didn't know if they'd have organized a second car by now, of if they'd have to call someone to organize backup. He just knew he didn't want to be driving anywhere much now that they were on to him. So he headed into the center of town. Close combat, he was thinking as he headed for his revised destination.

The Thirty Arms had a parking lot, but Reeve parked on the street outside. They didn't hand out parking tickets after six o'clock. Locals called it the Thirsty Arms, but the pub's true name was a reference to the fifteen men in a rugby side. It was the closest this quiet lochside town had to a "dive," which was to say that it was a rough-and-ready place which didn't see many female clients. Reeve knew this because he dropped in sometimes, preferring the drive via Inveraray to the busier route. The owner had a tongue you could strike matches on.

"Go get that red fuckin' carpet, will you?" he said to someone as Reeve entered the bar. "It's been that long since this bastard bought a drink in here I was thinking of selling up."

"Evening, Manny," said Reeve. "Half of whatever's darkest, please."

"An ungrateful sod of a patron like you," said Manny, "you'll take what I give you." He began pouring the drink. Reeve looked around at faces he knew. They weren't smiling at him, and he didn't smile back. Their collective stare was supposed to drive away strangers and outsiders, and Reeve was most definitely an outsider. The surliest of the local youths was playing pool. Reeve had noticed some of his mates outside. They weren't yet old enough looking to fool Manny, so would wait at the door like pet dogs outside a butcher's shop for their master to rejoin them. The smell of drink off him was their vicarious pleasure. In Inveraray, there wasn't much else to kill the time.

Reeve walked over to the board and chalked his name up. The youth grinned at him unpleasantly, as if to say, "I'll take anybody's money." Reeve walked back to the bar.

Two more drinkers pushed open the creaking door from the outside world. Their tourist smiles vanished when they saw the sort of place they'd entered. Other tourists had made their mistake before, but seldom stayed long enough to walk up to the bar. Maybe these ones were surprisingly stupid. Maybe they were blind.

Maybe, Reeve thought. He still had his back to them. He didn't need to see them to know they were the two from the car. They stood next to him as they waited for Manny to finish telling a story to another customer. Manny was taking his time, just letting them know. He'd been known to refuse service to faces he didn't like.

Reeve watched as much as he could from the corner of his eyes. From the distorted reflection in the beaten copper plate that ran the length of the bar behind the optics, he saw that the men were waiting impassively.

Manny at last gave up. "Yes, gents?" he said.

"We want a drink," the one closest to Reeve said. The man was angry already, not used to being kept waiting. He sounded English; Reeve didn't know which nationality he'd been expecting.

"This isn't a chip shop," said Manny, rising to the challenge. "Drink's the only thing we serve." He was smiling throughout, to let the two strangers know he wasn't at all happy.

"I'll have a double Scotch," the second man said. He was also

English. Reeve didn't know whether it was done on purpose or not, but the way he spat out "Scotch" caused more than a few hackles in the bar to rise. The speaker purported not to notice, maybe he just didn't care. He looked at the door, at the framed photos of Scottish internationals and the local rugby team — the latter signed — and the souvenir pennants and flags.

"Somebody likes rugby," he said to no one in particular. No one in particular graced the remark with a reply.

The man closest to Reeve, the one who'd spoken first, ordered a lager and lime. There was a quiet wolf whistle from the pool table, just preceding the youth's shot.

The man turned towards the source of the whistle. "You say something?"

The youth kept quiet and made his next shot, chalking up as he marched around the table. Reeve suddenly liked the lad.

"Leave it," the stranger's companion snapped. Then, as the drinks were set before them: "That a treble." He meant the whiskey.

"A double," Manny snapped. "You're used to sixths; up here we have quarters." He took the money and walked back to the register.

Reeve turned conversationally to the two men. "Cheers," he said.

"Yeah, cheers." They were both keen to get a good look at him close up, just as he was keen to get a look at them. The one closest to him was shorter but broader. He could've played a useful prop forward. He wore cheap clothes and had a cheap, greasy look to his face. If you looked like what you ate, this man was fries and lard. His companion had a dangerous face, the kind that's been in so many scraps it simply doesn't care anymore. He might've done time in the army — Reeve couldn't see Lardface having ever been fit enough — but he'd gone to seed since. His hair stuck out over his ears and was thin above his forehead. It looked like he'd paid a lot of money for some trendy gel-spiked haircut his son might have, but then couldn't be bothered keeping it styled. Reeve had seen coppers with haircuts like that, but not too many of them.

"So," he said, "what brings you here, gents?"

The taller man, Spikehead, nodded, like he was thinking: Okay, we're playing it like that. "Just passing through."

"You must be lost."

"How's that?"

"To end up here. It's not exactly on the main road."

"Well, you know . . ." The man was running out of lies already, not very professional.

"We just felt like a drink, all right?" his partner snapped.

"Just making conversation," Reeve said. The edge of his vision was growing hazy. He thought of the pills in his pocket but dismissed them instantly.

"You live locally?" Spikehead asked.

"You should know," Reeve answered.

Spikehead tried a smile. "How's that?"

"You've been following me since Oban."

Lardface turned slowly towards him, fired up for confrontation or conflagration. A pool cue appeared between them.

"You're up," the youth said.

Reeve took the cue from him. "Mind my drink, will you?" he asked Lardface.

"Mind it yourself."

"Friends of yours?" the youth asked, beer glass to his mouth as they walked to the pool table.

Reeve looked back at the two drinkers, who were watching him from behind their glasses the way men watched strippers — engrossed, but maybe a little wary. He shook his head, smiling pleasantly. "No," he said, "just a couple of pricks. Me to break?"

"You to break," the youth said, wiping snorted beer foam from his nose.

Reeve never really had a chance, but that wasn't the point of the game. He stood resting his pool cue on the floor and watched a game of darts behind the pool table, while the youth sank two striped balls and left two other pockets covered.

"I hate the fuckin' English," the youth said as Reeve lined up a shot. "I mean a lot of the time when you say something like that you're having a joke, but I mean it: I *really* fuckin' hate them."

"Maybe they're not too fond of you either, sunshine."

The youth ignored the voice from the bar.

Reeve looked like he was still lining up his shot; but he wasn't. He was sizing things up. This young lad was going to get into trouble. Reeve knew the way his mind was working: if they wanted to fight him, he'd tell them to meet him outside — outside where his pals were waiting. But the men at the bar wouldn't be *that* thick. They'd take him in here, where the only backup worth talking about was Reeve himself. There were a couple of drunks playing darts atrociously, a few seated pensioners, Manny behind the bar, and the road sweeper with the bad leg on the other side of it. In here, the two Englishmen would surely fancy their chances.

"You see," the youth was saying, "the way I see it the English are just keech . . ." He said some more, but Lardface must have understood "keech." He slammed down his drink and came stomping towards the pool table like he was approaching a hurdle.

"Now," Manny said loudly, "we don't want any trouble."

Spikehead was still at the bar, which suited Reeve fine. He spun from the table, swinging his cue, and caught Lardface across the bridge of his nose, stopping him dead. Spikehead started forward, but cautiously. Reeve's free hand had taken a ball from the table. He threw it with all the force he had towards the bar. Spikehead ducked, and the ball smashed a whiskey bottle. Spikehead was straightening up again when Reeve snatched a dart out of one player's frozen hand and hefted it at Spikehead's thigh. The pink haze made it difficult to see, but the dart landed close enough. Spikehead gasped and dropped to one knee. Reeve found an empty pint glass and cracked it against a table leg, then held it on front of Lardface, who was sprawled on the floor, his smashed nose streaming blood and bubbles of mucus.

"Breathe through your mouth," Reeve instructed. It barely registered that the rest of the bar had fallen into stunned silence. Even Manny was at a loss for words. Reeve walked over to Spikehead, who had pulled the dart from his upper thigh. He looked ready to stab it at Reeve, until Reeve swiped the glass across his face. Spikehead dropped the dart.

"Christ," gasped Manny, "there was no need —"

But Reeve was concentrating on the man, rifling his pockets, seeking weapons and ID. "Who are you?" he shouted. "Who sent you?"

He glanced back towards Lardface, who was rising to his feet. Reeve took a couple of steps and roundhoused the man on the side of his face, maybe dislocating the jaw. He went back to Spikehead.

"I'm calling the polis," Manny said.

Reeve pointed at him. "Don't."

Manny didn't. Reeve continued his search of the moaning figure, and came up with something he had not been expecting: a card identifying the carrier as a private investigator for Charles & Charles Associates, with an address in London.

He shook the man's lapels. "Who hired you?"

The man shook his head. Tears were coursing down his face.

"Look," Reeve said calmly. "I didn't do any lasting damage. The cut isn't deep enough for stitching. It's just a bleeder, that's all." He raised the glass. "Now the next slash *will* need stitches. It might even take out your eye. So tell me who sent you!"

"Don't know the client," the man blurted. Blood had dripped into his mouth. He spat it out with the words. "It's subcontracting. We're working on behalf of an American firm."

"You mean a company?"

"Another lot of PIs. A big firm in Washington, DC."

"Called?"

"Alliance Investigative."

"Who's your contact?"

"A guy called Dulwater. We phone him now and then."

"You bugged my house?"

"What?"

"Did you bug my house?"

The man blinked at him and mouthed the word *no*. Reeve let him drop. Lardface was unconscious. Reeve regained his composure and took the scene in — the prone bodies, the silence, the horror on Manny's face . . . and something like idolatry on the youth's.

"I could've taken them," the youth said. "But thanks anyway."

"The police . . . ," Manny said, but quietly, making it sound like a request.

Reeve turned to him. "I'll see you all right about the breakages," he said. He looked down at Spikehead. "I don't think our friends here will be pressing charges. They were in a car smash, that's all. You might direct them to the nearest doctor, but that'll be the last you hear about this." He smiled. "I promise."

He drove south until he reached a pay phone, and called Joan to check she was all right. She had arrived safely at her sister's, but still wanted to know what he was going to do. He remained vague, and she grew angry.

"This isn't just about you, Gordon!" she yelled. "Not now. It's about Allan and me, too. I *deserve* to know!"

"And I'm saying that the less you know the better. Trust me on this." He was still trembling, his body pumping adrenaline. He didn't want to think about how good he had felt laying into the two private eyes.

It had felt wonderful.

He argued a few more minutes with Joan, and was about to plead that he was running out of money when she remembered something.

"I called an hour or two ago," she said. "I got the answering machine, so checked it for messages."

"And?"

"There was one there from a woman. She sounded foreign."

Marie Villambard! He'd forgotten all about her. He'd left his home telephone number on her machine.

"She left a number where you can reach her," Joan said.

Reeve cursed silently. That meant whoever was bugging his phone would have her number, too. He took down the details Joan gave, told her he had to go, and dug in his pockets for more change.

"Allo?"

"It's Gordon Reeve here, Madam Villambard. Thank you for getting back to me, but there's a problem."

"Yes?"

"The line was compromised." Two cars went past at speed. Reeve watched them disappear.

"You mean people were listening?"

"Yes." He looked back along the dark road. No lights. Nothing. The only light, he realized, was the bare bulb in the old-style phone booth. He pulled a handkerchief out of his jacket and used it to disconnect the bulb.

"It is a military term, *compromised?*"

"I suppose it is. I was in the army." The darkness felt better. "Listen, can we meet?"

"In France?"

"I could drive overnight, catch a ferry at Dover."

"I live near Limoges. Do you know it?"

"I'll buy a map. Is your telephone —?"

"Compromised? I think not. We can make a rendezvous safely."

"Let's do it then."

"Okay, drive into the center of Limoges and follow signs to the Gare SNCF, the station itself is called Bénédictins."

"Got it. How long will the drive take from Calais?"

"That depends on how often you stop. If you hurry . . . six hours."

Reeve did a quick calculation. If he didn't encounter congestion or construction, he might make it to the south coast in eight or nine hours. He could sleep on the boat, then another six hours. Add a couple of hours for sailing, embarkation and disembarkation, plus an hour because France was one hour ahead . . . seventeen or eighteen hours. He'd flown to Los Angeles in about half that. The luminous hands of his watch told him it was a little after eight.

"Late afternoon," he said, allowing himself a margin.

"I'll be waiting in the station at four," she said. "I'll wait two hours, best look for me in the bar."

"Listen, there's one more thing. They recorded your call; they know your name now."

"Yes?"

"I'm saying be careful."

"Thank you, Mr. Reeve. See you tomorrow."

His money was finished anyway. He put down the receiver, wondering how they would recognize each other. Then he laughed. He'd have driven a thousand miles straight; she'd recognize him by the bloodshot eyes and body tremors.

But he *was* worried that "they" would know she'd called. He should have destroyed the transmitters as soon as he located them. Instead, he'd tried playing games, playing for time. These were not people who appreciated games. He pushed the light-bulb home and opened the iron-framed door.

One more thing worried him. The private eyes. They were working for an outfit called Alliance, an American outfit, and he had no idea who'd hired Alliance in the first place.

Plus, if Lardface and Spikehead hadn't planted those bugs . . . who had?

TWELVE

JEFFREY ALLERDYCE WAS LUNCHING WITH one of the few United States senators he regarded with anything other than utter loathing. That was because Senator Cal Waits was the only *clean* senator Allerdyce had ever had dealings with. Waits had never had to call on Alliance's services, and had never found himself under investigation by them. He didn't appear to be in any corporation's pocket, and had little time — at least in public — for Washington's veritable army of slick besuited lobbyists.

Maybe that was because Cal Waits didn't need the money or the attention. He didn't need the money because his grandfather had owned the largest banking group in the Southwest, and he didn't need the attention because his style in the Senate got him plenty of that anyway. He was a large middle-aged man with a store of homespun stories that he was keen on recounting, most of them very funny, most of them making some telling point about the subject under discussion in the Senate. He was always being quoted, sound-bitten, edited into fifteen seconds of usable television for the midevening news. He was, as more than one newspaper had put it, "an institution."

They ate at Allerdyce's favorite restaurant, Ma Petite Maison. He liked the crab cakes there; he also had a 10 percent share in the place (though this was not widely known), and so liked to keep an eye on business. Business wasn't bad, but at short notice Allerdyce had still been able to get a booth, one of the ones at the back usually reserved for parties of five or more. A journalist from the *Wall Street Journal* had been moved to one of the lesser tables, but would be kept sweet by seeing his eventual tab reduced by 10 percent.

Allerdyce couldn't tell Cal Waits that he'd had someone moved. Some luncheon companions would have been impressed, honored — but not Waits. Waits would have protested, maybe even walked out. Allerdyce didn't want him to walk, he wanted him to talk. But first there was the other crap to be got through, the so-called excuse for their lunch engagement: catching up on family, mutual acquaintances, old times. Allerdyce noticed how some of the other diners stared at them, seeing two scarred old warhorses with their noses in the feedbag.

And then the main courses arrived — cassoulet for Waits, *magret d'oie* for Allerdyce — and it was almost time.

Waits looked at his plate. "The hell with healthy eating." He chortled. "This health kick we've been on for the past — what? — twenty years: it's killing this country. I don't mean with cholesterol or whatever new bodily disaster or poison the scientists are coming up with, I mean people aren't eating for fun anymore. Dammit, Jeffrey, eating used to be a pastime for America. Steaks and burgers, pizzas and ribs . . . fun food. Surf 'n' turf, that sort of thing. And now everybody looks at you in horror if you so much as suck on a drumstick. Well hell, I told my doctors — you notice you don't just need one doctor these days, you need a whole rank of them, same thing with lawyers — I told them I wouldn't diet. I'd do anything else they told me to do, but I would not stop eating the food I've been eating my whole goddamned life."

He chewed on a fatty piece of ham to prove his point.

"How much medication are you on, Cal?" Allerdyce asked.

Cal Waits nearly choked with laughter. "About a bottle of pills a day. I got little pink ones and big blue ones and some capsule things that're white at one end and yellow at the other. I got red pills so small you practically need tweezers to pick them up, and I got this vast pastel tablet I take once a day that's the size of a bath plug. Don't ask me what they do, I just gobble them down."

He poured himself another half-glass of '83 Montrose. Despite hailing from California, Waits preferred the wines of Bordeaux. He was rationed to half a bottle a day, and drank perhaps twice that. That was another reason Allerdyce liked him: he didn't give a shit.

Allerdyce could see no subtle way into the subject he wanted to raise, and doubtless Cal would see through him anyway. "You were raised in Southern California?" he asked.

"Hell, you know I was."

"Near San Diego, right?"

"Right. I went to school there."

"Before Harvard."

"Before Harvard," Waits acknowledged. Then he chuckled again. "What is this, Jeffrey? You know I went to Harvard but pretend you *don't* know where I was born and raised!"

Allerdyce bowed his head, admitting he'd been caught. "I just wanted to ask you something about San Diego."

"I represent it in the Senate, I *should* know something about it."

Allerdyce watched Waits shovel another lump of sausage into his mouth. Waits was wearing a dark-blue suit of real quality, a lemon shirt, and a blue silk tie. Above all this sat his round face, with the pendulous jowls cartoonists loved to exaggerate and the small eyes, inset like a pig's, always sparkling with the humor of some situation or other. They were sparkling now.

"You ever have dealings with CWC?"

"Co-World Chemicals, sure." Waits nodded. "I've attended a few functions there."

"Do you know Kosigin?"

Waits looked more guarded. The twinkle was leaving his eyes. "We've met." He reached for another roll and tore it in two.

"What do you think of him?"

Waits chewed this question over, then shook his head. "That's not what you want to ask, is it?"

"No," Allerdyce quietly confessed, "it isn't."

Waits's voice dropped uncharacteristically low. His voice box was the reason Allerdyce had needed a table away from other diners. "I feel you're getting around to something, Jeffrey. Will I like it when we arrive?"

"It's nothing serious, Cal, I assure you." Allerdyce's magret was almost untouched. "It's just that Kosigin has hired Alliance's services, and I like to know about my clients."

"Sure, without asking them to their face."

"I like to know what people think of them, not what *they* would like *me* to think of them."

"Point taken. Eat the goose, Jeffrey, it's getting cold."

Allerdyce obeyed the instruction, and sat there chewing. Waits swallowed more wine and dabbed his chin with the napkin.

"I know a bit about Kosigin," Waits said, his voice a quiet rumble seeming to emanate from his chest. "There's been an investigation, not a big one, but all the same . . ."

Allerdyce didn't ask what kind of investigation. "And?" he said instead.

"And nothing much, just a bad feeling about the whole operation. Or rather, about the way Kosigin's headed. It's like he's building autonomy within the corporation. The only person he seems to answer to is himself. And the people he hires . . . well, let's just say they're not always as reputable as you, Jeffrey. This Kosigin seems to like to hang around with minor hoods and shady nobodies."

"You think CWC is in trouble?"

"What?"

"You think something's going to blow up." It was a statement, not a question.

Waits smiled. "Jeffrey, CWC is one of the largest chemical companies in the world. And it's American. Believe me, *nothing*'s going to blow up."

Allerdyce nodded his understanding. "Then the investigation . . . ?"

Waits leaned across the table. "How can the authorities protect American interests unless they know what problems might arise?" He sat back again.

Allerdyce was still nodding. Cal was telling him that the powers — the FBI, maybe the CIA — were keeping tabs on CWC in general and Kosigin in particular; not to root out illegalities, but to ensure those illegalities — whatever shortcuts Kosigin was taking, whatever black economy he was running — never, ever came to light. It was like having the whole system as your bodyguard! Jeffrey Allerdyce, normally so cool, so detached, so unflappable, so hard to impress . . . Jeffrey Allerdyce sat in Ma Petite Maison and actually whistled, something no diner there — not even his old friend Cal Waits — had ever seen him do. Something they might never see him do again.

He gathered his thoughts only slowly, picking at the goose. "But," he said at last, "they wouldn't protect him from every contingency, surely? I mean, if he became a threat to the standing of CWC in the world, then he wouldn't —?"

"He'd probably lose their protection," Waits conceded. "But how far would he have to go? That's a question I can't answer. I just know that I keep out of the guy's way and let him get on with getting on." Waits wiped his mouth again. "I did hear one rumor . . ."

"What?"

"That Kosigin has agency *privileges.*"

"You mean he's special to them?" Allerdyce knew who Waits meant by "agency": the CIA.

Cal Waits just shrugged. "What was he asking you to do anyway?"

"You know I can't answer that, Cal. I wish I could tell you, but I'm bound by a vow of client confidentiality."

Waits nodded. "Well, whatever it is, just do a good job, Jeffrey. That's my advice."

A waiter appeared at that moment. "Mr. Allerdyce? I'm sorry, sir, there's a telephone call. A gentleman called Dulwater — he said you'd want to speak to him."

Allerdyce excused himself.

The telephone was on the reception desk. A flunky held it out towards him, but Allerdyce just pointed to the receiver.

"Can you have that call transferred to the manager's office?"

The flunky looked startled. He didn't want to say no, but didn't want to say yes either.

"Never mind," Allerdyce snarled, snatching the telephone from a palm that was starting to sweat. "Dulwater?"

"Some bad news, sir."

"Better not be." Allerdyce looked around. "I'm in a public place; I'm sure cursing is frowned upon."

"The UK operatives proved to be disadvantaged."

"In plain English?"

"They weren't up to it."

"You assured me they were."

"I was assured they were."

Allerdyce sighed. "Should've sent our own men."

"Yes, sir."

Both of them were well aware that the decision had been Allerdyce's; he'd wanted to save money on flights. So they'd used some firm in London instead.

"So what's the damage?"

"They were confronted by the subject. They sustained a few injuries."

"And the subject?"

"Apparently uninjured."

Allerdyce raised one eyebrow at that. He wondered what sort of man this Reeve was. A grade-A tough bastard by the sound of it. "I take it they lost him?"

"Yes, sir. I doubt he'll return home. Looks like he's packed his wife and son off."

"Well, it's snafued, isn't it, Dulwater?"

"We can try to pick up his trail." Dulwater sounded unconvinced. He wasn't sure why Allerdyce was so interested anyway. To his mind it was a wild goose chase.

"Let me think about it. Anything else?"

"Yes, sir. One of the men said Reeve asked him about his house being bugged, asked if our operative was responsible."

"What?"

"Somebody bugged Reeve's domicile."

"I heard you the first time. Who?"

"Do you want an educated guess?"

"Let's see if we agree."

"Kosigin."

"We agree," said Allerdyce. He thought for a moment. "Makes sense. He's a clever man, doesn't like loose ends, we already know that. Now he's got one, and it's unraveling fast."

Allerdyce was intrigued. If he kept close to Kosigin's operation, he could well end up with information, with the very power he wanted over Kosigin. Then again, it might mean mixing it with some powerful agencies. Allerdyce didn't know everybody's secrets; there were some agencies he probably couldn't fix . . . Stay close, or take Cal Waits's advice and back off? Allerdyce had always been a careful man — cautious in his business, prudent in his personal life. He could see Cal sitting at the distant table pouring yet more wine. A warhorse, unafraid.

"Keep close to this, Dulwater."

"Sir, with respect, I advise we —"

"Son, don't presume to advise Jeffrey Allerdyce. You're not far enough advanced on the board."

"Board, sir?"

"Chessboard. You're still one of my pawns, Dulwater. Moving forward, but still a pawn."

"Yes, sir." A hurt pause. "Pawns aren't very flexible, are they, sir?"

"They just inch their way forward."

"But if they inch far enough, sir, isn't it right that they can turn into more important pieces?"

Allerdyce almost laughed. "You've got me zugzwanged, son. I'm going back to my lunch." Allerdyce dropped the receiver. He was beginning not to detest Dulwater.

Back at the table, Cal Waits was in conversation with a leggy blonde who'd paused to say hello. She was standing in front of the booth, leaning down over the senator. It was a gesture hinting at intimacy, carried out solely so the other diners would notice. It wasn't supposed to embarrass Waits; it was supposed to flatter *her*. She wore a blue two-piece, cut just about deep enough so Waits could see down the front.

She smiled at Allerdyce as he squeezed none too gently past her and resumed his seat. "Well, I'll leave you to your meal, Cal. Bye now."

"Bye, Jeanette." He released a long sigh when she'd gone.

"Dessert, Cal?" Allerdyce asked.

"Just so long as it ain't jelly on a plate," Cal Waits said before draining his wine.

THIRTEEN

REEVE MADE THE CALL FROM THE FERRY TERMINAL. It was either early morning or else the middle of the night, depending on how you felt. He felt like death warmed up, except that he was shivering. He knew the time of day wouldn't matter to the person he was calling. When he'd been a policeman, Tommy Halliday's preferred shift had been nights. He wasn't an insomniac, he just preferred being awake when everyone else was asleep. He said it gave him a buzz. But then he resigned, changed his mind, and found the force wouldn't take him back — just like what had happened with Jim and his newspaper. Maybe the force had discovered Halliday's drug habit; maybe news had leaked of his wild parties. Maybe it just had to do with staffing levels. Whatever, Halliday was out. And what had once been a recreation became his main source of income. Reeve didn't know if Tommy Halliday still dealt in quantity, but he knew he dealt in quality. A lot of army-types — weekenders and would-be mercenaries — bought from him. They wanted performance enhancers and concoctions to keep them awake and alert. Then they needed downers for the bad time afterwards, times so bad they might need just a few more uppers . . .

Reeve had few feelings about drug use and abuse. But he knew Tommy Halliday might have something he could use.

The phone rang for a while, but that was normal: everyone who knew Tommy knew he let it ring and ring. That way he only ended up speaking to people who knew him . . . and maybe a few utterly desperate souls who'd let a phone ring and ring and ring.

"Yeah." The voice was alert and laid-back at the same time.

"It's Gordie." All Tommy's callers used first names or nicknames, just in case the drug squad was listening.

"Hey, Gordie, long time." Halliday sounded like he was lighting a cigarette. "You know a guy called Waxie? Came to see you for one of your long weekends."

Henry Waxman. "I remember him," Reeve said. This was typical of Halliday. You phoned him for a favor from a pay phone and spent half your money listening to his stories. Through the terminal's windows, Reeve saw a greasy sky illuminated by sodium, a blustery wind buffeting the few brave gulls up there.

"He's become a good friend," Halliday was saying. Which meant Waxman had become a serious user of some narcotic. It was a kind of warning. Halliday was just letting Reeve know that Waxman might not be as reliable as he once was. Halliday was under the misapprehension that Gordon Reeve trained mercenaries. Reeve had done nothing to correct this; it seemed to impress the dealer.

"Sorry to ring you so early. Or do I mean late?"

"Hey, you know me. I never sleep. I'm right in the middle of *Mean Streets*, trying to figure out what's so great about it. Looks like a home movie. I dunno." He paused to suck on his cigarette and Reeve leapt into the breach.

"Tommy, I'd like you to get Birdy for me."

"Birdy?"

"Can you do that?"

"Well, I haven't seen him in a while . . ." This was part of the Drug Squad game, too. Birdy wasn't a person. Birdy was something very specialized, very rare.

"I've got something for him." Meaning, I can pay whatever it takes.

"I dunno, like I say, he's not been around much. Is it urgent?"

"No, I'm going to be away for a few days. Maybe I'll call you when I get back."

"You do that. I'll see if I bump into him, maybe ask around. Okay, Gordie?"

"Thanks."

"Sure, and hey, do me a favor. Rent out *Mean Streets*, tell me what's so great about it."

"Three words, Tommy."

"What?" The voice sounded urgent, like it mattered.

"De Niro and Keitel."

He slept for three-quarters of an hour on the ferry crossing. As soon as the boat came into Calais and drivers were asked to return to their vehicles, Reeve washed down some caffeine pills with the last of his strong black coffee. He'd made one purchase onboard — a hard-rock compilation tape — and he'd changed some money. The boat was nearly empty. They took the trucks off first, but within five minutes of returning to his car, he was driving out onto French soil. Back at a garage outside Dover, he'd bought a headlight kit, so he could switch beam direction to the other side of the road. Driving on the right hadn't been a problem to him in the USA, so he didn't think it would be a problem here. He'd jotted down directions so he wouldn't have to keep looking at the map book he'd added to his purchases at the garage.

He headed straight for Paris, looking to take one of the beltways farther out, but ended up on the *périphérique*, the inner ring. It was like one of the circles of Dante's Hell; he only thanked God they were all traveling the same direction. Cars came onto the road from both sides, and left again the same way. People were cutting across lanes, trusting to providence or some spirit of the internal combustion engine. It was a vast game of "Chicken": he who applied the brakes was lost.

Still hyped from the caffeine and loud music, and a bit dazed from lack of sleep, Reeve hung on grimly and took what looked like the right exit. The names meant nothing to him, and seemed to change from sign to sign, so he concentrated on road numbers. He took the A6 off the *périphérique* and had no trouble finding the A10, which called itself *l'Aquitaine*. That was the direction he wanted. He celebrated with a short stop for refueling — both the car and himself. Another two shots of espresso and a croissant.

When he started hallucinating — starbursts in his eyes — still north of Poitiers, he stopped to sleep. A cheap motorway motel looked tempting, but he stayed with his car. He didn't want to get *too* comfortable, but it didn't make sense to turn up for his meeting with Marie Villambard unable to concentrate or focus. He wound the passenger seat as far back as it would go and slid over into it, so the steering wheel wouldn't dig into him. His eyes felt gritty, grateful when he closed them. The cars speeding past the service area might as well have been serried waves crashing on the shore, the rumble of trucks a heartbeat. He was asleep inside a minute.

He slept for forty deep minutes, then got out of the car and did some stretching exercises, using the car's hood as his bench. He took his toothbrush to the toilets, scrubbed his teeth, and splashed water on his face. Then back to the car. He was a hundred miles from his destination, maybe a little less. Despite his stops, he'd made good time. At the back of his map book there was a plan of Limoges. It had two railway stations: the one he wanted — gare des Bénédictins — was to the east, the other to the west. He headed south on the N147 and came into Limoges from the north. Almost at once the streets started to hem him in. They either bore no signposts or identifiers, or else were one way. He found himself shunted onto street after street, twisting right and left and right . . . until he was lost. At one point he saw a sign pointing to gare SNCF, but after following it didn't see another sign, and soon was lost again. Finally he pulled over, double-parking on a narrow shopping street, and asked a pedestrian for directions. It was as if he'd asked the man to talk him through open-heart surgery: Bénédictins was difficult from here, he'd have to retrace his steps, the one-way system was very complicated . . .

Reeve thanked the man and started driving again, waving at the complaining line of drivers who'd been waiting to pass him.

Eventually he crossed a bridge and saw railway lines beneath him, and followed those as best he could. Then he saw it, a huge domed building with an even higher clock tower to one side. Bénédictins. It looked more like an art gallery or museum than a city's railway station. Reeve checked his watch. It was half past five. He found a parking space, locked the car, and took a few seconds to calm himself and do a few more exercises. His whole body was buzzing as though electricity was being passed through him. He walked on to the station concourse, looked over to the left and saw the restaurant and bar.

He paused again outside the bar itself, looking around him as though for a friend. Actually, he was seeking out the opposite, but it was hard to judge from the people milling around. There were down-and-outs and students, young men in military uniform and businesspeople clutching briefcases. Some stared anxiously at the departures board; others sat on benches and smoked, or browsed through a magazine. Any one of them could be putting on an act. It was impossible to tell.

Reeve walked into the bar.

He spotted her immediately. She was middle-aged, wore glasses, and was chain-smoking. There was a fog of smoke in the bar; walking through it was like walking through mist. She sat in a booth facing the bar, reading a large paperback and taking notes in the margin. She was the only single woman in the place.

Reeve didn't approach her straightaway. He walked up to the bar and settled himself on a stool. The barman had already weighed him up and was reaching for the wine bottle. He managed not to look surprised when Reeve ordered Perrier.

There were six other men in the bar, eight including the waiters. Reeve studied them all. They'd stared at him collectively on his arrival, but that was only natural in a French bar as in bars around the world. Mostly they were drinking short glasses of red wine; a couple of them nursed espressos. They all looked like they fitted right in; they looked like regulars. Then he saw that someone else was watching him. She'd put down her book and pen and was peering at him over the top of her glasses. Reeve paid for the water and took his glass to her booth.

"Mr. Reeve?"

He sat down and nodded.

"A good journey?" There was irony in the question.

"First-class," Reeve replied. He would place her in her early fifties. She was trim and well dressed and had taken care of herself, but the lines around the neck gave it away. Her hair was salt-and-pepper, swept back over the ears from a center part and feathered at the back of her head. She had the word *executive* stamped on her.

"So," she said, "now you will tell me about your brother?"

"I'd like to know a bit about you first," he said. "Tell me about yourself, how you came to know Jim."

So she told him the story of a woman who had always been a writer, ever since her school days, a story not dissimilar to Jim's own life. She said they'd met while she was on a trip to London. Yes, she'd known Marco in London, and he'd told her his suspicions. She had come back to France and done some research. In France the farming lobby was even stronger than that in the UK, with close ties between farm owners and their agrichemical suppliers, and a government — no matter whether left- or right-wing — which bowed to pressure from both. The investigation had been hard going; even now she wasn't much further forward, and had to leave the story for long periods of time so she could do work that would earn her money. The agrichem story was her "labor of love."

"Now tell me about Jim," she said. So Reeve told his side of it, a seasoned performer by now. She listened intently, holding the pen as if about to start taking notes. The book she'd been reading was the biography of some French politician. She tapped the cover absentmindedly with the pen, covering the politician's beaming honest face with myriad spots, like blue measles. The barman came over to take another order, and tutted and pointed. She saw what she'd been doing, and smiled and shrugged. The barman seemed not much mollified.

"Do you know this man?" she asked Reeve. She meant the politician. Reeve shook his head. "His name is Pierre Dechevement. Until recently he was responsible for agriculture. He resigned. There was a young woman . . . not his wife. Normally, such a thing would not be a scandal in France. Indeed, there was no trace of a scandal in Dechevement's case. Yet he still resigned."

"Why?"

She smiled. "Perhaps because he is a man of honor? That is what his biographer says."

"What do you say?"

She stabbed the pen at him. "You are shrewd, Mr. Reeve. For years Dechevement took *bribes* from the agrichemical companies — well, no, perhaps bribes is too strong. Let us say that he enjoyed hospitality, and received *favors*. In my opinion one of those favors was the young lady in question, who turns out to have been a sometime prostitute, albeit high-class. Dechevement was quite brazen; she accompanied him to functions here and abroad. He even became her employer, giving her a position on his private staff. There is no record that she contributed any work, but she was paid a generous salary."

Marie Villambard lit a fresh Peter Stuyvesant from the stub of the old one. Her ashtray had already been emptied twice by the barman. She blew out a stream of smoke.

"Dechevement's closest ties were to a company called COSGIT, and COSGIT is a French subsidiary of Co-World Chemicals."

"So Dechevement was in CWC's employ?"

"In a manner of speaking. I think that's why he was told to resign, so no one would bother to backtrack and find that the young prostitute had been paid for by Co-World Chemicals. *That* might have created a scandal, even in France."

Reeve was thoughtful. "So you weren't working along the same lines as my brother?"

"Wait, please. We have not yet . . . scratched the surface."

Reeve sat back. "Good," he said as his second Perrier arrived.

"In a sense, Dechevement is only a very small part of the whole," Marie Villambard said. The waiter had brought her a new pack of cigarettes, which she was unwrapping. Reeve noticed that all the customers who'd been in the bar on his arrival had now been replaced by others — which didn't necessarily mean there wasn't surveillance.

"I have become," she went on, "more interested in a man called Owen Preece. *Doctor* Owen Preece. Your brother was interested in him, too."

"Who is he?"

"He's dead now, unfortunately. It looked like natural causes. He was in his seventies — a cardiac crisis. It could happen to anyone that age . . ."

"Well then, who was he?"

"An American psychiatrist."

Reeve frowned; someone else had mentioned a psychiatrist in connection with CWC . . .

"He headed what was supposed to be an independent research team, funded partly by government and partly by agrichemical companies, to look into BSE, what you call mad cow disease."

Reeve nodded to himself. Josh Vincent had mentioned something similar — research funded by CWC itself, using psychiatrists as well as scientists.

"This was in the early days of the scare," Marie Villambard was saying. "The team comprised neurologists, viral specialists, experts in blood diseases, and psychologists. Their initial reports were that the disease ME — 'Yuppie Flu' as it was called at the time — was not a disease at all but was psychosomatic, an ailment brought on by the sufferer for some complex psychological reason."

"They were working on prion protein?"

"That is correct, and they found no evidence to link prion proteins found in organophosphorus substances, or any pesticides currently in use, to any of the range of diseases that other scientists claim *are* closely linked to them."

"They were got at by CWC?"

"Not exactly, but there is good reason to believe Dr. Preece was in the employ of CWC, and he was head of the team. He gave the final okay to their results. He had access to all the data . . ."

"And could have tampered with it?"

"One member of the team resigned, claiming something along those lines. He was killed in a boating accident only weeks later."

"Jesus. So Preece falsified tests and results? And all this was partly funded by the U.S. government?"

Marie Villambard nodded throughout. "The initial idea had come down from someone in the middle ranks of Co-World Chemicals. Some of us assume this man was responsible for putting Preece in charge. Dr. Preece was in some ways an excellent choice — he was a psychiatrist of some renown. He is also thought to have carried out experiments for the CIA."

"Experiments?"

"On humans, Mr. Reeve. In the fifties and sixties he was part of a team which tested the effects of various hallucinogens on the human nervous system." She saw something close to horror on Reeve's face. "It was all perfectly legal, believe it or not. The subjects were patients in lunatic asylums. They had few rights, and no one to fight for what few rights they had. They were injected with all manner of chemicals; we can't even say which. Preece was a small part of this. It only came to light recently, after his death, when some CIA files were released. It made some of us wonder about his involvement with various committees and research projects post-1960. This man had something to hide, some shame in his past, and those with a past can always be bought."

"And the CWC employee who suggested all this . . . ?"

"Kosigin," said Marie Villambard. "A Mr. Kosigin."

"How do you know?"

"Your brother found out. He interviewed a lot of people under the pretext of writing a book about Preece. He spoke to scientists, government agencies; he tracked down people who had been involved in the original project. He had evidence linking Preece to Kosigin, evidence of a massive cover-up, something concerning every person on the planet." She lifted her cigarette. "That's why I smoke, Mr. Reeve. Eating is too dangerous, to my mind. I prefer safer pleasures."

Reeve wasn't listening. "Whatever evidence my brother had has gone to the grave with him."

She smiled. "Don't be so melodramatic — and for goodness' sake don't be so *silly.*"

Reeve looked at her. "What do you mean?"

"Your brother was a *journalist.* He was working on a dangerous story, and he knew just how dangerous. He would have made backups of his disks. There will be written files somewhere. There will be *something.* In an apartment somewhere, or left with a friend, or in a bank vault. You just have to look."

"Supposing the evidence has been destroyed?"

She shrugged. "Then the story is not so strong . . . I don't know. Maybe it is impossible to find a publisher for it. Everywhere we look, in every country which uses these chemicals and pesticides, we find some government connection. I do not think the governments of the world would like to see this story published." She stared at him. "Do you?"

He stayed silent.

"I do not think the agrichemical conglomerates would like to see the story appear either, and nor would agencies like the CIA . . . Maybe we should all just get back to our ordinary lives." She smiled sadly. "Maybe that would be safer for us all."

"You don't believe that," he said.

She had stopped smiling. "No," she said, "I don't. It has gone too far for that. Another good reason for smoking. I am like the condemned prisoner, yes?"

And she laughed, the terror showing only in her eyes.

She had some information she could give him — copies of documents — so he followed her in his car. They left the city traveling towards a town called Saint Yrieix. This is all I need, thought Reeve, more driving. The road was a succession of steep ups and downs, and a couple of times they found themselves stuck behind a tractor or horse trailer. At last Marie Villambard's Citroën Xantia signaled to turn off the main road, but only so they could twist their way along a narrow country road with nothing but the occasional house or farmstead. It was a fine evening, with an annoyingly low sun and wide streaks of pale blue in the sky. Reeve's stomach complained that he'd been shoveling nothing but croissants and coffee into it all day. Then, to his amazement — out here in the middle of nowhere — they drove past a restaurant. It looked to have been converted from a mill, a stream running past it. A few hundred yards farther on, the Xantia signaled left, and they headed up a narrower, rougher track made from hard-packed stones and sand. The track led them into an avenue of mature oak trees, as though this roadway had been carved from the forest. A couple of roads leading off could have been logging tracks. At the end, in absolute isolation, stood a small old single-story house with dormer windows in the roof. Its facing stones hadn't been rendered, and the shutters on the windows looked new, as did the roof tiles.

Reeve got out of his car. "This is some spot," he said.

"Ah, yes, my grandparents lived here."

Reeve nodded. "He was a timberman?"

"No, no, he was a professor of anthropology. Please, come this way."

And she led him indoors. Reeve was dismayed to see that security was lax. Never mind the isolation and the fact that there was only one road in and out — the house itself was protected by only a single deadbolt, and the shutters had been left open, making for easy entry through one of the windows.

"Neighbors?" he asked.

"The trees are my neighbors." She saw he was serious. "There is a farm only a couple of miles away. They have truffle rights. That means the right to come onto the land to search for truffles. I only ever see them in the autumn, but then I see them a *lot*."

There was a bolt on the inside of the door, which was something. There was also a low rumbling noise. The rumble turned into a deep animal growl.

"*Ça suffit!*" Marie Villambard exclaimed as the biggest dog Reeve had ever seen padded into the hall. The beast walked straight up to her, demanding to be patted, but throughout Marie's attentions its eyes were on the stranger. It growled again from deep in its cavernous chest. "His name is Foucault," Villambard explained to Reeve. He didn't think it was time to tell her he had a cat called Bakunin. "Let him smell you."

Reeve knew that this was the drill — same with any dog —

don't be a stranger. Let it paw over you and sniff your crotch, whatever it takes, until it has accepted you in its territory. Reeve stretched out a hand, and the dog ran a wet, discerning nose over the knuckles, then licked them.

"Good dog, Foucault," Reeve said. "Good dog."

Marie was rubbing the monster's coat fiercely. "Really I should keep him outside," she said. "But he's spoiled. He used to be a hunting dog — don't ask me which breed. Then his owner had to go into hospital, and if I hadn't looked after him nobody would. Would they, Foucault?"

She started to talk to the dog — Reeve guessed part Alsatain, part wolfhound — in French, then led it back to the kitchen, where she emptied some food from a tin into a bowl the size of a washbasin. In fact, as Reeve got closer, he saw that it *was* a washbasin, red and plastic with a chewed rim.

"Now," she said, "my thinking is that you need a bath, yes? After your first-class journey."

"That would be great."

"And food?"

"I'm starving."

"There is an excellent restaurant, we passed it —"

"Yes, I saw."

"We will go there. You are in France only one night, you must spend the time wisely."

"Thanks. I've some stuff in my car; I'll just go fetch it."

"And shall I begin your bath."

The bathroom was a compact space just off the hall. There was a small kitchen, and a small living space that looked more like an office than somewhere to relax. It had a look of organized chaos, some kind of order that only the owner of such a room could explain.

"You live here alone?" Reeve asked.

"Only since my husband left me."

"I'm sorry."

"I'm not. He was a pig."

"When did he leave?"

"October eleventh, 1978."

Reeve smiled and went out to the car. He walked around

the house first. This was real "Hansel and Gretel" stuff: the cottage in the woods. He could hear a dog barking, probably on the neighboring farm. But no other sounds intruded except the rustling of the oak trees in the wind. He knew what Marie thought — she thought the very secrecy of this place made her safe. But where she saw secrecy, Reeve saw isolation. Even if she wasn't in the telephone book, it would take just an hour's work for a skilled operative to get an address for her. An Ordnance Survey map would show the house — might even name it. And then the operative would know just how isolated the spot was.

There were two small outbuildings, one of which had been a bakery at one time. The bread oven was still there, the large wooden paddles still hung on the walls, but the space was used for storage these days. Mice or rats had chewed the corners out of a tower of empty cardboard boxes. The other outbuilding was a woodshed, and maybe always had been. It was stacked with neat piles of sawn logs. Reeve peered into the forest. A covering of dry leaves on the forest floor wouldn't be enough to give warning of anyone approaching the house. He'd have had trip wires maybe. Or . . .

Sudden beams of light flooded the shade. He blinked up and saw that halogen lamps had been fastened to some of the trees. Something or someone had tripped them. Then he saw Marie Villambard standing beside the house, arms folded, laughing at him.

"You see," she said, "I have protection."

He walked towards her. "They're movement-sensitive," he said.

"That's right."

He nodded. "All connected to a single source?"

"Yes."

"Then they'd be easy to disable. Plus, what do they do? They light up the trees. So what? That's not going to stop someone from advancing."

"No, but it gives Foucault something to aim at. He stays out here at night."

"He's just one dog."

She laughed again. "You are a security expert?"

"I used to be," Reeve mumbled, going back into the house with his bag.

He changed into his spare set of clothes, wrapping his soiled shirt around Lucky 13. He wasn't planning on staying here. He'd head off after dinner, find a hotel somewhere on the route. So he took his bag back out to the car and put it in the trunk, out of sight. Marie Villambard had put together a cardboard box full of papers.

"These are all copies, so I do not need them returned."

"Fine," he said.

"And I don't know if they will tell you anything I haven't."

"Thanks anyway."

She looked like she had something awkward to say, her eyes avoiding his. "You know, you are welcome to stay here tonight."

He smiled. "Thanks, but I think I'll head off."

"You are sure?" Now she looked at him. She didn't look like an executive anymore; she looked lonely and tired, tired of solitude and stroking Foucault, tired of long wakeful nights wondering if the sky would suddenly burst open with halogen. Tired of waiting.

"I'll see how I feel after dinner," he conceded. But he loaded the box of files into the trunk anyway.

"Shall we take my car?" she asked.

"Let's take mine. It's blocking yours anyway." He helped her on with her coat. "It looked like a very nice restaurant." Making conversation didn't come easily. He was still getting over the feeling of being flattered that she wanted him to stay. She locked the door after them.

"It is an excellent restaurant," she said. "And a very good reason for moving here."

"It wasn't sentimentality then?" He opened the passenger door for her.

"You mean because the house belonged to my grandparents? No, not that. Well, perhaps a little. But the restaurant made the decision easy. I hope they have a table." Reeve started the engine and turned the car around. "I tried calling, but the telephone is acting up again."

"Again?"

"Oh, it happens a lot. The French system . . ." She looked at him. "You are wondering if my phone is tapped. Well, I don't know. I must trust that it is not." She shrugged. "Otherwise life would be intolerable. One would think oneself paranoid . . ."

Reeve was staring ahead. "A car," he said.

"What?" She turned to look through the windshield. There was a car parked fifty or sixty yards away — French license plate; nobody inside.

"*Merde,*" she said.

Reeve didn't hesitate. He slammed the gearshift into reverse and turned to navigate through the back window. There was a logging trail behind him, and another car darted from it and braked hard across the road.

"Gordon . . . ," Marie said as he stopped the Land Rover. It was the first time she'd used his name.

"Run for it," Reeve said to her. He released both their seat belts. The men in the rear car were reaching into their jackets, at the same time opening their doors. "Just get into the woods and run like hellfire!" He was shouting now, pumping himself up. He leaned across her, pushed open her door, and thrust her out of the car. "Run!" he yelled, at the same time hitting the accelerator with everything he had and pulling his foot off the clutch. The wheels spun, and the car started to fly backwards, weaving crazily from side to side. The men were halfway out of the car when Reeve hit them with everything his own vehicle had. One of the men slipped, and Reeve felt his back wheels bump over something that hadn't previously been on the road. The other man slumped back into the car, either dazed or unconscious.

Reeve looked out of his windshield. Men had appeared beside the car in front. They'd been hiding in the woods. He checked to his left and saw Marie scurrying away. Good: she was keeping low. But the men in front were pointing towards her. One of them headed back into the trees, the other two took aim at Reeve's car.

"Now," he told himself, ducking and opening his door. He slipped out of the car and started crawling towards the trunk just as the first shots went off. There was a body lying under the car, between the front and back wheels. Most of it was intact. Reeve patted it down but found no gun. It must have been thrown during the collision. He couldn't see it anywhere nearby. Another shot hit the radiator grille. Would they hear shots at the neighboring farm? And if they did, would they think them suspicious? The French were a nation of hunters — truffles not their only prey.

The collision had thrown open the back of the Land Rover. He couldn't hope to carry the box of papers, but snatched his overnight bag. They were closing on him, walking forward with real purpose and almost without caution. He could try the other car, there might be guns there. He was on the wrong side of the track to follow Marie, and if he tried crossing over they'd have a clean shot at him. His first decision had to be right. He knew what standard operating procedure was: get the hell away from the firefight and regroup. If you had to go back in, come from a direction the enemy would least expect.

It made sense, only it meant leaving Marie. I can't help her dead, he thought. So he took a deep breath and, crouching low, made for the trees. He was like a figure in a shooting gallery to the two gunmen, but they only had handguns and he was moving fast. He reached the first line of trees and kept running. It was nearly dark, which was both good and bad: good because it made it easier to hide; bad because it camouflaged his pursuers as well as himself. He ran jaggedly for three minutes and was still surrounded by oaks. He hadn't been trying to run stealthily or silently, he just wanted distance. But now he paused and looked back, peering between the trees, listening hard. He heard a whistle, then another — one way over to his right, the other to his left, much closer. Only two whistles; only two men. He was getting farther and farther away from Marie. It could take him hours to circle back around to her. He was doing something he'd vowed to himself he'd never do again: he was running away.

He held out his hands. They were shaking. This wasn't one of his weekend games; his pursuers weren't using blanks. This was *real* in a way that hadn't been true since Operation Stalwart. Return or retreat: those were the options facing him now. He had seconds to decide. He made the decision.

He looked down at his clothes. His pullover was dark, but the shirt beneath was white and showed at the cuffs and neck. Quickly he tugged off the pullover and took off his shirt, then put the pullover back on. Trousers, shoes, and socks were dark, too. He put the shirt back in his bag, then unwrapped Lucky 13. He used the damp and mud beneath the leaves to cover his face and hands and the meat of the dagger's blade. They might have flash-lights, and he didn't want a glint of metal to give him away. The dark was closing in fast, the tree cover all but blocking out the last light of day. Another whistle, another reply. They were far enough apart for him to walk between them. They'd hardly be expecting him to double back.

But he was going to do just that. He left the bag where it was and set off.

He took slow, measured paces so as not to make noise, and he went from tree to tree, using each one as cover so he could check the terrain between that tree and the next. He had no landmarks to go by, just his own sense of direction. He'd left no tracks that he could follow back to the road, and didn't want to follow tracks anyway: they might belong to a truffle hunter; they might belong to a pursuer.

But the whistled messages between his two pursuers were as good as sonar. Here came the first call . . . then the response. He held his breath. The response was so close he could hear the final exhalation of breath after the whistle itself had ended. The man was moving slowly, cautiously. And very, very quietly. Reeve knew he was dealing with a pro. His fingers tightened around Lucky 13.

I'm going to kill someone, he thought. Not hit them or wound them. I'm going to kill them.

The man walked past Reeve's tree, and Reeve grabbed him, hauling him down by the head and gouging into his throat with the dagger. The pistol squeezed off a single shot, but it was wild. Still, it would have warned the others. Even dying, the man had been thinking of his mission. Reeve let the body slump to the ground, the gaping wound in the neck spurting blood. He took the pistol from the warm, pliant hand and looked at the man. He was wearing camouflage, black boots, and a balaclava. Reeve tore off the balaclava but couldn't place the face. He did a quick search but came up with nothing in the pockets.

It was time to go. Another whistle: two sharp staccatos. Reeve licked his lips and returned it, knowing it wouldn't fool his adversary for longer than half a minute. He set off quickly now, hoping he was heading towards the cars. But he knew his direction was off when he came out into a clearing he knew. There was the house, sitting in darkness. He looked up but couldn't see any halogen lamps hidden in the trees. Maybe the enemy had disabled them.

Had they taken Marie back to the cottage? It looked unlikely, there were no lights in there. He walked forward to check . . . and now there was a burst of halogen, lighting the scene like a stage-set in a darkened theater.

"Drop the gun!"

A shouted command, the first words he'd heard for a while. It came from the trees. Reeve, standing next to the cottage window, knew he hadn't a chance. He pitched the automatic pistol in front of him. It landed maybe six feet away. Near enough for him to make a dive to retrieve it . . . if there was anything to shoot at. But all he could see were the trees, and the halogen lamps pointing at him from high up in the oaks. Great security, he thought — works a treat. And then a man walked out from the line of trees and came towards him. The man was carrying a pistol identical to the one on the ground. He carried it very steadily. Reeve tried to place the accent. American, he thought. The man wasn't saying anything more though. He wanted to get close to Reeve, close to the man who had slaughtered his comrade. Reeve could feel the blood drying on his hands and wrists, dripping off his forearms. I must look like a butcher, he thought.

The man kept looking at those hands, too, fascinated by the blood. He gestured with the pistol, and Reeve raised his hands. The man stooped to retrieve the other automatic, and Reeve swung an elbow back into the window, smashing the glass. The man stood up quickly, but Reeve stood stock-still. The man grinned.

"You were going to jump through the window?" he said. Definitely American. "What, you think I couldn't've hit you? You think maybe the telephone's working? You were going to call for help?" He seemed very amused by all these suggestions. He was still advancing on Reeve, no more than three feet from him. Reeve had his hands held up high now. He'd cut his elbow on the glass. His own blood was trickling down one arm and into his armpit.

The man held his gun arm out straight, execution-style, the way he'd maybe seen it done on the Vietnam newsreels. Then he heard the noise. He couldn't place it at first. It sounded motorized, definitely getting closer.

Reeve dived to his right as Foucault flew out through the window, sinking his jaws into the man's face. The force of the dog knocked him flat on his back, the dog covering his whole upper body. Reeve didn't hang around to watch. He snatched up the pistol and ran back towards the track. A few hundred yards would take him to the cars. He heard another vehicle in the distance, something bigger than a car. Maybe it's the cavalry, he thought, someone from the farm.

But now there was another whistled command. Three low and long, two higher and shorter. Repeated five or six times. Reeve kept on moving forwards. Van doors closing. Engine revving. As he turned a bend he saw the car he'd smashed into and his own vehicle. He couldn't see anybody lying under the Land Rover, and there was nobody in the smashed car.

There was a sudden explosion. It threw him backwards off his feet. He landed heavily but got up quickly, winded but still aiming his pistol at whatever the hell had happened. His Land Rover was in flames. Had they booby-trapped it maybe? Then he saw what they'd done. They were disabling it — that was all — so it would be here when the police arrived. The police would find evidence of a firefight, maybe bodies, certainly blood, and a missing journalist. They would also find a British car . . . a car belonging to Gordon Reeve.

"Sons of bitches," Reeve whispered. He moved past the burning wreckage and saw that the front car had gone, along with whatever vehicle had turned up towards the end. He kept hearing that whistled command. It sounded like the opening of a tune he recognized . . . a tune he didn't want to recognize. Five beats. Dahh, dahh, dahh, da-da. It was the opening to "Row, row, row your boat." No, he was imagining it; it could have been another song, could have been random.

He wondered about checking the woods for Marie Villambard's body. Maybe she was alive, maybe they'd taken her with them. Or she was lying somewhere in the woods, and very dead. Either way, he couldn't hope to help. So he set off the other way until he recovered his bag. He had a landmark this time though. The corpse with the cut throat was still lying slumped on the ground.

Row, row, row your boat. He detested that song, with good reason.

Then he froze, remembering the scene outside the crematorium in San Diego: the cars turning up for the next service, and a face turning away from him, a face he'd thought was a ghost's.

Jay.

It couldn't be Jay. It couldn't be. Jay was dead. Jay wasn't alive and breathing anywhere on this planet . . .

It was Jay. That was the only thing, crazy as it seemed, that made sense.

It was Jay.

Reeve was shaking again as he headed back to the cottage. There was a body cooling on the ground next to the window, but no sign of Foucault. Reeve looked into Marie Villambard's Xantia and saw that the keys were in the ignition. Car theft probably hadn't been a problem around here. Nor had warfare and murder, until tonight. He got in and shut the door. He was turning the key when a vast bloodied figure pounced onto the hood, its face framed by pink froth, growling and snarling.

"Got a taste for it, huh?" Reeve said, starting the engine, ignoring the dog. He revved up hard and started off, throwing Foucault to the ground. He watched in the rearview, but the dog didn't follow. It just shook itself off and headed back towards the cottage and what was left of its supper.

Reeve edged the Citroën past the two wrecked, smoldering cars. There was black smoke in the night sky. Surely somebody would see *that*. He scraped the Xantia against tree bark and blistered metal, but managed to squeeze past and back onto the road. He allowed himself a cold glint of a smile. His SAS training told him never to leave traces. When you were on a deep infiltration mission, you'd even shit into plastic bags and carry them with you. You left nothing behind. Well, he was leaving plenty this mission: at least two corpses, and a burned-out Land Rover with British plates. He was going to be leaving a stolen car somewhere, too, with blood on its steering wheel. And these, it seemed to him, were the very least of his problems.

The very, very least.

He drove north, heading away from a horror he knew would surely follow.

His arms and shoulders began to ache, and he realized how tense he was, leaning into the steering wheel as if the devil himself were behind him. He stopped only for gas and to buy cans of caffeinated soft drinks, using them to wash down more caffeine tablets. He tried to act normally. In no way could he be said to resemble a tourist, so he decided he was a businessman, fatigued and stressed-out after a long sales trip, going home thankfully. He even got a tie out of his bag, letting it hang loosely knotted around his throat. He examined himself in the mirror. It would have to do. Of course, the driver of a French car should be French, too, so he tried not to say anything to anyone. At the gas stations he kept to *bonsoir* and *merci;* ditto at the various *péage* booths.

Heading for Paris, he caught sight of signs for Orly. He knew either airport, Orly or Charles de Gaulle, would do. He was going to ditch the car. He figured the ports might be on the lookout for a stolen Xantia. And if the authorities weren't checking the ports, he reckoned his attackers almost certainly were. In which case they'd be checking the airports, too. But he had a better chance of going undetected on foot.

He drove into an all-night parking garage at Orly. It was a

multistory, and he took the Xantia to the top deck. There were only two other cars up here, both looking like long-stayers or cars which had been ditched. The Xantia would be company for them. But first of all he knew he needed sleep — his brain and body needed rest. He could sleep in the terminal maybe, but would be easy meat there. He reckoned there'd be no planes out till morning, and it wasn't nearly light yet. He wound the car windows open a couple of inches to help him hear approaching vehicles or footsteps. Then he laid his head back and closed his eyes . . .

He had a dream he'd had before. Argentina. Grassland and mountain slopes. Insects and a constant sea breeze. Two canoes paddling for shore. In the dream, they paddled in daylight, but really they'd come ashore in the middle of the night, faces painted. Supposedly in silence, until Jay had started singing . . .

The same song he'd sung when they landed on the Falklands only a week before, taken ashore by boat on that occasion. Splashing onto the beach, meeting no resistance. And Jay humming the tune he'd been ordered to stop singing.

> Row, row, row your boat
> Gently down the stream.
> Merrily, merrily, merrily, merrily,
> Life is but a dream.

A dream? More like a nightmare when Jay was around. He was supposed to be a good soldier, but he was a firing pin short of a grenade, and just as temperamental.

Just as lethal.

They'd sent for them after that firefight in the Falklands. They wanted to mount a two-man mission, deep surveillance. They were briefed onboard HMS *Hermes*. Their mission would be to keep watch on Argentinian aircraft flying out of Rio Grande. (Reeve was told only afterwards that another two-man unit was given the same brief with a different location: Rio Gallegos.) Nobody mentioned the words *suicide mission*, but the odds on coming back alive weren't great. For a start, the Argentinians on the Falklands had been equipped with direction-finding equipment and thermal imagers; there was little to show that the same equipment wouldn't be available on the mainland.

Therefore, their radio signals out would be monitored and traced. Meaning they would have to stay mobile. But mobility itself was hazardous, and the possibility of thermal imagers meant they wouldn't even be able to rest at night. Getting in would be easy, getting out a nightmare.

Jay only demurred when his request for a few Stinger shoulder-launched antiaircraft missiles was rejected out of hand.

"You're going in there to watch, not to fight. Leave the fighting to others."

Which was just what Jay didn't want to hear.

Row, row, row your boat . . .

And in the dream that's what they did, with a line of men waiting for them on the beach. For some reason, the men couldn't locate them, though Reeve could see them clearly enough. But Jay's singing got louder and louder, and it was only a matter of time before the firing squad by the water's edge let loose at them.

Row, row, row your boat . . .

Reeve woke up in a sweat. Christ . . . And the true horror was that the reality had been so much worse than the dream, so awful that when he'd finally made it back to *Hermes* they'd refused to believe his version. They'd told him he must be hallucinating. Doctors told him shock could do that. And the more they denied the truth, the angrier he got, until that pink haze descended for the first time in his life and then lifted again, and a doctor and two orderlies were lying unconscious on the floor in front of him.

He sensed movement, something low to the ground and in shadow, over beside one of the other cars. He turned his headlights on and picked out a thin, hungry-looking fox. A fox scavenging on the top floor of a multistory parking garage. What was wrong with the fields? Had things got so bad for the foxes that they were moving into high-rises? Well, Reeve could talk: he was *hiding* in a garage. Hiding because he was being hunted. Right now, he was being hunted by the bad guys; but all too soon the good guys — the so-called forces of law and order — would be hunting him, too. He turned off the headlights and got out of the car to exercise. Sit-ups and push-ups, plus some calisthenics. Then he looked in his traveling bag. He didn't have much left in the way of clean clothes. At the first service station on the route he had scrubbed away the blood. There were dried stains on his sweater, but his white shirt was still clean. He was wearing it now. He'd tried cleaning his shoes, not very successfully. They looked like he'd been playing football in them.

In his bag he found Lucky 13. The dagger was a problem. He knew he couldn't hope to get it past airport security. It would have to stay here. But it was a murder weapon; he didn't want it found. He walked with the dagger over to the elevator, and pressed the button for it to ascend. Then he wiped the dagger with his handkerchief, rubbing off fingerprints, and held it with the handkerchief. When the elevator arrived, he leaned in, pressed the button for the floor below, and stepped out again as the doors were closing. He slipped the blade of the dagger into the gap between the doors and, as soon as the elevator started to descend, used the blade to prize open the doors a couple of inches. Then he simply pushed the hilt and handle through the gap and let the dagger fall onto the roof of the elevator, where it could lie until maintenance found it — always supposing these elevators *had* any maintenance.

It was still early, so he sat in the car for a while. Then he got out and went over to the far wall, and leaned out so he could see the terminal building. There were two terminals, separated by a monorail, but this was the one he wanted, and he could walk to it. There were bright lights inside, and movement, taxis pulling up — the start of another day. He hadn't heard any flights leave in the past half hour, excepting a few light aircraft. But they would start leaving soon. During the night some larger planes had landed. At that hour, they had to be package operators or cargo.

Reeve made a final check on the contents of his bag, finding nothing immediately incriminating or suspicious. So he walked through the cool morning air towards the terminal building. He was starving, so he bought coffee and a sandwich first thing. He slung the bag over his shoulder so he could eat and drink as he walked. He walked among businessmen, all looking bleary-eyed and regretful, like they'd spent the previous night being unfaithful. He'd bet none of them had spent a night like his, but at least he was blending in better than expected. Just another disheveled traveler up too early.

He felt a little more confident as he walked to the desk to buy a ticket. He just hoped they'd have a ticket to spare. They did, but the saleswoman warned him he'd have to pay full business rate.

"That's fine," he said, sliding over his credit card. He was running up a huge bill on the card, but what did that matter when he might not be around come time to pay? Intimations of mortality bred a certain recklessness. Better financial recklessness than any other kind. He waited while the deal was done, looking for recognition in the woman's eyes as she took details of his name from his passport. But there was no recognition; the police weren't on to him yet. She handed back the passport and credit card, and then his ticket and boarding pass. Reeve thanked her and turned away.

There was a man watching him.

Or rather, he had *been* watching him. But now the man was staring at the morning headlines in his paper. Only he didn't look like he was reading them; Reeve would bet the man couldn't even read French. He could walk over and reassure himself of that with a couple of questions, but he couldn't cause a fuss here on the concourse, not when his flight was still some time away. So he walked casually in the direction of the bathrooms.

The bathrooms were up a passageway and around a corner, out of sight of the concourse. They faced each other, the Ladies and the Gents. There was a sign on a trestle outside the Ladies, saying the place was closed for cleaning and could customers please use the other toilets at the far end of the building. Reeve shifted the sign to the Gents and walked in.

He was lucky; there was nobody about. He set to work fast, looking around at the possibilities. Then he went to the sink nearest the door and turned the tap on full, stuffing the plughole with toilet paper. The sink started to fill. On the wall by the door there was an electric hand-dryer. Perfect. On the far wall were some vending machines. Reeve dropped a ten-franc piece into one and pulled the drawer. The small package contained a tiny toothbrush, tube of toothpaste, Bic razor, and comb. He threw the toothpaste and comb aside and got to work, smashing the head of the razor against the sink until he'd snapped off the plastic. He pushed half the blade's length into the head of the toothbrush until he was sure it was firmly lodged there. Now, holding the toothbrush by its handle, he had a scalpel of sorts.

Water was pouring onto the floor. He wondered how long it would be before his watcher would get suspicious and wonder what the hell was going on. Maybe he'd suspect another door, some sort of exit from the toilets. He would come to look. Reeve just hoped he wouldn't call in first, letting his boss or bosses know the score. He wanted one-on-one. He sat up on the edge of the sink, right in the corner of the room, and reached over to the hand-dryer. An electric lead curled out from it and disappeared into the wall. Reeve pulled on the end of the cord nearest the dryer, tugging it hard. Eventually it came away, but he kept on pulling. As he'd hoped, there was cable to spare inside the wall cavity. Electricians did that; it made it easier later if the unit had to be moved. He pulled out as much of the cable as he could. Then he waited. Water was still pouring onto the floor. He hoped the bastard would come soon, or maintenance might get nosy, or a businessman's breakfast coffee might work its way through . . .

The door opened. A man splashed into the water. It was the watcher. Reeve flicked the live end of the cable into his face, then hauled him into the room. With his hands up to his face, the man slipped on the wet floor and nearly fell. Reeve let the cable drop from his hand to the floor, connecting with the water, making the whole floor live. The man's face went into a rictus spasm, and he fell to his knees, hands on the floor, which only made things worse. The electricity jerked him for another couple of seconds, until Reeve hauled the cord away and rested it on the sink tops. Then he slid from his perch, crouched in front of the man, and held the blade to his throat.

The man was shaking all over, sparks still flying around inside. Some people got to like it, apparently. Reeve had been trained in interrogation techniques, and one of the instructors had told him that some prisoners got hooked on those jolts so that afterwards they kept plugging themselves into the socket, just for old times' sake . . .

"Who are you?" Reeve asked quietly. "Who are you working for?"

"I don't know anything."

Reeve nicked the throat, drawing a bead of blood. "Last chance," he hissed.

The man swallowed. He was big, and had probably been hired for that reason alone. But he was not smart — not really a professional to Reeve's mind — he'd fallen too easily. Reeve searched his pockets. The man was carrying cash, but nothing else, no papers, no ID, no telephone or radio.

"When's your RV?" Reeve asked.

"Noon," the man said.

So he knew what RV meant; a lot of Americans would have taken the letters to mean "recreational vehicle." So he'd served time in the armed forces.

"That's when your relief takes over?"

The man nodded. He could feel blood running down his throat but couldn't see any, not at the angle his face was at. Reeve would bet the cut felt worse than it actually was.

"What do you do if I'm spotted?"

"Watch you," the man said, his voice unsteady. He was losing color from his face. Reeve thought maybe the bastard was about to faint.

"And?"

"Call in to report."

"Have you called?"

The man swallowed. "Not yet."

Reeve believed him, and was thankful. "When you call in, what's the number?"

"It's in Paris."

"Give it to me."

The man recited the number.

"Who's on the other end of the phone?"

"I don't know." More pressure with the blade, a fresh trickle of blood. "He hired me in L.A.," the man said quickly, "at my gym. I don't know his name, I only know an initial."

"Jay?"

The man blinked at him, then nodded. Reeve felt his own temperature plummet. It was true; of course it was true. Reeve drew back his fist and hit the man solidly on the side of the jaw. The head jerked, and all resistance went out of the body. Reeve dragged him into a stall and locked the door, then hauled himself up and over the door. He tossed the blade into a washbasin and pulled open the door. A man was standing outside, briefcase in hand. He wasn't sure about the sign. Reeve showed the man the floor.

"Flooding," he said. "Toilet's out of order."

Then he walked back to the concourse and made straight for his departure gate.

PART FIVE
BIRDY

FOURTEEN

REEVE TRIED TO EAT the proffered breakfast on the plane but found he had no appetite. Instead he asked for an extra orange juice, and then for another after that. Heathrow was busier than Orly had been, but he still couldn't spot anyone waiting for him. He went down to the Tube station and made the call from the telephones there.

"Hello?" a voice answered.

Reeve waited.

"Hello?"

"Hello, Jay," he said.

"I think you must have a wrong number."

"Oh?"

There was a long pause at the other end. Reeve watched the units on his card click away. The voice came back on.

"Hey, Philosopher, is that you?"

"Yes."

"What's new, pal?"

Like they'd spoken only last week and had parted the best of friends. Like Jay wasn't in charge of a band of mercenaries with orders to hunt Reeve down and terminate him. Like they were having a conversation.

"I thought you were dead," Reeve stated.

"You mean you wish I was."

"Every day," Reeve said quietly.

Jay laughed. "Where are you, pal?"

"I'm at Orly."

"Yeah? Then you must have met Mickey."

"He gave me your number."

"I hope he charged you for it."

"No, I charged him."

"Well, I knew you'd be tough, Gordon."

"You don't know how tough. Tell your paymasters that. Tell them I'm taking this personally. Not a job, not a mission, just personal."

"Gordon, you're not really at Orly are you? Don't make me run all the way out there."

"Maybe we'll talk again."

"I don't think so, Philosopher."

And Jay put the phone down first.

Reeve took the Tube into central London.

He thought about Jay. Paddling ashore with him in darkness, hitting the coast just south of Viamonte. Their target, Rio Grande, was twenty miles to the north. They were on the Isla Grande de Tierra del Fuego, the western half of which belonged to Chile. If their escape route back to Viamonte was compromised, their best bet was to head west. A forty-mile walk from Rio Grande would take them into Chile.

Jay was carrying the transmitter, Reeve most of the rest of their kit. It was a 100-pound load. Additionally, he carried his M16 rifle and 200 rounds. The M16 came fitted with an M203 grenade launcher. The other armaments consisted of a 66mm antitank missile, fifteen HE grenades, a 9mm Browning, and an assortment of SAS flash-bangs, more for cover than anything else.

He carried binoculars, a night-sight and tripod-mounted 60x telescope, a sleeping bag and quilted trousers, a change of clothing, Arctic dried rations and compo rations, plus a hexamine stove for cooking the latter.

And the song Jay had been singing had somehow stuck in his head, so he couldn't think straight.

They'd begun their march under cover of darkness, aiming to complete it before dawn. That first night, they knew they probably wouldn't reach a good spot for an OP. They'd just find a good hiding place, maybe making a scrape and lying doggo all the next day under their netting and camouflage. And that was what they did. They maintained radio silence throughout. If only Jay was as easy to shut up . . .

"Fucking Argies better not expect *me* to eat their scummy corned beef again. You know how they make that stuff? I read about it in the *Sun* or somewhere. Makes sausages look like best fillet steak, I swear to God, Philosopher."

He was a good-looking man, a bit heavy in the face, but with short fair hair and greeny-blue eyes. His looks were his best feature. Reeve didn't like him and didn't know too many men who did. He was a braggart, cruel and bullying; he followed orders, but always with his own agenda hidden in there somewhere. Reeve didn't know if he was a good soldier or not; he just knew he didn't like him.

But there was something else about Jay. Early on in the conflict, he'd been part of a team dropped by Wessex helicopter onto the Fortuna Glacier. It was an important reconnaissance mission. They landed in near-whiteout conditions and sixty-mile-per-hour winds. Snow turned their guns to ice. They somehow had to cross the glacier. In the first five hours they progressed less than half a mile. To save them from freezing to death, they erected tents, but these blew away. Finally, the order came to abandon the mission. A helicopter sent in to lift the men out crashed in the blizzard conditions, killing three. A second chopper eventually succeeded in getting everyone out. Most of the survivors were suffering from exposure and frostbite. Jay's cheek had been slashed in the crash and required seven stitches.

He should have been out of action for days, weeks even, but insisted he wanted straight back in. The command applauded his readiness, and a psychologist could see no aftereffects from the ordeal. But Jay wasn't the same. His mind was on revenge, on killing Argentines. You could see it behind his eyes.

"You know, Philosopher," Jay said in the scrape that first

night, "you may not be the most popular man in the regiment, but I think you're all right. Yes, you'll do me."

Reeve bit off a question. He's just trying to wind me up, he thought. That's all. Let it go. The mission's all that counts.

Jay seemed to read his thoughts. There was a roaring in the sky east of them. "Rio Grande's getting plenty of action tonight. Wasn't that a film, *Rio Grande*? John Wayne and Dean Martin."

"Just John Wayne," Reeve told him.

"Now Dean Martin, there's an actor for you."

"Yes, a fucking awful one."

"You're wrong. Ever see Matt Helm? Or those comedies he did? Great actor."

Reeve just shook his head.

"Don't shake your head, I'm serious. You can't let anybody else have a say, can you? That's why you're not popular. I'm only telling you for your own good."

"Fuck off, Jay." He liked to be called Jay. Most of the Regiment were known by their first names, but not Jay. He liked people to use his surname. Nobody knew why. He called Reeve the Philosopher after finding him reading Nietzsche. The nickname had stuck, though Reeve hated it.

The second evening, they set up the OP properly with a half-decent view of the airfield. That night, they sent out their first signals, then moved again double-quick, an eight-man Argentinian patrol heading in their direction.

"They were fast," Jay conceded, carrying the half-packed transmitter.

"Weren't they though," said Reeve, almost slipping under the weight of his rucksack. They must have picked up the transmission straight off. It had been no more than a burst of a few seconds. Whatever direction-finding equipment they had down at the airport, it was earning its keep. Jay had sent a "burst transmission": a coded message, its contents predetermined, which could be transmitted to sea in a split second. Prior to transmission, he'd keyed the scrambled message on a machine which looked like a small electronic typewriter. In theory, the Argentines shouldn't have been able to use the direction finder on them given the brevity of the transmission. Theory was a wonderful thing, but fuck all use on the ground. The Argentines obviously had some new bit of kit, something they hadn't been told about, something that Green Slime — the Intelligence Corps — had missed.

There was aircraft noise overhead as they moved. Skyhawks, Mirage jets. Earlier there had been Pucaras, too. The Argentine Air Force was keeping itself busy. Both men knew they should be noting the flights in and out, ready to send the information on. But they were too busy moving.

The main problem was the terrain. As with most airfields — and with good reason — there weren't many hills around. Flat grassland and brush with some outcrops, this was their territory. Hard territory in which to remain undiscovered for any length of time. They shifted a couple of miles and scraped themselves another hide. They were farther away from the airfield, but still able to see what was flying out. Reeve stood guard — rather, *lay* guard — while Jay got some sleep. They didn't dare brew up for fear of the steam being seen. Besides, you never knew what a heat-seeking device could find. So Reeve drank some cold water and ate raw rations. He was carrying out conversations in his head, all of them in Spanish. It might come in handy later. Maybe they could bluff . . . no, his Spanish wasn't that good. But he could use it if they were caught alive. He could show willing. Not that he was obliged to, not under the Geneva Convention, but then Geneva was a long way from here . . .

Reeve blinked his eyes. The Tube compartment was full to bursting. He looked over his shoulder out of the grimy window and saw the station sign: Leicester Square. He got up and pushed his way out of the train, making for the Northern Line. Standing-room only for the first couple of stops. He stood next to a very beautiful young woman, and stared at her reflection in the glass, using her to take his mind off the past.

He alighted at Archway and, after a couple of questions, found Harrington Lane and Pete Cavendish's house. Cavendish was still in bed, but remembered him. When Reeve apologized and said what he wanted, Cavendish gave him the key and told him to bring it back when he was finished. He didn't need to ring the bell, just stick it through the mail slot.

"Thanks," Reeve said. Cavendish nodded and closed the door again.

It took him a little while to figure out how to access the lane behind Cavendish's street, but eventually he found a road in and walked down the lane until he saw what looked like the right garage, empty cans and bottles and all. He unlocked the garage door and pulled it up. It took him a few goes, and a few gentle applications of a half-brick on to the rollers, but eventually the garage was open. Dogs were barking in a couple of the walled back gardens, making as much noise as he'd done.

"Arnie! Shuddup!" someone yelled. They sounded fiercer than any dog.

Reeve unlocked the car, fixed the choke on, and turned the ignition. It took a while, reconditioned engine or not, but the car finally started, shuddering a little at first, then smoothing itself out. Reeve took it into the lane and kept it running while he went back to shut the garage door. This set the dogs off again, but he ignored them, relocked the garage, and got back into the Saab. He drove slowly to the end of the lane, avoiding glass and bricks and sacks of rubbish. A couple of lefts took him back into Cavendish's street, and he left the car long enough to put the garage key through the mail slot.

He searched for a London street map, but didn't find one. The glove compartment didn't have one, and there was nothing under the seats. The car was what he'd call basic. Even the radio had been yanked out, leaving just wires and a connector. Basic maybe, but not as basic as his own Land Rover, its carcass somewhere in France. A lot had happened this past day and a half. He wanted to sit down and rest, but knew that was the last thing he should do. He could drive to Jim's flat; maybe Fliss Hornby would be there. But he couldn't do that. He didn't want to put her in any danger, and he'd already seen what a visit from him could do to a woman on her own . . .

The tank was nearly empty, so he stopped in a gas station, filled up, and added a newspaper to his purchase. He sat flicking through, looking for a news story from France, finding nothing. He wondered how long it would take the French authorities to link the torched car to its owner. He guessed a couple of days max, which gave him today and maybe tomorrow. Maybe, but not for certain. He had to get moving.

He only had the one plan: advance. He'd tried a tactical retreat last night, and it had cost several lives, including, for all he knew, that of Marie Villambard. Now that he knew he was up against Jay, he didn't want to hide anymore, and didn't think he *could* hide — not forever. Not knowing Jay was out there. There-fore, the only tactic left was to advance. A suicide mission maybe, but at least it was a mission. He thought of Joan and Allan. He'd have to phone Joan; she'd be worried about him. Christ, what lies would he concoct this time? He couldn't possibly tell her about Marie Villambard. But not to tell her might mean that the first she'd hear of it would be the police knocking at her sister's door, asking his whereabouts. She'd hear their side of it, but not his.

Marie Villambard . . . Marie had said Jim would've kept copies of his working notes. He wouldn't have entrusted all his informa-tion to disks alone. He wondered if Marie herself had kept an extra set, maybe with another journalist. Would someone else pick up her baton? A safe place, she'd said: maybe a friend's flat or a bank vault. Reeve turned back and headed to Pete Cavendish's. Cavendish couldn't believe it.

"This is a nightmare," he said. "I told you to stick the key through the letterbox."

"I did that," Reeve said, pointing to the spot on the floor where the key lay.

"What then?"

"It's just, my brother trusted you with his car. I wondered if you were keeping anything else safe for him."

"Such as?"

"I don't know. Some files, a folder, papers . . . ?"

Cavendish shook his head.

"Maybe he told you not to tell anyone, Pete, but he's dead and I'm his brother —"

"He didn't give me anything, all right?"

Reeve stared into Cavendish's eyes and believed him. "Okay, sorry," he said starting back down the path.

"Hey!" Cavendish yelled after him.

Reeve turned. "What?"

"How's the motor running?"

Reeve looked at the idling Saab. "Sweet as a nut," he said, wondering how soon he could ditch it.

Tommy Halliday lived in Wales, because he thought the air and drinking water there were better; but he didn't have much affection for the Welsh, so lived as close to the border with England as he could while remaining near a funny place-name. Halliday lived in Penycae; the funny place-name was Rhosllanerchrugog. On the map it looked like a bad batch of Scrabble tiles, except that there were way too many letters.

"You can't miss it on the map," Halliday had told Reeve, the first time Reeve was planning a visit. "They always like to put Rhosllanerchrugog in nice big bold letters, just to show what silly fuckers the Welsh are. In fact, everybody around here just calls it Rhos."

"What does it mean?" Reeve had asked.

"What?"

"The word must mean something."

"It's a warning," Halliday had said. "It says, the English are coming!"

Halliday had a point. Penycae was close to Wrexham, but it was also within commuting distance of Chester, Liverpool, even Stoke-on-Trent. Consequently, English settlers were arriving, leaving the grime and crime behind, sometimes bringing it with them.

All Halliday had brought with him were his drug deals, his video collection, and his reference books. Halliday hated films but was hooked on them. Actually, more than the films themselves he was hooked on the film *critics*. Barry Norman was god of this strange religion, but there were many other high priests: Maltin, Ebert, Kael; *Empire*, *Premier*, and *Sight & Sound* magazines. What got Reeve was that Halliday never went to a movie. He didn't like being with other people, strangers, for two darkened hours. He rented and bought videos instead. There were probably six or seven hundred in his living room, more elsewhere in the semidetached house.

For Halliday, films were not entertainment. His tussle with the movie form was like a student tackling some problem of philosophy. It was as though, if Halliday could work out films — why some were good, others bad, a few works of genius — then he would have solved a major problem, something that would change his life for the better and for always. When Reeve turned up at the house, Halliday was in a tizzy. He'd just found an old *Guardian* review by Derek Malcolm panning Tarantino's *Pulp Fiction*.

"You should see the reviews in *Empire* and *Premiere*," he said irritably. "They loved that film."

"What did you think of it?" Reeve waited in the hall while Halliday triple-locked the reinforced front door. He knew Halliday's neighbors thought the reason his curtains were always closed was that Halliday was busy watching films. There was a rumor Halliday was writing a film of his own. Or that he was some English director who'd made a fortune in Hollywood and decided to retire young.

He looked younger than his years, with thinning short red hair, a faceful of freckles, and tapering ginger sideburns plus dark red mustache. He was tall and lanky, with arms that seemed to be controlled by someone else. He flapped them as he led Reeve down the short hall into the living room.

"What did I think of it? I agreed with *Empire*."

Halliday seldom had an opinion of his own — only what he'd gleaned from the reviewers and the theorists. There was a homemade bookcase, precariously angled, which held his store of film knowledge. There were library books and books he'd bought or lifted from shops. There were bound volumes of magazines, scrapbooks full of reviews from newspapers and magazines. He had video recordings of several years' worth of Barry Norman and the other film programs. He slumped into his large easy chair and jerked a hand towards the sofa. There was, of course, a film playing on the TV.

"Going through your Scorsese period?" Reeve asked. He recognized the film as *Mean Streets*. "How many times have you watched this one?"

"About a dozen. There are a lot of tricks he does here that he uses again in other films. Look, this slo-mo run through the bar. That's in *Goodfellas*. Later there's a good bit with Harvey Keitel pissed. How come Keitel plays Catholics so often?"

"I hadn't noticed he did."

"Yeah, I read that somewhere . . ." Halliday's eyes were on the screen. "Music, too, the way he uses music in this film, like he does in *Goodfellas*."

"Tommy, did you get the birdy?"

Halliday nodded. "You're not going to like it."

"How do you mean?"

Halliday just rubbed his thumb and forefinger together.

"Not cheap, huh?"

"Not cheap. The Colombians I used to deal with, they aren't around anymore. They worked for the Medellin cartel, but the Medellin people got shafted by the Cali cartel. So now I seem to be dealing with Cali, and they're not quite so — I don't know — friendly. Plus, as you know, this stuff is thick on the ground in Colombia but thin on the ground over here . . ." He looked at Reeve and smiled. "Thank God."

"So what did it cost?"

Halliday told him.

"What, did I buy the whole fucking crop?"

"You bought enough to get you into bed with the Dagenham Girl Pipers."

Looking around the living room, or indeed the rest of the house, you would not suspect Tommy Halliday of being a dealer in everything from drugs to arms. That was because he kept absolutely nothing incriminating on the premises. Nobody knew where the cache was hidden, but Reeve guessed it was another reason for Tommy's choice of this part of Wales. There was a lot of countryside around, mountains and forests frequented by hikers and picnickers — a lot of potential hiding places in those sorts of terrain.

No, the only things about Tommy's house that might make someone suspicious were the antisurveillance devices and the mobile phone. Tommy didn't trust British Telecom, and in the house he used the phone with a portable scrambler attached. The scrambler was U.S. Intelligence Corps standard, and Reeve guessed it had been "lost" during the Iraqi war. A lot of armed forces equipment had been lost during the campaign; a lot of Iraqi gear had been picked up quietly and tucked away for resale back in Britain.

Most of the arms Tommy dealt in, however, were eastern bloc: Russian and Czech predominantly. He had a consignment of Chinese stuff for a while, but couldn't give it away it was so unreliable.

Halliday glanced at his watch. "Wait till this film's over, all right?"

"I've got all the time in the world, Tommy," Reeve said. He didn't mean it, but he found that the time spent in the living room was time well spent. He cleared his mind and relaxed his muscles, did a little bit of meditation, some breathing exercises Joan had shown him. He gathered himself. And when he'd finished, there was still half an hour to go.

"Mind if I use the equipment?" he asked.

"You know where it is."

So he headed upstairs into the spare bedroom, where Tommy kept his weights and a couple of exercise machines. Reeve worked up a sweat. Sweat was the quickest way to void toxins from your body, assuming you weren't in the mood for sticking two fingers down your throat. From now on there was a regime he would follow: exercise when he could and eat well. Keep his mind and body pure. He would guess Jay had kept fit. He'd recruited from a gym: no mere accident. He probably frequented a few gyms. Reeve had to prepare as best he could. He considered taking steroids, but ruled them out quickly: their effects were short-lived, the side effects long-lasting. There was no "quick fix" when it came to fitness. Reeve knew he was pretty fit; family life hadn't completely destroyed him, it had just robbed him of a little willpower.

Joan — he should call Joan. When he got downstairs the film was finished, and Halliday was on his computer. The computer was new, and boasted CD-ROM. Halliday was studying some kind of film encyclopedia, open at *Mean Streets*.

"Look here," he said, pointing feverishly at the screen. "Maltin gives it four stars, 'a masterpiece'; Ebert gives it four; *Baseline* gives it four out of five. Even Pauline bloody Kael likes it."

"So?"

"So it's a film about a couple of arseholes, one smarter than the other, but both of them plainly fucked from the start. This is supposed to be great cinema?"

"What did you think of De Niro?"

"He played it the same way he always plays those roles, eyes all over the place, demented smile."

"You think he's like that in real life?"

"What?"

"What do you think his background is?"

Halliday couldn't see where this was leading, but he was prepared to learn. "Street punk, a kid in Brooklyn or wherever, same as Scorsese." He paused. "Right?"

Reeve shook his head. "Look up De Niro."

Halliday clicked the cursor over the actor's name. A biography and photograph came up.

"See?" Reeve said, pointing to the relevant line. "His parents were artists, painters. His father was an abstract expressionist. This isn't a street kid, Tommy. This is a well-brought-up guy who wanted to be an actor."

"So?"

"So he made you believe in his *character*. You got no inkling of his background; that's because he submerged it. He became a role. That's what acting is." Reeve watched to see if any of this sank in. "Can I use your telephone?"

Halliday flapped an arm towards the windowsill.

"Thanks."

Reeve walked over to the window.

"So you know about films, huh?" Halliday called.

"No, Tommy, but I sure as shit know about acting." He picked up the telephone and dialed Joan's sister. While he waited for an answer, he pulled the curtains apart an inch and looked out on to the ordinary lower-middle-class street. He'd parked the Saab outside another house: that was an easy rule to remember. Someone answered his call.

"Hi there," he said, recognizing Joan's voice. The relief in her next words was evident.

"Gordon, where are you?"

"I'm at a friend's."

"How are you?"

"I'm fine, Joan. How's Allan?" Reeve watched Halliday get up from the computer and go to a bookshelf. He was searching for something.

"He's missing you. He's hardly seen you lately."

"Everything else okay?"

"Sure."

"No funny phone calls?"

"No." She sounded hesitant. "You think they'll find us here?"

"I shouldn't think so." But how difficult would it be to track down the wife of Gordon Reeve, to ascertain that she had one brother and one sister, to locate addresses for both? Reeve knew that if they needed a bargaining chip, they'd resort to anything, including ransoming his family.

"You still there?"

"Sorry, Joan, what did you say?"

"I said how much longer?"

"I don't know. Not long, I hope."

The conversation wasn't going well. It wasn't just that Halliday was in the room; it was that Reeve was fearful of saying too much. In case Joan worried. In case someone was listening. In case they got to her and wanted to know how much she knew . . .

"I love you," she said quietly.

"Same goes," he managed, finishing the call. Halliday was standing by the bookcases, a large red volume in his hand. It was an encyclopedia. Reeve walked over and saw he had it open at Art History, a section about abstract expressionism. Reeve hoped he hadn't set Halliday off on some new tangent of exploration.

He touched Halliday's shoulder. "The birdy," he said.

Halliday closed the book. "The birdy," he agreed.

*　　*　　*

Birdy was their name for *burundanga*, a drug popular with the Colombian underworld. It used to be manufactured from scopolamine extracted from the flowers of the *borrachero* tree, *Datura arborea*, but these days it was either mixed with benzodiazepine, or else it was 100 percent benzodiazepine, this being safer than scopolamine, with fewer, less harmful side effects.

Reeve followed Halliday's car. Tommy Halliday was as cautious as they came. He'd already taken Reeve's money and left it at the house. Reeve had made a large withdrawal in a London branch of his bank. They'd had to phone his branch in Edinburgh for confirmation, and even then Reeve had taken the receiver and spoken to the manager himself. They knew each other pretty well. The manager had come on one of Reeve's tamer weekends.

"I won't ask what it's for," the manager said, "just don't spend it all in London."

They'd had a laugh at that. It *was* a large amount of money, but then Reeve kept a lot of money in his "sleeper" account; an account he kept hidden from Joan and from everyone else, even his accountant. It wasn't that the sleeper money was dirty, it was just that he liked to have it as a fallback, the way SAS men often took money with them when they went on missions behind enemy lines — gold sovereigns usually. Money for bribes, money for times of desperate trouble. That's what Reeve's sleeper fund was, and he judged this to be exactly the sort of time and occasion it was meant for.

He hadn't been expecting the birdy to cost quite so much. It would put a big dent in his bankroll. The rest of the money was for contingencies.

It would give the police something else to mull over, too, once they'd connected him to the mess in France. They might well find the account — his bank manager wouldn't lie about it — and they'd wonder about this large withdrawal, so soon after the killings. They'd be even more suspicious. They'd most definitely be "anxious" to talk to him, as they put it in their press releases.

Well, Tommy Halliday had some of that money now.

And once he'd handed over the powder, that would be good-bye. Reeve wouldn't be allowed to return to Halliday's house, not carrying drugs. So Reeve had asked his questions beforehand. Like, was it scopo, benzo, or a mix?

"How the fuck do I know?" Halliday had replied. "It's tough to get scopo these days, so my guess is pure benzo." He considered. "Mind, these Colombians have good stuff, so maybe it's ten, fifteen percent scopo."

"Enough to put someone in a psychiatric ward?"

"No way."

The problem with scopolamine was, there was just the one antidote — physostigmine — and neither man knew how readily available it was to hospitals and emergency departments, supposing they were able to diagnose *burundanga* poisoning in the first place. The drug was little known and little used outside Colombia; and even when it was used outside that country, it was normally used by native Colombians. No one in the British Army would admit to ever having used it as an interrogation aid. No, no one would ever admit that. But Reeve knew about the drug from his days in the SAS. He'd seen it used once, deep undercover in Northern Ireland, and he'd heard of its use in the Gulf War.

"Is there any physostigmine with it?"

"Course not."

Tommy Halliday drove into the hills. He drove for half an hour, maybe a little more, until he signaled to pull into the half-full parking lot of a hotel. It was a nice-looking place, well lit, inviting. The parking lot was dark, though, and Halliday pulled into the farthest, gloomiest corner. Reeve pulled up alongside him. They wound their windows down so they could talk without leaving their cars.

"Let's give it a couple of minutes," Halliday said, "just to be on the safe side." So they waited in silence, headlights off, waiting to see if anyone would follow them into the lot. No one did. Eventually, Halliday turned his engine on again and leaned out of his window. "Go into the bar, stay there one hour. Leave your boot slightly open when you go. Does it lock automatically?"

"Yes."

"Right, that's where the stuff will be. Okay?

"One hour?" Reeve checked the time.

"Synchronize watches," Halliday said with a grin. "See you next time, Reeve."

He backed out of the space and drove sedately out of the lot.

Reeve had half a mind to follow. He'd like to know where the cache was. But Halliday was too careful; it would be hard work. An hour. He'd guess the stuff was only ten minutes away. Halliday would take his time getting there though, and he'd take his time coming back. A very careful man; a man with a lot to lose.

Reeve locked the car, opened the trunk, and walked in through the back door of the hotel, into warmth, thick red carpeting, and wood-paneled walls. There was a reception area immediately ahead, but the bar was to his right. He could hear laughter. The place wasn't busy, but the regulars were noisy as only regulars are allowed to be. Reeve prepared smiles and nods, and ordered a half of Theakston's Best. There was a newspaper on the bar, an evening edition. He took it with his drink to a corner table.

He was thinking about the long drive ahead, back to Heathrow, not much relishing the idea. It would be good to stay put for a night, tucked between clean sheets in a hotel room. Good, but dangerous. He checked the newspaper. On one of the inside pages there was a "News Digest" column, seven or eight single-paragraph stories. The story he'd been dreading was halfway down.

FRENCH FARMHOUSE MURDER MYSTERY
French police confirmed today that a burned-out car found at the scene of a murder had UK license plates. Three bodies were discovered near a farmhouse in a densely wooded area of Limousin. One unidentified victim had been savaged by a dog, which belonged to one of the remaining two victims, a local journalist. The journalist was killed by a single bullet to the head, while the third victim was stabbed to death.

Reeve read the story through again. So they hadn't taken Marie — or if they had, they hadn't taken her far. The first thing the police would have done was shoot the dog. Reeve felt bad: Foucault had saved his life. And Marie . . . well, maybe she'd have died anyway. She was almost certainly on somebody's list. Police would have linked the deaths to the Land Rover. Maybe they'd think one of the other bodies was that of the owner. It depended on the other car, the one Reeve had backed into. He doubted they'd be able to track it down. It had probably been stolen. But they could track *his* car down.

He went into the lobby and found a telephone. There were three of them, each in its own booth with stool, ledge, writing pad and pen. Reeve phoned Joan again.

"What is it?" she said.

"Something I've got to tell you. I was hoping I wouldn't have to so soon."

"What?"

"The police may come asking questions. The thing is, I had to leave the Land Rover in France."

"France?"

"Yes. Now listen, there were some bodies at the scene." He heard her inhale. "The police are going to come looking for me."

"Oh, Gordon . . ."

"It may take them a few more days to get to you. Here's the thing: you don't know where I was going, you only know I said I had to go away on business. You don't know what I'd be doing in France."

"Why didn't you tell me any of this before?" She wasn't crying; crying wasn't her style. Angry was her style — angry and let down.

"I couldn't. Last time I phoned, there was someone else in the room."

"Yes, but you could have told me before now. Look, is this all about Jim?"

"I think so."

"Then why not just tell the police your side of it?"

"Because my side of it, as things stand, doesn't amount to anything. I've no evidence, no proof; I've nothing. And the men who did it, the police would have trouble finding them."

"You know who did it?"

"I know who's responsible." Reeve was running out of money. "Look, just don't tell the police any more than you have to. They may think one of the bodies is mine. They may ask you to identify the body."

"And I just go along with it, like we haven't spoken? I have to look at this dead man?"

"No, you can say we've spoken since, so you know it can't be me."

She groaned. "I really think you should go to the police, Gordon."

"I'm going to the police." Reeve allowed himself a small smile.

"What?"

"Only not here."

"Where then?"

"I can't tell you that. Look, trust me, Joan. You're safest if we play it this way. Just trust me, okay?"

She didn't say anything for a long time. Reeve feared his money would run out before she did say something.

"All right," she said, "but Gordon —"

The money ran out.

Back in the bar, no one had touched his drink or his paper. He left the paper folded at the crossword, but now opened it up again and read, or at least stared at the headlines. He didn't think they'd be watching the airports yet — well, the police wouldn't. Jay and his team might, but he thought they were probably gone by now. Regrouping, awaiting new orders. One mission was over for them, only a partial success. He guessed they'd be back in the States, maybe in San Diego.

Which was exactly where he was headed.

After sixty minutes, he went back out to his car. At first he couldn't see anything in the trunk. Halliday had tucked it deep underneath the lip. It was nothing really, a small packet — white paper, folded over. Reeve got into the car and carefully unfolded the A4 sheet. He stared at some yellowy-white powder, about enough for a teaspoon. Even with the interior light on, the stuff didn't look pure. Maybe it was diluted with baking soda or something. Maybe it was just a benzo-scopo mix. There was enough of it though. Reeve knew how much he needed: just over two milligrams a dose. Three or four per dose to be on the safe side; or on the *un*safe side if you happened to be the recipient. He knew the stuff would dissolve in liquid, becoming only very slightly opalescent. He knew it had no flavor, no smell. It was so perfect, it was like the Devil himself had made it in his lab, or dropped the *borrachero* seeds in Eden.

Reeve refolded the paper and put it in his jacket pocket.

"Beautiful," he said, starting the car.

On the way south, he thought about how Tommy Halliday might have stitched him up, or been stitched up himself. The powder could be a cold remedy, simple aspirin. Reeve could take it all the way to the States and find only at the last crucial minute that he'd been sold a placebo. Maybe he should test it first.

Yes, but not here. It could wait till America.

"Another bloody night in the car," he muttered to himself. And another airplane at the end of it.

FIFTEEN

ALLERDYCE HAD TAKEN WHAT FOR HIM was a momentous, unparalleled decision.

He'd decided he had to tread carefully with Kosigin and Co-World Chemicals. As a result, there was to be no more discussion of either topic within the walls of Alliance Investigative — not in his office, not in the corridors, not even in the elevators. Instead, Dulwater had to report, either by telephone or in person, to Allerdyce's home.

Allerdyce had always kept his office and home lives discrete — insofar as he never entertained at home, and no Alliance personnel ever visited him there, not even the most senior partners. No one except the dog handlers. He had an apartment in downtown Washington, DC, but much preferred to return daily to his home on the Potomac.

The house was just off a AAA-designated "scenic byway" between Alexandria and George Washington's old home at Mount Vernon. If streams of tourist traffic passed by his house, Allerdyce didn't know about it. The house was hidden from the road by a tall privet hedge and a wall, and separated by an expanse of lawn and garden. It was a colonial mansion with its own stretch of riverfront, a jetty with a boat in mooring, separate servants' quarters, and a nineteenth-century ice house, which was now Allerdyce's wine cellar. It wasn't as grand as Mount Vernon, but it would do for Jeffrey Allerdyce.

Had he chosen to entertain clients there, the house and grounds would have served as a demonstration of some of the most elaborate security on the market: electronic gates with video identification, infrared trip beams surrounding the house, a couple of very well-trained dogs, and two security guards on general watch at all times. The riverfront was the only flaw in the security; anyone could land from the water. So the security men concentrated on the river and let the dogs and devices deal with the rest.

The reason for all the security at Allerdyce's home was not fear of assassination or kidnap, or simple paranoia, but that he kept his secrets there — his files on the great and good, information he might one day use. There were favors there that he could call in; there were videotapes and photographs which could destroy politicians and judges and the writers of Op-Ed pages. There were audio recordings, transcripts, scribbled notes, sheafs of clippings, and even more private information: copies of bank statements and bounced checks, credit card bills, motel registration books, logs of telephone calls, police reports, medical examination results, blood tests, judicial reviews . . . Then there were the rumors, filed away with everything else: rumors of affairs, homosexual love-ins, cocaine habits, stabbings, falsified court evidence, misappropriated court evidence, misappropriated funds, numbered accounts in the Caribbean islands, Mafia connections, Cuban connections, Colombian connections, wrong connections . . .

Allerdyce had contacts at the highest levels. He knew officials in the FBI and CIA and NSA, he knew secret servicemen, he knew a couple of good people at the Pentagon. One person gained him access to another person, and the network grew. They knew they could come to him for a favor, and if the favor was something like covering up an affair or some sticky, sordid jam they'd gotten into — well, that gave Allerdyce just the hold he wanted. That went down in his book of favors. And all the time the information grew and grew. Already he had more information than he knew what to do with, more than he might use in his lifetime. He didn't know what he'd do with his vast (and still increasing) store of information when he died. Burn it? That seemed a waste. Pass it on? Yes — but to whom? The likeliest candidate seemed his successor at Alliance. After all, the organization would be sure to prosper with all that information in the bank. But Allerdyce had no successor in mind. His underlings were just that; the senior partners aging and comfortable. There were a couple of junior partners who were hungry, but neither seemed right. Maybe he should have fathered some children . . .

He sat in the smaller of the two dining rooms and considered this, staring at a portrait of his grandfather, whom he remembered as a vicious old bastard and tightfisted with it. Genes: some you got, some you didn't. The cook, a homely woman, brought in his appetizer, which looked like half a burger bun topped with salmon and prawns and a dollop of mayonnaise. Allerdyce had just picked up his fork when the telephone rang. Maybe two dozen people knew his home telephone number. More knew his apartment number, and he kept in touch by monitoring the answering machine there morning and evening. He placed his napkin on the brightly polished walnut table and walked over to the small antique bureau — French, seventeenth century, he'd been told — that supported the telephone.

"Yes?" he said.

There was a moment's pause. He could hear static and echoes on the line, like ghostly distant voices, and then a much clearer one.

"Sir, it's Dulwater."

"Mm-hm."

"I thought I'd let you know the situation here."

"Yes?"

"Well, I kept watch on the house, but nobody's been near. So I decided to take a look around."

Allerdyce smiled. Dulwater was an effective burglar; he'd used the skill several times in the past. Allerdyce wondered what he'd found in Gordon Reeve's home. "Yes?" he repeated.

"Looks like they've moved out for a while. There's a litter tray and a bunch of cat food, but no cat. Must've taken it with them. The cat's name's on the food bowl. Bakunin. I checked the name, thought it was a bit strange; turns out the historical Bakunin was an anarchist. There are books on anarchism and philosophy in the bedroom. I think maybe they left in a hurry; the computer was still on in the kid's bedroom. The telephones were bugged, sure enough — hard to tell who did it; the mikes are standard enough but they *are* U.S.-sourced."

Dulwater paused, awaiting praise.

"Anything else?" Allerdyce snapped. He sensed Dulwater was saving something.

"Yes, sir. I found a box of magazines, old copies of something called *Mars and Minerva*." Another pause. "It's the official magazine of the SAS."

"SAS? That's a British army unit, isn't it?"

"Yes, sir, mostly counter-revolutionary warfare: hostage rescue, deep infiltration behind enemy lines in time of war . . . I've got some stuff from the libraries here."

Allerdyce studied his fingernails. "No wonder Reeve dealt so diligently with the two personnel. Have you spoken to them?"

"I made sure their boss got the picture. They've been kicked out."

"Good. Is that everything?"

"Not quite. There was some action in France — a journalist was killed. Her name was Marie Villambard. I recognized the name because it was thrown up during our background search on James Reeve. He'd had some contacts with her."

"What happened?"

"I'm not absolutely certain. Looks like a firefight. A couple of burned-out cars, one of them British. The Villambard woman was shot execution-style, another guy had his face ripped off by a guard dog. Last victim had his throat cut. They found other bloodstains, but no more bodies."

Allerdyce was quite for a minute. Dulwater knew better than to interrupt the silence. Finally, the old man took a deep breath. "It seems Kosigin has chosen a bad opponent — or a very good one, depending on your point of view."

"Yes, sir."

Allerdyce could tell Dulwater didn't understand. "It seems

unlikely Reeve will give up, especially if police trace the car back to him."

"Always supposing it's his car," Dulwater said.

"Yes. I'm trying to think if we have contacts in Paris . . . I believe we do."

"I could go down there . . ."

"No, I don't think so. What is there to find? We'll have Paris take care of that side of things for us. So Reeve is ex-army, eh? Some special unit. What some would call a tough nut to crack."

"There's just one more thing, sir."

Allerdyce raised an eyebrow. "More? You've been busy, Dulwater."

"This is conjecture."

"Go on."

"Well, the muscle Kosigin's using, the one from L.A. He's supposed to be English."

"So?"

"So, he's also supposed to have been in the SAS."

Allerdyce smiled. "That could be interesting. Dulwater, you've done remarkably well. I want you back here."

"Yes, sir."

"And Dulwater?"

"Sir?"

"Upgrade your flight to First; the company will pay."

"Thank you, sir."

Allerdyce terminated the call and returned to the dining table, but he was too excited to eat right away. He didn't know where this story was headed, but he knew the outcome would be anything but mundane. Allerdyce could foresee trouble for Kosigin and CWC. They might have need of Alliance's services again; there might be a favor Kosigin would need. There might well be a favor.

Maybe he'd underestimated Dulwater. He pictured him in his mind — a large man, quiet, not exactly handsome, always well dressed, a discreet individual, reliable — and wondered if there was room for a promotion. More than that, he wondered if there was a necessity. He finished his water and attacked the food. His cook was already appearing, wheeling a trolley on which were three covered silver salvers.

"Is it chicken today?" Allerdyce asked.

"You had chicken yesterday," she said in her lilting Irish brogue. "It's fish today."

"Excellent," said Jeffrey Allerdyce.

PART SIX
CLOSED DOORS

SIXTEEN

REEVE HAD FLOWN into New York's JFK. It had been just about the only route open to him at such short notice. The good news was he'd been offered a cheap seat that had been canceled at the last minute. The woman behind the desk had seemed to take pity on him. He put the flight on his credit card. He couldn't know if Jay and his men — or whoever they worked for — had access to his credit card transactions, or to flight information and passenger lists; if they did, it would take a day or two for his name to filter down to them. And by then he wouldn't be in New York anymore.

The passport control at JFK had taken a while, lots of questions to be answered. He'd filled in his card on the plane. The officer at passport control stapled half of it back into his passport and stamped it. They'd done that last time too, but no one had checked his passport going home. The officer had asked him the purpose of his visit.

"Business and pleasure," Reeve said.

The official marked that he could stay three weeks. "Have a nice trip, sir."

"Thank you."

And Reeve was back in the United States.

He didn't know New York, but there was an information booth in the terminal, and they told him how to get into town and that there was another booth offering tourist accommodation along the other end of the concourse.

Reeve changed some money before heading for the bus into Manhattan. The information booth had provided him with a little pocket map, and his hotel was now circled on it in red. So he'd asked for another map, clean this time, and had torn the other one up and thrown it away. He didn't want anyone knowing which hotel he'd be staying at — if someone so much as looked over his shoulder, it would have been easy with the marked map. He was gearing himself up, ready for whatever they threw at him. And hoping maybe he could throw something at them first.

He was wearing a roomy pair of sneakers he'd bought duty-free at Heathrow. He'd divvied the birdy up into halves, folded each into a torn section of paper towel, and secreted one in either trainer, tucked into the cushioned instep. He'd also bought a clean polo shirt and sports jacket — again on the credit card. He wanted to look like a tourist for the authorities at JFK, but since he didn't want to look like a tourist on the streets of New York, he'd kept his old clothes so he could change back into them.

His hotel was on East 34th, between Macy's and the Empire State Building, as the man in the booth had informed him. He tried not to think about how much it was costing. It was only for one night after all, two at most, and he reckoned he deserved some comfort after what he'd been through. Christ alone knew what lay ahead. The bus dropped him off outside Penn Station, and he walked from there.

It was morning, though his body clock told him it was mid-afternoon. The receptionist said he shouldn't really check in until noon, but saw how red his eyes were and checked her computer, then phoned maid service. It turned out she could give him a room after all, freshly cleaned — she'd just have to tweak a reservation. He thanked her and headed upstairs. He lay down on his bed and closed his eyes. The room spun around him in his darkness. It was like the bed was on a turntable set to 17 rpm. Jim's first record player had been a Dansette with a setting for 17 rpm. They'd played Pinky & Perky records on it. The pigs had sounded like ordinary people. It was just a matter of slowing them down.

Reeve got up and ran a bath. The water pressure was low. He imagined a dozen maids all rinsing baths at the same time, preparing rooms for new guests, guests who came and went and left nothing behind.

He remembered a quote he'd read in one of his books: something about life being a river, the water never the same for any two people who walked through it. He'd remembered it, so it must have meant something to him at the time. Now he wasn't so sure. He studied his face in the bathroom mirror. It was getting ugly, all tensed and scowling. It had looked that way in Special Forces: a face you prepared for when you met the enemy, a permanently pissed-off look. He'd lost it over time as he'd let his muscles relax, but he was getting it again now. He noticed that he was tensing his stomach muscles, too, as though readying to repel a punch in the guts. And his whole body tingled — not just from jet lag; senses were kicking in. You might call them a sixth sense, except that there was more than one of them. One told you if someone was watching you, one told you someone you couldn't see was near. There was one that told you whether to run left or right to dodge gunfire.

Some of his colleagues in Special Forces hadn't believed in the senses. They'd put it down to sheer luck if you beat the clock. For Reeve it was instinct, it was about picking open part of your brain normally kept locked. He thought maybe Nietzsche had meant something similar with his "Superman." You had to unlock yourself, find the hidden potential. Above all, you had to live dangerously.

"How am I doing, old man?" Reeve said out loud, slipping into the bath.

In Queens, the fashion accessory of choice was the stare.

Reeve, though dressed in his needing-a-wash nontourist clothes, still got plenty of stares. His map of downtown Manhattan wouldn't help him here. This was a place they told strangers to avoid. His cab driver had taken some persuading; the yellow cab had been idling outside the hotel, looking for a fare up to Central Park or over to JFK if he was on a roll, but when Reeve had asked for Queens, the man had turned to examine him like he'd just asked to be taken to Detroit.

"Queens?" the man had said. He looked Puerto Rican, a ribbon of black curly hair falling from his oily baseball cap. "Queens?"

"Queens."

The driver had shaken his head slowly. "Can't do it."

"Sure you can, we just need to discuss the fare."

So they'd discussed the fare.

Reeve had spent a lot of time with the Yellow Pages, and when he couldn't find what he wanted in Manhattan, he'd switched to the outer limits: the Bronx and Queens. The third store he tried had sounded about right, so he'd asked for directions and written them down on a sheet of hotel notepaper.

So he sat with them in the back of the cab, listening to the wild, angry dialogue of the two-way radio. Whoever was manning the mike back at HQ was exploding. He was still exploding as the cab crossed the Queensboro Bridge.

The cab driver turned around again. "Last chance, man." His accent, whatever it was, was so thick Reeve could hardly make out the words.

"No," he said, "keep going." He repeated the words in Spanish, which didn't impress the driver. He was calling in, the mike close to his mouth.

The street they were looking for, the one Reeve directed the driver to, wasn't too deep into Queens. They stuck close to the East River, as though the cabbie didn't want to lose sight of the Manhattan skyline. When the cab stopped at lights, there were usually a few men hanging around, leaning down to peer into the back like they were at an aquarium. Or looking into a butcher's cabinet, thought Reeve. He preferred the idea of the aquarium.

"This is the street," Reeve said. The driver pulled over immediately. He wasn't going to cruise looking for the shop, he just wanted to dump Reeve and get out of there.

"Will you wait?" Reeve asked.

"If I stop longer than a red light, the tires'll be gone. Shit, *I'll* be gone."

Reeve looked around. The street was run-down, but it didn't look particularly dangerous. It was no Murder Mile. "What about giving me your card," he said, "so I can call for another cab?"

The man looked at him levelly. Reeve had already paid and tipped him. It was a decent tip. He sighed. "Look, I'll drive around. No promises, but if you're right here at this spot in twenty minutes, maybe I'll be back here to pick you up. No promises, you hear? If I catch another fare, that's it."

"Deal," Reeve said.

Twenty minutes might cover it.

He found the store on the other side of the street. Its window made it look like a junk shop — which in part it was — but it specialized in militaria and survivalist goodies. The hulk behind the padlocked counter didn't look like he was going to be mugged. Brown muscled shoulders bulged from a tight black T-shirt with some Nazi-style emblems and writing on the front. There were tattoos on the man's arms, variously colored. The thick veins ran through them like roads on a map. The man had a bulbous shaven head but a full black beard and mustache, plus a large looped earring in one ear. Reeve immediately pictured him as a pirate, cutlass between his teeth in some old black-and-white movie. He nodded a greeting and looked around the shop. What stock there was the mostly boxed, but the display cabinet behind which the owner — Reeve presumed he was the owner — sat was full of just what he'd come here for: knives.

"You the one that phoned?"

Reeve recognized the man's voice and nodded. He walked towards the display case. The knives were highly polished combat weapons, some with extremely mean-looking serrated edges. There were machetes, too, and butterfly knives — even a foreshortened samurai sword. There were older knives among the flashing steel; war souvenirs, collectibles with dubious histories.

The man's voice wasn't as deep as his frame would suggest. "Thought you must be; we don't get too many customers midweek. Lot of our stuff goes out mail order. You want I should put you on the computer?"

"What computer?"

"The mailing list."

"I don't think so."

"You see anything you like?"

Reeve saw plenty. He'd considered buying a gun, but wouldn't have known how to go about it. Besides, a knife was just about as good, so long as you got close. He was hoping to get *very* close . . .

"Nothing exactly like what I'm looking for."

"Well, this is just a selection." The man came from behind the counter. He was wearing gray sweatpants, baggy all the way down to his ankles, and open-toed sandals showing one toe missing. He went over to the door and locked it, turning the sign to CLOSED.

"Was it a bullet or shrapnel?" Reeve asked.

The man knew what he meant. "Bullet. I was rolling, trying to get to cover, bullet went into the toe of my damned boot."

"Through the steel toe cap?"

"I wasn't wearing steel toe caps," the man said, smiling. "This didn't happen to me in the army." He was leading Reeve through the shop. The store was narrow but went back a long way. They came to a section of clothing: disruptive patterns, plain olive greens, stuff from all over the world. There were boots, too, and a lot of equipment for wilderness survival: compasses and stoves and pup tents, binoculars, reels of filament for making trip wires, rifle sights, crossbows, balaclavas . . .

This, Reeve realized, was going to take more than the twenty minutes his cabbie had allotted him. "No guns?" he asked.

"I'm not licensed for them."

"Can you get them?"

"Maybe if I knew you better. Where you from anyway?"

"Scotland."

"Scotland? You guys invented golf!"

"Yes," Reeve admitted, not sure why the hulk was suddenly so excited.

"Ever played St. Andrews?"

"I don't play golf." The hulk looked bemused by this. "Do you?"

"Hell, yes, got me a five handicap. I *love* golf. Man, I'd like to play some of those courses over there."

"Well, I'd be happy to help you."

"But you don't play."

"I know people who do."

"Well, man, I would surely love to do that someday . . ." He unlocked a door at the back of the store. It had three locks, one of them a padlock attached to a central bolt.

"Not the rest rooms?" Reeve said.

"Yeah, the head's back here, but then so is a lot of other stuff."

They entered a small storeroom with barely enough space for the two of them. There were three narrow doors with piles of boxes in front of two of them. A box sat on the small table in the middle of the room.

"I already looked these out; thought they might be more your thing." He lifted the lid from an innocuous brown cardboard box, the size of a shoe box. There were layers of oiled cloth inside, and between the layers lay the knives.

"Nice balance," Reeve said, handling one. "Bit too short, though." After handling each knife, he handed it to the hulk for repolishing. Reeve peeled off another strip of cloth near the bottom of the box and saw what he'd been looking for: an eight-inch blade with five-inch handle. He tried it for weight and balance. It felt almost identical to his German knife, his Lucky 13.

"I like this one," he said, putting it to one side. He checked the remaining knives out, but none came close. "No," he said, "it has to be this one."

"That's a good knife," the hulk agreed, "a serious knife."

"I'm a serious person."

"You want a scabbard for it?"

Reeve considered. "Yes, a scabbard would be useful. And I want to check out some of your other lines, too . . ."

He spent another hour in the front of the shop, adding to his purchases. The hulk had introduced himself as Wayne and said that he used to be a professional wrestler, on TV even. Then he asked if Reeve was still interested in a gun.

Reeve wasn't sure. It turned out all Wayne had to offer was a revolver, a pump-action and an assault rifle, so Reeve shook his head, glad the decision had been taken for him.

Wayne handed him some leg straps so he could fasten the scabbard onto his leg if he wanted. "On the house," he said.

Then he added up the total, and Reeve took out some cash.

"Running around Queens with a bankroll," Wayne said, shaking his head, "no wonder you need a knife."

"Could you call me a cab?" Reeve asked.

"Sure. And hey, write down your address, just in case I ever do make that trip." He pushed a pad of papers towards Reeve.

Reeve had already given a false name. Giving a false address was easy.

The rest of the day was quiet. Reeve stayed in his room, slept for as long as he could, and exercised when he couldn't. About midnight, feeling fine, he walked the streets around the hotel and up as far as Times Square. The city felt more dangerous at night, but still not *very* dangerous. Reeve liked what he saw. He liked the way necessity had reduced some of the people to something edgier, more primeval than you found in most British cities. They all looked like they'd stared into the abyss. More than that, they looked like they'd bad-mouthed it as well. Reeve was not offered drugs — he didn't look the type — but he was offered sex and other sideshows. He stood on the fringes watching a man play the three-card trick. He couldn't believe people were making bets, but they were. Either they had money they didn't need, or they needed money very badly indeed. Which just about summed up the people he saw.

There were tourists about, looking like tourists. They were getting a lot of attention. Reeve liked to think that after a day in the city, he was fitting in, picking up less attention, fewer stares. Here he was, behind enemy lines. He wondered if the enemy knew it yet . . .

*　　*　　*

Next morning, he took a bus south 235 miles to Washington, DC. This was where Alliance Investigative had its headquarters, according to Spikehead. The private eye might have been lying, but Reeve didn't think so.

Reeve's own hotel in New York had a sister hotel in Washington, but that would have made him too easy to trace. Instead, he called a couple of other chains until he found one with a room in its Washington hotel.

He took a cab to the hotel itself, and asked at reception for a street map. In his room he got out the phone directory and looked up Alliance Investigative, jotting down the address and telephone number. Spikehead hadn't been lying. He found the address on his map but didn't mark it, committing it to memory instead. He looked up Dulwater next, but didn't find an entry. The man who had been Spikehead's contact at Alliance was ex-directory. Knowing what he was going to do, he heaved the Yellow Pages onto the bed and looked at the list of private investigation agents and agencies. There were plenty to choose from. Alliance had a small, understated ad which only said that they specialized in "corporate management." He went for one of the small ads, and steered clear of anything that boasted having been "long established." For all he knew, PIs were every bit as clubby as lawyers or accountants. He didn't want to contact a PI only to have that PI telephone Alliance with the news.

As it turned out, he chose remarkably well.

"You've come to the right person, Mr. Wagner."

Reeve was calling himself Richard Wagner. He was sitting in the rented office of a Mr. Edward ("please, call me Eddie") Duhart. Duhart was interested to speak to a European. He said he'd been researching his name and was positive it was originally DuHart and that he was somehow related to a big Bordeaux distillery.

"I think you mean vineyard," Reeve had said.

Eddie Duhart was in his late twenties, nicely enough dressed but not wearing the clothes with ease. He kept moving in his chair, like he couldn't get comfortable. Reeve wondered if the guy was a cokehead. Duhart had cropped blond hair, shiny white teeth, and baby-blue eyes. You could see the child in him peering out from a college-football body. "Well, yeah, vineyard. Sure I mean vineyard. See, I think these Duharts came over here to further their, you know, trade. I think they settled here, and"— he opened his arms wide — "I'm the result."

"Congratulations," said Reeve. The office was small and looked impermanent. There was a desk and a filing cabinet, a fax machine, and a coatrack on which hung something looking suspiciously like a fedora. There was no secretary, probably no need for one. Duhart had already informed him that he was "fairly fresh" to the business. He'd been a cop three years but got bored, liked to be his own operator. Reeve said he knew the feeling. Duhart said he'd always loved private-eye stories and movies. Had Reeve ever read Jim Crumley or Lawrence Block? Reeve admitted the gap in his education. "But you've seen the movies, right? Bogart, Mitchum, Paul Newman . . . ?"

"I've seen some movies."

Duhart accepted this as a truism. "So I decided to become a PI, see how I made out. I'm making out pretty good." Duhart leaned back in his creaking chair, folding his hands over a gut that did not yet exist. "That's why, like I say, you've come to the right person."

"I'm not sure I follow." Reeve had admitted that he wanted to know a little about Alliance Investigative.

"Because I'm not stupid. When I decided to set out in this game, I did some reading, some research. Foreknowing is forearmed, right?"

Reeve didn't bother to correct the quotation. He shrugged and smiled instead.

"So I asked myself, who's the best in the business? By which I mean the richest, the best known." Duhart winked. "Had to be Alliance. So I studied them. I thought I could learn from them."

"How did you do that?"

"Oh, I don't mean I spied on them or asked them questions or anything. I just wanted to know how they'd gotten so big.

I read everything I could find in the libraries, how old man Allerdyce started from nothing, how he cultivated friends in high *and* low places. Know his motto? 'You never know when you'll need a friend.' That is so true." If he leaned back any farther in his chair he was going to tip it. "So, like I say, if you want to know about Alliance, you've come to the right guy. Only thing *I'm* wondering is, why do you want to know about them? They done you wrong, Mr. Wagner?"

"Do you believe in client confidentiality, Mr. . . . Eddie?"

"Sure, Rule One."

"Well, then I can tell you that, yes, I think they may have done me wrong. If I can prove that . . . well, that might put both of us in an interesting position."

Duhart played with a cheap pen, handling it like it was rolled-gold Cartier. "You mean," he said, "that we could both use information about Alliance to our separate advantages?"

"Yes," Reeve said simply.

Duhart looked up at him. "Going to tell me what they did?"

"Not just now, later. First, I want to know what you know."

Duhart smiled. "You know, we haven't discussed my charges yet."

"I'm sure they'll be fine."

"Mr. Wagner, you know something? You're the first interesting damned client I've had. Let's go get a coffee."

As Reeve had feared, the fedora was not just an ornament. Duhart wore it as far as the coffee shop on the corner, then placed it on the Formica-topped table, checking the surface first for grease marks and coffee spills. He touched the brim of the hat from time to time with his fingernails, like it was his talisman. He watched from the window as he talked about Alliance. Nobody, it seemed, had any dirt on the company. They operated cleanly and for a client roll that included most of the city's top companies and individuals. They were the establishment.

"What about their structure?" Reeve asked. So Duhart told him a little about that. He *had* done his research, and he retained knowledge well. Reeve wondered if it was the police training.

"Have you ever heard of someone called Dulwater working for Alliance?"

Duhart frowned and shook his head. "It'd only take two seconds to check though." He slipped a portable telephone out of his pocket. "You don't happen to know Alliance's number, do you?"

Reeve recited it. Duhart pressed some buttons and took another sip of coffee.

"Mm, yes," he said at last, "Mr. Dulwater's office please." He waited, staring at Reeve. "Is that right? No, there's no message, thank you, ma'am." He cut the connection and put the telephone back in his pocket.

"Well?" Reeve asked.

"Seems he's not in the office today."

"But he does work there?"

"Oh yeah, he works there. And one other thing she told me."

"What?"

"The name's pronounced *Doo-latter*."

"Let me put something to you," Reeve said, after their second coffees had appeared, along with a slice of pie for Duhart.

"Shoot."

"Say Alliance wanted some work done overseas. Say they hire a couple of PIs from another firm based overseas to do some surveillance work."

"Mm-hm." Duhart scooped pie into his mouth.

"Well, who'd have the authority to put that sort of operation together?"

Duhart considered, swallowing the pie with some sour black coffee. "I get your question," he said. "I'd have to make an educated guess."

"Go ahead."

"Well, it'd have to be at senior-partner level, and for that they might even have to go to the old man himself."

"His name's Allerdyce, you said?"

"Yeah, Allerdyce. He plays his cards close, you know? He likes to keep tabs on everything the company's doing, every operation. I know the names of the senior partners; Dulwater ain't one of them."

"So Allerdyce would have to sanction something like that?"

"That's my guess."

"Even if he didn't actually originate the plan?"

Duhart nodded. "That what happened to you, Mr. Wagner? I mean, I notice your accent and all. You're British, right? Did they come and do a number on you?"

"Something like that," Reeve said thoughtfully. "Okay, Eddie, what about telling me everything you know about Allerdyce?"

"Where do you want me to start?"

"Let's start with where he lives . . ."

SEVENTEEN

WORKING SHIFTS, Reeve and Duhart kept a watch on the offices of Alliance Investigative.

It wasn't easy. For a start, parking outside was restricted to loading and unloading. Added to which, one person couldn't cover all the angles: the main entrance faced one street, but the entry / exit ramp for the underground parking garage was around the corner, on a different street altogether. It took them the best part of a day to figure that Allerdyce *never* entered or left the building on foot.

Additionally, Reeve worried that he might not recognize Allerdyce. All Duhart had shown him were newspaper and magazine photographs of the scowling figure. Plus, neither Duhart nor Reeve knew what Allerdyce's vehicle of choice would be. If a black stretch limo came crawling up the ramp, fair enough that was probably the boss. But it could just be a client. Tinted windows didn't mean anything either. Like Duhart said, if you were going to see Alliance and you were a Washington "name," you probably didn't want people recognizing you.

In the end, they switched tactics and kept watch on Allerdyce's apartment, but that was no more fruitful.

"Bastard's got a house somewhere on the Potomac," Duhart conceded that night. "Looks like he prefers it to the apartment."

"Where's the house exactly?"

"I don't know."

"Could we go look?"

"It's pretty exclusive real estate."

"Meaning?"

"Meaning several things. One, people don't have their name written on the mailbox or anything. They figure the postman *knows* who they are. Two, the houses are surrounded by lawns you could host the Super Bowl on. You don't just cruise past and peer in through the window."

Reeve thought about this. "It's on the river?" Duhart nodded. "Then why *can't* we just cruise past? I mean literally."

Duhart was wide-eyed. "You mean a boat?"

"Why not?"

"I've never been on a boat in my life, excepting a couple of ferries."

"I've been on boats a lot. I'll teach you."

Duhart looked skeptical.

"It's worth a shot," said Reeve. "Besides, I'm paying, remember?"

Which was about as much argument as Eddie Duhart needed.

Next day, on their way to rent a boat, they passed the Watergate Hotel. The rental place was actually a club, and not supposed to rent, but Eddie had promised quiet cash and the boat back within a couple of hours. The owner wanted a deposit, too, and that had to be negotiated. But eventually it was agreed. They had their boat.

It was a two-person motorboat, though the motor wasn't exactly powerful. There was a rowing club next door, and Reeve feared they'd be overtaken by scullers. They were in possession of a good map, which showed they were about fifteen miles from Mount Vernon. According to Duhart, they'd come to the house before that. Neither man discussed how they would actually *recognize* the house as belonging to Jeffrey Allerdyce. Reeve was trusting to instinct. And at least they were *doing* something. He didn't mind reconnaissance when there was something to reconnoiter, but so far they'd been staring at smoke.

It was a fine day of sharp sunshine and scudding thin wisps of high cloud. There was a stiff breeze at their back as they puttered down the Potomac. They passed Alexandria on their right, and Duhart said they'd be coming to the district soon where Allerdyce had his home. Reeve had brought a small pair of green rubberized binoculars. They were discreet but powerful. They hadn't been cheap, but as Wayne had said, they were marine-standard. Reeve had them around his neck as he steered, giving the throttle an occasional twist to push up the revs on the engine. He was wearing his tourist clothes today, plus sunglasses purchased on the plane from London and a white sailing hat borrowed from the boat's owner.

After they'd left Alexandria behind, Reeve slowed the boat down. "Remember," he said, "we'll get two stabs at this, so don't fret. Try to look casual."

Duhart nodded. The breeze had kicked around and was rocking the boat a bit. Duhart hadn't gone green at the gills exactly, but he wasn't saying much, like he was concentrating on his breathing.

They came to a row of palatial houses, two- and three-storied, with pillars and porches, gazebos and landing decks. Most carried polite signs warning boats against mooring. Reeve saw rectangular black arc lights dotted on lawns — movement-sensitive, he guessed. He saw an elderly man pushing a lawn mower across grass which looked like green baize. Duhart shook his head to let him know it wasn't Allerdyce, as if he needed telling.

On one of the wood-slatted sundecks, a man lazed with his feet up on a stool, a drink on the arm of his chair. Behind him on the clipped lawn, a large dog chased a punctured red ball tossed by another man. The dog's jaws snapped on the ball and shook it from side to side — your basic neck-break procedure. Reeve waved jauntily towards the man on the deck. The man waved back with three fingers, keeping one finger and a thumb around his glass, a very superior gesture. I'm up here, he was saying, and that's a place *you'll* never be.

But Reeve wasn't so sure about that.

He was still watching the two men and the dog when Duhart puked.

It came up pink and half-digested, a half-sub special and a can of cherry Coke. The $3.49 brunch floated on the surface of the water while Duhart rested his forehead against the side of the boat. Reeve cut the engine and shuffled forward towards him.

"You okay?" he said, louder than was necessary.

"I'll be fine — feel better already."

Reeve was crouching close by him, his head angled as though staring at his friend's face. But through the thick black lenses he was studying the layout of the garden where the man and the dog still played. He saw another dog pad around the side of the house, sniffing with its nose to the grass. When it saw there was a game in progress, it bounded onto the lawn. The first dog didn't look too thrilled, and they snapped at each other's faces until the man with the ball barked a command.

"Be still!"

And they both lay down in front of him.

The man on the deck was still watching the boat. He'd made no comment, hadn't even wrinkled his face at the sudden jetsam. Reeve patted Duhart's back and returned to the back of the boat, restarting the outboard. He decided he had an excuse to turn back, so brought the boat around, bringing him closer to where the dogs were now playing together.

"Hey," the man with the dogs called to his friend, "your turn to check if Blood's crapped on the front lawn!"

It was the sort of confirmation Reeve needed. The two men weren't owners — they weren't even guests — they were guards, hired hands. None of the other houses seemed to boast the same level of protection. He'd been told that Allerdyce was a very private man, an obsessive — just the kind of person to have security men and guard dogs, and maybe even more than that. Reeve scanned the lawn but couldn't see any obvious security — no trips or cameras. Which didn't mean they weren't there. He couldn't explain it, but he got the feeling he'd located Allerdyce's house.

He counted the other homes, the ones between Allerdyce's and the end of the building land. There were five of them. Driving out from Alexandria, he would pass five large gates. The sixth gate would belong to the head of Alliance Investigative.

Reeve was looking forward to meeting him.

They set off back to the boat club, then drove back out towards Allerdyce's home. Duhart hadn't said much; he still looked a bit gray. Reeve counted houses, then told him to pull over. To the side of the gate was an intercom with a camera above it. Behind the gate, an attack dog loped past. The stone walls on either side of the gates were high, but not impossible. There was nothing on the top of them, no wire or glass or spikes, all of which told Reeve a lot.

"You wouldn't go in for all the security we've seen, then leave the walls around your house unprotected," he said.

"So?"

"So there must be some sensing devices."

"There are the dogs."

Reeve nodded. "There are the dogs," he agreed. But when the dogs weren't around, there would be other measures, less visible, harder to deal with. "I just hope they're a permanent feature," he said.

The inflatable dinghy was big enough for one fully grown man, and a cheap buy.

That night, Duhart drove Reeve out to Piscataway Park, on the other side of the Potomac from Mount Vernon.

"Half of me wants to come with you," Duhart whispered at water's edge.

"I like the other half of you better," Reeve said. He was blacked up — clothes, balaclava, and face paint bought at Wayne's — not because he thought *he'd* need it, more for the effect he thought it might have on Allerdyce. And on anyone else for that matter. All he had to do was paddle across the river and upstream a mile or so — in silence, under cover of darkness, without anything giving him away. He hoped there were no garden parties in progress, no late-night drinks on the sundeck. He hoped there wasn't too much traffic on the Potomac this time of night.

He felt the way he had done at the start of so many missions: not scared at all, but excited, energized, ready for it. He remembered now why he'd loved Special Forces: he'd lived for risk and adrenaline, life and death. Everything had a startling clarity at moments like this: a sliver of moon in bristling reflection on the edge of the water; the moist whites of Duhart's eyes and the creases in his cheek when he winked; the tactile feel of the plastic oar, its grip grooved out for his four fingers. He splashed ankle deep into the water and eased into the dinghy. Duhart waved him off. The PI had his instructions. He was to go somewhere they knew him — a bar, anyplace. It had to be some way away. He was to stay there and get himself noticed. Those were his instructions. *If* anything went wrong, Reeve didn't want any of the shit hitting Duhart.

Which didn't mean he didn't want Duhart back here — or, more accurately, parked outside Allerdyce's gates — in three hours' time . . .

He paddled upriver, keeping to the bank opposite the houses. In darkness it was hard to differentiate one house from the other; they all seemed to have the same huge expanse of garden, the same jetty, even the same gazebo. He paddled until the dwellings ended, then counted back to the house he was betting belonged to Allerdyce. The homes on either side looked to be in darkness. Reeve checked for river traffic. A boat was chugging upriver. He hugged the bank, trusting to darkness. There were a couple of people on the boat deck, but they couldn't see him.

Finally, when all was quiet again, he paddled across the width of the river until he reached the house on Allerdyce's right. He got out of the dinghy and deflated it, letting it float away, pushing the paddle after it. He was next to the wall which separated the two estates. It was a high stone wall covered with creepers and moss. Reeve hauled himself up and peered into the gloom. There were lights burning in Allerdyce's house. He heard a distant cough, and saw wisps of smoke rising from the gazebo. He waited, and saw a pinpoint of red as the guard sucked on a cigarette.

Reeve lowered himself back into the neighbors' garden and produced a package from inside his jacket, unwrapping the two slabs of choice meat that he'd drugged using a mixture of articles freely available in any pharmacy. He tossed both slices over the wall and waited again. He was prepared to wait awhile.

In fact, it took about five minutes for the dogs' keen noses to locate the tidbits. He could hear them slobbering and slavering. There were no human sounds; the other guard wasn't with them. They were free to wander the estate. This was good news: it meant the movement-sensitive lights and other devices had almost certainly been kept switched off. They'd be for use only when the dogs weren't around. Reeve heard the eating sounds stop, the noise of sniffing — greedy things were looking for more — then silence. He gave it another five minutes, then hauled himself over the top of the wall and into Jeffrey Allerdyce's garden. There was no sign of the dogs. The sleeping draft would have taken its time to act. They'd be elsewhere. He hoped they were sleeping somewhere they couldn't be seen.

He stayed close to the wall, feeling it at his back, and moved towards the gazebo. The guard was sitting facing the water, his back to Reeve. Reeve moved quickly and quietly across the muffling lawn. He held the dagger by its scabbard, the handle showing, and swung it, clubbing the guard across the side of his head. The man was dazed, but not quite out. He was half-turning, opening his mouth, when Reeve's fist caught him full in the face. The second blow knocked him cold. Reeve got out tape and did the man's ankles, wrists, and mouth, making sure the nose wasn't broken or blocked, making sure the guard wouldn't suffocate. He felt in the pockets for a gun, but there wasn't one, just loose change and cigarettes. He didn't recognize the face; it figured — there had to be two shifts, maybe three.

He looked around. There were French windows to the back of the house. He wondered if they were locked. He also wondered where the second guard was. Indoors? He ran in a crouch towards the French windows. Lights shone inside. He was looking through the glass when he heard a growl behind him. One of the dogs. It looked very alert. Too alert. So only one of them had found the meat. The dog galloped towards him, and he pointed an arm at it.

"Be still!"

The dog stopped short, a little confused. It recognized the words but not the person uttering them, but then it was used to obeying more than one master . . . Reeve plunged the dagger two-handed into the top of its head, just behind the skull. The dog's legs buckled and it went down, Reeve maintaining the pressure. He glanced through the window to see if anyone had been roused. All he saw was the reflection of a man blackened up so that the brightest things about him were the whites of his eyes, his gritted teeth, and the blade in his hands.

He pulled the knife out and wiped it on the dog's coat. The French windows were unlocked. He took off his boots, left them hidden below the level of the porch, and let himself into the house.

His socks left no marks on the carpet, and the floor was solid, so his weight did not cause it to creak. The room was a dining room. He noticed that the small table had only one place setting, and there was only one chair. He was surer than ever that this was the right house.

He opened the door to a large octagonal hall with several doors off of it. A staircase led up to a landing, similarly octagonal, with more doors. Music was playing somewhere, behind one of the doors on the ground floor. Reeve walked over to the door, all too aware that if anyone stepped out of a room upstairs they would see him immediately. He had to be quick. He peered through the keyhole and saw a man sitting on a sofa, reading a magazine and nodding to the music. It was on a personal stereo, and must have been turned up all the way; even from here Reeve could recognize it: "Don't Fear the Reaper." The man was short and wiry: he didn't look like prime bodyguard material.

Reeve knew his best bet was to rush him. His hand tightened on the door handle. A clock in the room started to chime. Reeve burst in.

In a mirror above the fireplace, Reeve saw what the man could see: a massive snarling intruder with a bloodied knife so big you could quarter a buffalo with it. The man stood up, mouth gaping, the stereo dropping to the floor, the headphones falling from his ears.

"No noise," Reeve said quietly over the chimes. "Just lie down on the floor with your hands —"

Half a second before the man sprang into action, Reeve saw the change in his face — saw that the surprise had worn off already and he wasn't ready just to lie down. The man's body twisted, sending a powerful leg towards Reeve's groin. Reeve twisted too, the blow landing on his thigh, almost dead-legging him.

Small: yes; wiry: yes — but this guy had some martial arts training. The second blow, a fist this time, was already coming, aiming to disable the dagger. Blue Öyster Cult was still erupting from the headphones. All that was left of the chimes was an echo. Reeve dodged the fist and lashed out a roundhouse of his own. He wished he'd kept his shoes on. The blow glanced off the man's chest. The heel of a shoe slammed down onto Reeve's unprotected foot. His opponent was fast *and* smart. Reeve dummied with the dagger and swung his free hand into the man's throat. That felt better. The man's face and neck reddened as the oxygen tried to get through. Reeve followed up with a kick to the right knee and was readying to use an elbow, but the man hurled himself over the sofa and got to his feet again quickly. They hadn't made much noise yet; you didn't when you were concentrating. You hadn't time to think about screaming. Reeve hoped Allerdyce wasn't pushing some panic button somewhere. He had to make this quick.

His opponent had other plans. He tipped the sofa over so that Reeve had to dodge it: he was hemming Reeve in, making it awkward for him to move. Reeve launched himself over the sofa and hit the man full in the stomach, knocking him backwards onto the carpet. Reeve stuck the tip of the dagger to the man's stomach, just below the rib cage.

"I'll gut you like a fish," he snarled. He was kneeling on the man's legs. "Ask yourself, is he paying you enough?"

The small man considered this. He shook his head.

"Lie on your front," Reeve ordered. "I'm only going to tie you up."

The man obeyed, and Reeve got out the tape. He was breathing hard, his hands shaking slightly. And he had eyes only for the man on the floor; he didn't want the bastard trying anything else. After he'd taped wrists, ankles, and mouth — using double runs on the wrists and feet — he pulled the sofa upright and lifted the man's stereo by its headphones, bringing it over and clamping the 'phones to the man's head. He checked the pockets again. No gun.

But the man standing in the doorway had a gun.

"Who are you?" the man said. He was wearing a paisley dressing gown with frilled tassels hanging from the cord, pale pink pajamas, and burgundy slippers. He fitted the description Duhart had given.

"Mr. Allerdyce?" Reeve said, like they were meeting over canapés.

"Yes." It was a small-caliber revolver, the kind molls kept in purses in the books Duhart read. But Allerdyce was holding it steadily enough.

"My name's —"

"Let's get rid of the dagger first."

Reeve threw the dagger onto the sofa. He didn't have his hands up yet, but Allerdyce gestured with the gun, so he raised them.

"My name's Reeve, Gordon Reeve. I wanted a word with you."

"You could have come to my office, Mr. Reeve."

"Maybe. But this was personal, not business."

"Personal? I don't understand."

"Yes you do. Men hired by your organization have been following me." Reeve paused. "Are you sure you want to talk about this in front of witnesses?"

Allerdyce seemed to see the guard for the first time. The music was still blaring, but there was no telling what else he could hear.

"I should telephone for the police."

"Yes, sir, you should," Reeve agreed.

Allerdyce thought about this. Reeve stared at him levelly throughout.

"Upstairs," Allerdyce said at last.

Reeve preceded him up the staircase.

They went to a small sitting room. Allerdyce motioned for Reeve to sit down.

"Is it okay if I take my sock off?"

"What?"

"The guy downstairs stomped me pretty hard; I want to check the damage." Allerdyce nodded, keeping his distance. Reeve rolled down the sock. The foot wasn't that bad, some swelling, and there'd be a good bruise, but nothing was damaged. He made it look worse than it was, easing the sock off with infinite slowness, grimacing as he manipulated his toes.

"Looks sore," Allerdyce agreed.

"That bastard knew his stuff." Reeve put the sock back on. He saw bottles and glasses on top of a walnut-veneered cabinet. "Can I have a drink?"

Allerdyce considered this, too. Then nodded.

Reeve hobbled over to the cabinet, whistling as he examined the bottles. "Royal Lochnager — you have good taste."

"You're Scottish, Mr. Reeve?"

"You know damned well I am. You've probably got a big fat file on me. I'd like to know why."

"I assure you I don't know the first thing about you."

Reeve turned his head and smiled. "Do you want one?"

"Why not?"

Reeve fixed both drinks and turned toward Allerdyce.

"Leave mine on the cabinet," Allerdyce said. He waited until Reeve had hobbled back to the sofa, then backed his way to the cabinet, keeping the revolver on Reeve. Maybe the thing wasn't even loaded, but Reeve didn't want to take that risk, not yet. Allerdyce picked up the glass and came back around to face Reeve.

"*Slainte,*" Reeve said, drinking deep.

"*Slainte,*" Allerdyce echoed, like he'd used the toast before.

"You going to call the police?" Reeve asked.

"I think I'd better, don't you? A man has broken into my house, overpowered my dogs and my guards; that sounds like a man the police should know about."

"Will they allow me one phone call?"

"What?"

"In Britain, we get one phone call."

"You'll get a phone call."

"Good, I wonder which paper I'll call."

Allerdyce seemed amused.

"See," Reeve went on, "those two deadbeats you had following me in Scotland, they didn't just tell me they were working for you, they told a whole pub. Witnesses, Mr. Allerdyce. A precious commodity." He worked his injured foot again.

Allerdyce took another sip of whiskey. "I don't know what you're talking about."

"No? Are you quite sure? I mean, if you're sure then I owe you an apology. But you'll have to tell me about CWC first."

"Excuse me?"

"Co-World Chemicals. They murdered my brother. Or maybe they hired *your* people to kill him."

"Now wait a minute —"

"Or maybe all you did was compile a dossier on him. I believe that's your specialty. And then you handed it over and washed your hands. Don't you think you should have gone to the police? I mean, when my brother was found dead. Oh, no, you couldn't have done that, could you? The police might have had you for conspiracy, or aiding and abetting. Not a very good advertisement for Alliance Investigative." Reeve finished the whiskey.

"Your brother . . ." Allerdyce choked off the sentence.

"What?" Reeve raised his eyebrows. "You did know about him, didn't you?"

"Yes, I . . ." Allerdyce was perspiring. "No, I've never heard of . . . your brother." His face had lost its color, and he was having trouble focusing. "I think I'm . . ."

Reeve stood up and went to fix another drink. Allerdyce didn't try to stop him. The gun was hanging by his side, the empty glass held loosely in his other hand.

"Hope I didn't give you too much," Reeve said from the drinks cabinet.

"Too . . . much . . . what?"

Reeve turned towards him, smiling again. "Too much birdy," he said. "I had a little packet of it in my sock."

"Birdy?"

"Know what? Maybe you should know all about birdy. It could revolutionize your business." Reeve raised his replenished glass. "*Slainte.*"

This time the toast was not returned.

*   *   *

The thing about *burundanga* is, it is not just a truth drug. It makes the victim completely compliant. Completely suggestible. The victim becomes a sleepwalker. Men and women have been gang-raped after being tricked into taking it. They return to their senses forty-eight hours later and have no recollection. Amnesia. They could have been holding up banks, or emptying their own accounts, or playing in porno movies, or carrying drugs across borders. They'll do what they're told, no qualms, and will wake up with little more than a bad feeling, a feeling like their mind's not their own. That was why you had to judge the doses just right, so as not to do too much damage to the victim's mind.

It wasn't simply a truth drug the way sodium pentothal was — it was so much better than that.

"Sit down," Reeve told Allerdyce. "Take the weight off. I'm just going to look around. Anywhere special I should be looking?"

"What?"

"Do you keep any files here? Anything about me or my brother?"

"All my files are here." Allerdyce still looked confused. He was frowning like someone on a geriatric ward faced with their children, not recognizing them.

"Can you show me where?" Reeve said.

"Surely." Allerdyce got up again. He wasn't overly steady on his pins. Reeve hoped he hadn't given him too much. He hoped he hadn't just given this old man a massive dose of scopolamine.

They walked out of the room and took a left. Allerdyce slipped a hand into the pocket of his dressing gown.

"What have you got there, Mr. Allerdyce?"

"A key." Allerdyce blinked his moist yellow eyes. "I keep this room locked."

"Okay, unlock the door." Reeve took a look over the rail. The hall below was empty and quiet. Mr. Blue Öyster Cult probably wasn't worrying about anything. He'd seen his employer train a gun on the intruder. He'd be waiting either for a shot or for the police to arrive.

Allerdyce pushed open the door. The room was part library, part office. There was a lot of shiny new plastic around — fax, photocopier, shredder — but also a lot of antique wood and leather. The chair behind the desk was immense, more throne than chair, and covered in buttoned red leather. There was a matching sofa. The walls were book-lined, floor to ceiling. Some of the shelves were behind glass, and these housed the most precious-looking volumes. There were no filing cabinets, but there were files.

A lot of files.

They stood in towers which threatened to topple at any moment, slueing paper everywhere. Some of the towers were six feet high, resting in the corners of the room, giving it a musty, unventilated smell. There were more files on the sofa, and on the floor in front of it, and others beside the desk. Older files had been tidied away into big cardboard boxes — ordinary grocery boxes like you picked up in supermarkets, advertising chili beans and dishwasher powder and Planters peanuts.

"Have you never heard of computers, Mr. Allerdyce?" Reeve said, looking around him.

"I don't trust computers. With the right equipment, you can tap into a computer from a distance. To get this lot, someone would have to get very close indeed."

"Well, you've got a point. Where are the relevant files?"

"*File*, singular. It's on the desk. I was browsing through it earlier tonight, doing some updating."

"Why don't you sit on the sofa, Mr. Allerdyce?"

But there was no space. Allerdyce just stared at the sofa like a pet who'd been given an impossible command. Reeve cleared off some of the files so Allerdyce could sit down. Then Reeve sat behind the desk.

"You know about my brother?" he asked.

"Yes."

"Did your people kill him?"

"No."

"Then who did?"

"There's no proof he didn't kill himself."

"Take it from me, he was murdered."

"I don't know anything about it."

Reeve accepted this. He opened a gray folder and started separating the handwritten sheets. There were photographs there, too. "But you have your suspicions?"

"Surely."

"CWC?"

"It's feasible."

"Oh, it's feasible all right. Who's Dulwater?"

"He works for me."

"Why did you have me followed?"

"I wanted to know about you, Mr. Reeve."

"Why?"

"To see what Kosigin was up against."

"Kosigin?"

"You're reading his file."

Reeve picked up one of the photographs. It showed a boyish young man with steel-rimmed glasses and salt-and-pepper hair. He turned the photo towards Allerdyce, who nodded slowly.

Marie Villambard had spoken about Kosigin, how he'd set up the rigged investigation involving Preece and the others. Reeve had expected him to be older.

"What can you tell me about Kosigin?"

"It's all there in his file."

Reeve read it through.

"You've been following him," he said.

"Yes."

"Why?"

"I want him."

"I don't understand."

"I want him for my . . . collection." Allerdyce looked around the room.

Reeve nodded. "You're a blackmailer? That's your hobby?"

"Not at all, I just like to collect people, people who may be useful to me."

"I get it." Reeve kept reading. Then he came to the other photographs. One of them showed two men on a marina, sailboat masts sticking up behind them. One of the men was Kosigin.

The other was Jay.

"Housey-housey," Reeve said. He got up and took the picture over to the sofa. "You know this man?"

"Kosigin has hired him to do some work. I think he's called Jay."

"That's right. Jay."

"I don't know much more. He's rumored at one time to have been in the SAS." Allerdyce's eyes seemed to focus for a moment. "You were in the SAS, too, Mr. Reeve."

Reeve breathed in. "How do you know that?"

"Dulwater broke into your house. He found some magazines."

"*Mars and Minerva?*"

"Yes, that's the name."

"Did your man plant any bugs?"

"No, but he found some."

"Who do you think was bugging me?"

"I presume Kosigin."

Reeve went back to the desk and sat down. "Is Dulwater still watching my house?"

"No, he knew it was empty. Your wife and son are elsewhere."

Reeve sucked in breath again. "Do you know where?"

Allerdyce shook his head. "They're of little concern to me. My concern in all this is Kosigin."

"Well then, we're on the same side . . . as far as that goes." Reeve checked his watch. "What about you, Mr. Allerdyce?"

"What about me?"

"Do *you* have any secrets? Any skeletons?"

Allerdyce shook his head slowly but firmly.

"Where's Dulwater now?"

"I'm not entirely sure."

"You're not?"

"No. He's just returned from the UK. He's probably at home asleep."

Reeve checked his watch again. "Mr. Allerdyce, I'd like you to do something for me."

"Surely."

"Could you switch on your photocopier and copy this file for me?"

Allerdyce got up from the sofa and went to switch on the machine. "It takes a moment to warm up."

"That's fine. I'll be back in a minute."

Reeve went out onto the landing and looked down on Mr. Blue Öyster Cult, who was wriggling his way across the hall. He stopped when he saw Reeve looking at him. Reeve smiled and started down the stairs. The man was moving with more urgency now, trying to get to the door. Reeve walked beside him for a foot or two, then swept a leg back and kicked him on the side of the head with the meat of his stockinged heel. He dragged the unconscious figure back into the room, used more tape to bind him to the heaviest-looking table, and picked up the dagger.

Outside, he pulled his boots on and went and found the drugged dog. It was lying in front of some bushes near the gates. Anyone walking past could have seen it, but then nobody walked around here. Reeve dragged it deep into the shadows and taped its legs together, then wound more tape around its mouth. It was breathing deeply throughout, almost snoring.

Around the back of the house again, the guard in the gazebo looked like he'd been struggling for a while. It was good tape; the U.S. Postal Service used it for taping parcels. It had nylon crosspieces — you could cut it, or tear it with your teeth, but no way could you snap it. This hadn't stopped the guard from trying.

Reeve walked up to the man and punched him unconscious again.

Back in Allerdyce's den, the old man had nearly finished the copying. Reeve found an empty folder and put the warm copies into it.

"Mr. Allerdyce," he said, "I think you'd better get dressed."

They went to the old man's bedroom. It was the smallest room Reeve had seen so far, smaller even than the bathroom which adjoined it.

"You're a sad old bastard really, aren't you?" Reeve was talking to himself, but Allerdyce heard a question.

"I never consider sadness," he said. "Nor loneliness. Keep them out of your vocabulary and you keep them out of your heart."

"What about love?"

"Love? I loved as a young man. It was very time-consuming and not very productive."

Reeve smiled. "No need to bother with a tie, Mr. Allerdyce."

Allerdyce hung the tie back up.

"How do the gates open?"

"Electronically."

"We're walking out of the gates. Do we need a remote?"

"There's one in the drawer downstairs."

"Where downstairs?"

"The Chinese table near the front door. In a drawer."

"Fine. Tie your shoelaces."

Allerdyce was like a child. He sat on the bed and worked on the laces of his five-hundred-dollar shoes.

"Okay? Let me look at you. You look fine, let's go."

True to his word, Duhart had come back. The car was parked outside, blocking the gates. His jaw dropped when he saw the gates open and Reeve come walking out, dressed like something from a Rambo film, with Jeffrey Allerdyce following at his heels.

"Get in the back, Mr. Allerdyce," Reeve ordered.

"Jesus Christ, Reeve! You can't kidnap him! What the fuck is this?"

Reeve got into the passenger seat. "I've not kidnapped him. Mr. Allerdyce, will you please tell my friend that you've come with me of your own volition."

"Own volition," Allerdyce mumbled.

Duhart still looked like a man in the middle of a particularly bad dream. "What the fuck is he on, man?"

"Just drive," said Reeve.

Reeve cleaned up a bit in the car. They went to Duhart's apartment, where he cleaned up some more and put on fresh clothes. Allerdyce sat on a chair in a living room probably smaller and less tidy than anywhere he'd ever been in his adult life. Duhart wasn't comfortable with any of this: here was his idol, his god, sitting in his goddamned apartment — and Reeve kept swearing Allerdyce wouldn't remember any of it.

"Just go get the stuff," Reeve said.

Duhart giggled nervously, rubbed his hands over his face.

"Just go get the stuff." Reeve was beginning to wish he'd given Duhart a dose of birdy, too.

"Okay," Duhart said at last, but he turned at the door and had another look at the scene within: Reeve in his tourist duds, and old man Allerdyce just sitting there, hands on knees, like a ventriloquist's dummy waiting for the hand up the back.

While Duhart was away, Reeve asked Allerdyce a few more questions, and tried to work out where they went from here, or rather, *how* they went from here. Allerdyce wouldn't remember anything, but the two guards would. Then there was the corpse of the dog to explain. Reeve didn't reckon Mr. Blue Öyster Cult had heard much, if anything, of his short dialogue with Allerdyce. So all they'd know was that there'd been an intruder — an intruder who'd fucked with Allerdyce's mind. They'd be wondering what else he'd fucked with.

Duhart was back within the hour, carrying a shoe box. Reeve opened it. Smothered in cotton wool, like a schoolboy's collection of bird eggs, were listening devices of various shapes, sizes, and ranges.

"They all work?"

"Last time I used them," Duhart said.

Reeve rooted to the base of the shoe box. "Have you got the recorders to go with these?"

"In the car," Duhart said. "So what about Dulwater?"

"I want *you* to keep tabs on *him*."

Duhart shook his head. "What am I into here?"

"Eddie, by the time you've finished, you'll have so much dirt on our pal here he'll have to give you a senior partnership. Swear to God."

"God, huh?" Duhart said, staring at Allerdyce.

Duhart brought his car to a stop beside the entry / exit ramp of the Alliance Investigative building. Reeve told Eddie Duhart to stay in the car, but not to leave the engine idling. They didn't want him stopped by nosy cops. It was four in the morning: he'd have some explaining to do.

"Can't I come with you? Man, I never been in there."

"You want to be the star of *Candid Camera*, Eddie?" Reeve turned in the passenger seat. Allerdyce sat so quietly in the back it was easy to forget him. "Mr. Allerdyce, does your building have security cameras?"

"Oh, yes."

Reeve turned back to Duhart. "I don't mind them seeing me; Allerdyce is already going to have a grudge against *me*. Do you want him to have a grudge against you, Eddie?"

"No," Duhart said sullenly.

"Well, okay," said Reeve, picking up his large plastic carrier bag and getting out of the car. He opened the back door for Allerdyce.

"Which way would you usually go in?"

"Through the garage and up the elevator."

"Can you open the garage?"

Allerdyce reached into his coat and produced a chain of about a dozen keys.

"Let's do it," Reeve said.

He briefed Allerdyce as they walked the few steps to the garage entrance. "I'm a friend, in from England, if anybody asks. We've been up drinking half the night, tried but couldn't sleep. I asked you to show me the offices. If anyone asks."

Allerdyce repeated all this.

"The only guard is in the lobby," Allerdyce said, "and he's used to me coming in at all hours. I prefer the building when it's empty; I don't like my staff."

"I'm sure the feeling's mutual. Shall we?"

They stood in front of the garage's roller door. There was a concrete post to one side with an intercom, a slot for entry cards, and a keyhole to override everything. Allerdyce turned the key, and the door clattered open. They walked down the slope into the Alliance Investigative building.

Allerdyce was right: there was no guard down here, but there were security cameras. Reeve put an arm around Allerdyce and laughed at some joke the old man had just told him.

"The cameras," he said, "are the screens up in the lobby?"

"Yes," Allerdyce said. Reeve grinned again for the cameras. "And do they just show or do they record as well?"

"They record."

Reeve didn't like that. When the elevator arrived and they got in, Allerdyce slotted another key home.

"What's that for?"

"Executive levels. There are two of them — offices and penthouse. You need a key to access them."

"Okay," Reeve said as the doors slid closed.

Reeve guessed the security man would be watching the elevator lights. At the second story from the top, the elevator opened and they got out. Allerdyce's office door was locked by a keypad. He pushed in four digits and opened it.

Reeve got to work. There were no security cameras up here — the senior partners obviously didn't like to be spied on. Reeve placed one bug inside the telephone apparatus and taped another to the underside of the desk. The phone rang suddenly, causing him to jump. He answered it. It was the front desk.

"Good evening," Reeve said, drawing out each word, like he'd had a few.

"Mr. Allerdyce there?" the man asked, pleasant but suspicious, too.

"Would you like to speak to him? Jeffrey, there's a man here wants to speak to you."

Allerdyce took the phone. "Yes?" he said. He listened, Reeve listening right beside him. "No, it's just an old friend. We've been drinking, couldn't sleep. I'm showing him around." A pause to listen. "Yes, I know you have to check. It's what I pay you for. No trouble, good night."

Reeve took the receiver and put it back in its cradle.

"Nice one, Jeffrey," he said.

"These security men," Allerdyce said, yawning. "I pay them too much. They sit on their asses all night and call it working."

"We're finished in here," Reeve said. Then he saw the headed letter paper on the desk. "No, wait — sit down, Mr. Allerdyce. I want you to write something. Will you do that?" He lifted a pen and handed it to Allerdyce, then placed a sheet of the elegant paper in front of him. "Just write what I tell you: 'I invited Mr. Gordon Reeve to my home and took him on a tour of my business premises. I did these things of my own free will and under no restraint or coercion.' That's all, just sign it and date it."

Reeve plucked the paper from him and folded it in four. It wasn't much — he wasn't even sure it qualified as insurance — but if the cops ever *did* come asking, at least he could make things a bit sticky for Allerdyce . . .

They took the elevator down a couple of floors to where Alfred Dulwater shared an office. The door was locked, but Allerdyce had a key for it.

"Do you have keys to all the offices?" Reeve asked.

"Of course."

"Do you ever come here at night and rifle everyone's drawers?"

"Not everyone's."

"Jesus, no wonder you're a PI."

Reeve opened his bag, took out the shoe box and tool kit, and got to work again. Another bug in the telephone, another under Dulwater's desk, and one for good measure under his colleague's desk. There was nothing in the room about either James or Gordon Reeve, nothing about Kosigin or CWC, which was what he'd expected. Like Allerdyce had said, Dulwater reported directly to him. As little in writing as possible.

They started downstairs again. Reeve had another idea. He told Allerdyce what to do, and then pressed the button for the lobby. The two of them marched up to the front desk. The guard there stood up and straightened his clothes; he was obviously in awe of Allerdyce. Allerdyce went to say something, but yawned mightily instead.

"Late night?" the guard said with a smile. Reeve shrugged blearily.

"Donald," Allerdyce said, "I'd like the video of tonight."

"The recording, sir?"

"Alan here has never seen himself on TV."

The guard looked to "Alan." Reeve shrugged again and

beamed at him. Allerdyce was holding out his hand. "If you please, Donald?"

The guard unlocked a door behind him, which led to a windowless room with nothing but screens and banks of video recorders. The man ejected a tape, put in a fresh one, and came back out, locking the door after him.

"Thank you, Donald," Allerdyce said.

Reeve dropped the cassette into his bag. "Thanks, Donald," he echoed.

As they walked back towards the elevator, he heard the guard mutter: "The name's Duane . . ."

Outside, Duhart was waiting for them.

"Any trouble?" Reeve asked.

"No. You?"

Reeve shook his head. "I just hope those bugs are working."

Duhart smiled and held up a cassette player. He punched the Play button.

"Good evening." It was Reeve's own voice, tinny but clear.

"Mr. Allerdyce there?"

"Would you like to speak to him? Jeffrey . . ."

Reeve smiled an honest smile at Duhart, who began laughing.

"I can't believe we just did it," he said at last, wiping tears from his eyes. "I can't believe we just bugged the buggers!"

Reeve shook the shoe box. "There are a few left." He turned to the backseat. "Let's take Mr. Allerdyce home . . ."

They were aware, of course, that the Alliance building was swept top to bottom for bugs quite regularly. They were aware because Mr. Allerdyce told them so in answer to a question. The last debugging had been a week ago. The building would be swept again, of course, if Allerdyce discovered he'd paid this middle-of-the-night visit to his offices — but that would depend on the guard mentioning the visit. Allerdyce himself wouldn't remember a damned thing about it, wouldn't even know he'd left his own house. And the night-duty guard, Duane, might not mention the incident to anyone. It wasn't like it was going to be public knowledge around Alliance that Jeffrey Allerdyce had been drugged and used in this way.

No, Allerdyce wouldn't want *anyone* to know about that.

Reeve didn't want either of the guards at Allerdyce's home to see Duhart, but at the same time they couldn't leave the car outside for too long. A private police patrol cruised the vicinity once an hour, so Allerdyce said, so they took the car in through the gates and up the gravel drive. Duhart came with them into the house, and Reeve warned him not to go into one particular room downstairs, not to say anything, and not to leave his fingerprints. Duhart made the sign of zipping his lips.

They took Allerdyce upstairs to his bedroom.

"Mr. Allerdyce," Reeve said, "I think you must be exhausted. Get undressed and put your pajamas back on. Go to bed. Sleep well."

They closed the bedroom door after them and went to the office, which Reeve unlocked. Inside, they bugged the telephone, the underside of the desk, the underside of the photocopier, and the leg of the sofa.

Downstairs, they bugged the other telephones but none of the rooms — they'd run out of bugs. They got back into the car and started down the driveway.

"What the hell is that?" Duhart gasped.

It was a dog, its mouth, front and back legs taped, jerking across the lawn towards the driveway.

Reeve pushed the button on the remote and the gates swung silently inwards. After they'd driven out, he used the remote to close the gates, then rolled down his window and tossed the thing high over the stone wall.

He hoped it would miss the dog.

PART SEVEN
CONFESSIONAL

EIGHTEEN

REEVE DIDN'T HANG AROUND for the aftershock.

He flew out to Los Angeles that morning, grabbed a cab at the airport, and told the driver he wanted a cheap rental service.

"Cheapest I know is Dedman's Auto," the cabbie declared, enjoying showing off his knowledge. "The cars are okay — no stretch limos or nothing like that, just clean sedans."

"Dead man's?"

The cabbie spelled it for him. "That's why he keeps his rates so low. It's not the sort of name would leap out at you from Yellow Pages." He chuckled. "Christ knows, with a name like that would *you* go into car rental?"

Reeve was studying the cabbie's ID on the dashboard. "I guess not, Mr. Plotnik."

It turned out that Marcus Aurelius Dedman, the blackest man Reeve had ever seen, operated an auto-wrecking business, and car rental was just a sideline.

"See, mister," he said, "I'll be honest with you. The cars I get in here ain't always *so* wrecked. I spend a lot of time and money on them, get them fit for battle again. I hate to sell a car I've put heart and soul into, so I rent them instead."

"And if the client wrecks them, they come straight back for hospitalization?"

267

Dedman laughed a deep, gurgling laugh. He was about six feet four and carried himself as upright as a fence post. His short hair had been painstakingly uncurled and lay flat against his head like a Cab Calloway toupee. Reeve reckoned him to be in his early fifties. He had half a dozen black kids ripping cars apart for him, hauling out the innards.

"Nobody strips a vehicle quite like a kid from the projects," Dedman said. "Damned clever mechanics, too. Here's the current options." He waved a basketball player's arm along a line of a dozen dusty specimens, any of which would be perfect for Reeve's needs. He wanted a plain car, a car that wouldn't stand out from the crowd. These cars had their scars and war wounds — a chipped windshield here, a missing fender there, a rusty line showing where a strip of chrome had been torn off the side doors, a sill patched with mastic and resprayed.

"Take your pick," Dedman said. "All one price."

Reeve settled for a two-door Dodge Dart with foam-rubber suspension. It was dull green, the metallic sheen sanded away through time. Dedman showed him the engine ("reliable runner"), the interior ("bench seat'll come in handy at Lover's Point"), and the trunk. Reeve nodded throughout. Eventually, they went to Dedman's office to clinch the deal. Reeve got the feeling Dedman didn't want the project kids, no matter what their mechanical skills, to see any money changing hands. Maybe it would give them ideas.

The office was in a ramshackle cinder-block building, but surprised Reeve by being immaculately clean, bright, air-conditioned, and high-tech. There was a large black leather director's chair behind the new-looking desk. Dedman draped a sheet over the chair before sitting, so as not to dirty the leather with his overalls. There was a computer on the desk with a minitower hard disk drive. Elsewhere Reeve glimpsed a fax and answering machine, a large photocopier, a portable color TV, even a hot drinks machine.

"Grab a coffee if you want one," Dedman said. Reeve pushed two quarters into the machine and watched it deliver a brown plastic cup of brown plastic liquid. He looked around the office again. It had no windows; all the light was electrical. The door, too, was solid metal.

"I see why you keep it padlocked," Reeve said. Dedman had undone three padlocks, each one barring a thick steel bolt, to allow them into the office.

Dedman shook his head. "It's not to stop the kids seeing what's in here, if that's what you're thinking. Hell, it's the kids who bring me all this stuff. They get it from their older brothers. What am I supposed to do with a computer or a facsimile?" Dedman shook his head again. "Only they'd be hurt if I didn't look like I appreciated their efforts."

Reeve sat down and put the cup on the floor, not daring to sully the surface of the desk. He reached into his pocket for a roll of dollars. "I'm assuming you don't take credit cards," he said.

"Your assumption is correct. Now, there's no paperwork, okay? I don't like that shit." Dedman wrote something on a sheet of paper. "This is my name, the address here, and the telephone number. Anyone stops you, the cops or anybody, or if you're in a crash, the story is you borrowed the car from me with my blessing."

"Insurance?"

"It's insured."

"And if I break down?"

"Well" — Dedman sat back in his chair — "for another thirty, you get my twenty-four-hour call-out service."

"Does it stretch as far as San Diego?"

Dedman looked at the roll of notes. "I guess that wouldn't be a problem. That where you're headed?"

"Yes. So how much do I owe you?"

Dedman appeared to consider this, then named a figure Reeve found comfortably low. Reeve counted out the bills and made to hand them over, but paused.

"The Dart isn't hot, is it?"

Dedman shook his head vehemently. "No, sir, it's aboveboard and legal." He took the bills and counted them, finding the sum satisfactory. He looked at Reeve and smiled. "I never rent a hot car to a tourist."

*   *   *

Dedman had warned Reeve that he might get lost a few times on his way out of Los Angeles, an accurate assessment of Reeve's first hour and a half in his new car. He knew all he had to do was follow the coast, eventually picking up I-5, but finding the coast was the problem initially, and keeping to it proved a problem later. The freeway system around Los Angeles was like a joke God was playing on the human brain. The more Reeve focused his mind, the less sense things made. Eventually he let his eyes and mind drift into soft focus, and found himself miraculously on the right road, heading the right way. He wasn't on the coast, he was inland on I-5, but that was fine. I-5 was fine.

He had both windows open and wished he had a radio. One of Dedman's mechanics had offered him one, installation included, for fifty bucks, but it would've meant hanging around the break-ing yard for another hour or so, and Reeve had been keen to get going. Now he wished he'd taken the teenager up on the offer. Everything about the Dart was fine except the axles. The steering wheel juddered in his hands at speeds above fifty, and it felt like the problem led directly from the axles, either front or back. He hoped a wheel didn't spin off and roll away ahead of him.

Once on the interstate, it was a quick run to San Diego. He came off near the airport and took Kettner Boulevard into the downtown district. He wanted a different hotel from last visit, and something more central, something much closer to the CWC building. His first choice, the Marriott, had rooms. Reeve swallowed hard when told the price, but was too tired to go look-ing anywhere else — the previous night had been a long one, after all. He took his bag up to the room; pulled open the curtains, flooding the room with light and a spectacular view of the bay; and sat down on the bed.

Then he picked up the telephone and rang Eddie Duhart.

He didn't identify himself. He just asked, "What's happening?"

Duhart couldn't wait to tell him. "*Everything's* happening! Allerdyce is running around like there's a cactus up his ass and all the proctologists are in Hawaii. He knows something happened to him last night, only he doesn't know what."

"He's back to himself?"

"Seems to be. First thing he did was sack the bodyguards. Then he decided that was too lenient, so they're back on the payroll till he can find a worse fate. Next he phoned for a vet and a van to take away the carcass."

"But he doesn't remember any details from last night?"

"Not a one. Man, I should get my hands on some of that stuff. He's spent all day trying to put together the pieces. You should hear him. Man is he wild! He dropped into a private hospital, checked in as an emergency. He wanted them to run tests on him. He's been doing everything. He thought maybe he's been hypnotized, so he's got a hypnotherapist coming over to the house to try to get him out of it."

"Hmm, he may have stumbled onto something."

"You think the hypnotist can help him remember?"

"I don't know. I've never heard of anyone trying it before."

"Christ, I hope he *doesn't* remember. He's been to my apartment!"

"Don't fret, Eddie. Has he been into the office?"

"No, and nothing from the bugs in Dulwater's office either, except that whoever he shares the space with has a flatulence problem."

"Allerdyce hasn't tried contacting Dulwater?"

"Well, he's made some calls and not gotten an answer; maybe he's been trying to catch him."

"And he hasn't contacted the police?"

Duhart clucked. "No, sir, no cops."

"Which tells you something."

"Yeah, it tells me a man like Jeffrey Allerdyce doesn't *need* cops. He knows someone broke into his house last night; it won't be long before he gets a gang in to sweep for clues. They'll find the bugs."

"Doesn't matter."

"How are you doing anyway?"

"Fine."

"Where are you?"

"Best you don't know. Remember, if . . . *when* the bugs are found, I want you to lie low, okay? That's the point at which you drop the investigation."

"Yeah, you said."

"I mean it. Allerdyce will be cagier than ever. He'll know he's being watched. Just step back and leave it alone."

"And then what?"

"Wait for me to get back to you. You've got other clients, right? Other cases you could be working on?"

"Sure, but I could work till I was a hundred and seventy, I'd never get another case like this. Hey, what if I need to contact you?"

"I'll phone twice a day, morning and evening."

"Yeah, but —"

Reeve broke the connection. He wasn't sure he'd ever call Duhart again.

There was a low late-afternoon sun beaming in on downtown San Diego, casting shadows between the blocks and lighting the windows of the buildings. The streets were busy with shoppers on their way home, standing sag-shouldered at bus and trolley stops. No office workers — this was the weekend. Reeve had an espresso in a coffee shop right across the street from the Co-World Chemicals building. There was an office-supply store next door to the coffee shop. It sold computers and other machines, plus mobile communications equipment. A cheap sign in the window said that it rented, too.

Reeve had rented a cellular phone. It wasn't much bigger than the palm of his hand. He'd put it on his credit card and handed over some cash as a deposit. The man in the store hadn't been too bothered about Reeve's lack of credentials. Maybe that was because he dealt with a lot of foreign business. Maybe it was because he knew he could always cancel Reeve's personal cell phone number, negating the little black telephone altogether. Hookup to the system was immediate.

So Reeve sat in the coffee shop and punched in some numbers. He tried Eddie Cantona's home first, but there was no answer. With the coffee shop's phone book in front of him on the window-length counter, he tried a couple of the bars Cantona had said he used. At the second bar, whoever had answered the call growled Cantona's name. Eddie Cantona picked up the telephone.

"Hello?" It sounded like he'd said "yellow."

"So they let you out?"

Cantona sucked in breath, and his voice dropped to a mumble. "Soon as you left town. That nice detective said I could go, but not to go talking to strange men anymore."

"This was Mike McCluskey?"

"The same. Where the fuck are you?"

"You think anyone's keeping tabs on you?"

"Well, hell, it wouldn't be hard. I only knew *you* a coupla days first time around, and how long did it take you to find me?"

"Three calls. This is the third."

"There you go. I got to tell you, Gordon, I've been drinking steadily and seriously for some days now. My excuse is that it's in memory of Jim — a one-man movable wake. But maybe it's because I took a jolt myself."

"I don't want to get you mixed up in anything. I just want to hire you for a day or so."

"Oh, is that all?" Cantona said, slipshop voice full of sarcasm. "Maybe you didn't hear what I just said."

"I heard."

The voice dropped low again. "I was *scared* back there, Mr. Reeve."

"I'm not asking you to do anything dangerous." Reeve had his free hand cupped around his mouth and the mouthpiece. Nobody in the coffee shop seemed interested in him; they were buying takeout cups for the walk to the bus stop. Traffic rumbled past, and the air-conditioning rattled like teeth in a glass. Reeve was in no danger of being overheard. "I just want you to sit in a coffee shop for a while. I want you to keep watch. If you see a man answering the description I give you, call me. That's it."

"You want me to follow him?"

"Nope."

"You just want to know when he leaves this building?" Cantona sounded far from convinced.

"Well, I'd rather know when he goes in. Come on, who else in this town can I trust? The only danger you'd be in is from caffeine poisoning, and they do a great decaf espresso here."

"No liquor license?"

"No liquor license. Hey, I'd want you sober."

"I don't work drunk!"

"Okay, okay. Listen, what do you say?"

"Can we meet? Maybe talk about it over a beer?"

"You know that's not a good idea."

"In case they're watching me, right?"

"Watching you or watching me. Safer if we don't meet."

"You're right. Okay, let's give it a stab."

This would not have been Reeve's favored choice of words.

He gave the details over the phone to Cantona — once Cantona had located some paper and a pen that worked. He told Cantona the address of the coffee shop, gave him its opening hours, and then described Kosigin, closing his eyes and picturing the photographs in Allerdyce's file. On the off chance, he described Jay, too. Finally, he gave Cantona his mobile number, and checked for him — Cantona was sobering fast — not only that there was a public pay phone in the coffee shop, but that it was working, too.

"Oh-seven-thirty hours," Cantona said. "I'll be in position. Guess I'd better go home now and dry out."

"Thanks."

"Hey, you'd do the same for me, right?"

Reeve wasn't sure about that. His next call was to the San Diego Police Department. McCluskey wasn't in the office, and they said they couldn't patch any calls through to him.

"Well, can you get a message to him? He'll want to hear it, believe me."

"Go ahead, I'll see what I can do." The woman had a high, whining voice, utterly without personality.

"Tell him Gordon Reeve would like to speak to him." He spelled his surname for her. It took three goes. "I'll keep trying."

"Sure."

"Thank you very much."

The young woman in charge of the coffee shop was relieved by the next shift. She seemed furious about something, maybe the fact that she'd been working on her own and they'd been really busy. Two people her own age — one male, one female — took her place, and soon had a rhythm going. One of them took the orders and the money, the other worked the machine. When the line had been served, the female walked over to Reeve with a pot of coffee and asked if he wanted a refill. Reeve smiled at her and shook his head, then watched her retreat, clearing a couple of the cramped tables as she did. He felt touched by her offer. He knew a lot of places in the United States had the same policy, the offer of coffee refills, but it seemed an act of kindness, too, and he hadn't been close to much kindness recently. He could feel defenses inside him, barricades he'd hastily erected. They tottered for a moment, but held. He thought of Bakunin and Wagner again, side by side on the barricades of Dresden. The anarchist Bakunin, and Wagner — the friend of Nietzsche. Nietzsche: the self-proclaimed first amoralist. When necessary, when events dictated, they had fought alongside each other. The anarchists would call that proof of the theory of mutual aid. They would say it repudiated Nietzsche's own theory, that the will to power was everything. Opposites reconciled, yes, but momentarily. Look at the role of Russia in World War Two: what happened afterwards was a descent into mistrust and selfishness. Just because you were allies didn't mean you didn't hate each other's guts.

"Jay," Reeve said quietly, staring at nothing beyond the smudged glaze of the window, the words "Donuts 'n' Best Coffee" stenciled on it in muted red.

Then he tried McCluskey again, and got through to the same woman.

"Oh, yes, Mr. Reeve. He said for you to give me your number there and he'll get back to you."

"No," Reeve said, and broke the connection again. He got up to leave the coffee shop, and realized by the stiffness in his legs how long he'd been sitting there. As he passed the cash register, he saw a glass tumbler beside it, half-filled with tips, nothing bigger than a quarter. He reckoned the shifts were college kids, and pushed a dollar into the glass.

"Hey, have a nice evening," the young woman said. She was choosing some music for the tape machine.

"You too."

Reeve crossed at the lights with the other pedestrians and checked his reflection in the windshield of a stopped bus. He didn't look any different from anyone else. He kept pace with a short woman in clacking high heels, so it almost looked like they were together but didn't know each other real well. He was half a step behind her as they passed the steps up to the glass revolving door, which led into the foyer of the CWC building. Above the revolving door, the CWC symbol was etched into the glass. It looked like a child had taken a line for a walk, so that a single doodle managed to spell out the letters *CWC*, like the CNN logo on a bad night.

The woman scowled at him eventually, figuring he was trying to pick her up by mime alone, and at the next street crossing, he took a right as she went straight ahead. It was another half a block before he realized someone was keeping half a pace behind *him*. He didn't look around, didn't make eye contact; he kept his gaze to the pavement, and that way could watch the man's feet: polished brown shoes with leather soles, charcoal suit trousers above them. Reeve took another right, into a quieter street. The shoes and trousers kept with him.

Must have picked me up outside the CWC building, he thought. It had to be Jay or one of his men. Thing was, they were too close for it to be mere surveillance. They didn't just want to follow him, they wanted contact. Reeve started fast, shallow breathing, oxygenating his blood, and loosened his shoulders, tightening his fists. He walked briskly, hoping he could get his retaliation in first. A couple of pedestrians were coming towards him. He stared hard at them as though trying to see into their souls. He was seeking accomplices. But all the couple saw was an angry man, and they moved out of his way.

It was as good a time as any. Reeve stopped abruptly and swiveled on his heels.

He hadn't noticed that the man in the charcoal suit had slowed his pace a few yards back, and was now standing still, seemingly at ease, his hands out in appeasement. He was a tall man with slick black hair, thinning at the temples. He had a sharp face and sallow cheeks, and the slightly narrowed eyes of one who sported contact lenses.

"This is just where I'd have chosen," the man was saying, "for the showdown, the confrontation."

"What?" Reeve was looking around upwards, looking for an assassin's gunsight, a slow-moving car with tinted windows, looking for danger. But all there was was this tall well-dressed man, who looked like he'd be comfortable trying to sell you a spare vest to go with your suit.

"Who the fuck are you?" Reeve snarled.

"I knew you'd come back here. That's why I flew direct, saved time. Don't ask me how I knew, I just felt it."

"What are you, a clairvoyant?"

"No, Mr. Reeve, I study personalities, that's all."

Reeve blinked. "Dulwater?"

The man made a small bow with his head. "I've been watching outside CWC for three hours."

"You should've stopped for a coffee."

"Ah, you were in the coffee shop?"

"What do you want?"

"Well, you seem to know who I am. I'm guessing you know what I want."

"Indulge me."

Dulwater took a step forwards. "I want to know what you did to my employer, Mr. Reeve."

Reeve frowned, trying to look puzzled.

Alfred Dulwater just smiled. "Might *I* make a guess?" he said.

"Go ahead."

Dulwater pouted thoughtfully. "I think it's know as *burundanga*."

Reeve tried not to look impressed.

"I've heard of it," Dulwater continued, "but this is the first occasion I've known someone to use it."

"I don't know what you're talking about."

"Mr. Allerdyce caught up with me an hour ago, by telephone. He had a very strange story to tell. Did the two London operatives tell you my name?" Reeve said nothing, which seemed to be what Dulwater was expecting. "They told me they hadn't, but I didn't believe them."

Though Reeve had been looking Dulwater in the eye, his peripheral vision had all been for the man's clothes. Dulwater didn't look armed, and he didn't look particularly dangerous. He was tall, a head taller than Reeve, but while his face showed cunning and intelligence there wasn't anything else there, nothing physical. Reeve reckoned he could take him out. He didn't relax, but he felt a little better.

"I know what you're thinking," Dulwater said.

"What?"

"You're thinking about violence. In particular, you're thinking of violence which might be perpetrated by you upon me. I shouldn't take that thought any further." Dulwater smiled again. "I've seen the psychiatric report."

Reeve remembered that Dulwater had been in his house. He knew what the man was talking about. He was talking about the warning. Any more fits of violence and Reeve might well be committed.

"I mean," said Dulwater, "after the scene in the bar . . ."

"Your men started it. I've got witnesses."

"Terrible mess those two are in — and you, Mr. Reeve, you don't have a scratch on you. How's the foot by the way? Kaprisky says he stomped on the intruder's bare foot."

Reeve stared levelly at Dulwater. "Nothing wrong with either foot," he said.

"I'm glad to hear it."

"So, what now?"

"Now? Now we go somewhere and have a talk. You see, we have a lot in common. We're both after information on Kosigin. And more than that . . ."

"Yes?"

Dulwater smiled. "Neither of us much likes Jeffrey Allerdyce."

*   *   *

They went to a bar. It might've been a bar Jim Reeve used to drink in, Gordon Reeve couldn't remember. While Dulwater went to the men's room, Reeve tried the Police Department again. This time he got through to Mike McCluskey, who sounded out of breath.

"Hey, Gordon," McCluskey said as if they were old friends, "where are you?"

"Near San Diego," Reeve told him.

"Yeah? Any reason for that?"

"I never do anything without a reason, McCluskey. I want us to talk."

"Sure, no problem. Let me take down your —"

"Later tonight." A waitress was advancing with the beers they'd ordered. Dulwater, rubbing his hands, was right behind her. "Say midnight."

"Midnight? Well, that's a funny —"

"La Jolla, remember that place we went for a drink after you showed me where my brother was murdered?"

"Now, Gordon, you know there's not one shred of evidence —"

"Outside there at midnight. If you're not alone, I don't show."

Dulwater sat down as Reeve cut the call. "What was that?" he asked.

"A sideshow," said Reeve, taking one of the glasses. He gulped an inch of liquid and licked his lips. "So why are we having this good-natured drink, Mr. Dulwater? How come you don't have me trussed up in a crate on my way back to Washington?"

Dulwater lifted his own beer but did not drink. "I like my job, Gordon; I like it fine. But I have ambition just like anyone else."

"You want to set up for yourself?"

Dulwater shook his head. "I want a promotion."

"Well, if you take me back to Allerdyce, I'm sure you'd be well placed . . ."

"No, that's not the way Allerdyce works. He'd only want

more. Besides, what are you to him? You're a one-night irritant, like a mild allergic reaction. You're not the prize."

"Kosigin?"

Dulwater nodded. "I get the feeling if I stick close to you, I'll get Kosigin."

"And then you hand Kosigin to Allerdyce?"

"But not all at once. He wouldn't be grateful if I just handed that bastard over. One little piece at a time."

Reeve shook his head. Everybody wanted something: Duhart wanted something on Allerdyce; Dulwater wanted something *over* Allerdyce; Allerdyce wanted Kosigin; Kosigin and Jay wanted Reeve.

And what did Gordon Reeve want? He thought of Nietzsche again: the will to power. Power was what most of these games were all about, the desire for power, the fear of loss of power. Reeve wasn't a part of the game. He was on another board with different pieces. He wanted *revenge*.

"You know," he said, "I'm not even sure I should be talking to someone who broke into my damned house."

Dulwater shrugged. "I wasn't the first. Alliance didn't plant those bugs, Kosigin's men did. Besides, what have you to lose by cooperating? You surely don't think you can do anything to harm Kosigin on your own."

"I'm not on my own."

"You've got help?" Dulwater thought for the merest second. "Cantona?" Reeve's face failed to disguise his surprise. "Cantona's a deadbeat. You think you can put him up against Kosigin?"

"How do you know about Cantona?"

"You forget, Kosigin hired Alliance to compile a dossier on your brother. We're very thorough, Gordon. We not only did a full background check, including family, we watched him for a couple of weeks. We watched him get to know Cantona."

"Then you handed the lot over to Kosigin and he had my brother killed."

"There's no evidence —"

"Everybody keeps telling me that!"

Dulwater still hadn't touched his drink. He ran his thumb around the rim of the frosted glass. "A good argument for letting me help you. The courts aren't going to be any use. You're never going to have enough evidence to go to court with. The best you can hope for is that someone else makes Kosigin's life hell. Kosigin lives for power, Gordon. If someone else gains power over *him* it's the worst torture he could ever imagine, and it will last the rest of his life." He sat back, argument over.

Reeve sighed. "Maybe you're right," he lied. "Okay, what exactly do you propose?"

Dulwater stared at him, measuring his sincerity. Reeve concentrated on the beer. "Why did you come back here?" Dulwater asked.

"I wanted to speak to a few people. I intend speaking to one of them tonight. You can help."

"How?"

"Two things: one, I need a video camera, a good one, plus a couple of recorders, more if you can get them. I want to make copies of a videotape."

"You need these tonight?"

Reeve nodded.

"Okay, I don't foresee a problem. What's the other thing?"

"I need you to keep lookout for me."

"Where?"

"In La Jolla." Reeve paused. "About two miles away from where I'll actually be."

"I think you've lost me."

"I'll explain later. You're sure you can get the equipment?"

"Pretty sure. It may take a few phone calls. It may have to be brought down from L.A. Are you in a hotel here?"

"Same one I stayed in last time, the Radisson."

"I'm in the Marriott," Dulwater informed him. Reeve's face was a mask. "It's more central. We'll set the gear up in my room if that's all right with you."

"Fine," Reeve said dryly.

At last Dulwater took a sip of his beer. He pretended to savor it as he framed another question. "What is it you're going to video exactly?"

"A confession," Reeve said. "One man unburdening his soul."

"Film at eleven," Dulwater said with a smile.

NINETEEN

REEVE PARKED THE DART a couple of streets away from where he wanted to be.

There was a pizza delivery van parked curbside, a little boxy three-wheeler which looked like it might use an electric motor. He hadn't seen anyone inside it as he'd driven past, and he didn't see anyone in it now. He gave it another couple of minutes — maybe the delivery boy was having trouble making change. But he knew there was no delivery boy really. What there was was an undercover cop, keeping watch on the bungalow, except he'd been called to another job just a couple of miles away. The electric motor wouldn't take him there, so his buddies had come and picked him up.

Reeve checked his watch. It was quarter to midnight. He didn't have much time. Having already noted the delivery van, he hadn't bothered bringing the video camera with him. It was still locked in the Dart's trunk. He walked down the street then back up the other side. There was no one about, no neighborhood patrol or crime watch. Reeve stopped for a moment beside the delivery van. It boasted a radio with handset attached. He saw now why they'd used a delivery van: there was nothing particularly odd about such a van having a radio. It might have been so the driver could keep in touch with base.

Indeed, that was just what it was for.

Lights were burning in the bungalow, but not brightly. A reading lamp maybe. The curtains were closed, the light seeping out from around the edges of the window. Reeve opened the slatted wooden gate, hearing bells jangle from a string attached to the back of it. He walked up to the bungalow and rang the bell. He was hoping there would be someone home. With the journalist dead, he was betting they'd have let the scientist come home. He heard a chain rattle. A security chain. The door opened a couple of inches, and Reeve stepped back to give it the meat of his shoe heel. It took two blows till the door burst open.

He had wanted the elderly man shocked, surprised, scared. He was getting all three.

"Dr. Killin?" he said to the figure cowering in the short hallway, holding a book over his head. The title of the book was something to do with molecular biology.

The old man looked up, blinking spaniel eyes. Reeve hit him just hard enough to send him to sleep.

He left the body where it lay and went back outside. There was still no one about. The houses were separated by high hedges. Somebody might have seen him from the house across the way but it was in darkness, and besides, the pizza van hid Dr. Killin's doorway from general view. Reeve jumped the gate rather than bothering to open it, and jogged back to his car. He brought it around to Dr. Killin's house, parking next to the pizza van. The old man didn't weigh much and was easy to carry out to the car. Reeve dropped him onto the backseat, then went back to the house, switched off the lamp beside Killin's chair, and pulled the front door closed. In the shadow of the covered porch, you could hardly notice the splintered wood of the surround. From out on the pavement, you couldn't see it at all.

Reeve got into the Dart and drove north on a local road that seemed to parallel I-5 but kept closer to the edge of the Pacific Ocean. Just south of Del Mar, he pulled the car into a rest area sheltered from the road but with a view of the ocean. Not that you could see anything much, but with the window rolled down Reeve could hear the waves. He got out of the car and opened the trunk, bringing out the video camera and the replacement for Lucky 13. Back in the driver's seat, he swiveled so he was facing Killin. Then he switched on the car's interior lights. Dulwater and he had discussed lighting, but this camera had a good low-light facility and even a spot beam of its own — though using it would drain the batteries fast. Reeve switched the camera to ready, removed the lens cap, and put his eye to the viewfinder. He watched the old man stirring. The needle on the viewfinder told him the lighting was poor, but not unusable. Reeve put the camera down again and picked up the dagger. It was the first thing Dr. Killin saw when he woke up.

He sat upright, looking terrified. Reeve wondered for a moment if the knife would be enough to slice the truth from the man.

"What's going on?" the doctor asked shakily. "Where am I? Who are you?"

"This knife," Reeve said quietly, "could bisect you from skull to scrotum and still have an edge on it."

The doctor swallowed and licked his lips.

"I have some questions," Reeve said. "I want answers to them. You're being watched, round-the-clock protection. Why?"

"That's absurd. Why would anyone watch me?"

Reeve smiled without a trace of humor. "You worked for Co-World Chemicals, didn't you? Did you ever meet Dr. Owen Preece?"

"I'm sorry, I want to help you, but I don't know that name."

Reeve angled the dagger so light glinted off the blade, causing Killin to squint. The doctor licked his dry lips again.

"Fear can do that," Reeve told him. "It stops the saliva getting to your mouth. Here." He reached into his left-hand jacket pocket and handed Killin a small plastic bottle of mineral water. Killin took the bottle and stared at it. "Can't answer questions with a dry mouth," Reeve said. He drew out an identical bottle from his right-hand pocket. "Can't ask them either." He broke the seal and unscrewed the top. Killin was still staring at him. "You don't want it?" Reeve said. "Want mine instead?"

Killin thought about it then shook his head, broke the bottle's seal, and unscrewed the top. He sipped at the water, tasting it, then gulping a mouthful. Reeve put his own bottle on the passenger seat and lifted the video camera. To do so meant putting down the dagger.

"Now," he said, "I hope you've noticed this car has no back doors. Your only exit is past me, and I don't think you want to try that."

"Look, I'll answer your questions if I can, but I want to know what's going on."

Killin was growing either testier or more confident — confident that Reeve wasn't the type to kill him.

"I'll tell you," Reeve said. "I want to know about Co-World Chemicals. I want to know about Dr. Owen Preece and the work he did for CWC. I want to know about a man called Kosigin who set the whole thing in motion. I want to know about pesticides, Doctor. I want to know what *you* know."

Killin took his time answering. "It's true," he said, nursing the bottle, "that I worked for CWC. I headed the R & D team for four years, but I'd worked for the company for fifteen years before that. You are correct that a man called Kosigin also works for CWC, though in what capacity I'm not sure. He may not still be there; I don't keep in touch with CWC, and I believe executives in most companies flit about from competitive salary to competitive salary. And that," he said, "is all I *do* know."

"Did a man called Reeve ever come to see you?"

"I don't recollect." Killin sounded impatient.

"A British journalist? He came to your house wanting to ask questions."

"If he did, I didn't let him in." He tapped his forehead. "My memory's not what it . . ." His fingers stayed on his forehead, rubbing at beads of sweat which were appearing there. He blinked hard, as though trying to focus. "I don't feel well," he said. "You should know that my heart has been giving me trouble. There are some pills back at my home . . ."

"You're all right, Doctor. You're just drugged." Reeve hadn't started the tape running yet, but he had his eye to the viewfinder. Even in color, Killin's face looked gray, like he was acting in a black-and-white movie. "You don't need to break the seal to inject something into a plastic bottle. You just need a dot of glue to seal the bottle up again."

"What?" The doctor lost the faculty of speech for a moment. Reeve took the doped bottle from him and replaced it with his own.

"Here, drink this, it'll help."

"I don't feel well."

"You'll feel a lot better when you clear your conscience. The birdy will help with that. Now, where were we? Yes, Co-World Chemicals." Reeve started the tape running. "You were telling me, Dr. Killin, that you worked for CWC — what was it — nineteen years?"

"Nineteen years," Killin agreed, his voice dull and metallic.

"The last four of those heading the company's R & D?"

"That's right."

"Did you know a man called Owen Preece?"

"Dr. Preece, yes, he was a psychiatrist."

"Well respected?"

"They might have invented the word *eminent* with him in mind."

"Did he do any work for CWC?"

"Yes, he headed a research team looking into pesticides."

"Specifically?"

"Specifically side effects."

"And these pesticides were . . ."

"Organophosphorus."

"So he was looking at PrPs?"

"Well the *team* examined all aspects of a great many pesticides. Its conclusions were published in several journals."

"And those conclusions were accurate?"

"No, they were faked." The doctor stared out of the car's back window. "Is that the ocean out there? Doesn't it sound angry?"

"Yes, it does," Reeve said.

"It should be angry. We dump so much dangerous trash into it. Our rivers trickle mercury and other poisons into it. You wouldn't think you could kill an ocean, would you? But we'll do it one day. That's how negligent we are."

"Is CWC negligent?"

"Monstrously so."

"Why haven't you spoken out about it?"

"To protect my career, for one thing. I discovered early in my professional life that I was a coward, a moral coward. I might seethe inside, but I'd do nothing to upset the status quo. Later, after I'd retired, I could have done something, but that would have meant admitting my silence, too. You see, I'm just as culpable as anyone. Preece was a psychiatrist, not a scientist; it was easy for him to believe that the cause of certain diseases might lie in the mind itself. Even today there are people who refuse to acknowledge the existence of ME as a valid disease. They say it's psychosomatic. But Preece's group, the scientists — we had *proof* that pesticides and certain neurological diseases were causally linked."

"You had proof?"

"And we let them cover it up."

"Who's them?"

"CWC." He paused, gathering himself. "Kosigin primarily. I've never been sure whether those above him knew about it at the time, or are any wiser now. He operates within his own sphere. Those above him allow him this leeway . . . Perhaps they have an inkling of what he's like, and want to distance themselves from him."

"What is he like, Doctor?"

"He's not evil, that's not what I'm suggesting. I don't even think he's power-mad. I believe he thinks everything he does is in the genuine interests of the company. He is a corporation man, that's all. He'll do all he can — anything it takes — to stop damage being done to CWC."

"Did you tell him about the journalist, James Reeve?"

"Yes, I did. I was frightened."

"And he sent men to guard you?"

"Yes, and then he told me to take a short vacation."

"There's still a man guarding your house, isn't there?"

"Not for much longer. The threat has disappeared."

"Kosigin told you that?"

"Yes, he told me to put my mind at rest."

"Do the guards work for CWC?"

"Oh, no, they're policemen."

"Policemen?"

"Yes. Kosigin has a friend in the police department."

"Do you know his name?"

"McCluskey. If there's any trouble, any problem, I can always phone this man McCluskey. You know something? I live about a half a mile from the ocean, but I've never heard it sound so angry."

"They're just waves, Dr. Killin."

"You do them an injustice." He sipped undoped water. "We all do."

"So let me get this straight in my head, Dr. Killin. You're saying you were part of a cover-up instigated by Kosigin?"

"That's right."

"And you're not sure whether anyone higher up in CWC knew about it at the time, or knows about it now?"

The old man nodded, staring out of the window. Reeve recorded his face in profile, the face of a sad old man who had little to be proud of in his life.

"We're poisoning everything. We're poisoning the very food we eat. All over the world, from the biggest agribusiness to the smallest sharecropper, they're all doing business with the chemical companies, companies like CWC. In the richest countries and the poorest. And we're eating the results — everything from daily bread to a nice juicy steak. All tainted. It's like the sea; you can't see the damage with the naked eye. That makes it easy to hide the problem, easy to cover it up and just deny, deny, deny."

Slowly, methodically, Killin started to beat his forehead against the side window.

"Whoa," Reeve said, pulling him away. "It's not your fault."

"Oh, but it is. It is!"

"Look, everything's going to be all right. You're going to forget all about this."

"I can't forget."

"Well, maybe not, but trust me on this. What about Agrippa? What does it have to do with any of this?"

"Agrippa? Agrippa has everything to do with it, don't you see? Agrippa has several patents pending on genetically engineered crop strains, with many more patents to come in the future. Do you realize what those will be worth? I don't think it's an exaggeration to say billions. Genetics is the industry of the future, no doubt about it."

Reeve nodded, understanding. "And if Kosigin's dirty tricks came to light, the licensing authorities might take a pretty dim view?"

"CWC could lose existing patents *and* be banned from applying for others. That's why the cover-up is imperative."

"Because it's good for the company," Reeve muttered. He made to switch off the camera.

"Aren't you going to ask me about Preece?"

"What?"

"Preece. That's what the reporter wanted to talk about."

Reeve stared at Killin, then put the viewfinder back to his eye and watched as the lens refocused itself on the old man. "Go on, Doctor. What about Preece?"

"Preece had a reputation to think of. You think he'd have worked for Kosigin, covered everything up, and signed his name to the lies if there had been an alternative?"

"There wasn't an alternative?"

"Kosigin had information on Owen. He'd had people do some digging. They found out about Preece and his patients. The ones at the hospital in Canada."

"What about them?"

"Preece had for a time advocated a kind of sexual shock treatment. Sex as a means to focus the mind, to pull it back to reality."

Gordon Reeve swallowed. "Are you saying he raped patients?"

"He had sex with some of them. It was . . . it was experimental. He never published anything, naturally enough. Still it was never the best-kept of secrets. These patients were unpredictable. Preece had to have orderlies in the room to hold them down."

"Jesus Christ."

"The psychiatric community got to know about it, and the stories spread out until even people like me heard them."

"And no one kicked up a stink?"

"These patients were incarcerated. They were fair game for experiments."

"So Kosigin found out and used the information as a lever?"

"Yes. He had a private detective work on Preece's history."

"Alliance Investigative?"

"I don't know . . ."

"A man called Jeffrey Allerdyce?"

"The name sounds familiar."

Reeve thought for a moment. "My brother knew this?"

"Your brother?"

"The reporter."

"Yes, he knew some of it."

"How could he know?"

"I take it he'd talked to a few people. As I said, it was not the world's best-kept secret. If the reporter had been looking into Owen's past, he would have stumbled on it eventually. I mean, he would have known about Owen and his patients."

And would have put two and two together, Reeve thought. Jim hadn't only been trying to blow the pesticide story open, he'd made things more personal. He'd been homing in on Kosigin as manipulator *and* blackmailer. Kosigin wasn't protecting CWC, he was protecting *himself*. Reeve turned the camera around so it was pointing at him, and waited for the autofocus to pick out his face. Then he spoke.

"This is being kept nice and safe, a long way from you," he said. "I drugged the old man, that's why he's been talking. The drug's called *burundanga*; it's Colombian. You can check on it. You might even want your R & D people to do something with it. But listen to this; if you do anything to Dr. Killin I'll know about it, and a copy of this tape goes straight to the police. And I don't mean the San Diego PD. We know now how much of *that* outfit you own, Kosigin. Okay?"

Reeve sought the right button and turned the recorder off. He wound it back a little and pressed Play. Peering into the viewfinder again, he saw his own face, muddy but definable. His voice came from the small built-in speaker.

"You can check on it. You might even want your R & D people to —"

Satisfied, he switched off the camera and laid it on the passenger seat. "Dr. Killin," he said, "I'm going to take you back now."

They drove in silence, Killin nodding off in the backseat, his head sliding lower and lower down the backrest. Reeve stopped the car three streets away from Killin's bungalow, opened the passenger door, and pulled the back of the passenger seat down. Then he shook Killin awake.

"Get out of the car, Doctor. You'll know where you are. Just walk home and go to bed. Get some sleep."

Killin staggered out of the car like he was drunk. He stood up straight, staggered a little more, and looked around him like he was on the moon.

"Look at all the stars," he said. There were plenty of them up there. "So many," he said, "you'd never think you could poison them all." He bent down to peer into the car. "But give us a chance and we'll do it. There are hundreds of tons of space junk flying around up there already. That's an excellent start, wouldn't you say?"

Reeve closed the passenger door and drove off.

Dulwater sat on his bed, watching the television. He'd boosted the brightness and adjusted the color and contrast. There was nothing wrong with the sound. Dr. Killin was on the screen, saying his piece. Dulwater was watching the performance for the third time, and saying "This is fucking unbelievable" for the seventh or eighth.

The tape that was playing was simultaneously being recorded onto the third blank tape of a box of five.

"Fucking unbelievable," Dulwater said.

Reeve watched the tape counter. Dulwater's room was three floors down from his own. He'd been nervous coming here, but none of the staff had recognized him. It was a big hotel after all, and he'd done nothing to make himself memorable.

"Of course," Dulwater said, "you could never use this in a court of law. Killin's obviously been drugged."

"You already said we'd never get Kosigin into a courtroom anyway."

"Well, that's true, too."

"I don't particularly *want* him to stand trial. I just want him to know I have this on record."

They'd come to the bit where Killin asked if Reeve didn't want to hear about Preece.

"Anyway," said Reeve, "what do you care? You've got what you wanted right there. Your boss compiled one of his famous dossiers on the dark side of Owen Preece's history, and this opened Preece up to blackmail."

"Yes."

"You should be happy. You've got something on your boss."

"I suppose so." Dulwater swung off the bed and went to the table. He had a bottle of whiskey there, and helped himself to another glass. Reeve had already refused twice, and wasn't going to be given a third chance. "What about you?" Dulwater asked between gulps. "What're you going to do with the tapes?"

"One for me, and one for Kosigin."

"What's the point of sending him one?"

"So he knows I know."

"So what? He'll only send that buttfuck Jay after you."

Reeve smiled. "Exactly."

"Doesn't that bastard have a surname?" Dulwater sounded three-fifths drunk.

"Jay is his surname."

"You really know him then?"

"I know him. Tell me again about the bar."

Dulwater smiled. "Half the damned police department must have been there. You told McCluskey you wanted one on one? You got a hundred on one. Cars, vans, armed to the teeth. Man, he was ready for you and then some. You should have seen how angry he was when he figured it was a no-show. And his pals weren't too happy with him either."

"He'll be worse when he finds out I've walked into Killin's house after he pulled the guard away."

"Oh, yeah, he'll pop some blood vessels. And then Kosigin'll pop *him*."

"I hope so."

The tape was coming to its end, Reeve's face on the screen. Dulwater finished his drink and crouched in front of the machine. "You know, Gordon, I called the Radisson. I thought it was pretty dumb of you to stay in the same place you stayed last trip. But you're not that dumb, are you?"

"No, I'm not," Reeve said. He was right behind Dulwater, arms stretched out, when Dulwater stood up. As Dulwater turned, slowed by the alcohol, Reeve brought his hands together in what would have been a sharp clap, had Dulwater's ears not been in the way. Dulwater's face creased in sudden excruciating pain, and his balance went. He bounced off the bed and crumpled onto the floor, trying his best to rise again quickly.

Reeve kicked him once in the head and that dropped him.

"No, I'm not," he repeated quietly, standing over Dulwater. He didn't think he'd hit him hard enough to burst an eardrum. But then it wasn't what you'd call an exact science. The Nietzsche quote came to him: "Must one first shatter their ears to teach them to hear with their eyes?" Well, maybe he was one of Nietzsche's gentlemen after all.

He spent a few minutes getting everything ready. Then he called McCluskey.

"Hey, McCluskey," he said.

"You sonofabitch, where were you? I waited hours."

"Well, leastways you weren't lonely."

There was a pause. "What do you mean?"

"I mean all your boyfriends."

Another pause, then a sigh. "All right, Gordon, I admit it — but listen, and this is a friend speaking now, you're on Interpol's list, man. It came through after we spoke. The French police want to talk to you about some murders. Hell, when I read that I didn't know what to think."

"Nice story, McCluskey."

"Now wait —"

"I'm gone."

Reeve dropped the receiver onto the bed. He could hear McCluskey asking if anyone was still there. To drop a bigger hint, Reeve put the TV volume up. It was the insomniacs' shopping channel. It would take McCluskey time to trace the call, once he figured the phone had been left off the hook. Time enough for Reeve to check out of the hotel and into another. He took three copies of the video with him, leaving just the one.

He knew that if McCluskey and Dulwater sat down to watch the video together, they might find out it was better all around to destroy it. Or rather, McCluskey would want it destroyed, and he'd tell Dulwater that if he didn't let him destroy it, then Mr. Allerdyce might be appraised of the situation — such as what Gordon Reeve had been doing phoning from Dulwater's hotel room, and what part Dulwater had played in the videotaping . . .

So in all, Reeve felt he needed three copies. One for himself, one for Kosigin.

And one just to let Allerdyce know the score.

TWENTY

REEVE HEADED NORTH OUT of town on I-5, citing a "family crisis" as the reason he had to leave the Marriott at such an odd hour. On the way down from Los Angeles, he had picked out a number of dreary-looking roadside motels, just off I-5 on the coastal road which ran parallel with it. He checked the mileage as he drove, and came off the interstate near Solana Beach. He was twenty miles out from the Marriott. The motel had a red neon sign which was making a buzzing sound as he parked beneath it. The reception was all locked up, but there was a sign drawing his attention to the machine attached to the wall alongside. It looked like a cash machine but was actually an Automated Motel Reception. Reeve slipped his credit card into the slot and followed the onscreen instructions. The key which appeared from another slot was a narrow plastic card with holes punched in it. The machine flashed up a final message saying it wished him a pleasant night's sleep. Reeve wished the machine a pleasant night, too.

The rooms were around the far side of the building. Reeve drove slowly and picked out his room number with his headlights. There were four cars parked, and about twenty rooms. Reeve guessed they weren't doing great business at the Ocean Palms Resort Beach Motel. He also guessed that *resort* and *beach* were misnomers; the motel was a tired motorist's overnight stop, nothing more. The 1950s cinder-block construction told its own story. The building was in a gulch, closer to I-5 than any beach. The Cinder-Block Last Resort Motel would have been a more accurate name.

But the locks on the doors were new. Reeve slotted home his card, turned the handle, and pulled the card out. He had his bag with him and slung it over a chair. He checked the room over, tired as he was — just the one door and one window. He tried the air-conditioner and wasn't surprised when it didn't work. The lightbulb in the lamp fixed into the wall over the bedhead was dead, too, but he took out the dud and replaced it with a working bulb from the ceiling light. He went back out again, locking his door, and prowled the area. There was a small well-lit room at the end of the row. It had no windows and no doors and a bare concrete floor. There were humming machines in there, one dispensing cold drinks, another snacks, and the last one ice. When he lifted the lid he saw there was no ice, just a small metal paddle on a chain. He looked in his pocket for quarters, then went back to the Dart and found a few more. Enough for a can of cola, a chocolate bar, and some potato chips. He took his haul back to the room and settled on the sagging mattress. There was an ugly lamp on the table beside the TV, so he moved it where he couldn't see it. Then he switched on the TV and stared towards it for a while, eating and drinking and thinking about things.

When he woke up, the morning programs were on, and a maid was cranking a cart past his door. He sat up and rubbed his head. His watch told him 10:00 A.M. He'd been asleep the best part of six hours. He ran a tepid shower and stripped off his clothes. He stayed a long time in the shower, letting the water hammer his back and shoulders while he soaped his chest. He had fallen asleep thinking, and he was thinking now. How badly did he want Kosigin? Did he want Kosigin at all? Maybe Dulwater was right: the proper torment for Kosigin was to give someone else — Allerdyce, in this case — power over him. It was a right and just fate, like something Dante would have dreamed up for one of the circles of Hell.

But then Reeve liked Allerdyce little better than he liked Kosigin. He wished he had a solution, something that would erase them all. But life was never that simple, was it?

Checking out of the motel was as easy as dropping his key into a box. He'd been there about eight hours and hadn't seen a soul, and the only person he'd even heard was the chambermaid. It was everything he could have asked for.

By now he guessed McCluskey would be tearing up every hotel room in the city. He'd want details of Reeve's car, but Dulwater wouldn't be able to help him, and neither would anyone else. If he checked the automobile registration details at the Marriott, he'd see that Reeve had put down a false license plate attached to an equally fictitious Pontiac Sunfire. Reeve drove the Dart down to a stretch of beach and parked. He pulled off shoes and socks and walked across the sand to the ocean's edge. He walked the beach for a while, then started jogging. He wasn't alone: there were a few other men out here, mostly older than him, all of them jogging along the waterline. But none of them ran as far as Reeve did. He ran until he was sweating, then stripped off his shirt and ran some more.

Finally, he fell back onto the sand and lay there, sky swimming overhead, waves pounding in his ears. There were toxins in the sky and in the sea. There were toxins in his body. So much for the Superman. So much for Mutual Aid. Reeve spent the rest of the day on the beach, dozing, walking, thinking. He was letting McCluskey and Dulwater sweat. His guess was that they wouldn't go to Kosigin, not right away. They'd try to find Gordon Reeve first. At least McCluskey would. Reeve wasn't so sure about Dulwater; he was the more unpredictable of the two.

That evening he ate at a roadside diner, his waitress not believing him when he asked for soup, a salad, and some orange juice.

"That all you want, sweetheart?"

"That's all."

Even then, he wondered about additives in the juice, chemicals in the soup stock, residues in the salad vegetables. He wondered if he'd ever enjoy a meal again.

*   *   *

Reeve took the Dart back into San Diego. His face was still stinging from his day on the beach. The traffic was heavy heading into
town. It was a work week, after all. Eventually Reeve hit the
waterfront, parked in the first space he found, and went for a
walk.

He found the Gaslamp Quarter. He accosted the first non-
crazy-looking beggar who approached him and laid out his
scheme. The beggar forced the fee up a couple of notches from
the price of a drink to the price of dinner *and* a drink, but Reeve
reckoned he had dollars to spare. The beggar walked with him
up Fifth Avenue and west to the CWC building. Reeve handed
him the package.

It was pretty crude: a plastic carrier bag sealed shut with
Scotch tape, and MR. KOSIGIN: PRIVATE & CONFIDEN-
TIAL in felt-penned capitals.

"Now, I'm going to be watching, so just do what I told you,"
he warned his messenger. Then he stood across the street, on the
corner outside the coffee shop. He could see Cantona inside,
dunking a doughnut. But Cantona couldn't see him, and Reeve
kept it that way. He kept an eye open for Dulwater or anyone
else, but Dulwater was probably still tied up sorting out his own
problems. It was a risk, using the coffee shop. After all, Dulwater
knew Reeve himself had used the premises, and Dulwater knew
what Cantona looked like. But Reeve reckoned he was safe
enough. Meantime, the beggar had entered the CWC building.

Reeve waited a few minutes, then walked to another vantage
point and waited a few more. Nobody left the CWC building. As
he'd guessed would happen, an unmarked police car eventually
screamed to a halt outside the entrance. McCluskey got out, and
was met halfway up the steps by Kosigin himself.

It was Reeve's first real look at Kosigin, Allerdyce's photographs aside. He was a short, slim man who wore his suit like
he was modeling in a commercial. From this distance, he looked
as dangerous as a hamburger. But then after what Reeve had
learned lately, he couldn't be sure anymore just how safe a hamburger was.

Kosigin led McCluskey into the building. McCluskey looked tired, pasty-faced. He'd had a very long couple of days. Reeve wondered if the detective had slept at all. He hoped not. He knew the beggar was inside, probably sandwiched between two security men. They'd want to ask him questions. They'd maybe take the money away from him; or threaten to, if he didn't give a convincing description of his benefactor.

Reeve's mobile rang. He held it up to his ear. Unsurprisingly, Cantona's voice came over loud and clear.

"Hey," he said, "your man just came out of the building. But get this, only as far as the steps where he met up with that fucking detective. They've both gone back inside."

Reeve smiled. Cantona was doing his job. "Thanks," he said into the mouthpiece. "Keep watching."

"Sure. Hey, do I get to take a lunch break?"

"What? After that doughnut you just ate?"

There was silence on the line. When Cantona next spoke, he sounded amused. "You sonofabitch, where are you?"

"I'm just leaving." Reeve put away the telephone, turned on his heels, and headed into the shopping district.

The first thing he did was get a haircut. Then he bought some very plain clothes which all but made him invisible. The barber had given him a shave, too. If he hadn't been in fear of his life, Reeve would have felt great. He found a nice restaurant on the edge of Gaslamp and had lunch with the other business-people. His table was near the window, facing another table laid for two with a single woman eating at it. She smiled at him from time to time, and he smiled back. He had the sense that rather than flirting with him, she was acknowledging her right — and his, too — to dine alone. She went back to her paperback novel, and Reeve watched the street outside. During dessert, he saw his messenger slouch past, a dazed scowl on his face. The world had given him another punch in the teeth, and the man was trying to figure out how he'd walked into it. Reeve vowed that if he saw him later, he'd slip him a dollar without stopping.

Hell, maybe he'd make it two.

He gave Kosigin a couple of hours, then telephoned from his mobile. He was guessing they'd try to trace any calls made to Kosigin. Reeve sat on a bench in a shopping mall and made the call.

"Mr. Kosigin's office, please."

"Just one minute." The switchboard operator transferred him to a secretary.

"Mr. Kosigin, please."

"May I ask who's calling?"

"Sure, my name's Reeve. Believe me, he'll want to talk to me."

"I'll try his office, Mr. Reeve."

"Thanks."

The secretary put him onto one of those annoying music loops. He started to time how long he was kept waiting. He could visualize them setting up an extra telephone set so McCluskey could listen in, could see McCluskey busy on another line trying to get a trace on the call. Reeve gave it thirty seconds before he cut the connection. He walked to a coffee stand and bought a double decaf latte. He peeled off the plastic cover until he had a hole big enough to sip through, and window-shopped the mall. Then he sat on another bench and made the call again.

"Mr. Kosigin's office, please."

"Just one minute."

And then Kosigin's secretary again, sounding slightly flustered.

"It's Reeve again," he said. "I have an aversion to waiting."

"Hold the line, please."

Fifteen seconds later, a male voice came on the phone. "Mr. Reeve? This is Kosigin." The voice was as smooth as the suit Kosigin wore. "How can I help you?"

"What did you think of the video?"

"Dr. Killin was obviously drugged, delirious. I'd say he'd almost been brainwashed into that crazy story. Abduction is a very serious offense, Mr. Reeve."

"What did McCluskey think of it?"

That stopped Kosigin for a moment. "Naturally, I sent for the police."

"Before you watched the video," Reeve stated. "That's a bit suspicious, isn't it? Almost like you were expecting something. I take it you're recording this call, that's why you're acting innocent. Fine, act away. But Kosigin, I've got the tape. I've got *lots* of copies of it. You don't know who's going to receive one in the mail one of these fine mornings. Maybe they'll believe your version, maybe they'll believe Killin's."

Another pause. Was Kosigin taking instructions from someone? Maybe McCluskey.

Maybe Jay.

"Perhaps we should meet, Mr. Reeve."

"Yeah? Just the two of us, same as I was supposed to meet McCluskey? Only McCluskey turned up with his private personal army, and you, Kosigin, you'd turn up alone — right?"

"Right."

"Apart from Jay, of course, training a laser sight on my forehead."

Another pause.

Reeve was enjoying this. "I'll call back in ten minutes," he told Kosigin, then hung up.

He walked out of the mall into bright afternoon sun and a warm coastal breeze. He didn't think he'd ever felt more alive. He made the next call from outside the main post office.

"So, Kosigin, had any thoughts?"

"About what? I believe you're a wanted man in Europe, Mr. Reeve. Not a very pleasant situation."

"But you could do something about that, right?"

"Could I?"

"Yes, you could hand Jay over to the French authorities, you could tell them he set me up."

"You two know one another, don't you?"

"Believe it."

"There's some sort of enmity between you?"

"You mean he hasn't told you? Get him to tell you his version. It's probably so fake you could install it as a ride at Disneyland."

"I'd like to hear *your* version."

"I bet you would, and at length too, right?"

"Look, Mr. Reeve, this is getting us nowhere. Why don't you just tell me what you want."

"I thought that was obvious, Kosigin. I want Jay. I'll phone later with the details."

Reeve walked back to the office-supply shop and handed over the mobile, signing some more documents and getting back his deposit.

"Any calls will be charged to your credit card," the assistant told him.

"Thanks," Reeve said. He went next door to the coffee shop. Cantona was reading a crumpled newspaper. Reeve bought them both a coffee.

"Hell," Cantona said, "I didn't recognize you there."

Reeve reached into his pocket and drew out a miniature of whiskey. "Here's something to pep you up."

"I meant what I said, Gordon." Cantona's eyes were bloodshot and he hadn't shaved in a few days. His stubble was silver and gray. "I don't drink when I'm working."

"But you're not working anymore. I'm heading out."

"Where to?" Cantona received no reply. "Best I don't know, right?"

"Right." Reeve handed over the money from his mobile deposit.

"What's this for?"

"It's for looking after Jim, and taking some shit on my behalf last time I was here."

"Aw hell, Gordon, that wasn't anything."

"Put it in your pocket, Eddie, and drink up." Reeve stood up again, his own coffee barely touched. Cantona glanced out of the window. It had become a reflex.

"There's McCluskey," he said.

Reeve watched the detective get into his car. He didn't look happy. Reeve kept watching. If Jay walked out of the building, Reeve would finish it now. He'd leave the coffee shop, sprint between the traffic, and take the bastard out.

But there was no sign of Jay.

"Go home," Reeve told Cantona. It was like he was telling himself.

He drove to L.A.

It took him a while to find Marcus Aurelius Dedman's

Auto-Breakers. He'd phoned ahead, and Dedman was waiting for him.

Dedman gave the car a cursory inspection. "She drive all right?" he asked.

"Fine."

"No problems at all?"

"No problems at all," Reeve echoed.

"Well in that case," Dedman said. "I might as well use her to give you your ride."

Dedman had agreed to drive Reeve out to the airport. He insisted on driving, and Reeve was quite happy to rest in the passenger seat. On the way, Dedman talked about cars, using a language Reeve only half understood. He'd done a course in car mechanics as part of his SAS training, but that had been on elderly Land Rovers, and had been cursory at best. It seemed a long time ago.

Reeve shook Dedman's hand at the airport and watched him drive off. He didn't think they'd be expecting him to leave so soon. Kosigin would be waiting for the next call. Reeve walked around the concourse until he found a bulletin board. He scribbled a note on the back of a napkin he'd taken from the coffee shop, then folded the note over, wrote a surname in large capitals, and pinned the napkin to the bulletin board.

Then he checked himself onto the next available flight and made straight for the departure gate. There wasn't much to do at LAX; it was no Heathrow — which these days was more department store than airport. Reeve ate a pizza and drank a Coke. He bought a magazine, which he didn't read. There was no duty-free shop, so he sat by the row of public telephones until just before his flight was called.

Then he called Kosigin.

"Yes?" Kosigin said impatiently.

"Sorry to have kept you waiting."

"I don't like games, Mr. Reeve."

"That's a pity, because we're deep in the middle of one. Have somebody — Jay preferably — go to LAX. There's a public bulletin board in the departures hall, near the information kiosk. There's a note there."

"Look, why can't we just —"

Reeve cut the connection. His flight was being called over the loudspeaker.

He had probably got one of the last places on the aircraft. He was seated by the aisle in a middle row of three. Next to him were an Australian couple heading over to Ireland to trace the wife's ancestors. They showed Reeve some photographs of their children.

"Old photos, they're all grown now."

Reeve didn't mind. He smiled and ordered a whiskey, and watched the sharp blue sky outside. He was just happy to be away from San Diego. He was glad he was going home. When the in-flight movie started, he pushed his cushion down so it was supporting his lumbar, and then he closed his eyes.

Old pictures . . . He had a lot of those in his head: old pictures he would never forget, pictures he'd once dreamed nightly, the dreams breaking him out in a sweat.

Pictures of fireworks in Argentina.

PART EIGHT
STALWART

TWENTY-ONE

IT WAS THE THIRD NIGHT, and enemy activity was increasing still further. There were constant patrols, firing searing pink-burn flares into the sky. An order would be yelled, and a patrol would spray their designated area with bullets. Reeve and Jay knew the tactic. The Argentine soldiers were trying to rile them, flush them out. They were trying to break them.

Reeve understood the shouted orders and would shake his head at Jay, meaning there was nothing to worry about. But they were both nervous. They'd been kept so low by the patrols that sending any more data to the ship was impossible; it had been that way for the best part of the day. They'd been forced farther inland, away from the air base, so that they could no longer see the runway or any of the buildings, and the planes taking off and landing were droning flies.

In fact, *not* transmitting was the only thing keeping them alive. The patrols were so close they'd have DF'd the two-man team in seconds. Reeve and Jay maintained complete silence throughout. Reeve couldn't remember the last time either of them had spoken. Muscles were seizing up from being kept still and rigid for hours at a time. The back of Reeve's neck ached terribly, and he daren't crack it. The fingers on his M16 felt arthritic, and he'd already had two bouts of cramp.

Whenever he glanced over towards Jay, Jay would be looking at him. He tried to read the look in those eyes. They seemed to be saying, quite eloquently, "We're fucked," and they were probably right. But because Jay thought that, he was getting edgier and edgier, and Reeve suspected he might be on the verge of panicking. It was all about nerve now: if they lost theirs, the only possible outcome was "brassing up," blasting away at anything and anybody until your ammo ran out or you copped one.

Reeve fingered the two Syrettes of morphine which hung around his neck. They felt like a noose. He hoped he wouldn't need to use them. He'd rather put a bullet to his head first, though the regiment considered that the coward's way out. The rule was, you fought to the death, and if the enemy didn't kill you but captured you instead, then you did your damnedest to escape. Both men had been trained to withstand various interrogation techniques, but maybe the Argentines had a few tricks Hereford hadn't heard of. Unlikely, but then torture was a broad subject. Reeve reckoned he could withstand quite a bit of physical abuse, and even psychological wearing-down. What he knew he couldn't cope with — what no one could cope with — were the various chemical forms of torture, the drugs that fucked with your mind.

The name of the game was beating the clock. On the regiment's memorial clock back in Hereford were written the names of all SAS men killed in action. As a result of the war in the Falklands, there were already a lot of new names to be added to the clock. Reeve didn't want his to be one of them.

When he looked at Jay again, Jay was still looking at him. Reeve gestured with his head for Jay to return to watch. They were lying side by side, but facing opposite directions, so that Jay's boots rested an inch or so from Reeve's left ear. Earlier, Jay had tapped a Morse message with his fingers on Reeve's boot — "Kill them all" — repeating the message three times. Kill them all.

The ground was cold and damp, and Reeve knew his body temperature was dropping, same as it had done the previous night. A couple more nights like this and they would be in serious trouble, not so much from the enemy as from their own treacherous bodies. They had eaten only chocolate and drunk only water for the past thirty-six hours, and what sleep they'd taken had been fitful and short-lived.

Even when planning their escape route and emergency rendezvous they had not spoken, but had lain head to head with the map on the ground in front of them. Reeve had pointed to a couple of possible routes — if they were forced to withdraw from the OP in the midst of a firefight, chances were they'd be split up — then had tapped the map at the ERV. Jay had then traced a line with his unwashed finger from the ERV to the Chilean border, leaving no doubt what his route would be after the ERV.

Reeve wasn't so sure. Would the Argentine command expect them to make for the border or for the coast? They were still a lot closer to the coast than the border, so maybe the border *was* the best plan. Besides, there was no point reaching the coast if no ship had been alerted of your plight. They wouldn't be able to radio that message in the middle of brassing up, and if forced to retreat they would lighten their load, which meant leaving the rucksack and very probably the transmitter. Reeve had already mentally checked off the contents of his rucksack and had decided he needed nothing out of it but a few more rations. It was because he was thinking along these lines that he knew the mission was at an end. There'd be time later to wonder where and why it had gone wrong, always supposing he was still alive at the end of it all. The coast was closer; Reeve couldn't get that idea out of his head. He had an emergency beacon with him. If they could find a boat and head out to sea, they could switch on the beacon and then pray someone would pick up the signal. The problem with that was, it was as likely to be an Argentine plane returning to base as anyone else.

The sky turned pink again and started to fizz and crackle as the flare started its gentle parachute-borne descent. Reeve could see a four-man patrol five hundred yards off to his right. Reeve and Jay were lying beneath netting and local foliage, and the patrol would have to get a lot closer to see them, even with the help of the flare. There was a sudden shrill whistle, like one of the old tin-and-pea jobs football referees use.

"Half time," Jay whispered. He'd broken the code of silence, but he'd also broken the tension. Reeve found himself grinning, stifling laughter which wrenched itself up from his gut. The way Jay's feet were quivering, he was laughing, too. It became almost uncontrollable. Reeve took a deep breath and expelled it slowly. The patrol was moving away at speed — and there was nothing funny about that.

Then the first rocket thudded into the ground several hundred yards to Reeve's left. The earth beneath tried to buck his body into the air, and his face slammed down hard into the dirt.

"Shit," Jay said, not caring who heard him. Not caring because he knew, like Reeve knew, that there was no one around to hear: the patrols had been signaled to evacuate the area.

Another rocket landed, farther away this time. Then another, and another. Finally, a flare went up. Two blows on the whistle. Reeve guessed patrols were being sent into the freshly bombed area to look for bodies or fleeing survivors.

"What do you reckon?" Jay whispered.

"Lie doggo," Reeve said. His mouth felt strange when it worked. "A rocket's as likely to hit us up-and-running as lying still."

"You think so?" Jay sounded unsure. Reeve nodded and resumed watch. There was sweat in the hollow of his spine, trickling down towards the trouser line. His heart was beating ever more loudly in his ears. Then he heard a distant megaphone, a voice speaking heavily accented English.

"Surrender or we will kill you. You have two minutes to decide."

The two minutes passed all too quickly. Reeve flipped open the cover on his watch face and followed the sweep of the luminous dial.

"Very well," the megaphone said. Then another single blow on the whistle. Reeve could feel Jay trying to burrow deeper into the scrape, pressing himself hard against the ground.

Rockets whistled past to their left and right, causing deafening explosions on impact. Great clumps of earth fell on both men. More missiles, more gut-wrenching explosions. Between impacts, Reeve could hear nothing but a loud buzzing in his ears.

He'd been too late putting his hands over them, and was now suffering the consequence. He felt fingers tapping his leg, and half turned to see Jay starting to rise onto his knees.

"Get down!" Reeve hissed.

"Fuck this, let's go!"

"No."

More explosions caused them both to fall flat, but Jay scrambled up again straight after, dirt and grass and bits of bark falling like heavy dollops of rain.

"They send a patrol out to check this grid, they're bound to spot us," he spat.

"No."

"I say we go."

"No. We can't lose our bottle now."

The flare went up, the double whistle sounded, and Reeve pulled Jay to the ground. Jay started to struggle, giving Reeve two options: let him go, or slug him. Jay came to his own decision first, catching Reeve on the side of the head with his rifle butt. Reeve snatched at the rifle, letting go of Jay in the process, and Jay got to his feet, pulling the rifle out of Reeve's hands.

Reeve risked a glance around. The patrols would be on their way. Smoke was being blown all around them, but when it cleared they'd be as visible as targets at the fairground.

Jay was pointing his M16 at Reeve, finger just shy of the trigger. He was grinning like a monkey, his face blackened, eyes wide and white. Reeve noticed that there was a 40mm missile in the 203 grenade launcher. Jay raised the rifle above Reeve's head and fired the grenade into the sky. With the 203 there was no explosion or recoil, but a loud pop as the grenade was launched.

Reeve didn't use up precious seconds on watching the grenade's trajectory. He was up and moving. Jay had done it now; he'd let the enemy know they were there. They were fair game now for anything the Argentines threw at them. Reeve left his rucksack. He didn't care whether Jay left his or not, or even if he left the transmitter. It was time to move — and quickly. Behind them, the grenade made impact and exploded.

With his rifle carried low in front of him, Reeve ran.

"Where are you going?" Jay yelled at him, pouring bullets from his M16 towards where the enemy would be hunkered down, waiting for him to expend the lot. Reeve knew his partner had cracked. He'd never been sure of Jay in the first place, and now his worst fears were being realized. Everything Jay was doing was against the standard operating procedure . . . or any other procedure. Reeve wondered if he'd be justified putting a bullet into Jay himself. He dismissed the thought in less than a second.

"See you in Chile!" Jay yelled. Reeve didn't look back, but he knew from Jay's voice that he was moving too, taking a different line from Reeve.

Which suited Reeve just fine.

He knew the first few hundred yards, could have run them blind. He'd been staring at the route for the past twelve or so hours, since switching directions with Jay. They'd changed position so they would stay fresh and alert. Staring at the same spot for too long, you could lose your concentration.

But Reeve had focused his mind on the route, his escape route. He didn't know what was over the next rise, but the next rise was shelter from gunfire and night sights, and that was his primary objective: shelter. He knew from an earlier compass reading that he was running northeast. If he kept going, he'd reach the coastal road north of Rio Grande. He was taking a risk, since this direction meant he would have to skirt the northern perimeter of the airfield. Well, they wouldn't be expecting him anywhere near *there*, would they? More crucial, he had two obstacles to cross: a main road and the Rio Grande itself.

He didn't know why he'd set his sights on the coast, and if Jay was headed for Chile so be it. Jay would wait for him an hour or so at the ERV, then move off. Bloody good luck to him, too.

The bastard.

Reeve went over the rise on all fours, keeping low in case there were any nasty surprises waiting for him. But the Argentine bombing had done him a distinct favor by clearing out all the patrols. He scurried down the other side of the escarpment, sliding over loose rocks and pebbles. It didn't seem to be man-made.

It wasn't a quarry or a dump for unwanted stone and shale, it was more like the scree Reeve had come across on the glacial slopes of the Scottish mountains. He ended up going down the slope on his arse. Just when he thought there was no end to the drop he found himself on a road and crossed it hurriedly, remembering to turn around first, in case they came hunting him with flashlights. His footprints led back the way he'd just come. The other side of the track, he turned on his heels again, hit another uphill slope at a run, and powered his way to the summit. There was gunfire behind him, gunfire and rockets and grenades. The sky was full of pink smoke, like a fireworks display. Gunpowder was in his nostrils.

That stupid bastard.

There was someone over to his right, about seventy or eighty yards away. It looked like Jay's silhouette.

"Jay!" Reeve called.

Jay caught his breath. "Keep going!" he said.

So Reeve kept going. And the sky above him turned brilliant white. He couldn't believe it. Jay had let off a WP grenade. White phos made a good smoke screen, but you didn't use the stuff when you were already on your way out of a situation. Then Reeve realized what Jay had done, and his stomach did a flip. Jay had tossed the phos in Reeve's direction, and had headed off the other way. He was using Reeve as his decoy, bringing the Argentine troops over in Reeve's direction while he made his own escape.

Bastard!

And now Reeve could hear whistling, a human whistle. A tune he recognized.

Row, row, row your boat,
Gently down the stream . . .

And then silence. Jay was gone. Reeve could have followed him, but that would mean running straight through the smoke into God knew what. Instead, he picked up his pace and kept running the direction he'd been going. He wondered how Jay could have set off one way yet come back around to meet up with Reeve. It was crazy, Jay's sense of direction wasn't *that* bad . . .

Unless . . . unless he'd come back on purpose. The enemy had heard only one yelled voice, come under fire from just one rifle, one grenade launcher.

They didn't know there were two men out here!

Reeve saw it all. The safest way out of this was to lie low and let the enemy catch your partner. But that only worked if your partner *was* caught. Jay was just making sure. Back at Hereford, it would be one man's word against the other's . . . always supposing they both made it home.

Over the rise the ground seemed to level out, which meant he could move faster, but also that he could be spotted more easily. He thought he could hear rotors behind him: a chopper, maybe more than one, probably with searchlights attached. He had to reach cover. No, he had to keep moving, had to put some distance between himself and his pursuers. Relieved of his rucksack and most of his kit, he felt as though weights had been taken off his ankles. That thought made him think of shackles, and the image of shackles gave him fresh impetus. His ears still seemed blocked; there was still a hissing sound there. He couldn't hear any vehicles, any commands or gunfire. Just rotors . . . coming closer.

Much closer.

Reeve flung himself to the ground as the helicopter passed overhead. It was over to his right and moving too quickly to pick him out. This was a general sweep. They'd carry on until they were sure they were at a distance he couldn't have reached, then they'd come back, moving more slowly, hovering so the searchlight could play over the ground.

He needed cover right now.

But there was no cover. He loaded a grenade into the launcher, got up, and started running again. The rifle was no longer in both hands and held low in front of him: now it was in his right hand, the safety off. It would take him a second to swing the barrel into his other hand, aim, and fire.

He could see the beam of light ahead of him, waving in an arc which would pick him out when the chopper was closer. Reeve dropped to one knee and wiped sweat from his eyes. His knees hurt, they were stiff. The chopper was moving steadily now, marking out a grid pattern. They weren't rushing things. They were being methodical, the way Reeve would have done in their situation.

When the helicopter was seventy-five yards in front of him Reeve took aim, resting one elbow on his knee to steady himself. As soon as the helicopter went into a hover, Reeve let go with the grenade. He watched the bomb, like an engorged bullet, leave the launcher and head into the sky, but he didn't wait to see the result. He was running again, dipping to a protective crouch as the sky overhead exploded in a ball of flame, rotor blades crumpling and falling to the ground. Something hot fell onto Reeve's arm. He checked it wasn't phos. It wasn't — just hot metal. It stuck to his arm, and he had to scrape it off against the ground, taking burning flesh with it.

"Jesus Christ!" he gasped. The helicopter had hit the ground behind him. There was another explosion, which almost toppled him. More flying metal and glass hit him. Maybe bits of bodies were hitting him, too. He didn't bother looking.

His arm wasn't sore; the adrenaline and fear were taking care of that for the moment, the best anesthetics on the planet.

He'd been scared for a second, though, and what had scared him most was the fear that the heat on his arm had been white phos. The stuff was lethal — it would have burned straight through him, eating as it went.

Well, he thought, if Jay's smoke screen had hinted I was here, the helicopter was an open fucking invitation.

He heard a motor, revving hard: a Jeep, probably on the track he'd crossed a few minutes back. If it unloaded men, then those men would be that few minutes behind no more. No time to stop, no time to slow. He didn't have time to pace himself, the way he knew he should so he'd have some idea how far he'd traveled when he got a chance to stop and recce. You did it by counting the number of strides you took and multiplying by length of stride. It was fine in training, fine when they told you about it in a classroom . . .

But out here, it was just another piece of kit to be discarded.

He had no idea where Jay was. The last he'd seen of him was vanishing behind all that thick white smoke, like a magician doing a disappearing trick. Magicians always had trapdoors, and that's what Reeve was looking for now — a door he could disappear through. There was a small explosion at his back. Maybe it was the helicopter, maybe Jay launching another grenade, or the enemy redoubling its bombardment.

Whatever it was, it was far enough behind him to be of little concern. He couldn't hear the Jeep anymore. He wondered if it had stopped. He thought he could hear other vehicles in the distance. Their engine drones were just the right timbre to penetrate his blocked ears. Heavy engines . . . surely not tanks? Personnel carriers? He couldn't see any other searchlights. There had been only the one chopper. They might be ordering another from the airfield, but if the crew was sensible they would take their time getting here, knowing the fate of their comrades.

Reeve was thinking about a lot of things, trying to form some structure to the chaos in his mind. Above all he was trying to think of anything but his own running. On a grueling route march you had to transcend the reality. That was the very word his first instructor had used: *transcend*. Someone had asked if he meant it as in transcendental meditation, expecting to raise a smile.

"In a manner of speaking," the instructor had said in all seriousness.

That was the first time Reeve got an inkling that being a good soldier was more a state of mind, a matter of attitude, than anything else. You could be fit, strong, have fast reflexes and know all the drills, but those didn't complete the picture; there was a mental part of the equation, too. It had to do with spirit, which was maybe what the instructor had been getting at.

He came suddenly to the main road which ran from Rio Grande on the east coast all the way into Chilean territory. He lay low, watching army trucks roar past, and when the route was finally clear scuttled across the road like any other nocturnal creature.

His next obstacle was not far away, and it gave him a choice: he could swim across the Rio Grande — which meant ditching more equipment, including maybe even his rifle — or he could cross it by bridge. There was a bridge half a mile downriver, according to his map. Reeve headed straight towards it, unsure whether it would be guarded or not. The Argentines had known for some time now that there were enemy forces around, so maybe the bridge would be manned. Then again, would they have been expecting Reeve and Jay to make it this far?

Reeve's question was answered soon enough: a two-man foot patrol guarded the two-lane crossing. They were standing in the middle of the bridge, illuminated by the headlights of their Jeep. At this time of night there was no traffic for them to stop and check, so they were talking and smoking cigarettes. Their eyes were on the distance, the direction Reeve had just come. They'd heard the explosions, seen the smoke and flame. They were glad to be at this safe distance from it all.

Reeve took a look at the dark, wide river, the cold-looking water. Then he peered at the underside of the bridge, and made up his mind. He clambered down to the water's edge and made his way underneath the bridge. It was an iron construction, its struts a crisscrossed series of spars forming an arch over the water. Reeve slung his rifle over his shoulder and gripped the first two spars, pulling himself up. He climbed slowly, quietly, hidden from land but all too visible from the river, should any boat with a spotlight come chugging along. Where he could, he used his feet and knees for purchase, but as he climbed higher, he found himself hanging over the water below by his hands, moving one hand at a time, his legs swinging uselessly in space. He thought of training courses where he'd had to swing this way across an expanse of water or mud — but never this distance, never under these conditions. His upper chest ached, and the rusty metal tore into his finger joints. He thought his arms would pop out of their sockets. Sweat was stinging his eyes. Above him he could hear the soldiers laughing. He could pull himself up onto the bridge and open fire on them, then steal their Jeep or cross the rest of the bridge on foot. But he knew if he opted for this kind of action, he'd leave traces, and he didn't want that, he didn't want the enemy to know which way he'd come. So he kept swinging, concentrating on one hand, then the other, squeezing shut his eyes and gritting his teeth. Blood was trickling down past his wrists. He didn't think he was going to make it. He started to fantasize about letting go, falling into the water, about letting the river wash him all the way to the coast. He shook his head clear. The splash would be heard; even if it wasn't, what were his chances? He had to keep on moving.

Finally, he found purchase with his feet. He was at the far side of the span, where the struts started curving downwards towards the riverbank. He mouthed a silent "Jesus" as he took his weight on his feet and legs, easing the pressure on his shredded palms. He felt exhausted as he started his descent, and dropped when he reached solid ground, gasping and panting on all fours, his head touching the dank earth. He gave himself thirty precious seconds to get his breath back. He pressed some strands of grass against his palms and fingers, as much of a compress as he could manage.

Then he got to his feet and moved away from the water, heading northeast. He couldn't follow the river: for one thing, it led back towards the airfield; for another, he was more likely to encounter civilians close to a water source. Stumbling across a fisherman was not high on his Christmas-present list.

Reeve was running the way he'd been taught: not a sprint, because a sprint used up too many resources too quickly — this running was measured, paced, steady, more a jog than anything else. The secret was not to stop, not to falter — and that was the most difficult part of all. It had been difficult on the Brecon Beacons during those arduous training runs. Reeve had jogged past men he regarded as fitter and stronger than him. They'd be standing bent over, hands on knees, spewing onto the ground. They daren't sit down — with the amount of kit they were carrying they'd never get back up. And if they stopped too long they'd begin to seize up. It was something joggers knew. You saw them at traffic lights or pausing to cross the road, and they jogged on the spot.

Never stop, never falter.

Reeve kept running.

The terrain became much as it had been the other side of the river, steep ridges of loose shale with shallow valleys between. He didn't bother counting his steps, just kept moving, putting miles between himself and the river. He knew he couldn't outrun vehicles, but this terrain, inhospitable to a human, would be downright lethal for any vehicle other than the hardiest. No Jeep could take these slopes, and a motorcycle would slew on the loose stones. A helicopter was the enemy's best bet, and he'd probably wiped that option out for the meantime. He took strength from that fact.

He was climbing again, trying not to think about the pain in his hands, crossing the ridge, then sliding. At the bottom of the slide, he picked himself up and ran forward four paces.

Then he stopped dead.

He couldn't really see anything, but some sixth sense had told him to stop. He knew why: it was the nothingness itself that had warned him. He couldn't see the ground ahead, not even ten feet in front of him. He shuffled forwards, toeing the ground, until one foot stepped off into space.

"Christ!"

He took two steps back and got down on his hands and knees, peering into the darkness. He was on the edge of a gully. No . . . more than a gully: sheer sides dropped he didn't know how far. A ravine, a deep chasm. Even supposing he could climb down into it, he'd no idea whether he could scale the other side. He might be trapped. He'd have to go *around* it, but that might take hours. Damn it to hell. He tried to see something, anything down there, something that might tell him what was waiting for him. He unclipped the night scope from his belt and put it to his eye. Its range was limited, but he thought he could make out shapes at the bottom of the hole, rocks or boulders probably. The drop was pretty sheer, tapering off towards the bottom. In daylight, if he wasn't rushed, he could probably find enough hand- and footholds to climb out the other side. But in darkness with the enemy behind him . . .

He took the night scope away from his eyes and was confronted by the ravine's blackness again. It was taunting him.

Everybody, no matter how good, needs luck, it was telling him. And yours just ran out.

"Fuck that," he said, clipping the scope back onto his belt and standing up. His leg muscles complained. He had to make a decision soon, for all sorts of reasons. Turn left or right? Right, and he'd be heading vaguely in Jay's direction; left, and he might hit the coast. Was that correct? He screwed shut his eyes and concentrated. No: if he turned *right* he might hit the coast. He had to turn right.

He ran more slowly now, keeping close to the edge of the ravine so he'd know if and when it ended. The problem was, this close to the edge, he daren't pick up his pace. One stumble might send him over. The ground was dangerous enough as it was. He remembered the dirt track, and the scree, and the boulders at the bottom of the pit . . . it *was* a quarry! The landscape made sense now. And if he was right, then he could half-circle the pit without too much difficulty. Quarries weren't *that* big. There might even be places he could hide or, as a last resort, a vehicle he could hijack.

He heard voices ahead of him and stopped again, unclipping the night scope. A two-man patrol. Somehow they'd got ahead of him, which was very bad news. There could be any number of them between here and the coast road. One man had called to the other to let him know he was stopping to urinate. The other carried on. Both had their backs to Reeve. He walked forward in a silent crouch and, when he was near enough, reached down to lay his rifle on the ground. His right hand was already clutching Lucky 13.

The man was zipping himself up as Reeve came close. He'd had to lay down his own rifle while he was peeing. Reeve tensed and sprang, one hand over the man's mouth, the dagger chewing into the exposed throat below. The man's hands reached up from his fly too late. Reeve kept gouging at the neck, hot blood spilling over him. It splattered onto the ground like urine. He laid the body on the ground and retrieved his rifle. The other man was calling for his friend. Reeve made an affirmative sound and started jogging forward, like he had finished and was now catching up. His eyes burned into the enemy's back. The soldier was saying something about radioing in when Reeve grabbed him by the head and went to work with the knife. More steaming blood. Another body.

He'd killed them by the book. Quick and silent.

He rolled both bodies over the lip of the quarry, then started jogging again. There was not time for analysis or shock; he simply stuck the dagger back in its scabbard and ran. He had maybe four more hours of darkness.

He reached the other side of the quarry without incident. He'd presumed from the casual attitudes of his two kills that nobody was expecting him to get this far. The patrol hadn't been primed for sudden contact. At the other side of the quarry he got out his compass. He'd start heading east now, a direct line to the coast. From what he remembered of the map, there were no settlements of any size for thirty miles north of the town of Rio Grande. There was the coast road to cross, and he hoped that would be his next and final obstacle. He heard a chopper approaching, but it veered off again. Maybe there had been a sighting of Jay. He hoped the chopper hadn't found the bodies in the quarry, not so soon.

He felt good again. He gave himself a few seconds to think about the killings. They'd been necessary, he was sure of that. They wouldn't exactly trouble his conscience; he hadn't even seen the men's faces, just their backs. One of the trainers had said it was eyes that haunted you, that final stare before oblivion — when you kill, never look at the eyes: concentrate on some other part of the face if you have to, best if you don't look at all. Because the person you're killing is staring Death in the face, which makes *you* Death. It was not a role any man should be happy with, but sometimes it was a fact of conflict.

The blood was sticky on Reeve's hands. He had to pry his fingers off the rifle barrel. He didn't think about it at all.

He hit the coast road before dawn, and let the feeling of elation have its way for a few moments while he rested and checked the road for guards, patrols, or traffic. He could see nothing, but he could hear and smell the sea. He double-checked with his night scope that the route was clear, then picked himself up and jogged across the paved surface, his rubberized soles making little sound. He could make out the edge of the sea before him, and a ribbon of sand and shale. Lights south of him told the story: he was only five or so miles north of Rio Grande, which put him maybe twenty to twenty-five miles south of the next decent-sized settlement. Reeve knew what he wanted now — he wanted a boat. He doubted he'd find many between here and the next settlement north. He'd have to walk towards Rio Grande and, this close to the ocean and the road, cover was limited to say the least.

He had to use what darkness there was.

And he had to get a move on.

He picked up his pace, though every muscle in his body complained and his brain told him to go to sleep. He popped two caffeine tablets and washed them down with the last water from his canteen. His luck was holding. After barely a mile he came across a small cove filled with paddle boats. They were probably used for fishing, a single rower and lines or a net. Some of them bobbed in the water, attached by lines to several large buoys; others lay beached on the shale. An old man was putting his gear into one of the beached boats, working by the light of his lantern. Reeve looked around but saw no one else. It would be dawn soon, and the other fishermen would arrive. This old man was beating the rush.

The man looked up from his work as he heard Reeve crunch over the shale towards him. He prepared a glint of a smile and some remark about another early bird, but his eyes and mouth opened wide when he saw the soldier pointing a rifle at him.

Reeve spoke to the man quietly in Spanish, stumbling over the words. He blamed fatigue. The man seemed to understand. He couldn't take his eyes off the caked blood on Reeve's arms and chest. He was a man who had seen blood before. It was dried to the color of rust, but he knew what he was looking at.

Reeve explained what he needed. The man begged him to take another boat, but Reeve needed the man with him. He couldn't trust him not to raise the alarm as soon as his fellow fishermen arrived.

What Reeve did not say was that he was too tired to row. That was another reason he needed the old man. There was not yet light in the sky, but the darkness was not as black as it had been. Reeve didn't have any more time to waste. He pointed the rifle at the man, guessing that a dagger wouldn't suffice to scare someone who gutted fish. The old man put up his hands. Reeve told him to start hauling the boat out into the water. The man did as he was told. Then they both got into the boat and the old man slid the oars back and forth, finally finding his rhythm and working them strongly. There were tears in his eyes, not just from the wind. Reeve repeated that he wasn't going to kill the man. He just wanted to be taken out to sea.

The farther out they got, the safer Reeve felt on the one hand, and the more exposed on the other. He was beginning to have doubts that such a small boat could get far enough out into the ocean for any rescue ship to make a rendezvous. He took out the metal cylinder which contained the beacon and twisted off its cap. The beacon was simple to use. Reeve switched it on, watched the red light start to blink, and placed it on the tiny bench beside him.

The fisherman asked how far they were going. Reeve admitted he didn't know.

"There have been rumors of gunfire around the airport," the old man said. He had a voice thick with tobacco use.

Reeve nodded.

"Are you invading us?"

Reeve shook his head. "Reconnaissance," he told the man, "that's all it was."

"You have won the war, you know," the man said without bitterness. Reeve stared at him and found he believed him. "I saw on television. It will all end maybe today, maybe tomorrow."

Reeve found he was smiling, then laughing and shaking his head. He'd been out of contact for seventy-two hours. Some mission, he thought. Some bloody mission.

They began to chat quite amiably. Maybe the man did not believe a smiling man could kill him. The man spoke of his youth, his family, the fishing, about how crazy it was that allies like Britain and Argentina, huge wealthy countries, should fall to war over a place like the Malvinas. The conversation was pretty one-sided; Reeve had been trained to give away nothing. When he spoke, he spoke generally, and sometimes he did not answer the old man's questions.

"This is usually as far as I go," the old man said at one point.

"Keep going," Reeve ordered.

The old man shrugged. Later he said, "The sea is getting rough."

As if Reeve needed telling. The waves were knocking the little boat about, so that Reeve held on to the side with both hands, and the old man had trouble keeping hold of the oars. Reeve held the beacon securely between his knees.

"It will get rougher," the old man said.

Reeve didn't know what to say. Head back into calmer waters? Or stay here and risk being capsized? He didn't know how long it would take for someone to pick up the beacon's signal. It could take all day, or even longer if some final assault were taking place on the Falklands. Nobody would want to miss out on that.

In the end the old man made up his own mind. They retreated to water that was choppy, but not dangerous. Reeve could see land in the far distance.

"Will other boats come out this far?"

"Boats with engines, yes."

Reeve couldn't see any signs of activity on the water. "When?" He was forming an idea. He would make it look like the little boat was in trouble, and when one of the motorized boats came to help, he'd use his rifle to take command and head out farther into the South Atlantic.

"When?" The old man shrugged. "Who knows? An hour? Two hours?" He shrugged again.

Reeve was feeling the cold. He was wet and seriously fatigued. His core temperature was dropping again. He asked if the old man had any clothing on the boat. There was an oilskin beneath Reeve's seat. He put that on and immediately felt more sheltered from the stiff breeze. The old man signaled that there was food and drink in the canvas bag. Reeve rummaged and found bread, apples, chorizo sausage, and a bottle of something which smelled evilly of alcohol. The old man took a swig of this, and told Reeve he could eat what he liked. Reeve ate one apple and half a peppery sausage. The old man pulled the oars in and laid them on the floor of the boat, where they sat in two inches of water. Then he lifted up one of his rods and started to tie bait onto it.

"Might as well," he said. "While we're here. Do you mind me asking, what are we waiting for?"

"Friends," Reeve told him.

The old man laughed for some reason, and baited another rod.

An old man fishing from two lines, and another man huddled in a tattered yellow oilskin. That was the sight that greeted the rescue party.

Reeve heard the engine first. It was an outboard. He scanned the waves, but it was behind him. He turned his head and saw an inflatable dinghy scudding across the foam. It had no markings, and none of the three men in it wore distinguishing uniforms or insignia.

Reeve aimed his rifle at the boat, and two of the men onboard aimed their rifles back at him. When the two vessels were twenty feet apart, the man steering the dinghy asked a question in Spanish.

"What are you doing here?"

"Fishing," the old man said simply. He had rolled and lit himself a cigarette. It bobbed in his mouth as he spoke.

"Who are you?" the man on the dinghy demanded.

"Fishermen," the old man said.

Now the man commanding the dinghy stared at Reeve. Reeve held the stare. The man smiled.

"You look like hell," he said in English. "Let's get you back to the ship."

The debriefing took place while the Argentine garrison formally surrendered on the night of June 14. Reeve had been given a thorough physical by a doctor, then was allowed to eat, sleep, and clean up — in any order he liked. Mike Rose, 22 Battalion's CO, was not on the ship. Reeve was debriefed initially by three of his own officers, and again later by a couple of spooks. There would be a further debriefing next day.

They asked about Jay, and he told them the truth. They didn't like that. They made him go over the story several times, probing at various details like dentists seeking a pinprick of decay. Reeve just kept telling them the truth. It didn't go any further. A senior officer came to see him, one on one.

"You'll be up for a commendation," the officer said, "probably a medal."

"Yes, sir." Reeve didn't care a damn.

"But the regiment doesn't air its dirty linen in public."

"No, sir."

"No one's to know about Jay."

"Understood, sir."

The officer smiled and nodded, unable to keep the relief off his face. "You'll be looking forward to a bit of R & R, Gordon."

"I want out altogether," Reeve told the officer, quietly but firmly. "Out of the regiment and out of the army."

The officer stared at him, then blinked. "Well, we'll see about that. Maybe you should take some time to think about it, eh?"

"Yes, sir."

But Reeve knew he wouldn't change his mind.

Days and weeks passed. Jay never appeared — in Chile or anyplace else. He was eventually presumed dead, though the Argentine military authorities denied capturing him or killing him. It was as if he really had vanished in that puff of smoke, leaving nothing behind but a snatch of a badly whistled children's song.

A song Reeve had hated ever since.

And a man he'd hated with it.

TWENTY-TWO

JAY WORE HIS ARMANI-LOOK-ALIKE SUIT to LAX. He liked the way it was roomy: you could strap a holster to your ankle, tape a knife to your leg, and nobody would know. You could carry a small semiautomatic beneath your jacket, an Ingram or one of the folding-butt Kalashnikovs, especially if you had a special pocket and release strap sewn into the lining, as Jay had. The tailor in Singapore had made the alterations after Jay had been measured for the suit. Jay had drawn a picture of what he wanted, and what he wanted it for. The tailor had been bug-eyed, and had knocked a few dollars off his original estimate. It was a tactic Jay had tried since, with similar success.

He toted a Heckler & Koch MP5 to the airport, its stock fully retracted. He had a little snub-nosed revolver around his ankle, and ammo in his pocket. He was chewing gum and wearing Harley-Davidson sunglasses. He wore brown loafers and ice-blue socks with the yellow suit. He fitted right in.

He didn't carry his two-way radio or a telephone of any kind, but he was wearing a wire. He had three men in the terminal building and two more outside. Not that he was expecting trouble. He was grinning, the way he often did these days, though nobody but him got the joke. He tried to blow a bubble, but it was the wrong kind of gum. It was hard to find the right kind of gum these days. Jay whistled a little tune, knowing the guys listening in wouldn't appreciate it. He was wondering what kind of stunt Gordon Reeve would pull. Should have finished the fucker off in France. Funny the way fate threw old shadows in your face, blotting out the sun. In — where was it? Yes, Singapore, same trip he bought the suit — in Singapore he'd bumped into a guy he'd known in 2 Para, before he'd joined Special Forces. Jay had been sinking dark rums at some bar, maybe three in the morning, and this guy had literally bumped into him. They'd sized each other up, both keening for a fight; then the man took a step back and dropped his arms.

"Jay," he'd said. "Fuck me, it *is* you."

So they'd had a drink — a few drinks actually — then Jay had taken the guy, whose name was Bolter or Boulter or something like that, to a brothel he knew. It was just a small apartment of two bedrooms above an electrical shop, but it did such good business they had to wait in the rank hallway, plied with beer laced with Christ knew what, for twenty minutes, until Jay kicked down a door and dragged a weary punter off one of the girls. The service got better after that; they had a bloody good time after that. Then Jay and his pal went for a walk down by the docks. You'd never seen so many little boats bobbing on the water. It was getting on for six in the morning, and though both men were bushed, neither wanted to go to sleep.

"Here, this'll help," Jay had said, sliding a narrow-bladed knife into the back of his old colleague's neck. He dragged the body behind some trash cans, took a wristwatch and all the cash on the body, plus any papers he had with his name on them. He got rid of the stuff on his way back to his own hotel. Thing was, he couldn't have anyone from the old days knowing he was still around — the SAS would want to talk to him about desertion. They'd be terrifically keen to talk to him, and not just to catch up on the good old days. He didn't know what story Reeve had given, whether he'd told the truth or not; he hoped he'd never have to know.

Funny thing was, next time he was in Singapore and went back to the brothel, one of the girls complained that his friend had given her herpes. So Bolter or Boulter had left something behind. Everybody did.

Jay liked the life he had now, a life he'd carved out for himself — sometimes literally — in America. It hadn't been easy. In fact, it had been fucking hard — especially those first weeks in South America. On the run, a one-man slaughterhouse. He'd killed three Argentine soldiers that first night, one for each man who'd died on the glacier, but it hadn't been enough to erase the memory of that doomed mission. Jay had seen something on that glacier, his eyes peering into the whiteout. He'd seen the bland white face of Death. It was an absence, an uncaring void, and the more chilling for that, the more hypnotic. He'd stared at it for a long time, not bothering with goggles. When they'd lifted him onto the helicopter, he'd been snow-blind. But when the blindness receded, there was a clearer vision in its place, a knowledge of helplessness and the will to power. It had taken him all the way through Tierra del Fuego and into Chile.

He'd killed one poor bastard because he needed civvy clothes, and another for his motorcycle, which duly packed up after thirty miles, forcing him to walk for a while. Big fucking country Chile — north to south anyway. He'd stuck to the west coast, killing some bearded Australian backpacker for his passport. Jesus, backpacking in fucking Chile: that was asking for trouble.

He'd crossed into Peru, smiling for the border guards like the man in the picture in the passport, rubbing his chin and laughing, to show he'd shaved a lot of his beard off since the photo had been taken. They stayed somber throughout but let him go. The backpacker's body would never be found, not while it had skin on it, though one day the skeleton might be found. He bypassed Ecuador and went into Colombia. People in Peru had told him not to do it, but he didn't see why not — and it was lucky he didn't heed their warnings, because Colombia turned out to be a great place, and the site of his first civilian job. He'd met up with some hard cases in Cali and ran a few errands for them. He got to know the kingpin, Edouard, and Edouard told him there was always work for those willing to undertake personal risk.

"I've taken more risks than you'll ever know," Jay had said, though in fact he'd already told Edouard most of the Rio Grande story, exaggerating somewhat and turning Reeve into an early corpse.

Eventually, Edouard had given Jay a job which involved liaison with some Americans. The Americans took him with them to Venezuela and from there to Jamaica, where he decided to stay awhile and was duly passed to yet another new employer. He was learning fast what his employers wanted, and how to know if a proffered fee was a rip-off or not. He stayed in Jamaica more than a year and saved enough to buy an American identity. Later on, homesick, he bought himself a new British passport, too, and now he had a Canadian one as well — all in different names of course, none of them his own.

When the Jamaican police started asking questions about a headless, handless corpse that had been dragged out of a trash dump on the edge of Kingston, Jay left the island, not without regrets, and headed to the USA, feeling immediately at home in Miami. Jesus, what a madhouse. It was in Miami that he found himself talking like an American, even though most people he spoke to still mistook him for an Australian. Jay set up his stall in Miami, but found work hard to come by. It was all organized, mostly along clan lines: he wasn't Cuban, so the Cubans didn't want him; he wasn't Puerto Rican, so the PRs wouldn't take him. They had their own firepower, and if they needed freelancers, there were a hundred kids on the street, each one with something to prove and nothing to lose.

Jay got in touch with Edouard, who put him in touch with an old friend. Edouard had been good to Jay, and Jay had liked him. There was an affinity between them, two men who only ever liked to be called by a single name. The only hit Jay had ever turned down had been on Edouard.

Edouard's old friend brought Jay to L.A. The man's name was Fessler, and Jay had worked for Mr. Fessler — that was what you had to call him, Mr. Fessler; Jay sometimes thought even Fessler's wife called him that — for three years before setting up on his own. He liked the regular income, but itched to be his own boss. It was tough at first, but got easier after the first couple of jobs. In fact, the money got so good, Jay developed a nose-talc habit which he broke only with the aid of a lot of booze. A *lot* of booze. The booze had put some weight on him which no amount of workouts seemed able to shift, but he thought he carried it well enough, and in a baggy suit no one noticed, right?

La-La Land, that was what Jay called Los Angeles. He'd come across it in a book about snuff movies. The appellation stuck in his mind, and he pretended he'd made it up, even to people who knew he hadn't.

He liked La-La Land. He liked being his own boss. Above all, he liked working for big companies. Big companies paid well and let you get on with it. They didn't want to know the details, the procedures — they just wanted the job done. And they paid on the nail. No fuss, no mess, minimum paperwork. Jay's cover was as a "corporate restructuring adviser," and he'd even read books on the subject. Well, articles anyway. He bought the *Wall Street Journal* sometimes, too, and he was an avid reader of some bits of *Time*. He had letterheaded paper and knew a guy who could type up an expense sheet or an account if the employer really wanted one. These pieces of paper were art forms, full of terms like "workstation projection analyses" and "capital fluidity advisement," stuff Jay didn't understand, but the guy who did the typing swore they meant something.

Kosigin wasn't like anyone Jay had ever worked for. For a start, he wanted to know *everything* — every detail. And he would make Jay tell the story several times over. Jay was never sure if Kosigin was looking for him to make a mistake in the retelling, or if the guy just got off on the stuff Jay told him. Certainly, no matter how exaggeratedly gruesome Jay made the details, Kosigin never winced, never showed any emotion. He'd just stand there at his office window, or sit at his desk with his hands together as if in prayer, the tips of his fingers just touching his chin. The fucker was creepy, no doubt about that. No doubt at all.

But Jay reckoned he could learn a few things about deportment from Mr. Kosigin. He liked Kosigin's style. Kosigin was Brooks Brothers for work and L.L. Bean for casual moments, as buttoned-down as an oxford shirt. He would never feel right in Armani, even if it was original. He was aloof, but that just made him seem stronger. Jay liked to visit him in his office. He liked to study him.

It was like a message, when Kosigin gave him the job which led to Reeve being delivered unto him. It was like a dream. Jay could have taken Reeve out a dozen times since, any number of different ways, but he wanted a face-to-face. He wanted to know what had happened to Reeve, and what he'd told the brass. Just for his own personal satisfaction.

Then he'd kill him.

And if Reeve wouldn't tell, or made any rash first move . . . well, Jay would drop him without a second's hesitation.

"Where's this fucking bulletin board?" he murmured, walking through the packed concourse. It was like a demolition derby of luggage carts and parties of elderly couples, all with walkers and umbrellas and bags of golf clubs and raincoats folded over pencil-thin liver-spotted arms. Umbrellas in La-La Land! It was a madhouse, and the lunatics had been in charge so long that nobody bothered to question the system anymore.

"I love this town," he said out loud, maneuvering past the latest obstruction. He finally saw the information kiosk, though it was doing its best to blend in with the scenery. He passed a couple of his guys without acknowledging their presence, but when he got to the board, he stopped and turned on his heels, checking all around, studying the scene through the plate-glass window — a jam of cabs and minibuses and a frantic cop windmilling his arms at them. The cop had a whistle in his mouth, referee-style. Jay remembered that moment in the scrape, when he knew he had to jump and fight or he'd implode, he'd been lying there so long and so quiet. He knew that in technical parlance, he had "cracked" — but fuck that. Reeve was so tight-arsed he'd have lain there and let a bomb detonate between his cheeks. If Jay hadn't got up and run, very probably neither of them would still be alive. That was something else he wanted to tell Reeve; he wanted Reeve to thank him for getting him out of that situation. He reckoned he was owed a little respect.

He looked around him again, and up towards the ceiling, and nothing he saw looked like a trap.

So then he studied the bulletin board, both sides, and he smiled at the clerk at the information desk, just in case he had something to do with it. Then he turned his attention to the notices again, especially the folded paper napkin with the name *JAY* written on it. He touched it with a finger, ran the palm of his hand down it, feeling for a bump, maybe some tiny explosive device which would take off a couple of fingers or blind him in one eye. That sort of magnitude.

But there was nothing. He lifted one corner of the napkin, but the layers started to peel, and he had to take off another layer before he could make out that there was writing there. So then he licked his lips and hauled the napkin off the board in a single swift movement, so that the clerk looked at him quizzically. "All clear here," Jay said, as if to himself. Then he unfolded the note, the note telling him to fly to London. It gave the name of a hotel, and said a message would arrive there for him in the name of Rowe.

Rowe: that was a nice touch.

One of his hired hands came up, removing his earpiece as he approached. "So?"

"So nothing, just a fucking note."

They'd been all wound up. They'd been told of Reeve's rep. Jay had wanted them ready for anything. They were going to go away frustrated, pent-up, needing to unwind.

"Everyone to the cars," Jay said. "We'll go back to the gym, maybe hit a bar later. I just got to make a call first."

He went to the public pay phones and called Kosigin.

"Well?" Kosigin demanded.

Jay read the note out to him. "What do you want me to do?" he asked when he'd finished.

"Personally," Kosigin said, "I want you to follow the instructions."

"And what if I'm walking into a trap?"

"I thought you were clever enough to avoid traps?"

"I am, but I also don't believe in walking into them in the first place."

"Then what do you suggest?"

"I'll go, but I want to take some men with me. It won't be cheap."

"It never is."

"You want to come along for the ride?"

"Absolutely not."

"You still want me to go?"

"Absolutely," Kosigin said before hanging up.

Their conversation had gone exactly as Jay had known it would.

He looked around him for a sales desk, then walked over to the information kiosk.

"Which carriers fly to London?" he asked. He might have to try more than one. Could be difficult to make a block booking at such short notice . . .

PART NINE
BLOOD HUNT

TWENTY-THREE

THERE WERE POLICE ON DUTY at Heathrow, a lot of uniforms. Reeve would bet there were some plainclothes detectives around, too. Maybe they were looking for him. At this point, he could only trust to luck. Everyone deserved one lucky break per mission. They might have a description of him, but it would be pre-haircut. They couldn't have a recent photograph; ever since his days in the SAS, Reeve had been camera-shy. The weekend soldiers sometimes wanted photographs, and he didn't refuse. But before posing for their cameras, he would don a balaclava and dark glasses. The weekend soldiers loved it.

Reeve had a lot of planning to do. He wasn't too happy about returning to Jim's Saab, which he had parked in a long-term parking lot only a courtesy bus ride away from the Heathrow terminals. He didn't know how clever the police would be; he didn't think they would trace him as far as the Saab, but he couldn't be sure. To add to this, the car was a liability, and might break down at any minute. But he had very little alternative. He didn't want to rent a new car. That would mean handing over his credit card, and he guessed the police would be tracking its use. (They probably didn't know about his secret bank account, and even if they did they might not want to freeze it: if he accessed cash or wrote a check they'd have another way of tracking his movements.)

The people at the parking lot, on the other hand, knew only the false name he'd given them. He'd paid cash up front — so probably there wouldn't be a problem. But Reeve didn't enter the single-story office straightaway. First he took a look around the lot. He could see the Saab. It wasn't hard for him to spot among the shiny new Jags and BMWs and Rovers. The company had hemmed it in behind more expensive cars, reckoning them a better ad to potential customers. Reeve didn't blame them — he was actually relieved the Saab had been hidden from view during his time away.

He walked into the office.

"Had a good trip?" the girl behind the desk asked.

"Yes, thanks," he said. There was complimentary coffee on a table nearby, and he helped himself to a cup. There was powdered milk only, so he took it black. It was bitter, but it woke him up a bit.

"Now, Mr. Fleming, you didn't specify a return date, so we've not been able to valet your car."

"No problem. The dirt is the only thing holding it together."

She smiled and filled in the rest of the form, which he had to sign at the bottom. He couldn't recall what first name he'd given, but saw it printed at the head of the sheet. Jay. He'd called himself Jay Fleming.

"And here are your keys," the receptionist said, handing them over.

"I think you'll need to move a few of the other cars."

"Oh, you're blocked in. I'll get Tom to see to it."

Tom was outside, drinking tea from a flask. He wore overalls, a slicker, and Wellingtons, and was without doubt the valet. Reeve watched as he started up and moved a gleaming red BMW 635 and a silver Rover 200. He thanked him and trundled the Saab out of the parking lot and into the lanes of traffic. It was the start of what was going to be a long twenty-four hours.

He headed north, stopping only for gas and coffee and to read all the newspapers. He cursed the Saab's lack of a radio — he needed to know whether the police had connected him to the Marie Villambard killing. McCluskey had mentioned Interpol interest, but that could have been a bluff. But when he stopped near the border and bought some Scottish newspapers, he caught his first mention of the story, relegated to an inside page. Police, it said, were "anxious to contact Scots climbing instructor Gordon Reeve." There was no description, but they could have published one in a previous day's edition. He stopped at a Little Chef to replenish his caffeine level, and telephoned Joan's sister. Joan herself answered the phone.

"Joan, it's Bob Plant here, any sign of Gordon?"

She recognized his voice immediately. There was a slight pause as she came to understand what was going on. (She'd had a crush on Robert Plant of Led Zeppelin at one time.) "Bob," she said, "sorry, I'm not thinking straight."

"Are you all right, Joan?"

"I'm fine. It's just been a shock, with the police and everything."

"They've been asking you questions?" He sounded like a solicitous friend.

"Well, they just want to know where Gordon is. You know they found his car in France, near where three bodies were found, one of them a woman's."

"Gracious."

"They're keeping watch on the house here, just in case he shows up."

"They think he had something to do with the murders?"

"Well, Bob, what would *you* think if you were them? Gordon's Land Rover burned out and no trace of him anywhere."

"I suppose you're right."

"Bob, I'm worried about him."

"Gordon can take care of himself, Joan."

"Yes, I know, but — "

"Might he go back to the island?"

"I don't know. There are police watching the ferries."

"A real manhunt, eh?"

"They may even be watching the house."

"Ach, unlikely he'd head back there."

"Yes, I suppose so. But where else would he be? Where could he go?"

"You know him better than I do, Joan."

"Well, I thought I knew him, Bob."

Silence on the line.

"Joan," Reeve said, looking in at the diners — families mostly, "he'll be all right. I'm sure he's done nothing wrong."

"Try telling the police that."

"Maybe he needs evidence first, I mean before he can come back."

"Evidence?"

"Of his innocence."

Joan sniffed. He could tell she was crying.

"I'll phone again," he told her.

"I'm sorry," she said, wiping her nose.

"Maybe I shouldn't have called."

"No, I'm glad you did. It's been a while, Bob."

"Yes, it has. Is Allan all right?"

"Missing his dad. But at the same time — I know this is wrong — he seems to quite like the idea of having a father who's a wanted man." She laughed.

Reeve smiled, and blinked back tears. At one table, a father was admonishing his son, who still had a full plate of food in front of him. The kid was nine, maybe ten. The man spoke in a low voice, but his eyes were blazing.

"Bye, Joan," he said.

"Good-bye, Bob."

He kept the receiver to his ear after she'd put down the phone, and heard a double click and what sounded like a stifled sneeze. The bastards were listening in, just as he'd suspected. Not Jay or Kosigin this time, but the police. He ran through the conversation again, satisfied he hadn't given anything away. And he'd learned so much.

"Thanks, love," he said quietly, heading back to his table and a refill of coffee.

If they were watching the ferries, they'd be watching Oban and Tarbert on the mainland, both of which had direct sailings: Oban to South Uist and Tarbert to North Uist. The two islands were separated by the smaller island of Benbecula, and all three were linked by bridges. They might also be watching Uig, a small port on Skye. But to get to Skye he would have to take a short ferry ride from Kyle of Lochalsh, the bridge to Kylerhea, or the much longer ferry crossing from Mallaig. Unless there was manpower to spare, Reeve doubted anyone would be watching Mallaig.

Which was precisely why he ignored Oban and drove instead to Fort William and from there to Mallaig on the coast. There were no direct ferries from Mallaig to the Outer Hebrides.

At the same time, he couldn't afford to relax. His face was known in the town, and a few people even knew him by name. There would be police in the vicinity, maybe not in Mallaig itself, but nearby. And if his description had been in the papers . . .

He was there to seek out one of the people who knew him by name, an old rogue called Kenneth Creech. "Creech short for creature," Kenneth sometimes said in introduction — and he had a point. He reminded Reeve in particular of a lizard; all he was missing was the green skin.

Kenneth Creech had a narrow, jagged face that fell to two distinct points — his chin and the extruding tip of his nose. When you looked at him face-on, his nostrils couldn't be seen at all. His eyes bugged from his face, and his tongue, which slid an inch or two from his mouth between utterances, was thin and pointed like his face. He was known to cheat at cards, siphon gas from any unlocked fuel tank (to which end he sometimes carried a gallon drum with him, empty at the start of the evening), and be foulmouthed in front of the opposite sex, while nary a curse passed his lips in the company of his fellow men.

People steered clear of Kenneth Creech. Reeve had got to know him when Creech had tricked him out of some money which was to pay for the transportation of some stuff between North Uist and the mainland. Creech owned a couple of small boats and some creels and lobster pots. He never actually used these, but somehow managed to be the recipient of a European Community "Business Expansion Grant," which had paid for the second boat and kept Creech well-enough off besides.

In the summer, Creech sometimes tricked tourists into going

with him on one of the boats for what was supposed to be an all-day pleasure cruise around "the beautiful Hebrides." In fact, he'd head straight for the choppiest waters and most dangerous wind-torn straits, after which the tourists would beg to return to land. At this point, they'd be told there were no refunds. If they argued for their money back, Creech would pay them, then would drop them off somewhere on the far side of Skye, pretending they were a mile or so south of Mallaig.

Reeve liked Creech. He liked him so much he had eventually let Creech keep the money he'd been cheated of.

Creech hated mankind, but he surely did love money. Reeve was counting on this fact.

Kenneth Creech had a boathouse just north of the town. It was six in the evening when Reeve got there, having driven through town without stopping. The sky to the west, out over Skye and the Minch, was a palette of pinks and grays, thin threads of silver and softly glowing red. Reeve gave it all of a second of his time then kicked at the boathouse door, which rattled on its hinges.

The door was locked, but that didn't mean Creech wasn't inside. At last a bolt slid back and the door opened.

"You'll pay for any damage," Creech snapped, examining his door first and his visitor second. His mouth made an O when he recognized Reeve.

"Well now, Gordon," he said. "What brings you here?"

"Money," Reeve said, holding up a thickish fold of notes. "To wit, my desire to give you some."

Creech couldn't take his eyes off the cash. "Well now, Gordon," he said, the tongue darting in and out of his mouth, "you must be wanting a boat."

"How did you guess?"

Creech didn't say anything, just ushered him inside. The back of the boathouse opened onto the Sound of Sleat. Reeve could see the southern tip of Skye. The larger of the two boats was tied up in the water; it had bench seats both sides, and could carry a dozen passengers. In the middle of the deck stood the control console with a small steering wheel, like that of a sports car. In fact, if you looked closer, there was the MG insignia in the center of the wheel. Creech had stolen it from a crashed car south of the town. By the time the insurance investigators reached the vehicle, there hadn't been much left but a shell.

Creech's other boat was smaller, but boasted an outboard motor and was a lot nippier as a result. It had been hauled out of the water and now hung by winches over the wooden floor. Old newspapers were scattered beneath the hull, which Creech was in the middle of repainting.

"You're painting over the barnacles," Reeve told him. Creech was wiping his hands on a rag. The paint tin looked to Reeve like ordinary vinyl silk emulsion. The color, according to the lid of the tin, was taupe.

"Well, it's a sight easier than scraping them off."

Reeve nodded, and smiled at Creech, who looked nervier even than usual. He kept jerking his head and blinking his bulbous eyes.

"You know about me?" Reeve said.

Creech started to deny it. Denial was an instinct, like breathing. But then he broke off, knowing Reeve knew.

"I've heard a few stories," he said at last, sounding like it didn't bother him in the slightest.

Reeve looked around. "You've no phone here, Kenneth?"

Creech shook his head slowly, then spoke carefully. "I wouldn't turn you in, Gordon."

"That's unusually friendly of you, Kenneth. What's wrong, isn't there a reward?"

The momentary look in Creech's eyes told Reeve he'd never considered the possibility until now.

"Don't," Reeve warned him.

Creech got back some mobility and went over to the boat, picking up his paintbrush. He'd left it lying on the edge of the newspaper, and some paint had dribbled onto the floor. He wiped the spot with his rag, but that just spread the stain farther.

"I'm painting this boat," he said.

"I'd never have guessed." Reeve paused. "But that's the boat I want."

Creech glanced towards him. "Now?" Reeve nodded. "Can't it wait till I'm finished?"

"Do I look like a man who can wait?"

"No." The word took a long time coming out. "But you surely don't want to take a boat out at night?" Creech paused. "No wait, of course you do. There's less chance of them spotting you at night."

"Well done, Kenneth. How many police are there?"

Creech considered lying, but looked at the money again, the money Reeve was still holding in his hand.

"There's more where this came from," Reeve told him.

Creech wet his already glistening lips. "Well, there's nobody in Mallaig," he said, "but I've heard tell there are a couple of strange faces on Skye."

"Anywhere else?"

"Oh, aye, they were in Oban yesterday."

"And Tarbert?"

"I couldn't tell you about Tarbert."

"And on South Uist?"

"Well, they've been to your house a couple of times, that much I've heard. You're big news around here, Gordon."

"I didn't do anything, Kenneth."

"I don't doubt it, I don't doubt it, but the police used to have a saying in Glasgow: you don't arrest an innocent man. If they take you in, they'll try their damnedest to find *something* against you, even if it means planting the evidence."

Reeve smiled. "You sound like you've been there."

"I was in trouble enough in my early days. I'm from Partick, remember. One look at my face — I know it's no beauty — and the polis would stop me." Creech spat into the water.

"You'll help me?"

Creech considered the question. The tension left his shoulders. "Ach, maybe I'm too sentimental for my own good," he said. "Of course I'll help you."

And he held out his hand for the cash.

Reeve helped him move the boat back over the water and lower it in, so that its side scraped that of the larger vessel, leaving smears of paint on the wood. Creech went to check that the boathouse doors were locked. When Creech returned, Reeve was standing at the workbench, his back to him. Creech licked his lips again and moved forward quietly. When Reeve turned, Creech let out an involuntary gasp. Reeve was holding the biggest knife Creech had ever seen. He had it in his right hand, a coil of Creech's best rope in the other.

"What . . . what are you going to do?" Creech said.

Reeve showed him. He sliced through the thick braids like they were string, then let the long part of the rope fall to the floor. "I'm going to tie you up," he told Creech.

"No need for that, Gordon. I'll come with you."

"And you'd wait in the boat for me? You wouldn't for example sprint off the minute I was on dry land and head for the nearest mainland telephone?"

"No," Creech said. "You know I wouldn't."

But Reeve was shaking his head. "This way we both know where we stand. Or in your case, sit."

And he made Creech sit on the floor with his back to the workbench, tying his hands behind him around one thick wooden leg of the structure. For good measure, he cut another length of rope — "That stuff costs a fortune," Creech protested — and tied Creech's ankles. He thought of sticking the paint rag in Creech's mouth, but he wanted to restrain the man, nothing more. He doubted anyone would come to see Creech during his absence. Creech had no friends, no one who'd miss him; he spent most of his time in the boathouse, and had even put up a partition so he could sleep there, too. Reeve glanced into the "bedroom" to make sure there *was* no telephone. He'd seen no cables outside, but it was best to check. All he saw was a mattress and duvet on the floor, a candlestick, an empty whiskey bottle, and a pornographic magazine.

Satisfied, he brought his bag in from the car and got to work, changing into dark clothes and balaclava, donning face-blacking. Creech's face told him he had achieved the right effect. There was a good-sized moon in a clear sky. He wouldn't have any trouble navigating; he knew the islands and the potential obstacles pretty well. He had a choice of two routes: one would take him into the Sound of Eriskay so he could approach the western side of South Uist. The advantage of this route was that he'd have a shorter hike at the end of it, two or so miles, but it meant a lot more time spent in the boat than the second route, which would land him in Loch Eynort, a seawater loch. This way he would land farther away from Stoneybridge, maybe as much as a six-mile hike away. It made for a longer time on land, more time for him to be spotted. Plus, of course, if forced to retreat, he'd have a lot farther to run to reach the safety of the boat.

He decided in the end to head for Loch Eynort. If all went well it would cut hours off the mission time, being a much shorter boat crossing. He still doubted he'd complete his mission under the cover of darkness, but the sooner he started the better chance he'd have. He loaded spare fuel into the boat, and took one of Creech's better sets of rain gear, plus a flashlight and mooring rope. Then he cut himself a length of twine, and tied about a dozen knots in it, each one a couple of inches from its neighbor.

Finally he went back over to Creech, who'd been complaining throughout about aching arms. "I could always amputate," he said, showing Creech the knife. That shut him up. "What's the water in the Minch likely to be like tonight?"

"Cold and wet." Reeve inched the knife closer to Creech, who gave in quickly and told Reeve the prevailing winds and the forecast: it would be blustery, but far from unmanageable. Of course, he could have been lying, but Reeve didn't think so — it was in his interests for Reeve to return. For one thing, he might starve to death otherwise, since chances were nobody came near the boathouse from one week to the next. For another, he loved his boats too much. He wouldn't want one tipped and sunk in a gale, especially not the one with the expensive European Community outboard motor.

"Take care of her," Creech begged.

"Thanks for your concern," Reeve said, climbing down the ladder into the boat.

The crossing was worse than he'd anticipated, but that was typical of Little Minch: you thought it had done its worst, then it did a little more. He was glad he didn't have to tackle the sounds; Eriskay could be particularly hair-raising. He wondered no amusement park had sought to emulate it — talk about a white-knuckle ride. His own knuckles were quite white enough as he wrestled with the outboard. The only good news was that it wasn't raining. Still, he was glad he was wearing the rain gear, considering the amount of spray that was being washed over him. He kept close to the Skye coast for as long as he could before heading out into Little Minch proper. He was taking as direct a line as he could, hoping he would hit the coast in the right place. The way the wind was blowing, and without much in the way of navigation save his small compass, he knew he might be blown off course by as much as three or four miles, which would only add to the trek if he decided to land the boat.

He saw a couple of boats, warning lights flashing to let others know they were there, but they didn't see him, and they certainly couldn't hear him. He changed hands often on the outboard's throttle, but even so wished he'd thought to bring gloves. He used his breath to warm his fingers, then worked them in the raincoat's pocket, rubbing life back into them.

His mind was on nothing but the crossing itself. He couldn't afford not to concentrate his full attention on it.

Finally he saw land and, checking to the south, could make out the small island of Stuley, which meant he was just south of Loch Eynort. He'd been adjusting direction to account for the winds, and was pleased to find he had corrected his course wisely. The water was already much less choppy, and as he entered the inlet he felt the wind drop. He took the boat as far into the loch as he could. Stepping onto land was a relief and a strange sensation. He felt his feet weren't wholly connected to the ground, as though gravity had lost its grip. He knew the feeling would not last long. It was a trick his brain was playing on him.

Reeve grabbed his bag and headed along the road.

There were a couple of crofts nearby, but no signs of life in them. At this hour, the only things awake might be a few sheep and the night birds and animals. The road he was on would soon cross the A865. If he stayed on the road, he'd round the southern side of Loch Ollay and come to a junction. Left would take him to Ormiclate; right would take him towards Stoneybridge and home. He'd checked the time upon landing: he wanted to know how long the hike took. He was also pacing it out. He had the twine in his hand, and was counting his steps. Every hundred steps he slid another knot through thumb and forefinger. At the end of the piece of twine, he could then multiply by length of stride to find roughly how far he'd gone, which would help him estimate how fast he was traveling.

He didn't really need this information. What he *did* need was to feel like a soldier again. Because soon he'd be coming up against Jay, one way or another, and he had to be mentally sharp. At short notice, there wasn't much he could do to bolster his fitness or physique — the years had taken their toll. From what he'd seen of Jay, the man would be stronger than him: fighting him physically would be a lost cause. What Reeve needed to do was become strong mentally; he needed to hone his attitude and his instincts. He needed proper planning and procedure, starting right now.

Knowing the roads as he did, he made good time to the house. He could have shaved minutes off by crossing country, but he'd have been more likely to get lost, and running on a road was easier on the muscles than running over rough terrain.

He took his time approaching the house.

He did one full circuit around it at a distance of half a mile, then closed in and circled it again. If anyone was watching for him, they were well concealed. He knew policemen, and knew they weren't trained that way. For one thing, they liked their creature comforts; for another, they didn't have the necessary patience. There might be a presence inside the house, but he'd swear there was no one out here with him.

Silently, he entered the compound, crouching low, keeping to the shadows along the walls. There was an added advantage to staying close by the walls: the drive itself was gravel and noisy underfoot, but there was a two-foot border of earth between the driveway and the walls, a concession to Joan, who had planted small flowers and climbers there. Reeve crushed them underfoot in silence.

He had the keys he needed in his free hand, the keys to the killing-room door. But the police had been there first. They'd taken a sledgehammer to the door, which looked like it had resisted their onslaught bravely. The door swung inwards to the touch. He wondered what they'd thought when they'd found the room, with empty cartridge casings on the floor and shop-window dummies acting as hostages. He knelt down in front of the baseboard and shone the flashlight against it. It looked undisturbed. Reeve pulled it open and reached in, touching the oiled rags, feeling the metal bulk beneath their wrapping.

And he smiled.

He unwrapped the Beretta and found the right pack of ammo for it, filling his pockets as well as the gun. Pushing his hand back into the wall, he pulled out a package of plastic explosive with all the trimmings. The material itself was fairly fresh; he'd been using it to rig up explosions some weekends, to keep his soldiers on their toes. Reeve checked for detonators, wire, and wire cutters; everything he needed was in the package, including the crocodile clips, which acted as triggers. He put everything in his holdall, then replaced the baseboard and made sure he'd left no footprints.

He crossed the courtyard, moving slowly on the gravel and pebbles. Peering through the kitchen window, he saw nothing. He circled the house, looking in the windows on all four sides: still nothing. He couldn't tell about upstairs. It was just possible that a guard could be asleep in one of the bedrooms. The curtains in Allan's room were closed, but maybe he'd just forgotten to open them the morning they'd been cleared out.

Reeve unlocked the front door and entered the hall. He didn't need to disable the alarm: the police must already have done that. He wondered how long it had rung before they'd found a way to silence it. Not that it mattered out here; the nearest croft wasn't within hailing distance.

He double-checked the downstairs rooms then made for the stairwell. The second step from the bottom was the creaky one, so he avoided it, just as he avoided the middle of the third step from the top. He didn't use the banister for fear of a warning sound. On the landing, he held his breath and listened. There was no noise. He waited there three full minutes: when someone's asleep, they usually make some sort of sound every three minutes or so. Reeve suspected that a policeman would have *some* regard for property, so any guard would probably choose to sleep in the guest room. He opened the door slowly and pointed his pistol through the crack. The curtains weren't closed, and moonlight filled the room. The bed was made up, with several throw pillows and costume dolls arranged on it. Joan's work. She'd spent a lot of time lovingly decorating a room nobody ever came to stay in.

He turned and crossed the landing, opening Allan's bedroom door. The room was a mess: bedclothes thrown onto the floor, pajamas draped over the end of the bed, comics everywhere; the computer's power light shone lemon-yellow in the gloom. Either Allan had left it on, or the police had checked it and forgotten to turn it off. Reeve left the room and quickly checked the main bedroom and even the bathroom.

Then he breathed a sigh of relief.

Downstairs he found milk in the fridge, but it was sour. There was an unopened carton of orange juice, and he cut it open with scissors, then gulped from it. There was an unopened packet of ham in there, too, so he peeled it open and lifted out two slices, rolling them up and stuffing them into his mouth. Back in the living room, he assessed the visit by the police. They had dusted. Probably they wanted his fingerprints for the file they were opening on him. It looked like they'd shifted everything and put it back not quite in the right place. Searching for clues, he supposed. He unscrewed the telephone handsets. The bugging devices had been removed. He suspected this had been done by Dulwater rather than the police.

He didn't suppose anyone would be listening in, so he went upstairs and took a quick hot shower, thanking God for the instantaneous water heater. He left the light off in the bathroom, though he couldn't say why. Perhaps it was because it felt like procedure.

He dried himself off and searched for clean and, above all, *warm* clothes. There were a few other things he needed, but they were in his workshop. He walked into Allan's room again, restless, unable to sit down. The yellow light caught his attention. The screen was black, but when he nudged the mouse it came to life, showing him the games menu from the hard disk. There were a couple of good games there, and some which must have been new from the last time he and Allan had played together.

Then Reeve saw the game Allan had loaded from the disk sent to him by Jim. The game Allan couldn't get on with. It was called Prion.

"Jesus," Reeve whispered. Prion, as in PrP, as in the bad chemicals which had started this whole nightmare. His hand was fairly steady as he moved the pointer onto Prion and double-clicked to load the game.

When the title screen came up though, it wasn't called Prion at all. It looked like a fairly straight arcade game called Gumball Gulch, which is what Allan had called it, Reeve recalled. Which screen was it Allan had said he couldn't get past? Five? Six?

It took Reeve a while to follow the instructions and get into the game. As far as he could tell, he was a turtle in the Wild West, just made sheriff of the town of Gumball Gulch. In screen one, he rode into town and was voted sheriff after killing the three bad guys who had just shot the sheriff to bust their comrade out of the jail. In screen two, there was a bank robbery to foil. The graphics, so far as Reeve could judge, were pretty good, as were the sound effects, complete with voices.

After maybe half an hour, he was in screen four. In screen three he'd had the option of taking as deputy a one-legged drunk. Reeve had accepted "Stumpy," who now guarded the villains from the bank robbery.

Suddenly Reeve paused. "What the hell am I doing?" he asked himself. But he kept on going.

Screen four was a difficult one. Reelection time was coming up, and Reeve's popularity was only 40 percent, two of the bank robbers having escaped, and one innocent bystander having been gunned down during the shoot-out. Reeve granted a new license to the Brawlin' Barroom, which pushed his popularity to 50 percent. But then the rowdiness factor increased, and soon the cells were bursting. Reeve opted to take another deputy, a fresh-faced young kid.

"This is *Rio Bravo*," he muttered.

The real trouble started on screen five. There was a mass breakout attempt at the jail. Stumpy had the place locked tight with himself inside. He wasn't letting anyone in, the sheriff included, which left Reeve outside with one kid deputy, a restless populace, and a possible lynch mob. In a little while, the escaped bank robbers would be coming into town intent on revenge. Reeve's guns and ammo, of course, were in the jail.

And Stumpy was asking for the password.

Reeve tried a few obvious things, some only a *Rio Bravo* buff would know. Then he sat back, arms folded, and did some thinking. Jim had changed the name of the game to Prion. Why? Suddenly it became clear. As Marie Villambard had said, Jim was a journalist from his head to his toes. He would have kept files. He would have kept backups, and kept them well hidden.

Reeve knew now the purpose of the password. He typed in CWC, but it didn't work. He tried Co-World, then PrP, then Prion — to no avail. He tried Killin and Preece. Nothing.

So then he tried Kosigin.

And suddenly he wasn't in Gumball Gulch anymore. The bottom of the screen told him he was reading page one of twenty-eight. The print size was small; Jim had crammed a lot in. Single-spaced, too. At the top was a message in bold:

> I'll let you get back to the game soon, Gordon. I'm assuming it's you reading this, and if you are reading it then I'm most probably dead. If I am dead and if you are reading this, then you've probably been sniffing around and I thank you for your concern. The following may be of help. I'd dearly love to get it published. A friend called Marie in France may help; I'll give you her address at the end. But first, I have a story to tell you . . .

And what a story. Reeve already knew it, of course, but Jim had more information than anyone had suspected. There was the stuff about Preece's history, his "revolutionary" shock-sex therapy, and Kosigin's hiring of Alliance Investigative to dig up the details. Kosigin's blackmail of Preece had been implicit, but Jim's report made it explicit by actually interviewing two ex-investigators at Alliance who had worked on the job, as well as members of the original research team headed by Preece.

Including a Dr. Erik Korngold.

Jim had had two very cordial meetings with Korngold. It was Korngold who had admitted the blackmail. Preece had spoken to him about it at the time. But then Dr. Korngold had turned up dead, leaving Jim pretty well stuck unless he could get corroboration. The only other scientist he knew of from the original research team was Dr. Killin. So he'd started pestering Killin, and Killin had gone to Kosigin.

And Kosigin had decided the reporter had to be taken out of the game.

Jim's research was impressive — and scary. He detailed countries around the world where neurological diseases were on the increase, and showed how these increases correlated to the introduction of CWC herbicides and pesticides onto those countries' farms. There were snippets of interviews with farmers and doctors, agrichemical experts and environmentalists. Farmers everywhere were getting more and more ill. Stress, the skeptics had said. But Jim had found out different. And when the police *did* start to get curious about pesticide side effects, CWC simply shifted spheres, concentrating on third world countries.

Jim found a correlation with tobacco companies who, as western markets contracted after health scares, merely opened up new unsuspecting markets — Africa, Asia . . . CWC was doing the same thing with chemicals. What was more, Jim had been getting, at the time of writing, inklings of crooked deals to introduce pesticides into third world countries. Deals were done with governments, regimes, and dictators, money slipped into secret bank accounts, and import barriers suddenly disappeared. Jim hinted at links between CWC and the CIA, since the CIA wanted a presence in countries that CWC was opening up. It was a global conspiracy, encompassing governments, the scientific community, and everyone who had to eat.

Jim had worked hard and fast building up his case. He did so for a simple reason, one he stated towards the end of the file: "I think some people would kill to keep this secret, because while bits and pieces are well-enough known, certainly among the environmental pressure groups, no one has really been able to link it *globally*. They say you are what you eat. In that case, we're poison."

At the end, Jim gave Marie Villambard's address, and beneath that were some instructions. They told Reeve where he would find the "hard evidence." Jim had hidden all the documents — transcripts, notes, archive material, and tapes of interviews. They were in a box at Jilly Palmer's farm outside Tisbury. Jilly Palmer: Reeve remembered her long braid of chestnut hair, her rosy-red cheeks. Jim had been introduced to her by Josh Vincent, and had trusted her from the off. He'd asked her to store a large box for him, and to say nothing to anyone about it unless they told her they'd read about it on the disk.

"I'm keeping copies of some of the stuff with me," Jim concluded, "so that if any burglaries suddenly and mysteriously occur, they'll think they got what they came for."

Then a final message: "To access the next game level, press Ctrl+N. To quit, press Esc."

Reeve hit the Escape button and shut down the computer. The story had been here all the time, here under his own roof. His legs weren't the steadiest as he got to his feet. He couldn't think, couldn't concentrate on anything but his brother. He got down to the kitchen somehow and made himself a hot drink, then sat at the table sipping it, staring at nothing.

The mug was one-third empty when he started to cry.

He planned to call Jay's hotel that evening, which gave him a full day to prepare. High on his list was sleep, but first he had to return to the boat.

The early-morning waters were calmer, and the dawn made navigation easier. He made good time back to Mallaig. He could tell Creech had been sleeping, but he was awake now, looking miserable. Even so, he studied the boat carefully as Reeve brought her home.

"Not a scratch on her," Reeve said, clambering out with his stuff. He checked Creech's wrists. They were red-ringed, the skin broken at a couple of points. "Trying to escape, eh?"

"Wouldn't you?" Creech snarled. Reeve had to agree. "Man my age and condition, trussed like a Christmas turkey." Reeve untied him and told him to put the kettle on. When Creech came back, Reeve was laying out bank notes on the workbench.

"What's that for?" Creech tried not to sound too interested.

"I need your help, Kenneth. I'm sorry I had to tie you up, but to be honest I'd very little option. If I'd taken you with me, you'd've had to walk from Loch Eynort to Stoneybridge and back. But now I'd like you to help me. If you do, you pocket this money for starters."

Creech eyed the money. "How do you mean, starters?"

"I'll give you some passengers. They'll pay you whatever you ask. They'll just want to take one of your boats, perhaps both. Like I say, you can name your price."

The kettle was boiling. Creech didn't go to switch it off.

"What do I have to do?" he said.

There were old wooden boards lying around the place. It wasn't difficult to find two or three the right size, along with some fixing poles. They used the taupe paint to put a few words on the boards and, when it was dry, used a hot-air gun to peel some of it back off. Creech got some earth and rubbed it into the boards. In the end, they looked fairly authentic.

Then Reeve dipped into his bag and brought out a packet of red powder he'd brought from his workshop. It was like powdered paint, but mixed with a little water, it produced a thick bubbly liquid which looked just like blood. He used it some weekends, laying a fake trail for his soldiers. He didn't tell Creech what it was, or what it was for.

They stopped for more tea. Creech kept asking about these men who'd want to hire his boats. How did Reeve know about them? When would they come?

"I'll tell you later," Reeve said, standing up. "First though, I'm going to borrow your mattress for an hour or two. Okay?"

Creech nodded vigorously. Reeve lifted the Beretta out of the bag, waved it at Creech, and took it and his tea with him to the mattress.

Creech decided not to move from the table until Gordon Reeve awoke, no matter how long that took.

Reeve took Creech with him when he went to make the telephone call. Not because he didn't trust Creech, but because Creech didn't trust *him*. Creech wanted to hear him make the call.

They squeezed into a telephone box at the end of a farm road, and Reeve made the call.

A hotel receptionist answered, and Reeve asked to be put through to Mr. Rowe's room. Jay answered on the first ring.

"It's me," Reeve said icily.

"Who else? I want to thank you, Philosopher. I've always wanted an excuse to come back home. And all-expenses paid, too."

"Kosigin's a generous man. You weren't worried I'd sic the regiment onto you?"

"I don't think that's what you want."

"You're right."

"So when and where do we meet?"

"An island. Not far from my home."

"You want home advantage, eh? Well, I'd do the same. Give me the details."

"Head to Mallaig." Reeve spelled it out. "Just north of the town, there's a boathouse with an old Saab parked outside. You'll see it easily enough. The boathouse is owned by a man called Creech." He spelled this, too. "He'll hire you a boat."

"A boat? Hey, do I get to row it, like in the song?"

Reeve ignored this. "Will you need just the one boat?"

Jay laughed. "It's just you and me, Philosopher."

"I'll bet. Creech will know where you're to go. He'll give you directions. Naturally, he'll want paying for the hire." Reeve watched Creech's tongue flick momentarily from his mouth.

"Naturally. I'm looking forward to seeing you again. We've got a lot to catch up on."

Reeve blinked away the pink fog. Soon, he thought. Soon. But he mustn't let the anger get the better of him. He had to control it.

"Kosigin must really want those tapes," he said.

Jay just laughed. "Come on, Philosopher, we both know this isn't about the tapes. Screw the tapes. Screw Kosigin. This is about you and me, am I right?"

"You're a clever man, Jay."

"Not as clever as you, Philosopher, but I've been trying."

Reeve put down the receiver and pushed his way out of the box.

"Is he coming?" Creech asked.

"He's coming."

"When?"

"As long as it takes him. Come on."

"Where to?"

"The boathouse. I want you to drop me off somewhere."

"An island?" Creech guessed.

"Yes."

"Which one?"

So Reeve told him.

TWENTY-FOUR

JAY AND HIS MEN took three cars from London.

They drove steadily, without saying much. The front car had a map. All three cars were equipped with comms: two-way radios, cell phones, beepers.

"And if those don't work," one man had said, "we'll just have to whistle."

There were ten men altogether. Jay split them as two four-man patrols and one two-man patrol. His was the two-man patrol. His second-in-command was an ex-L.A. cop called Hestler. Hestler was very good; Jay had worked with him before. However, Jay hadn't been given much notice of the mission, had needed men in a hurry, and a few of the others in the group were unknowns. There were a couple who weren't much more than street kids, ex–gang members. They looked mean, but looks counted for very little. Reeve could sneak up from behind them and take them out. The first he'd see of their mean looks, their eyes would already be glazed over.

Jay and his squad hadn't flown direct to Heathrow. He knew Heathrow customs could be tough. They'd flown to Paris instead, and got a French operative to organize cars to take them across the channel by ferry. It was slow, but it meant no one checked the contents of the large metal cases they'd brought with them from the French capital.

The cases were polished aluminum, the sort of rigid carrier camera equipment was often shipped in. There could have been video cameras inside, but there weren't. Instead, the cases were packed with the same equipment they'd taken on the Villambard mission.

Everyone was tired, Jay knew that. They'd hardly checked into the hotel before Reeve's phone call had come. Probably Reeve was playing on that factor. He would keep Jay moving, keep him from sleeping. Jay had considered staying put in London, getting some rest and setting off next morning. But he was keen to get this over and done with. He was good and ready. There'd be plenty of time for sleep afterwards.

He knew his own enthusiasm wasn't shared by everyone. The car passengers were trying to sleep. They'd switch drivers every hour, and stop every two hours for a stretch and some coffee. The map was a Collins road atlas, and it showed them that Mallaig was in the Scottish Highlands, a hell of a way from London but very close to Reeve's own home. Reeve wanted them on his territory. Mallaig was coastal, not quite wilderness. Jay didn't mind. When he wasn't working, he liked to take off east out of L.A. to the forests and mountains of San Gabriel and San Bernardino. There was no terrain he didn't know. He was an adept skier, climber, and runner. Last fall he'd taken off into the wilds for fifteen days, not coming across another living soul for fourteen of them. He knew Reeve had been running survival courses, but doubted they could be anything near as arduous as his own survivalist training. Plus, of course, Jay had been through the same training as Reeve, the same grueling marches over moor and mountain. He didn't think the Highlands would faze him.

But that was another thing about his troop — they were city dwellers for the most part, used to street-fighting and gun law. Only two, Jay apart, had served in armed forces. One of these was Hestler, the other was a big but paunchy Native American called Choa whose main line of work these days was as a bouncer at a nightclub on Sunset Boulevard. Some actor had died there a while back, but Choa's name hadn't been mentioned . . .

Reeve had done all right so far. He'd handled himself pretty well. But he'd been operating swift strikes, vanishing again afterwards. Jay didn't think he'd cope with confrontation quite so well. The odds still favored Jay, which was the only way he'd play them.

They reached Mallaig at ten in the morning. It had been raining ever since they'd crossed the border. The windshield wipers were on full and still were barely coping. There wasn't much of a road north out of Mallaig, and the next settlement along, Mallaigvaig, was the end of the line. The only thing you could do when you got there was turn back to Mallaig itself.

But just before they reached Mallaigvaig, they saw the boathouse and the Saab.

"Hestler, with me," Jay said. At the last service station, they'd opened the metal cases, and when the two men left the front car, each carried a Heckler & Koch MP5 set at three-round burst. They ran to the boathouse door, and Jay banged on it with his shoe. Then they stood to either side of the door, and waited for someone to answer.

When the door started to open, Jay shouldered it inwards, throwing Kenneth Creech onto his back, from which position he peered up into the mouth of the submachine gun.

"Are you Creech?"

"Sweet Jesus."

"Are you Creech?"

Creech eventually managed to nod that he was. Hestler had recced the shed and now said, "All clear," then went to the door to signal for the others to come in.

"You know someone called Reeve?"

Creech nodded again.

"What did he tell you?"

"He said you'd . . . you'd need a boat."

"To go where?"

"Skivald. It's a small island off South Uist."

Jay turned to Hestler. "Tell one of them to bring the map." He turned back to Creech. "I notice you've wet yourself." The stain on Kenneth Creech's trousers was spreading fast. Jay smiled. "I like that. Now, Mr. Creech, how big is Skivald?"

"About a mile and a half by three-quarters of a mile."

"Small."

"Aye." Choa handed the map book to Jay, who put it on the floor and crouched down to flick its pages. The MP5 was still trained on a point between Creech's eyes. "I don't see it," Jay said at last. "Show me." Creech sat up and looked at the map. He pointed to where Skivald was, north of Loch Eynort.

"There's nothing there."

"No," Creech said, "it's not marked. You won't find it on a map."

Jay narrowed his eyes. "What's going on, Mr. Creech?" The tip of the gun touched the bridge of Creech's nose. Creech screwed shut his eyes, which were watering. "Dear me, Mr. Creech, you're leaking from every orifice."

The men who had gathered around laughed at this. Creech didn't feel any better for them being there, but he could hardly feel worse about their massive presence either.

"He's ugly," said one of the street-gang youths. He'd been wearing his uniform of sawn-off black T-shirt and sleeveless denim jacket for most of the trip, but had insisted they stop at a service station just south of Carlisle so he could find something warmer to wear. The others had stayed in their cars.

"I doubt the shops here will sell clothes," Jay had murmured. But the street youth had come out with a wool-lined brown leather jacket. Jay didn't ask where he had found it. He knew he should be angry; it was a very public announcement of their presence, ripping off someone's jacket. But he doubted the victim would run to the police, who would have to listen to a story about an American Blood on the loose in Carlisle . . .

"I fucking hate ugly people, man," said the youth, shuffling his feet.

"Hear that, Mr. Creech?" Jay asked. "He hates you. Maybe you'd better help me pacify him, or you never know what he might do."

As if in answer, the youth, whose name was Jiminez, expertly flicked open a gold-colored butterfly knife.

"Reeve made me take him to the island," Creech spluttered.

"Yes? When was this?"

"Last night."

"Does he have any way off the island?"

Creech shook his head.

"Are you sure?"

"Positive. He could always swim, but that's about it."

"Anything else, Mr. Creech?"

Creech licked his lips. "No," he said.

Jay smiled and stood up. "Cut him," he ordered. Jiminez had been waiting. The knife flashed across Creech's thigh and he winced, covering it with his hand. Blood squeezed out from between his fingers.

"We can do you a lot of damage, Mr. Creech," Jay said, walking around the boathouse. "You have some nice tools here, any one of which could be turned on you. All it takes is a little . . . creativity." He picked up the hot-air gun. "Now, where's the socket?"

"I swear to God!" Creech said.

"What did he take with him, Mr. Creech?" Jay asked. "You say you took him to this island, you must at least have seen what he took with him."

"He had a bag, a holdall sort of thing. It looked heavy."

"And?"

"And he had . . . he had a gun."

"Like this one?" Jay asked, waving the MP5.

"No, no, just a pistol."

"A pistol? Is that all?"

"It's all I saw."

"Mmm. You didn't see anything else? No traps?"

"Traps?"

"Yes, for catching animals."

"I didn't see anything like that."

Jay had finished his tour of the room. He crouched down again in front of Creech. This was *his* show. He wasn't performing so much for Creech — who had been terrified from the outset anyway — as for his own men. He wanted to impress those among them who didn't know him. He needed their respect, their loyalty, and even a measure of fear. That was how to command.

"Anything else, Mr. Creech?"

He knew if he kept asking Creech would keep telling. He'd tell until he was telling the tiniest details, because he knew if he stopped he might start to bleed all over again.

"Well," Creech said, "he made some signs."

"Signs?" Jay frowned. "What sort of signs?"

"He made them so they'd look old. They were danger warnings, warning about the island."

"Warning of what exactly?"

"That it was out-of-bounds. That it was infected with anthrax."

Jay stood up again and laughed. "That's crazy!" he said. He turned to Hestler, who was smiling without knowing what the joke was. Hestler had cropped black hair, a long black beard, and a face whose blotchiness was disguised by a year-round tan. "You know what he's doing?" Jay asked. Hestler admitted he didn't. "He'll scatter those signs around half-hidden, like he's pulled them up. When we come across one, we're supposed to panic. And while we're panicking, he picks us off with his toy pistol."

"What's anthrax?" the other Chicano asked.

"A poison," Jay explained. "A tenth of a millionth of a gram can kill you. The army *did* experiment with it in the fifties." He turned to Creech again. "Isn't that right?"

Creech nodded. "But the island you're thinking of is north of here."

"And not on any map?" Creech nodded again. "Yes, maybe that was his thinking. He chooses an island the map-makers haven't bothered with and makes it look infected. Too elaborate, Gordon. Way too elaborate." He turned to Choa. "Take Watts and Schlecht and start bringing the stuff in." Choa led the two men outside. Watts was tall and as thin as a reed, but deceptively strong. Jay had come up against him in an arm-wrestling contest in the gym, and had bet $300 on himself to win inside half a minute. Watts had beaten him in eleven seconds flat.

Schlecht was someone Watts knew, and that was about as much as Jay knew. He was small, but with massive biceps and a bull neck, an Ollie to Watts's Stan Laurel. Schlecht even had

Hardy's mustache, but his face was like an animal's, nicked and scarred and mean.

The other three in the team had been suggested by Hestler, which was good enough for Jay. They were brothers: Hector, Benny, and Carl. For some reason, they didn't reveal their surname. They looked like the weakest links, wide-eyed during the flight from L.A., amazed to be visiting hotels and Paris and car rental offices, like Europe was one giant theme park. One of them had even brought a camera with him, which Jay had confiscated straight off.

Hestler agreed that they acted like kids, but he'd seen them in fights. Once they got going, he said, they were real bastards. He thought they'd had their whole moral training from video games and spaghetti westerns.

It took a couple of trips to bring all the stuff in. Everyone was damp, and not liking it.

"Start unpacking," Jay ordered.

Hestler looked at him. "Are we going now?"

"Why not?"

"It's raining hard!"

"Hestler, we're going to be in a fucking boat. We'd get wet even if the sky was blue as a South Carolina morning. I bet you're the sort who runs out of the swimming pool when the rain starts."

There was more laughter at this. Hestler didn't appreciate being its butt, but he stopped questioning Jay's decisions.

Jay turned to Jiminez. "See if you can find any oilskins."

Jiminez nodded and set to work. Choa, Watts, and Schlecht were handing out armaments. Each man had a submachine gun, either the MP5 or a Cobray M11. They also received a pistol, ammo, and knife. Jiminez refused the knife, preferring his own blade. Hestler and Jay were the only two to be given grenades — Jay's orders. The other men could be professional baseball pitchers, he still wouldn't have trusted them with a grenade.

"We take those three bags with us," Jay said, pointing to the ones he meant. "If you have dry clothes with you, put them in a backpack."

Watts and Schlecht handed out the backpacks. They were day-walker spec, big enough for a change of clothes and some provisions. Belts and holsters were next. Creech could hardly believe the evidence of his own eyes. He didn't feel so bad now about ratting out Reeve. After all, Reeve hadn't warned him what he was getting him into.

All Creech hoped now was that he'd get out of this alive. Jiminez had found some waterproof clothing, not quite enough to go around. Jay examined the two boats, only one of which was big enough to accommodate all of them. He decided they should take both: a backup was always useful.

"Are these ready to go?" he asked Creech.

"Might need some fuel," Creech said, trying to be helpful.

"Do it. Hector, you watch him. Benny and Carl, go move the cars, see if you can get them out of sight."

The three brothers nodded. Jay still didn't know which of them was which. He bit his bottom lip thoughtfully. This mission was costing Kosigin dearly; he didn't want one single fuck-up.

"Hey, Hestler, you ever skippered a boat?"

"Some," Hestler said. Hestler had done most things in his life, one reason why he was so useful.

"Okay," Jay said, "you take the motorboat. You can take the three stooges with you. The rest of us will take the bigger boat." He looked down on Creech, who was carrying a canister of fuel down the short metal ladder that led to both boats. "You're in charge of the bigger boat, Mr. Creech."

Creech managed to nod. "Er . . . ," he said. But then he swallowed. He'd been about to ask about the hire fee, but looking into Jay's eyes it suddenly didn't matter anymore.

It was a terrible day to be in a boat. The Minch was notorious anyway, and this was the sort of day which merely added to its reputation. The two boats kept in radio contact, for though they were only thirty feet apart, there was no way a shout could be heard from one to the other, and even hand signals were difficult, since most of the men were holding on with both hands to stop from being pitched over the side.

"I think we should go back!" Jay had heard Hestler say more than once. He'd just shaken his head towards Hestler's boat, not caring whether Hestler saw him or not. The Chicano whose name Jay had forgotten was puking over the side, his face close to green. Jiminez didn't look too good either, but stared ahead, refusing to acknowledge he was having any problem. Watts and Schlecht had sailed before, "but never when we weren't carrying dope." Choa was staring at the sea like he could control it with his anger, the way he could control people. He was learning a very old lesson indeed.

"What happens if we capsize?" the Chicano squealed, wiping his mouth with the back of his hand. "What happens then?"

Jay said something the youth couldn't make out. Jiminez repeated it for his friend.

"Fallback."

"Fallback? What fallback?" The youth turned to spew again, and that ended the argument.

"The wind's easing," Creech said. He was pale in the face himself, but not from the weather. "Forecast said it would be better in the afternoon."

"We should have waited," growled Choa.

Jay stared at him, then looked at the sea again. It was the same shade of gray they painted navy ships, with great spumes of white where the waves clashed. Yes, he should have waited. This way, they would land on the island less than a hundred percent ready to do battle. He wondered if the Philosopher had worked that out . . .

Hestler wiped stinging water out of his eyes; he was thinking much the same as Jay.

Jiminez and his friend were staring at Jay, not sure what to think. "What the fuck is he doing?" Jiminez's friend asked.

"He's singing," Jiminez told him. Jay was singing "Row, row, row your boat" at the top of his voice.

Nobody joined in.

"There!" Creech said eventually. "There's the island." He was as relieved as anybody, though he was filled with a certain dread, too. Hands tightened around guns; eyes peered at the coastline.

"There's only one real place for a landing, that wee bit of beach."

The beach was a narrow strip of sand so dark it might have been coal dust. The land adjoining it had been worn away, so that there was little more than a steep step up from the beach onto earth and grass.

"What do I do?" Creech asked.

"Beach the boat."

"She's not built for that."

"Then get us as close as you can and drop anchor. We'll wade ashore. Boots off, everybody!"

Choa was studying the pocket-handkerchief beach. Jay asked him what he thought.

"He's been here since last night," Choa said. "He'll be ready. If it were me, I'd pick us off as we go ashore."

"I don't see him."

"Like I say, he's had time to get ready."

"You mean camouflage?" Jay accepted the point and brought his binoculars up to his eyes. He scanned the horizon slowly, carefully. "He's not there," he told Choa, handing him the binoculars. Choa peered through them.

"Maybe," he said, "we should circle the island in the boats, see if we can spot anything. He could've booby-trapped the beach. No footprints, but with this wind and rain that's no surprise. Any footprints would be erased in minutes." Choa had a deep molasses voice, and looked like he knew his stuff; he came from a race of hunters and trappers, after all.

But Jay shook his head. "He won't play it that way."

He couldn't say why he felt so sure.

They tied the motorboat to the larger vessel and dropped anchor. "You're coming with us," Jay told Creech. "Don't want you buggering off and leaving us." Creech seemed resigned.

With trousers rolled up, they waded ashore, boots tied around their necks, packs on their backs, the first men in the water keeping their guns aimed at the beach, the men to the rear carrying the three large cases.

The rain was blowing almost horizontally as Jay gathered his troops around. "Remember," he said, "there are signs warning of anthrax. They're a bluff, so don't be surprised if you stumble across one, even if it's been well hidden. Okay? Let's get off the beach." He looked around, his eyes finding the nameless Chicano. "Stay here with Creech. Don't let him near the boats, understood?"

"Understood."

The rest of them set off towards a narrow trail which snaked up from the beach. The trail divided into two, and Jay split his men into two units.

The Chicano waved his friend good-bye, and turned his gun on Creech. "This is horrible country."

"You get used to it," Creech said, heading for the shelter of the step. It formed a nice windbreak, so that if you crouched down you were completely protected. The Chicano didn't sit beside him — he had to keep watch — but he didn't stray too far either. He paced the beach, alternating between keeping a lookout for Reeve, and keeping an eye on Creech. He knew they'd finish off the man eventually, probably as soon as they got back to the mainland. The youth shivered and shrugged his shoulders. He was freezing, and he noticed that Creech's jacket looked warm.

"Hey," he said, "you don't need that. Give it to me." And he used his gun instead of "please." Creech shrugged off the brown corduroy jacket. The Chicano had to put his gun down to put the jacket on. "Move and I kill you," he told Creech, who held up his hands peaceably. The Chicano placed his gun on the sand and stood up.

As he stood, he saw something incredible. The earth at the top of the step opened up and a man sprang to life, for all the world like a zombie. The man sprang forward and leapt on the youth, knocking him backwards. The young man wrestled to get his pistol out of its holster, then stopped suddenly, intent on the hilt of a dagger which was protruding from his chest.

Creech leapt to his feet, mouth open in a silent scream.

Gordon Reeve stood up and looked down at the youth, whose hands were fluttering around the grip of the knife like moths around a flame. Reeve placed a foot on the dying man's stomach and pulled out the dagger, blood spewing out of the slit. Creech turned away and threw up on the sand. The Chicano's eyes were starting to close when Reeve wiped the knife clean on Creech's jacket.

It had taken him some time to find the perfect spot, and then longer still to dig his foxhole. He'd used a collapsible spade, brought from his workshop, first scraping off a three-inch-deep layer of topsoil and grass. And when the hole was finished, and Reeve installed in it, he'd placed the section of turf back, convinced he was invisible.

He'd been in that hole the best part of ten hours, fearing trench foot as the water table rose and the rain kept coming down.

"One down," he said now.

"Th-there are t-ten altogether," Creech stammered, wiping his lips.

"I know, I saw you arrive." Reeve stared at him. "And I heard Jay talking about those signs we made."

"Ach, Mr. Reeve, I had to say *something*. I was shite-scared, I admit it."

"It's okay, Kenneth. I knew Jay would find out about them."

"What?"

"He was expecting a trap, and you handed him one. He wasn't so ready for another. Come on."

"Where?"

"Back to the boat."

Creech managed to let out a yip of relief. They waded into the water and were halfway to the boat when there was a roar from the island. Jiminez had come back to check on his friend. Now he was sprinting towards the body, yelling something in Spanish at the top of his voice.

"Hurry!" Reeve urged. As if Creech needed telling. They grabbed for the side of the larger boat and hauled themselves in, Creech finding an energy he hadn't used in years. There was a sudden explosion behind them, and Reeve turned his head to see smoke rising into the sky, and earth raining down all around.

"Looks like someone stumbled on one of my surprises."

He'd run trip wires across both paths. The explosive charges were big enough to take out two, maybe three men if they were close enough together. Only one explosion though; the other party had stopped short of the trip wire. They must have heard the scream and turned back towards the beach. They were starting to appear. Two ran straight to the water's edge, firing as they ran.

Creech started the engine. It was still warm and started quickly. Reeve dealt with the anchor by slicing the rope with a single hack of his dagger.

"Let's go!" he yelled.

They went, the motorboat trailing after them. When they were out of the range of bullets, Reeve ordered Creech to cut the engine. Creech had to be told twice; even then he couldn't believe what he was hearing.

"Why?"

"Because I want to watch." Reeve had a backpack of his own, and took from it a small pair of powerful binoculars. Jay seemed to be talking to his men as they stood around the cooling body. From the looks on their faces, Reeve knew he had scored an important victory. They didn't look angry or set on revenge; they looked horrified. Doubts would now start to enter their minds. There were four of them, including the Hispanic-looking youth who'd run onto the beach first. Four. Which meant the explosive had been tripped by a unit of the remaining five men. The Hispanic had recovered a little and was yelling at Jay, waving his arms at him accusingly. Tears were streaming down his face.

Reeve moved the binoculars and saw the survivors of his little group come staggering down onto the beach. There were only two of them, both spattered with blood and badly wounded. One man had a branch sticking out of his leg; the other looked to have lost an ear. They were the only two to emerge.

Reeve took a moment to slip his boots back on before putting the binoculars back to his eyes. Jay was standing on the beach, his own binoculars trained on Reeve.

And he was smiling.

The smile seemed to anger the Hispanic youth still further.

He turned Jay around so they were face to face. Reeve saw what the young man, so close to Jay, could not. He saw Jay's hand go to the holster, saw him ease the gun out. Saw him take a step back, raising his gun hand, and blow a hole in the young man's forehead. Then Jay turned around again, so he was looking towards Reeve.

Reeve got the message.

"What're they doing?" Creech said. "Shooting each other?"

"Getting rid of excess baggage," Reeve corrected him grimly.

Through the binoculars, he watched Jay order the two uninjured men remaining to open one of the cases. The two others, the ones injured in the blast, were huddled together, seated on the sand. Jay looked towards them, but wasn't about to offer any comfort. He was more intent on the metal case. Then Reeve saw why, and saw, too, why Jay had been happy Reeve and Creech had stuck around.

A grenade launcher.

"Oh, shit," he said.

"What is it?" Creech came to the side to see. "What are they doing?"

"Get us out of here," Reeve said quietly. His voice fell away as he saw the contents of the other cases.

Two small dinghies, gas-inflatable, and the paddles to go with them.

Creech was at the wheel. The beach faced the South Uist coastline, and Creech was headed there in as straight a line as he could navigate.

"Can they hit us at this distance?" Creech yelled.

"Depends what model of launcher they've got. Knowing Jay, it'll be a good one."

Reeve could do little but watch. It wouldn't help, but he wished he'd brought the dead man's Cobray with him. The success of his own "trap" had led him to underestimate Jay. The bastard wasn't stupid.

"Proper planning," Reeve muttered. Jay had taken charge of the grenade launcher. He was crouched by the water's edge, one knee on the sand, his eye busy at the sight's crosshairs.

"Here it comes," Reeve said, watching the wisp of smoke as

the first grenade was launched. It flew past the boat and hit the water a hundred yards ahead.

"That answers your question," Reeve told Creech, who was now steering wildly, serpentining the boat and throwing Reeve about.

A second grenade came over, landing short of their boat but hitting the motorboat full on. There was an explosion, wood and metal rising into the sky above a pall of black smoke.

Creech let out a shriek. Reeve thought he was panicking, until he saw the jagged point of wood protruding from his shoulder. Reeve went to help him, but the boat started circling. He had to get them out of range. He pulled the splinter out of Creech's shoulder with no ceremony, then pushed Creech aside and gripped the wheel tight, setting them back on course.

Another grenade just reached the boat, hitting it aft and blowing a hole in the wooden structure. Water started pouring in.

"Can you swim?" Reeve asked Creech, who nodded, his teeth gritted against the pain. "Even with one arm?"

"I'll be all right. How far are we from land?"

Reeve looked up. The answer was less than half a mile. He took his boots off again and put them in his backpack, zipping it tight. It was waterproof, and didn't weigh very much. As a last resort, he would ditch it and trust to his dagger, which was in its scabbard attached to his leg.

"Come on then," he told Creech, "let's go for a swim."

They swam away from the sinking boat. Creech couldn't help but look back at it, watching the hull tip, seeing barnacles and wood that was in dire need of repainting.

They swam together. Reeve couldn't see, but he guessed Jay would be setting out in the dinghies by now, bringing his two remaining men with him. Reeve had taken seven men out of the game.

But at a price.

They were swimming across the current, which made half a mile seem like three times that. Creech grew quickly exhausted, and Reeve had to help him. This is great, he thought, just what I need. Lying in a foxhole all night, and now a half-mile swim pulling an injured man with me.

Meantime, Jay would be paddling, not straining himself. The odds were turning against Reeve all the time.

He eventually pulled Creech ashore. Creech wanted to lie down and rest, but Reeve hauled him to his feet and slapped his face a couple of times.

"You've got to get out of here!" he yelled. Creech's leg wound, the slice the Chicano had given him, had opened up again. They were six or seven miles shy of the nearest village, but Reeve knew there was a croft to the south, maybe three miles distant. "Keep to the coast," he told Creech. "Don't try crossing the hills. Okay?"

He waited till Creech had nodded. The man made to stumble away, but Reeve grabbed his arm. "Kenneth, I'm sorry I got you into this."

Creech shrugged free and started to walk. Reeve watched him go, trying to feel something for him. But the soldier had taken over. Creech was a casualty; that didn't mean you had time for flowers and sympathy. It was sink or swim. Really, Reeve shouldn't even have helped him ashore. He should have conserved his own energy, which was what he did now. He took off his wet clothes and wrung them out, then lay them out to dry. They wouldn't have time to get really dry, but the wind might help. The things in his backpack were almost completely dry, which was good fortune. He trained the binoculars on the dinghies. There were two men in the front one, only one in the second. The man with Jay looked grim with a large black beard, the man paddling alone looked American Indian. Reeve scanned the boats for armaments: pistols and submachine guns; no rocket launchers that he could see. Nothing heavy. But there was something on Jay's lap . . . He'd thought at first it was a transmitter, but saw now that it was a cassette player.

"What the hell is that for?" he asked himself.

He examined his surroundings. He knew this area fairly well, which was to his advantage. The hill range had two peaks, Hecla to the north and Beinn Mhor to the south, each at about two thousand feet. Reeve had managed to go unnoticed for whole weekends when tracked by up to a dozen men, and he'd only had part of this wilderness to play with. But now he had to assume he was up against professionals.

This time, he really was playing for his life.

Creech was out of sight. Reeve knew Jay wouldn't bother with him anyway: he couldn't afford to lose one-third of his force. But just in case, Reeve bided his time until Jay and his men could see him clearly. He pulled on trousers, socks, and boots, and tied the arms of his shirt around his neck, so it flapped like a cape. It would dry quicker that way. Then he picked up his backpack and pistol and headed into the hills, making sure his pursuers could see the direction he was taking.

He heard the bullet crack behind him but didn't slow down. His pursuers were carrying MP5s; Reeve knew the things were as accurate as rifles up to about a hundred yards, but he was well out of that range. They were just wasting ammo, and soon realized it. Reeve came to the top of the first rise and turned his head to watch. They were close to the shore now. He had maybe four or five minutes on them.

He started running.

TWENTY-FIVE

JAY WAITED TILL THE LAST POSSIBLE MOMENT before leaping out of the dinghy onto land. He was still fairly dry, and wanted to stay that way. The others didn't mind splashing into the knee-deep water, clambering over the rocks onto land. They brought the inflatables with them, and weighed them down with rocks so they wouldn't be blown back to sea.

"Do we split up?" Choa asked.

"Let's stick together," Jay said. "If it becomes necessary later, we can split up." He had torn a page out of their map book — the one showing the Western Isles — but it was a driver's map, not a walker's. It didn't tell him much about the terrain except that they were a long way from civilization.

"Let's go," he said, folding the map back into his pocket. "Choa, check your ammo clip."

Choa had been the one who had blasted away at Reeve, on the principle that if you could see your target, you were as well to have a go at hitting it. Choa had never used the MP5 before. He'd liked firing it so much he was itching to fire it again. He held it ready, safety catch off.

"Space out," Jay told his men. "Let's not make any easy targets. Choa, you watch our backs, in case he comes around us."

"You don't think he'll just run?" Hestler asked.

"It would make sense," Jay admitted. "He's wet and most probably tired. He knows the odds. But I don't think he'll run. He wants this over as badly as I do."

"No matter who wins?"

Jay looked at Hestler. "No matter who wins," he said. "It's playing the game that counts."

They marched in silence after that, Jay using hand signals to show when he thought they were bunching up too much. They didn't march in a line, but spread themselves out, making a more random pattern which would be harder for an enemy to hit. Jay wondered if Reeve had a plan. Reeve's house was only five or so miles distant; it made sense that, running an adventure center, he'd know these hills better than they did. He might know them very well indeed.

Jay knew it was three against one, but taking everything else into account, those weren't ideal odds. He wished he had an Ordnance Survey map of the area, something that would give him a better idea of what they were up against. But all he had were his eyes and his instincts.

And the knowledge that Gordon Reeve had almost got them both killed.

The rain started again, like mischievous needles jabbing the skin. They walked into it face-on. Jay knew Reeve wouldn't keep moving in a straight line; that direction would take him to civilization too quickly. He'd be circling around at some point, either towards Hecla or Beinn Mhor. If there had been three men with him, Jay would have split the group in half, a two-man patrol in either direction, but he only had two men left. He didn't regret killing the Chicano, not for an instant, but another man would have been useful. He had Benny and Carl's word for it that their brother Hector, plus Watts and Schlecht, were lying dead back at the scene of the explosion. Jay had promised to come back for the two injured men. He wasn't sure if it was a promise he would fulfill.

He'd been right about one thing: the phony anthrax signs *had* been crazy. The Philosopher had known what he was doing. Creech had been allowed to know about them, and had spilled his guts to Jay . . . and Jay had been tricked into thinking he knew something important. They'd been a ruse, nothing more, the *real* trick had been the trip wires. He guessed now that his own unit had stopped just short of encountering one.

Nice, Gordon — very nice.

Jay and his two men came to a high point and looked into the deep valley below. There was no sign of Reeve and no visible hiding place. But Choa, with his hunter's eyes, spotted something, a dark shape against the hillside. They approached cautiously, but it was just a groove in the earth, maybe a foot deep, six feet long, and a couple of feet wide.

"It's a scrape," Jay said.

"A what?" Hestler asked.

"A hide. You scrape away the earth, then lie in the hole. Put some netting over you and you're hidden from a distance." Jay looked around, realizing. "He uses this area for his training courses. There must have been a manhunt at some stage. There could be dozens of these spread out across the hills."

"So he could be hiding?"

"Yes."

"So maybe we've walked right past him; maybe he's already behind us." Hestler eased his catch off. "I say we split up, that way we cover more ground. We could be here all night otherwise."

"Maybe that's what he wants," Choa offered. "Get us cold and lost, wet and hungry. Stalking us, just waiting for concentration to lapse."

"He's only one man," Hestler growled. He was still looking around, daring anything to move. Jay noticed Hestler's MP5 was set to full auto.

"All right," Jay said, "you two head north. I'll head south. There are two peaks. We each circle one and RV back at the dinghies. Keep in touch by two-way. It might take a few hours. It won't be dark by the time we finish. If there's no result, we think again."

"Sounds good to me," Hestler said, setting off. "Sooner we start, sooner we finish."

Choa gave Jay a doubting look, but set off after his partner.

Jay decided after they'd gone to make straight for the summit of Beinn Mhor. He'd be more of a target, but on the plus side he could take in the country below with a single sweep.

"Just do it," he told himself, beginning to climb.

"This is fucking unbelievable," Hestler told Choa. "There were ten of us at the start, how the fuck did we get to this?"

"Search me."

"Ten against one. He's fucked us up nicely. I'd like to tear him a new asshole."

"You think he needs two?"

Hestler turned to Choa. "He's likely to be shitting himself so much, maybe he will at that."

Choa said nothing. He knew words came free; as a result people talked too much. Sometimes people could talk themselves into believing they were superhuman. Talking could make you crazy.

The last they saw of Jay he was clambering on all fours up a steep slope. Then they rounded the hillside and lost him.

"This weather is the pits," Hestler said.

Choa silently agreed. The last time he'd known anything like it was up in Oregon, near the mountains there. Rain so thick you couldn't see through it. But afterwards, the trees had smelled so beautiful, pine and moss bursting underfoot. There weren't many trees here. There was practically nowhere to hide, except for these scrapes. He didn't like the idea of these invisible hides. "We're a long way from Los Angeles," he said quietly.

Hestler chuckled. "Killing's killing," he said. "Doesn't matter where you do it or who you do it for."

"Look," said Choa, pointing. He had good eyes. He'd been the first to spot the scrape, and now he'd noticed another small-ish patch on the ground. When they got up close, it was wet, greasy to the touch. It was blood.

"Bastard's winged!" Hestler said.

"Let's radio Jay and tell him."

"Fuck that, the bastard could be around the next bend. Let's get him."

Hestler set off, but Choa held back. He had the two-way hooked to his belt and now unclipped it.

"Got something here," he said. Then, with Hestler almost out of sight, "Hey! Hold on a minute!" But Hestler kept on going.

"What is it?" Jay's voice said. He sounded a little out of breath, but not much.

"Blood, very fresh."

"No way."

"I'm telling you —"

"I don't think he's hurt."

"One of the grenades maybe?"

"Not the way he swam to shore. I watched him, remember. He clambered up that first slope like a mountain goat."

"Well, it's blood." Choa rubbed some of it between thumb and forefinger. It was sticky and cold.

"Taste it," Jay said.

"What?" Choa couldn't believe what he was hearing.

"Put some on your tongue," Jay commanded.

Choa looked at his fingers.

"Do it!"

Choa put the tip of his tongue against the blood. He couldn't taste anything. He licked at it, tasted it, then spat.

"Well?"

Choa spoke into the radio. "Tastes funny," he said.

"Is it metallic, the way blood is?"

Choa had to admit it wasn't like that. "Sort of chalky," he said.

"Like paint?" Jay guessed.

"How did you know?"

"It's fake. He's laying a false trail."

Choa looked ahead of him. There was no sign of Hestler.

"Hestler!" he shouted. "Get back here!"

Then there was a single gunshot. Choa knew better than to run towards it, but he didn't freeze either. He moved off downhill and circled around towards the noise. He'd switched off the radio so it wouldn't give away his position. He carried his submachine gun cocked and ready.

There was a body ahead of him, lying in a gully. It looked like Hestler had taken a shortcut. Instead of rounding the gully, he'd headed down into it, which made him easy prey for anyone hiding just over the ridge. What was the phrase? Like shooting a pig in a tub.

Choa daren't descend into the gully. Besides, the hole in the back of Hestler's head was big enough and clear enough. He held the radio to his face.

"What?" Jay said quietly. He'd heard the shot.

"Hestler's down," Choa said simply.

"What happened?"

"Someone tore him a new mouth, wrong side of his head."

Choa cut the radio. He needed both hands for his gun. Reeve was nearby. He rounded the gully. There were so many dips and rises in the landscape, he couldn't see farther than eighty feet in any direction. Reeve could be as close as eighty feet. Apart from the rain hitting him and the wind in his ears, there was no noise at all. No birds, no leaves rustling. The sky overhead was like a slab of stone.

Choa came to a decision which seemed immediately right to him: head back to the dinghies and take one, then paddle away from here. The thought made him feel better. This was Jay's fight, not his. He felt like Reeve was watching him, even though he couldn't see a damned thing. His excellent eyesight didn't work so well in driving rain. A storm was directly over the island. Choa dropped the MP5 and his pistol, then started walking with hands held high above him. He guessed he was heading the right way; away from here seemed *exactly* the right way.

Reeve saw him go.

He was naked apart from his boots. His clothes were in the backpack, staying dry. He watched for a full ten minutes, then went to pick up the armaments. He scrabbled down the side of the gully and quickly unloaded Hestler's weapons, leaving them with the body but taking the ammo. Then he found the two grenades, and he took those, too. He liked these odds better now.

He knew the Indian had simply walked away from the fight, which was entirely sensible.

Then he heard the music. It was a long way off, but between the squalls, fragments of it drifted to his ears. It was Jay, and he was singing that damned song. Reeve made towards the sound, but he took his time. He knew it wasn't really Jay — it was the cassette recorder. Jay had recorded himself singing the song over and over again, his voice rising the longer the recording went on.

Reeve had to cross a wide valley between the two peaks, and knew he would be most vulnerable here. There was no sign of Jay, just the music, getting closer now. He edged around towards it, moving in a crouch, backwalking part of the way, staying to the shelter of slopes wherever he could. Until he came to the final slope. The music sounded just the other side of the ridge. Reeve crawled up the slope, hugging the ground.

There was a saucer-shaped dip beyond the ridge, and in the center sat the cassette recorder. Reeve lay there for a few minutes, until he could stand the music no longer. He took aim with the MP5 and hit the fat black box dead center.

The box exploded, flames shooting out radially from it. Booby-trapped. Maybe now Jay would come looking.

Suddenly there was another explosion, much closer to Reeve. The ground quivered, and divots showered down around him. For a split second he was back in the scrape in Argentina, and Jay was about to crack.

Now another explosion, very close. He realized what was happening. Jay was in hiding somewhere, and had guessed the direction of Reeve's burst of gunfire. Now he was tossing grenades in that direction, and they weren't landing far short of their target. Reeve stood up to see if he could spot the grenades in flight. Smoke from the explosions was being dispersed by the sharp breeze, but pungent tendrils still coiled up from the plastic remains of the cassette player.

Suddenly a figure stood up on the far side of the gully. Naked, body and face smeared with earth, white teeth grinning through the improvised face paint.

Jay.

Sixty feet away and firing from the hip.

Two bullets thudded into Reeve, pushing him off his feet. He rolled back down the slope, just managing to keep hold of his gun. He came to a stop on the gully floor, but knew he had no time to check the damage. He had to get out of the gully. He scraped his way up the other side, cresting the rise before Jay came into view. He just made it. Rain stung his eyes as he ran, feet slipping in mud. Another narrow valley, across a stream . . . he knew where he was going, knew where he'd end up. One bullet had caught him in the left shoulder, the other between shoulder and chest. They burned. The scabbard was still strapped to his right leg, but it slowed him down, so he undid the straps and drew out the dagger, discarding the scabbard.

"Hey, Philosopher!" Jay called, his voice manic. "You like hide-and-seek? You were always chicken, Philosopher! No guts."

Reeve knew what Jay was doing: trying to rile him. Anger made you strong in some ways, but so weak in others.

But there was no pink mist now, nothing in Reeve's heart but cool procedure and searing pain. He crested two more rises before he found himself at the chasm, a rupture in the land which ran in a jagged tear to the sea. At high tide, the base of the cavity filled with gurgling, murderous water. But just now it was a damp bed of jagged rocks. It was dark down there, no matter what time of day, whatever the weather above. A place of shadows and secrets never brought up into the light. Reeve walked its edge. He wasn't scared of it — it was too familiar to him — but he'd seen his weekend soldiers cower in its presence. He picked his spot and waited, taking time to examine his wounds. He was bleeding badly. Given time, he could create makeshift dressings, but he knew time was short.

"Hey, Philosopher!" Jay yelled. "Is this blood real?" A pause. "Tastes real, so I guess it is! Want to know something, Philosopher? I've done a lot of thinking over the years about Operation Stalwart. I've been wondering why they chose us. I mean, I was fucked up after that fiasco on the glacier. I should never have been allowed off the ship, never mind sent behind enemy lines. I wanted to kill those bastards so badly. And you . . . well, you weren't popular, Philosopher. You had too many ideas in your head, including your own ideas. You were the Philosopher, reading too much, turning yourself on to anarchism and all that other stuff. As far as the brass were concerned, there was half a chance you were becoming the enemy. See, Philosopher, we were both of a kind — loose wires, expendable. That was always going to be a one-way mission, and it would've turned out that way if I hadn't saved our hides."

The voice sounded maybe a hundred yards away. Two-thirds of a yard per stride . . . Reeve started counting, at the same time snaking his way back up the slope, listening intently for any clue as to the line Jay was taking. He guessed he would simply follow the trail of blood.

Reeve was just below the crest now. Suddenly he heard a grunt as Jay started to climb. In a few seconds he would crest the rise, Reeve just the other side of it, hugging the land. Reeve stopped breathing. Jay was so close, not even six feet away.

Reeve concentrated all his energies, closing his eyes for a moment, finally taking a deep breath.

"Hey, Philos—"

He threw out his good arm with all his strength, plunging the dagger through Jay's boot and into his foot. As Jay started to scream, Reeve yanked his ankles away from him, hurling him down the slope. Jay could see what was at the bottom of the slide and tried digging his heels, elbows, and fingers in, but the ground was slippery and he just kept on sliding. Reeve was sliding, too. The force of his momentum when he'd hauled Jay over the crest had sent him into a roll. His shoulder banged against the ground, almost causing him to pass out. Below him, he saw Jay slip three-quarters of the way over the precipice, his hands scrabbling for purchase. Reeve was rolling straight towards him. They'd fall into the ravine together.

Reeve struck out with his right hand, the hand which still held the dagger. The blade sank into the earth, but started to cut through it, barely slowing his descent. He twisted the blade so the meat of it was gouging into the wet soil. It was like applying a brake. He jolted to a stop, his legs hanging into space. He found the edge with his knees and started to pull himself up, but a hand grabbed one of his ankles. And now Jay's other hand let go of the lip of the ravine, and he used it to gain a better grip on Reeve, hauling himself up over Reeve's slippery legs while their combined weight started the dagger cutting through the earth again, so that as Jay climbed, Reeve slid farther over the edge.

He waited till Jay was preparing to slide farther up; while he was unbalanced, Reeve rolled onto his side, shrugging Jay off and at the same time lashing out at him with his feet. For an instant they were side by side, the way they had been that final night in Argentina, their faces so close Reeve could feel Jay's breath against his cheek.

"Well," Jay panted, trying to grin, "isn't this cozy? Just the two of us, like it was always meant to be."

"You should have died back in Rio Grande," Reeve spat.

"If we'd stayed in that damned trench, we'd have died," Jay hissed. "You owe me, Philosopher!"

"Owe you?" Reeve was clawing at the ground with the fingers of his left hand, feeling pain shoot through his shoulder. When he had a good handhold he started to ease the dagger out of the ground.

"Yes, owe me," Jay was saying, readying to pull them both over the edge and onto the rocks below.

Reeve raised the dagger and plunged it into Jay's neck. Blood gurgled from Jay's mouth, his eyes wide in amazement as one hand went to the wound. He lost all grip and started to slide over the edge.

Reeve watched him go, the head disappearing last of all, eyes still wide open. He didn't hear the body hit the ground. Reeve let out a roar which echoed down the chasm walls and up into the sky. Not a roar of pain or even of victory.

Just a roar.

"All debts repaid," Reeve said, digging the dagger back into the ground, and for some reason he saw Jim in his mind, content.

Then he started slowly, carefully, to climb back up the treacherous slope, not relaxing until he was at the top, his head and trunk hanging over the crest of the rise. He closed his eyes then and wept, not feeling the pain in his shoulder or the chill damp ground robbing him of his core temperature, degree by willful degree.

TWENTY-SIX

THERE WAS A LOT OF MESS still to be cleared up: Gordon Reeve knew that. The police might or might not accept his story. It sounded pretty farfetched when he thought about it. But he had Jim's computer file, and soon he'd have the documents to go with it, as soon as he could arrange a trip to Tisbury.

As for CWC itself and Kosigin . . . he didn't know what would happen. He only knew that *something* would. The same applied to Allerdyce and Alliance Investigative. He didn't really care anymore. He'd done what he could.

He made his way back home and staggered indoors. He knew he should clean his wounds, make fresh dressings, call a doctor. But he sat at the kitchen table instead. He wanted to phone Joan, wanted to tell her it was all right now, that Allan and she could come home. He wanted that most of all.

He wasn't sure what they'd do after that. Go back to the old routine? Maybe. Or maybe he'd dig up some of their land, turn it into a vegetable garden . . . go organic, and worry less that way. He didn't think so, though.

He started to laugh, resting his head on his forearms.

"I'm one of Nietzsche's gentlemen," he told himself. "I'll think of something."

Ian Rankin is the #1 bestselling mystery writer in the United Kingdom. He is the winner of an Edgar Award for *Resurrection Men*, and he is the recipient of a Gold Dagger Award for Fiction and the Chandler-Fulbright Award. He lives in Edinburgh, Scotland, with his wife and their two sons.